THE HEIGHTS
OF VALOR

David Tindell

Kevin,
Thanks for
climbing the
Heights! David
Tindell
4/22

Other books by David Tindell:

The White Vixen

Quest for Honor

The Red Wolf

Quest for Vengeance

To my grandfathers,
James L. Tindell and Alvin Carpenter.
Thanks for showing me how to live a life of honor.
See you soon.

Far better to dare mighty things, to win glorious triumphs, even though checkered by failure, than to take rank with those poor spirits who neither enjoy much nor suffer much, because they live in the gray twilight that knows neither victory nor defeat.

- Theodore Roosevelt

PROLOGUE

Platteville, Wisconsin
April 26, 1898

The white-haired man behind the desk threw the newspaper down on the blotter. "It is completely out of the question," Jeremiah Dawson said. He sat back in the leather chair and stroked his beard. "The semester is not yet over. If you fail to complete the term, you shall not graduate with your class next year."

The well-built young man sitting in front of his elder responded with a sober nod. "I am aware of that, Father. After my service in Cuba, I can return to the campus and take my final examinations. I have spoken to my professors. My standing in the class has earned me some measure of...leeway, let's call it."

"Charles, I–"

The young man leaned forward. "If you're concerned about me delaying my joining the firm, rest assured, Father, I have every intention of coming back here once I complete law school. When the new century dawns, I will be here, at your right hand. Just as you and Mother planned all these years." He sat back, crossed his legs and joined his hands. "I know that was her wish, God rest her soul."

"It was most certainly not her wish for her only son to become cannon fodder." The older man frowned, then stood, boosting himself up with a hand on the heavy oak desk. He reached for a cane. "You have no idea," he whispered, shaking his head. He walked to the display case on the far wall of the office, using a cane to compensate for his limp. Pausing before the case, he placed a hand on it. "Son, war is not a lark. It is not...not some grand adventure."

The young man stood, tugged at his waistcoat, and strode confidently to his father's side. He moved with the easy grace of an athlete, and indeed he was one of the best boxers at the University of Wisconsin. He'd also taken up polo, further developing the horsemanship skills he'd honed riding through the ridges and valleys of Grant County. Fully three inches taller than his father, he stood next to the old man and placed a hand on his shoulder. "I understand that, Father," he said. "Truly, I do."

"That is not possible. You have not seen the elephant." He flipped the latch and raised the glass lid. Reverently, he reached down and touched the old sword that rested on the red velvet. "We were like you. Fit as a fiddle, all of us hankering to whip the Reb. One battle was all we would need. It was a holy crusade, we were told. I shall never forget what Governor Randall told us at the camp we named after him in Madison." He stared at the flag on the wall behind the case, his eyes seeing through the mists of memory to a day thirty-seven years past. "He said we were instruments of God's vengeance, 'His flails wherewith on God's great Southern threshing floor, He will pound rebellion for its sins.'" The old soldier looked up at his son, and his eyes were hard. "Let me tell you something, boy, I was at Antietam, and Gettysburg, and a lot of other places where it seemed God was conspicuous by His absence. General Sherman said war is hell, and he was absolutely right. If it is glory and adventure you desire, Cuba is the last place you shall find it."

"But your father let you go, did he not?" Charles pointed to the citation printed on a plaque, below the bronze medal held by the red, white and blue ribbon. "Seventh Wisconsin Volunteer Infantry, Company C. The Platteville Guards. You were the same age as I, Father. A lieutenant, second in command to Captain Udelhofen. Assumed command of the company when he fell at Antietam, promoted to captain. And it was at Gettysburg that you won the Medal of Honor."

"One does not *win* the Medal of Honor, boy, it is *awarded*."

"Yes, through the mail. It should be worth more than that, Father. It should be presented by the President of the United States himself."

"Well, perhaps someday it will be. But do not mistake my pride in that medal with my purpose here today." He closed the lid and latched it, then stepped aside to face his son. "Do you know how many men we lost? Just at Gettysburg alone, the regiment went into action with three hundred and seventy men. We lost thirty-nine killed, one hundred and three wounded, fifty-two missing. You can do the arithmetic. Our casualty rate was more than one-half." He rubbed his right leg. "The Rebel ball I took on Cemetery Ridge is a reminder that is with me every moment of every day." His eyes misted. "One other man from the regiment was awarded the medal from that battle. Francis Coates, from Company H, the Badger State Guards. He was from Boscobel. Lost both his eyes on the first day, leading his men. He came home and then moved to Nebraska. Died at the age of thirty-six. I doubt if he ever thought war was glorious."

"I have no illusions about war, Father. But I do want to serve my country, and help free the Cuban from Spanish bondage, just as you fought to free the Negro from his. And I shall be honest: I want to prove myself, beyond what I can find in the boxing ring. Just like Mr. Roosevelt, I would suspect."

The older man raised his cane and pointed toward the newspaper on the desk, which in bold headlines announced that the United States was now officially at war with Spain. Another article on the front page took note of Roosevelt's appointment as lieutenant colonel of a volunteer regiment. "That four-eyed rich parlor soldier? Thinks he has to be the biggest toad in the pond. He has no more business leading a regiment than your little sister!"

Charles laughed. "You'd best not let Margaret hear that. And as for Colonel Roosevelt, I think he might very well be president one day."

The old soldier shook his head. "He is a lunatic. If he manages to survive this war, mark my words, the Republicans will not let him within a mile of the White House. Nobody takes him seriously." He pointed again at the paper. "Why, they are calling his regiment 'Roosey's Red-Hot Roarers'! In my day, we at least had some sense of dignity."

Charles led his father back to the desk. "It is the First U.S. Volunteer Cavalry, and I believe they will call themselves the Rough Riders." He turned his father toward him. "And I would like to join them, Father. But I need your help. You are acquainted with Senator Spooner. A letter from you, asking him to put my name forward to Secretary Roosevelt, would be extremely beneficial to my application."

Jeremiah sank into his chair. "Charles, I am to be sixty years old next year, assuming the Lord does not call me before then. I have no desire to bury my son. I have had to bury my wife and that was a hard thing. I....I do not know if I would have the strength to bury you." He folded his hands on the desk blotter, unable to stop them from trembling.

The young man came around the desk and placed his hand on his father's. "It may be that I am...naïve about this endeavor," he said, "but I intend to try. If I am not chosen by Roosevelt, then I shall do whatever else I can do. Please. I need to do this."

The old man was silent for a moment, then said, "I said much the same to my own father. He was a farmer, you know. Always wanted me to be more than a farmer. I promised him I would become a lawyer, if he would just give me his blessing to join the Guards."

"I have already given you that assurance," Charles said. "But I shall add another promise. First, though, I must ask you something I have always wondered about. Why have you never chosen to share your wartime experiences with me?"

Jeremiah looked up sharply. "It was a terrible thing! I saw men blown to bits in front of me! There is no romance on the firing line. The only glory comes with survival. And some of the boys could not handle that, either."

"Then I shall make sure my own sons, and all Dawson men into the future, know the truth of such an experience. You know I have been a diarist. I intend to continue this in my service. And I promise you that your grandson will know what it was like, so if his country calls, he can make a more informed decision than his father did." He squeezed the liver-spotted hands. "Or his grandfather."

There was silence. Charles heard the ticking of the grandfather clock in the corner. With each tick he felt the regiment slipping away, Cuba slipping away, his chance to prove himself...

"Very well," Jeremiah Dawson, Civil War hero, said. "I shall wire the senator tomorrow morning. The rest is in God's hands."

Charles felt his heart leap in his breast. "And in the hands of Assistant Secretary of the Navy Theodore Roosevelt."

CHAPTER ONE

Fox News Special: "The U.S. Army Fights to the End in Iraq"
March 31, 2011

Less than a year from now, all U.S. combat forces are scheduled to be withdrawn from Iraq. President Bush negotiated the Status of Forces Agreement in 2008, calling for a withdrawal by the end of 2011, and President Obama shows no signs of seeking an extension. So as the months wind down, the remaining U.S. forces concentrate on their duties: advising and assisting Iraqi forces in defense of their nation against terrorists and sectarian militias. This mission, while not as fraught with danger as those during the height of the war as little as three years ago, is still hazardous. War correspondent Shane Aubart recorded the stories of the men of G Troop, Thunder Squadron, 3rd Cavalry Regiment, after a firefight in Wasit Governate, southeast Iraq, March 2011.

SFC Lester Boudreau is the top sergeant of G Troop. A native of Louisiana, he speaks in a Cajun drawl and it doesn't take long for the Mesopotamian sun to cause beads of sweat to break out on his ebony skin. He's still built like the college football linebacker he once was.

G Troop got to the Sandbox in early March. Two dozen guys, about half of them on their first deployment, fresh from OSUT (*One Station Unit Training*). I came out of Tulane in '95, gave up my football ride for my last two years, lost my starting job in spring ball and said screw it, I know somebody else I can play for. So I went to Basic Training and then AIT (*Advanced Infantry Training*), these days they combine it into one. My opinion, the kids are better prepared than we were, 'specially 'cause they got lots of combat vets as instructors now. I did a tour myself at Fort Benning, whippin' kids into shape. Harder these days, you ask me, lots of fatties comin' in. I can still say that, can't I? They ain't fatties when we get done with 'em, no sir.

The newbies, they bitched about the heat, like they all do first time in country. Mornin' of the firefight wasn't so bad, we got rain night before. A coupla 'em, they asked me when we be gettin' some action, word was this area wasn't so hot. I say, you be losin' your virginity right damn soon, kiddo, don't be lookin' for it, this ain't your high school prom night. Wasit borders on Iran and word was the IRGC (*Iran Revolutionary Guard Corps*) was infiltratin' and had a lot of the Iraqi militias in their pocket. These Iranians, they called themselves Pasdaran, were tough mothers. I'd run into a few on my last tour. They'd go down, but always the hard way.

Dawson? No, he wasn't one of those cocky guys. Quiet guy, built. Wrestler in college, they said. I put him in 4th Squad, and two days after they got in, we got our first mission. Platoon of IAs (*Iraqi Army*), with us as backup, patrolling five klicks (*kilometers*) out to check out a couple villages, then back to the firebase. Easy chips, one of my veterans says, but the newbies didn't look too confident when we mustered that morning. It was startin' to get real for 'em.

One of the new guys, Murphy, he asks how many times over here for me. I tell him, "I lost count, kid." True enough. My first deployment was to Germany, then the Balkans, my first combat action. And yeah, I lost count after that, but my wife didn't. Got to be too many for her, she took my girls home to Louisiana and became my ex-wife. Got a nastygram from her that morning, fact is, then I nicked myself shaving, so I was double pissed when we saddled up. But it was a nice day, and I was back in the Sandbox. Didn't mind that. Lots of bad guys over here need killin', truth be told, and I'm good at it. Now, my turn to teach these kids to be good at it, too.

Wasn't supposed to be me leadin' that patrol, but my top staff sergeant, Tom Brill, had taken out patrols three days runnin' and needed down time. Next guy up was Ted Pretasky, but he was on the shelf a couple days, sprained an ankle in combatives training the day before. So I picked my guys. Doering, my commo corporal, to handle the radio.

Two veterans, Bender and Roberts, both on their third tour, they knew the score. Four slots for newbies: Dezotell, Solum, Murphy and Dawson. These kids looked pretty solid. Murphy and Dawson were tight, they'd gone through OSUT together, and Dawson, he was the wrestler, from Wisconsin. All-American, somebody said. Well, he could sure as hell handle himself in combatives. That's how Pretasky blew his ankle, trying to break it up when Dawson and one of the Iraqis went at it a little too hard. The Iraqi thought he was cock of the walk but Dawson twisted him in knots, broke contact when Teddy ordered, but the IA jerk comes back at him and Teddy stepped in on that sand and there goes the ankle. My only thing with Dawson was that he looked a little tentative with a real weapon in his hands. But I had the feeling he'd be all right. Just needed confidence. I'd known some wrestlers at Tulane, tough mothers, all of 'em, but it's one thing to be tough on the mat. Nobody shooting at you there. So yeah, I was a little concerned about Dawson.

CPL Rich Bender is on his third tour, twice now to Iraq, one to Afghanistan. His average height and build don't draw attention, but his eyes do. They have a distance, the same thing I've seen in many War on Terror veterans. Only twenty-seven, he's already seen much. Bender was born and raised in Iowa, worked on the family pig farm after trying a year of college, then joined the Army at twenty-three.

We moved out at 0830, got to the first vill in good time, only two klicks from the firebase. Everything looked quiet, far as I could see. We look for the little things: are there kids playing outside? Old men sitting outside their homes, smoking or reading and just generally watching the world go by? Or is everybody inside? Anybody pick up a cell phone when they see us go by? There's lots to look for, but the little things can tell you if it's gonna be a good day or maybe a real bad one.

I spotted a couple things and hustled up to the sarge. The IA troops were in the lead. The sarge had said he thought the IAs looked pretty squared away, but I had my doubts. Hell, I have my doubts about everybody over here who isn't wearing a U.S. flag patch. Well, the Brits are okay, but not too many of them around anymore.

There'd been a couple guys in the vill hitting their phones when we came through. Older guys. No military-age males to be seen. The sarge said he'd seen the same thing, so he asks Doering, our commo guy, about the terrain between the first vill and the next one. Doering says, "Two klicks to the vill, pretty open except for a stand of trees about a klick and a half down the road. I think there's a farmer's compound right across from the trees."

Well, the sarge, he doesn't want to have you *think* about something, he wants you to *know* about it, so he tells Doering to find the hell out, and Doering checks his map and sat photos and says yeah, there's a compound, about fifty meters before the trees on the opposite side of the road.

"Bender," the sarge says, "spread the word to stay frosty, I'm gonna talk to Lieutenant Abadi." That was the IA officer leading their platoon. So he heads up to the front of the column and I start making the rounds of our guys. A couple of the newbies were starting to look a little peaked, like my grandma used to say, and I told 'em to just pay attention, remember their training, follow the sarge's lead.

PFC Jake Dawson is a shade under six feet and certainly has a wrestler's build. From northern Wisconsin, he had a wrestling scholarship to the University of Wisconsin and was All-American his sophomore year, but then quit school and joined the Army. This is his first deployment. The word among the troopers is that Dawson has an interesting family history. He's talked about going Special Forces, like his grandfather, who was killed in Vietnam, and the legacy goes back a lot further, all the way to the Civil War. When asked, Dawson demurs, preferring to talk about the mission and his fellow soldiers, if he has to talk at all.

I saw Sergeant Boudreau talking with Bender and the radio guy, so I knew something was up. The radio guy—Doering, that's his name— checked his map, then the sarge headed up to the front of the column. I told my buddy Chet, "Something's going on, stay sharp, bro."

And of course he said, "Copy that." I had to smile at that. Chet was a big fan of *24,* the TV show. It was always Jack Bauer this, Jack Bauer that, and Chet was going Special Forces like Bauer had done before he went into counter-terrorism. Well, I want to go SF too, but my reasons are different. It's a tough road. Both of us had thought about going in as an X-ray. That's when you join the Army and go right into SF training, but we both figured that we should get a tour or two under our belts in the infantry first. Chet and I didn't meet until OSUT at Fort Benning, but we'd been on the same page all the way and we just sort of stayed on the same page.

Dawson looks away for a moment, blinks, fights to compose himself.

You know, before that day, the closest thing to combat I'd ever experienced was wrestling. State high school tournament back home, the best of the best in the state, and then a whole new level at Madison, the Big 10, the NCAAs. I thought I knew pressure. I thought I knew how to handle nerves before a big match, a big showdown. When I got to Iraq and started walking down that road, I realized I didn't know (deleted).

I thought about my grandfather, in Vietnam. I never met him, he was KIA (*killed in action*) when my own dad was only five. Was this how he felt, his first time? That's what I kept asking myself.

CPL John Roberts is called the "Chief Justice" in the outfit because of his name, but by the time of this mission, most everyone just called him "Chief." One reason is the name, the other is his weapon. Roberts is the soldier who carries the M249 LMG (light machine gun). It's a tough job because it's a big weapon and he's always one of the first men targeted by the enemy in any engagement. But the six-four former oilfield worker from North Dakota relishes the challenge.

Rich gave me the word about maybe some trouble up ahead, so I checked out my weapon. We were good to go. My weapon is my partner. In OSUT they talk all the time about being a partner with your weapon, but when it's just an M4, it's not that special, everybody has one. Not everybody has the M249. My uncle used the M60 in Vietnam, bigger and heavier than the M249, but he was a big guy. When my gun first came in, they called it the SAW, Squad Automatic Weapon. They don't call them that anymore, but that's what I call mine. We have some long talks, me and my uncle, when I'm home on leave. The things you see, the things you have to do…well, it helps a helluva lot to hear how a guy who's been there has dealt with it. You gotta listen to the voice of experience. What he's told me has helped me make it through my deployments, and I'll make it through this one, me and my SAW.

The guys call me the Chief Justice. The one with my name back home passes judgement on people in his courtroom. Over here, I pass judgement on people who get in our way. My judgement is more final, I'll tell you that. People walk out of the other guy's courtroom, but they don't walk out of mine.

So when Rich said there might be trouble up ahead, I said, "Ain't hardly a day over here without trouble, son." He couldn't help cracking a grin at me. He knows I like Jesse Ventura, the guy from the *Predator* movie. I grew up in Grand Forks, across the river from Minnesota, when Ventura was governor there. The guy was a badass, didn't take any (deleted) in the ring, or in the movies, or when he was governor. I haven't had a chance to use his favorite line yet: "I ain't got time to bleed." I was thinking, well, maybe today would be the day.

When I saw the trees up ahead, I knew we'd be in for something. Didn't look right. On your third tour, you get a sixth sense about these things. Mine hadn't failed me yet. The compound on our right looked like it had been abandoned a long time ago, falling apart, but it was quiet. I'd seen a couple of the IAs go in to check it out. They came out and gave the all-clear signal. But those trees, man, I didn't like those trees. I got my weapon ready. If the trees opened up, the IAs would be the first to get hit, but then I could start SAWing people. Hey, it's serious business, man. I can tell you don't like it, but that's what it is, when you carry a weapon in a war zone. Kill or be killed. Back home I did some godawful dirty work in the oil fields, but I got to go home every night, take a shower, have a beer, nice warm bed, maybe a lady to make it warmer. None of that over here. When this work gets godawful dirty, some of the people aren't going home, except in a metal box. Hey, what did Patton say? Something about not dying for your country, but making sure the dumb SOB on the other side dies for his country. That works for me.

PFC Dawson:

Bender came down the line and gave us the word to get ready. Boots Solum was at our six, and he looked kind of nervous. I don't know his real first name, everybody calls him Boots because he's always cleaning his, has the best-looking boots in the outfit. Nineteen, a farm kid from Kansas. I told him his nickname had panache. He liked that, although I don't think he really knew what it meant.

I heard the first shots coming out of the woods and my training just kicked in. You always wonder during training, what'll I do when the (deleted) really hits the fan? The DIs (*drill instructors*) are always on you about the training, making it realistic, doing it over and over. For me, it was a lot like wrestling. You learn what you have to do and you get out there on the mat and do it, over and over. It becomes second nature. And the firefight was just like that.

I went down into a crouch, brought my M4 up. I glanced behind me and Boots was still standing up. I yelled at him to get the hell down. There was a stain on the crotch of his pants, but he hit the dirt.

When I was a kid, I read every book our library had about Special Forces, because of my grandfather. I always wondered, what would I do if I got into it for real? On the mat, you might get hurt, but you won't get killed. There's a ref there to make sure nothing really bad happens. There aren't any refs out here, there's just your training and your buddies. You have to rely on both, and that's what I did, and everything started to click.

SFC Boudreau:

Abadi was one of the good ones. He listened to what we had to say, and I can't say that about all the IA officers we worked with. *Boudreau pauses, looks away, shakes his head, then continues.* But overall, they were getting better. The first guys I'd worked with, on my first tour here in '06, man, they were clueless. Even the guys who'd served in Saddam's army didn't know jack about real soldierin'. They'd proven that back in '91 when Desert Storm went through 'em like (deleted) through a goose. But Abadi, he knew the score. When I told him might be trouble up ahead, he said, "I will send men up ahead to clear trees." His English was passable. He started divvying his boys up into squads. He never got no further.

The first AK rounds came out of the trees and took him and his top sergeant down. I yelled, "Contact!" and dropped down to one knee and started returning fire. Didn't see the targets but they were there, sure as hell. I put four rounds on them and then hustled back toward my guys. Rounds are going past me, zip! I heard some of the IAs yelling, but not too many returning fire. I knew this was gonna be bad. Only good thing, the enemy had opened up too soon, they hadn't let us get into the kill box all the way. But we were still in the (deleted), that I knew.

PFC Matt Dezotell is from Michigan's Upper Peninsula. Like a lot of his fellow soldiers, he joined up after an unproductive year in college. Dezotell's grandfather fought with the Marines in Korea, so that branch was his first choice, but the Marine recruiter wasn't there when Dezotell walked into the recruiting office in Escanaba, and the Army recruiter was. Dezotell is nineteen, well-built and used to the outdoors after spending his youth hunting and fishing almost every day.

My first firefight. I'd been hunting since I was seven years old, shot plenty of small game, a lot of deer, a few bears, but none of them ever shot back, you know? But when I see the first Iraqis go down, three of them, my training takes over and I hit the dirt, bring my weapon around and start scanning for targets. A guy wearing black and carrying an AK (*AK-47, the enemy's primary infantry weapon*) steps out of the woods and I drop him with one shot, center mass. I was the top marksman of my class at OSUT and these targets were at about fifty meters, no problem, really. Two more come out and I drop them, too, one shot each.

I thought, holy Christ, I've just killed three guys.

The sarge comes running by, waving us over to the ditch on the side of the road, yelling "Move your ass! Move your ass!" He didn't have to tell me twice. I get up and run over there and trip on a rock and down I go, head first. There's water and mud at the bottom of the ditch and I get all of it. Some gets in my mouth and nose and I start choking, but then somebody grabs me by the collar and pulls me out, turns me around. It was Dawson, the guy from Wisconsin, the wrestler. Good thing, it would've been a helluva thing to drown in a ditch in Iraq, you know?

He says, "Matt, you okay?" And I cough a couple times and then say yeah, good to go. The ditch isn't that deep, maybe three feet, and we crawl up to the edge to see what's going on. Lots of gunfire, most of it AK. It's a very distinctive sound, not like our M4s, so I can tell right away the IAs are getting the worst of it. But our guys, the Americans, are getting into the ditch and the sarge, Boudreau, he's yelling at 'em, then he spins around like a top and goes down hard.

"Sarge's hit," Jake says.

So I think I should maybe go get him, so I start to climb out of the ditch and a round goes past my helmet, just an inch or so from my ear, and that drops me back down pretty damn quick. I say something like, "Jesus Christ!" And Jake says I'll be seeing him pretty soon if I don't stay down. Then he says he's gonna go get the sarge so I should give him some cover.

I'm at the edge of the ditch now and Jake, he's ready to go after the sarge. I sight on the flashes coming out of the woods and start returning fire, three-round bursts, no way do I want to go full auto, we're trained not to do that, stay under control. I notice that those three guys I dropped are still out there but their buddies are hanging back in the trees now. It's not just me returning fire, it's most of my buddies in the ditch. The IAs, they're in pretty tough shape out on the road. Most of 'em are down, some are crawling toward the ditch. Lots of moaning, crying out to their moms, at least I think so, I don't know any Arabic.

Jake says, "Okay, here I go!" He crawls out and then scrambles toward the sarge, low to the ground. Something moves to my right, and I risk a glance over there. It's the Chief, and he's up in firing position with that big son of a bitch of a machine gun he's got and he's really giving it to 'em, covering Jake as he gets to the sarge and picks him up and starts hustling him away. Boudreau, he's a pretty big guy himself, but Jake picked him up like he was nothing.

PFC Dawson:
I'd never seen a man get shot before, but I'd seen some leg injuries on the mat and I knew the sarge wasn't going to be running away from this one. The hajis were going to turn him into Swiss cheese if somebody didn't help him. They were already chewing up the IA wounded. Things were happening pretty fast. Rounds were kicking up the dirt and zipping past me. It was only ten or twelve meters to the sarge but it seemed like a couple miles.

But I got to him and he was alive. I picked him up by the belt and the collar of his vest and hustled him back to the ditch. Every step I'm thinking they're gonna get me, I'm gonna take some rounds in my legs and we'll bleed out and it'll all be over. Matt, the U.P. kid, his face was full of mud but he was providing covering fire. Chet was at the end of the line and then there was the Chief with his SAW, then Matt and then some other guys to my right, and between all of them it was just enough to keep the hajis in the woods pinned down and give me some cover. I gave Matt a nod when I went by him. One thing about Yoopers, they're tough kids, it's real wilderness up there and you learn fast what you need to do to get the job done. He was getting it done.

The thing about wrestling is, you've gotta have strong legs, a lot stronger than you might think. My legs were in great shape and so I didn't have a problem getting the sarge down into the ditch. I got him up into a fireman's carry and headed to the compound. I saw Doering down the line, yelling and waving us toward it.

CPL Marcus Doering is G Troop's communications expert. His wiry build speaks to his many days in the field, as well as his athletic background; this is his second deployment, and prior to joining the Army he was on the swimming team at Penn State.

When Boudreau went down, that left me in command of the American squad. I wasn't scared, because I went through the same thing a couple times in Afghanistan. Training and experience take over. I yelled at the men to fall back to the compound. About half of the Iraqis were down, the other half were booking it to the compound, nothing like an orderly retreat. A few of them brought along wounded buddies. Our guys were giving them decent cover but we had to get into the compound. I got down in the ditch and got on comms to call in air support. I had no idea how many hajis were in those woods but if they were there in platoon strength, we'd have a hard time defending that compound considering how depleted we already were, including the IAs.

My first call didn't get acknowledged. I had to get to the compound and repeat the call, maybe repair the radio if it had gotten banged up. I looked over the edge of the ditch and there was Dawson, hauling Boudreau off the road. The guys were laying down covering fire. Dawson got into the ditch, got the sarge up on his shoulders and I waved them toward the compound. I yelled at the guys to retreat. If we stayed out in the ditch, the hajis would try to flank us and if they cut us off from the compound, we were toast.

CPL Bender:

Maybe half the IAs made it to the compound. I stayed with Doering. That radio was our lifeline, if we lost that we'd have to slug it out with the hajis and at the moment, I didn't like those odds. I didn't know where any air assets might be, but Doering would find them.

I heard the Chief's SAW hammering away and risked a look outside the compound entrance. He was one of the last guys out there, and he was still in the ditch, although he'd moved several meters closer. The enemy was focusing their fire on the Chief, trying to knock his gun out of the fight. If they had an officer who had his (deleted) together, they could flank the Chief, take him out and then advance on the compound.

And damn if I didn't see about four of them, about twenty meters up the road, run across it and head for the ditch. The Chief saw them too, turned his gun on them and got one or two, forcing the rest back into the trees.

Dawson was carrying the sarge and hustling toward the compound. Dezotell was trailing him, stopping every few meters to drop to a knee and give them cover. Solum was already inside. That left just two Americans, the Chief and Murphy, out on the road. I looked past the Chief and saw Murphy fall back into the ditch. He'd been hit. The Chief slid back into the ditch and started running to the compound. He went down after two steps and I thought he'd bought it, but he got up and started running again. I found out later he'd taken a round to the helmet, glanced off the Kevlar.

Doering was making his call, getting through. Dawson put Boudreau down against a wall and checked him over, found the leg wound, and then one of the surviving IAs, the platoon medic, came over to treat the sarge. Dawson ran back to me at the gate. "Where's Chet?" he asked.

"Out there past the Chief," I said. "I think he took a round."

"I've gotta go get him," he said. "Cover me." Before I could say anything, he took off running toward the road.

I took a knee and sighted on the trees, fired a three-round burst. The hajis were coming out of the trees. They'd seen Murphy, too.

Sid Murphy looks like the Marlboro Man, except he doesn't smoke. He's a rancher in Cut Bank, Montana, and two years ago he dropped his son, Chet, off at the Missoula airport for his flight to Fort Benning and basic training.

Well, Chet was about the best son a man could hope to have. Always a great attitude, worked hard on the ranch, did well in school. Played football, went to Montana State, walked on the team there and played quite a bit. Starting safety by his junior year and they gave him a scholarship. It's a long drive, here to Bozeman, but his mother and I never missed a home game, saw some on the road, too. He got a degree in Animal Science, focusing on livestock management. He was all set to take over the ranch. His older brother and sister, they didn't love the ranch like Chet did.

But then he said, "Dad, I want to go into the Army, I'm not ready to come home just yet." I said okay. That was before his mom was diagnosed with breast cancer…

When I told him, he said he was gonna get out somehow, come home, but I said no, stay in and finish your hitch, then make your decision. Maybe he could've gotten out because of his mom, maybe not. She's doing okay, she's a fighter, like he is. Montana women, 'specially those raised up here on the High Line like her, they're tough. So Chet went overseas. I didn't have much advice for him. I did a hitch in the Navy, wanted to see the world, all that, and I did, but never saw combat. My dad, though, he was with the Marines in Korea, and he and Chet were close, so I know he gave my boy some good advice.

He was always a good shot. Plenty of varmints on the ranch, you know, and there was always hunting. Chet loved that, brought home deer and elk every year. We never lacked for venison in the freezer, that's a fact. So when they told me he got a few of those (expletive), I wasn't surprised. And when they told me he was the last guy on the line, in that ditch, to cover his buddies, well, that wasn't no surprise, either. Chet was a team player. Always had been. The ranch, football, then the Army. He was a team guy. The guy you'd want beside you when the chips were down.

CWO4 David Scott was aloft over Wasit Governate that day in his AH-64D Apache Longbow attack helicopter. Scott is a twenty-year Army veteran and was on his sixth deployment, third to Iraq.

It was supposed to be a training flight that day. My front seater, Swanson, had just arrived in the Sandbox from Fort Rucker. We had a full combat load and the Longbow was purring like a cat. Swanson was doing well. I was just about ready to return to base when we got a radio call, troops on the ground in contact, requesting air support. The commo guys do their best to stay calm but I could hear gunfire in the background and knew the (deleted) was hitting this guy's fan, so I acknowledged and confirmed we'd be there ASAP. I punched his coordinates into the computer and the readout told me I could do fifteen, maybe twenty minutes over the target before we had to RTB. I switched my frequency, reported to base that we were en route to engage, then told Swanson that we were diverting to assist, and his weapons were free.

CPL Roberts:

I was running low on ammo. I'd loaded up with STANAG mags, thirty rounds each, and I'd burned through two and was maybe halfway through my third. I had three more and that was it. Should've brought belts on this mission, but Boudreau had said I wouldn't need 'em. The sarge is a pretty smart guy but he made the wrong call on this one.

Dawson ran through the ditch behind me. There was one of our guys left out there, about twenty meters past me, around a little bend, and the hajis were almost on him. Dawson yelled for me to give him cover fire. I picked up my SAW and started following him. Ten meters out, I couldn't fire on the hajis coming after our guy, didn't want to risk hitting him, but I could keep their buddies from coming out, so I started hosing the woods again. Dawson would have to deal with those jokers on his own. I hoped he wouldn't be too late.

CPL Bender:

I was still about forty meters from our guys when I heard the most beautiful sound an infantryman can hear, and that's the sound of an Apache inbound. Doering had gotten one and help was on the way.

Up ahead, I saw the Chief firing on the hajis coming out of the woods. A few bodies were piled up on that side of the road but there was no telling how many were left in there. Still plenty of fire coming out of the timber, that's for damn sure. I saw the three hajis advancing across the road toward Murphy, and I had a better angle on them than the Chief, so I used a big rock for cover, sighted on the bad guys and my (expletive) gun jammed. I worked to clear the jam but I knew it was up to Dawson now.

Doering must've vectored the bird for the trees because his chain gun opened up. Two of the hajis were just outside the tree line, I saw them bring their AKs up to fire on the bird and then they were gone, they just sort of dissolved when those M230 rounds hit them. Don't take this the wrong way, man, but that was about the prettiest sight I'd seen all day.

CPL Roberts:
I heard the Apache coming in and hit the deck, just as its chain gun opened up. My SAW is a helluva weapon, but hey, it's nothing like that M230. That mother puts out six hundred rounds a minute, a thirty millimeter round that causes a lot of damage, and I mean a lot. The hajis were getting chewed up pretty good even if the rounds didn't hit them directly, just taking shell fragments and splinters from the trees. Heard some screams over the sound of the bird and the chain gun. Music to my ears, man. I'd seen Apaches work a lot and I'm damn glad the hajis don't have anything like 'em. Too bad for those guys, right?

The bird made its first pass in just a few seconds and there was smoke and dust coming out of the trees, but no enemy fire. Anybody left alive in there, they'd be on the run by now, because the bird was coming around for another run. That's the thing about these (expletive), they got nothing that can challenge the Apache and they know it, so when one shows up, they run like the fury of Almighty God is right on their ass, which it pretty much is.

I could hear Dawson's M4 to my right. He was engaging the three hajis who'd come after Murphy, giving them his personal attention, so I ran that way to help him.

Sid Murphy:
They told me Chet had taken a bullet to the shoulder, his gun shoulder, so they don't think he had a chance to fire his weapon after he fell down into that ditch. But I know he had his granddad's KA-BAR combat knife. My dad never talked too much to me about his time over in Korea, but he did tell me that he kept the knife clean because he'd gotten a lot of blood on it. That told me all I needed to know.

Chet knew how to use a knife, too. His granddad had taught him how to skin a buck with it, and I imagine he taught him how to use it on a man, too, if he had to. That day, they tell me, Chet was...*He sighs, and his lower lip trembles.* He was able to use what he'd been taught. My son was a fighter.

PFC Dawson:
I yelled for Chet to hang on, but over the sound of the helo and the chain gun, I don't know if he heard me. I saw the first haji jump down in the ditch and Chet pull his knife. That left two on the side of the road. I was still about fifteen meters away. I went full auto with my weapon and kept running.

CW4 Scott:
Making a second pass over the target was probably overkill, but I had the weapons and the fuel and our men down there were still in contact, so I brought the Longbow around again. This time it would be rockets. I've had too many missions to count, in Iraq and Afghanistan, and the chain gun usually does the job quite nicely against enemy infantry, but there was no use taking any chances.

We had a full load of Hydras, two dozen, half of them with flechette warheads. A flechette is a steel dart, about four grams in weight. Other weapons we had were designed to take out hardened targets, bunkers or armored vehicles, but there was no need for those now. I took the firing control for the launch. My helmet monocle let me focus on the target as I brought the aircraft around, all I had to do was follow the symbols in the monocle to aim the M261 rocket pods. I took one last look at the Americans, there were three or four still engaging the enemy from the ditch on the far side of the road. Plenty of clearance, so I walked the rockets through the woods. If there were any enemy still alive in there before, there wouldn't be now. I rather doubted there would be any virgins waiting for them, where they were going.

CPL Bender:
When I saw the Apache's rocket pods light up, I knew the firefight

was over and the good guys had won. But Dawson and Murphy were still down at the end of the line. I'd seen Dawson fire on the hajis coming across the road and then he jumped into the ditch. I'd cleared my M4's jam and ran like hell up the road. Two of the hajis were down on the road and I put two rounds in each one just to make sure they wouldn't cause any more trouble.

I got to the edge of the ditch and saw there was no need to fire any more rounds. The Chief was already there and he'd safed his weapon. I did the same with mine. I heard him say, "Goddamn it," kind of soft. I got down in the ditch, to see if I could help, but it was all over.

Dawson was down there in the mud, on his knees, and Murphy was in his arms. A haji was lying there next to them, Murphy's KA-BAR buried to the hilt in his gut, he was deader than a (deleted)bug, like my grandpa used to say.

Murphy's helmet was off and the front of his BDU, under his vest, was dark with blood. The haji must've gotten him with a knife, up and under his body armor. Had enough to do it, which was saying something, 'cause Chet had gotten him first. Knife fighting is like that, you're both gonna get cut, you just hope the other guy gets it worse. This time, they both got it worse.

I could hardly look at it. Chet's eyes were still open, looking up past Dawson, who was crying. "I was too late," he said. "I was too late to save him."

What could I say? What do you say to a brother when another one of your brothers is lying there? I put my hand on Dawson's shoulder and said, "You did what you could, man."

He just shook his head. "It wasn't enough," he said. "It wasn't…"

Bender breaks down, waves the camera away.

CHAPTER TWO

Northern Wisconsin
September 2013

When I saw her, I asked myself why in the hell I'd broken up with her all those years before. How long ago was it? We were juniors at Lakeland Union High, so that would be seven years. Samantha Peterson was good-looking back then, with long, toned legs, a light spray of freckles that gave her a bit of a little-girl look, sandy blonde hair, a figure that was starting to fill out. And now, it sure had.

"Jake! Why aren't you wearing your uniform tonight? You looked so good in it at church."

So she'd noticed me that morning after all. As she walked over to me, the party swirling around her, I couldn't keep my eyes from tracking up from the white pumps on her feet to those legs to her short denim skirt and the white sweater that displayed just the right amount of cleavage. Remembering that we were at my mother's house and not at a bar, I forced myself to focus on her face, and her great smile, and those hazel eyes. But on the way there I'd noticed that there wasn't a ring on her left hand.

The house suddenly seemed a little warmer. Outside, it was northern Wisconsin in late September, meaning it could be seventy degrees one day and snowing the next. Inside, all the people my mom had invited were chatting and having a drink or two, enjoying themselves. Old friends of the family, some classmates of mine—and the girls all looked prettier than ever—and even some wrestling opponents from nearby schools. Overall, a good slice of the kind of folks who lived in and around Minocqua, enjoying the lakes and everything else that small-town life offered. Sometimes I missed it. No, I missed it a lot of the time. It was good to be home, even if I wasn't going to be around much longer.

The uniform, she'd asked about the uniform. Focus. "Well," I said, "the official Army Service Uniform is only worn at prescribed functions when on duty, but for off-duty occasions, it's the soldier's choice. I figured I'd better dress up for God, I'm likely to need him where I'm going."

Her eyes went wide and she clutched the bottle of Leinie's she'd been sipping from. "Will it be dangerous? I mean, I know you're in the Army and you've already been over there, but, well…"

"I wouldn't worry, Sam," I said. "At least for a while. I'm heading down to Fort Benning on Thursday to start Ranger training."

Sam's eyes sparkled and her head tilted. She had the same "tell" she'd had back in the day, when I was a state-champion wrestler for the Lakeland Thunderbirds and she played first base on the softball team. She was intrigued, and signaling that she was also available. "I've heard about Rangers," she said. "On the news and everything. Pretty tough guys, huh?"

"Nothing your average Marine couldn't handle," a deep male voice said.

It was my great-uncle, and he'd snuck up on me like he always did. Damn, how did he do that? John Dawson was a former Marine— although he'd say there's nothing *former* about it, even though he hadn't worn the uniform for almost thirty years. At parties, there was an even chance he was close to being drunk, although Mom had told me in a letter about a year back that he'd gone on the wagon again and it seemed to be sticking this time. He appeared to be sober tonight, in fact a little more serious than usual.

"Hello, Uncle John, glad to see you," I said, and I meant it. I'd always thought of him as the grandfather I never had. We shook hands, and the old Marine's grip was as strong as ever. His gray eyes bored into me for a second, then turned back to Samantha. "Honey, if you'll excuse me, I have to borrow the guest of honor for a few minutes."

"Oh. Okay, sure."

"Don't go anywhere," I said over my shoulder as my great-uncle led me away by an elbow. And I didn't want her to go anywhere, at least not with anyone else. Why wasn't she married by now? I fully intended to explore that topic later, in private. Maybe, I thought, I should try to make amends for the last time we'd gone out. She had to remember it, because I'd never forgotten it: a blanket out by the lake, a warm summer night, and my only condom had broken at the moment of truth. She'd laughed at me, and worse yet, she told her friends about it, and within a few days everybody in the whole damn school seemed to know. That's how I remembered it, anyway, but tonight I just couldn't hold it against her anymore. Hey, we were kids back then, weren't we?

What the hell, it was a small town. People needed something to talk about, but I'd broken up with Sam right after that. During my senior year Angie Egan gave me a gift after I won my second straight state championship. That night the condom didn't break, by God.

Uncle John was leading me toward the sliding glass doors that opened onto the deck. On the way several more people wished me good luck, a couple of the men slapping me on the shoulder. We passed the dining room table, and the "Good Luck Jake!" cake, garish as it was in my school colors of black and white with Army green thrown in, was almost gone. Everybody seemed to be having a good time, and I had to admit that I was, too, and I'd been able to do it on only one beer, which had to be a new record.

And I suddenly realized that I was proud of that. In the past couple years, I'd been making some changes, tightening things up, getting more serious. Iraq showed me a lot about myself, a lot of which was good, some of it bad. The bad things, I'd started working on those. The drinking was one of them. Not that it had ever been out of hand, but now I was okay with one beer, instead of three or four. The women, too. Seeing Sam had been a real turn-on, but within seconds after that initial rush, I'd remembered more than just her body. I remembered the good times we'd had together, the laughter and the gentleness. On the mat and the diamond, we were holy terrors, focused and driven. We understood each other, and that was what had been best about us. Now,

I wondered if maybe, just maybe, we could put that one disastrous teenage summer night behind us and see what might be out there for us as adults.

I took a glance back toward the kitchen where my mom, the consummate homemaker, was making sure everyone had enough food. Next to her was Barry Templeton, her significant other, adding juice to the punch bowl. I could hardly believe my nearing-fifty mother referred to him as her "boyfriend." But I liked Barry, a guy so opposite from my dad that they might have come from opposite sides of the planet. Well, in essence they had, culturally-speaking. Barry was a local guy, owned the hardware store in Minocqua. He was down to earth, a Packer fan, voted Republican every election. My dad, and Monica Dawson's ex-husband, was Ronald Dawson, and he tolerated Wisconsin as long as he could spend most of his time down in cosmopolitan Madison. He considered football barbaric and wouldn't vote Republican if his life depended on it. As for me, I had always found the culture up here in the north woods to be a lot more comfortable than the one in the city my father inhabited down south.

Uncle John was already through the doors and out on the deck when I felt a soft hand touch my arm. "Hello, Jake."

I had to look down at the gray-haired lady smiling up at me. "Mrs. King? Hey, thanks for coming!" Our town librarian had always been one of my favorite people, and I wrapped her in a hug, taking care not to squeeze. She'd never been a big woman, and she seemed a lot frailer than I remembered. "Aren't you retired by now?"

"Five years ago, although I go back now and then to help out."

"Well, that's great." I had a lot of fond memories of Mrs. King, helping me search through the shelves for anything about the military, especially Special Forces. She'd even managed to find a picture of my grandfather's A-team from Vietnam, a photo that was still in a frame on the wall of my old bedroom, down the hall. And that memory reminded me of something. "Stay here, I'll be right back."

Twenty seconds later, I handed her a paperback book, its cover nearly in tatters. "I think this might be slightly overdue," I said.

She took it from me almost reverently. "*The Green Berets,* by Robin Moore." She beamed as she flipped carefully through the first few pages. "Why, this is the original one we got back in 1966. Jake, you must have read this a dozen times."

"Well, six or eight, at least. The last time I checked it out, I forgot to return it. I think it was senior year. I suppose I'll have a pretty hefty fine built up by now."

She nodded. "You've been kind of busy," she said, and handed it back to me. "Here. The statute of limitations has run out, I think."

I was touched. "Thank you," I said, and gave her another hug.

I stepped out on the deck to join my great-uncle, and the beauty of Bobcat Lake stretched out before us. I breathed in its scent, so familiar, so distinct. It was...comforting. The home on the lake had always been that to me, I had to admit. I figured I might as well embrace it, because I had no idea when—or if—I'd ever make it back. After Ranger School I'd be assigned to a combat unit, and I'd be overseas somewhere. Today's Army didn't want its newly-minted second lieutenants pushing paper stateside. And I knew that if I were to achieve my ultimate goal, Special Forces, getting that Ranger tab and then another combat tour or two was vital.

Uncle John leaned over against the railing, gazing out at the lake. Behind us, the sounds of the party were muffled. It was unseasonably warm for the final weekend of September, but that would change soon, it always did. Snow flurries usually made their first appearance up here by mid-October. By then I'd be packing a ruck through the woods of Georgia, and snow would be the furthest thing from my mind.

I saluted the lake with my bottle and drained the last of the Leinie's, stifled a burp and leaned on the railing next to him. "So, what's on your mind, Uncle John?"

"Sorry for taking you away from Miss July back there," he said, "but I wanted to make sure we had a chance to talk before time got away from us."

I looked over at my great-uncle. So serious now, unusual for him. John Dawson had always been the favorite uncle every boy wanted, a guy to hang out with, maybe play a video game or two, a guy you could talk to about things you couldn't talk to your own father about. And in my case, the age difference meant even more. I'd never known my own grandfathers, so my great-uncle filled the bill. Uncle John could be the life of the party one minute and the next he'd be the tough Marine sergeant he must've been thirty years before. How old was he now, anyway? Must've been pushing seventy, but he still looked to be in pretty good shape. I suddenly realized I might not know my great-uncle as well as I thought.

He asked, "When do you ship out?"

"Thursday morning," I said. "Flight out of Green Bay at ten. I'll be at Benning by late afternoon."

"Training starts when?"

"A week from tomorrow. I have to report on Sunday the sixth, but I wanted a couple extra days to get squared away, check out my gear."

Uncle John nodded. "Yeah." He sighed. "Listen, Jake, why don't you switch your flight, leave from Milwaukee instead?"

I looked at him, momentarily puzzled. "Why would I do that? Green Bay's a lot closer than Milwaukee."

"Yeah, but it's not that far from Madison." Those old gray eyes looked at me with a sharpness I suddenly found uncomfortable. Then I got it.

I waved my empty beer bottle. "Oh, no. You're thinking…nope. Not gonna happen, Uncle John. I'm surprised you'd even suggest it." The old Marine stood up straight. He was shorter than me by a good inch, but right now looked like he could still take me in a wrestling match. "You need to see your father, Jake. After Ranger School, you'll be deployed. And you know what could happen."

"Has he talked to you? Is that it, he asked you to talk me into going down there?"

Uncle John shook his head. "No. I haven't talked to your father in, what, three years? I called him after he lost his last election, just to tell him I was sorry."

I laughed and turned back to the lake. I had a powerful urge to throw the bottle as far out into the water as I could, but my discipline held me back. I'd first learned about discipline on the wrestling mat, from third grade all the way to college, and then with the Army, where it was taken to a whole new level. I took a deep breath, and inside me there was a struggle. A part of me knew that my great-uncle was right. But I couldn't admit it, not just yet.

"You were sorry he lost? Hell, Uncle John, you didn't vote for him."

"No, I didn't, mostly because I didn't live in his district. But he's family, Jake, and I know he enjoyed being in Congress. He worked hard. Family sticks together when one of them is going through a tough time. You know that."

I turned to face him, suddenly angry. "He served three terms, for crying out loud, and finally the voters got tired of him and threw his ass out. Times were changing and they didn't want an anti-war guy in there anymore. An anti-military guy. Did you know he voted against every defense appropriation? For six years, every goddamn time! He wanted to hang me and my buddies out to dry."

Uncle John took a step closer and put a hand on my shoulder. "Yeah, I knew. I heard about it often enough. But he's still your father, Jake, and you may not think so, but I know he loves you. And deep down inside, you–"

I shrugged the hand off. "Don't say it. Don't."

"Okay. Just think about it, all right? Anyway, that's not the only reason I wanted to talk to you before you left. Come on, let's sit down."

We pulled chairs out from the patio table. I'd offered to put the furniture away for the winter, but Mom had told me to wait till after the party. Well, I'd do it before I left. For Green Bay.

"I've been meaning to ask you something," Uncle John said. "I got three letters from you while you were in Iraq, and you never mentioned the firefight."

I tried to relax, but couldn't. The memory was still raw, more than two years later. I looked out at the lake, knowing where this was going. Finally, I asked, "Which one? There were a few."

"You know the one, Jake. The one where you got the Bronze Star."

When I didn't respond, he added, "Your mom told me about the medal. She didn't even know till some reporter from Green Bay called her."

I tried to shove the memory away and relax. A futile effort, although by now I had trained myself to hide it pretty well. I suspected, though, that my great-uncle, who knew me better than anybody, could see right through it. I shrugged. "Not much to tell, Uncle John. My squad got in a jam. I did what had to be done to help us get out. But…" My eyes were suddenly wet, and like a thousand times before I cursed myself for my weakness. I couldn't think of Chet without all the emotions flooding back. Sorrow, like I'd never known before, and anger, ready to boil up like lava if I didn't keep it capped. After a moment, I felt my great-uncle's hand on my shoulder again. This time, I left it there. It helped push the emotions back down, where I could control them.

"It's okay, Jake. You don't have to talk about it. I'm sorry I asked."

I shook my head. "Bronze Star, my ass," I said, almost whispering. I tried to focus on the loon out on the lake. Pretty late in the season for loons. As if reading my thoughts, the bird uttered a long, mournful call. "My buddy bled out in my arms," I blurted out. "Because I wasn't fast enough, wasn't tough enough. I got the medal, should've been him." What I didn't dare say, not even to my favorite guy in the world, was that Chet's death haunted me for more reasons than one. Everything I'd done since that terrible day was moving toward another day, when I'd again have to make the tough decisions, with men's lives at stake, and deep inside myself I wondered whether I'd make the right call the next time. As an officer, I'd be responsible for a lot of men when my next firefight came along. Would I be able to bring them all through it? Or would I fail, again? Would I have to write that letter home that no officer wanted to write?

I'd thought that going through Officer Candidate School would surely lead to the chance to redeem myself, but on my next tour, in Afghanistan, I was attached to a headquarters unit. In five months in-country I'd gone on only a couple dozen patrols, always as the second in command, and only twice had my unit come under fire. I hadn't lost any men, but both times I'd been bailed out by the commanding officer's smarts and leadership. I knew I should've been grateful for that, but the ultimate test of my own leadership, my courage, was still somewhere out there in the mountains and valleys. And Chet Murphy, my boot camp buddy, was still in his grave out in Montana, still waiting to be avenged.

We were silent for a minute. The loon called again. I was thinking that maybe, just maybe, I should lay it all out for Uncle John. If anybody would understand, he would, after three tours in Vietnam with the Marines. But he beat me to it. He coughed, then said, "I lost my buddy, too. Khe Sanh, seventh of February, 1968."

That got my attention. I'd rarely heard my great-uncle talk about his own wartime experiences. "What happened?"

Uncle John sighed, then said, "The NVA infiltrated one night, came through the wire and overran our OP. I was twenty feet away, taking a leak. Billy was dozing, I thought I'd only take a minute, then I'd be back. I got two or three of the bastards, but…" He sighed again. "I never got over that, Jake. A month later the relief column got through and I was rotated back to Saigon. Went to Bangkok on leave and started drinking before the plane's wheels touched the tarmac. If the Corps hadn't needed every single one of us, I'd've been drummed out for sure. Today they'd never tolerate it, and that's a good thing." There was another pause, where he seemed to be summoning up some kind of inner strength. "I did two more tours, sent a few more of those gomers down to roast with Uncle Ho, but none of that brought Billy back. Jake, you gotta put that behind you, son, I'm telling you." He was silent for a few seconds, then said, "Maybe there's somebody else who could tell you that better than me." He reached over near the grill and brought a paper bag out, setting it on the table.

"What's this, a going-away gift?" I asked.

"You might say that. I'm not much for gift wrapping, and this doesn't really need to be wrapped, anyway." Uncle John reached in side and pulled out a book, handing it over to me. "That's for you. Read it when you have some free time, although I suspect you won't have much of it for a while."

I held it up to the light coming through a window. The book was old, a faint mustiness interfering with the telltale scent of its leather binding. It seemed thicker than it should be, and then I realized that was because it was stuffed with things: letters, newspaper clippings, photographs. Even a pressed flower. At the very front was a folded letter, and a sepia-toned photo of a man in a nineteenth-century uniform. "What is this?"

"There's a letter inside that explains it. From your grandfather."

That got my attention. "Grampa Dennis?"

"Right. He gave it to me just before he went back to 'Nam in 'seventy-two." Uncle John was sitting back in the chair, relaxed, but now sat forward slowly, bowing his head. His eyes blinked several times, then he sat back, letting out a sigh. "Damn. Sorry about that. I get kind of emotional when I think of him."

"Hey, nothing to be sorry about." He had told me some stories about my long-dead grandfather, but from when they were kids, not about his time in the Army. Once or twice I had asked him about that, but Uncle John just closed up, shook his head, said not now, maybe someday.

That day had come. Uncle John talked for the next thirty-five minutes. He held back the tears for thirty-three.

CHAPTER THREE

Central Wisconsin
October 2013

My last morning at home, and I was up before dawn. By ten I'd run the gamut of Wisconsin fall weather: I did my two-mile run through snow flurries, and it had turned to drizzle by the time I hit the road after one last breakfast with Mom. Now, the sun was shining as I pulled my rented Camry off Highway 51 into a truck stop just north of Stevens Point. It was warm enough that I had to take off my uniform jacket when I got out to gas up.

I'd made good time, but still had two hours ahead of me to Madison. After filling up the car, I had to empty myself, so I went inside to use the facilities. When I got back behind the wheel and slipped a paper cup of cappuccino into the holder on the console, I saw the Rough Rider's diary on the seat, all by itself. The corner of a letter peeked out from inside the front cover.

Last night, before I turned in one last time in my old bedroom, I'd opened the book and took the letter out. It was the first of several inserted within the book's original pages, and it looked a little yellowed and brittle. I unfolded it carefully and turned it toward the light from my bedside lamp, the same lamp I'd used to read *The Green Berets* and so many other books when I was a kid. Uncle John had told me this letter was the first thing I should read, since it was the most recent addition to the diary.

I'd seen plenty of pictures of my grandfather, even some old home movies from the sixties, but had never read his words. I read the letter twice, and had some difficulty getting to sleep. The guy in the photos, the guy who was represented by that folded flag on my shelf, the guy whose rank pins and medals were displayed on my wall...he finally came alive for me.

I started the car and put it in gear, but I didn't swing it around toward the highway. Instead, I pulled ahead into a parking space, turned off the engine and picked up the letter. I had to read it again.

The letter of Sgt. Maj. Dennis Dawson, U.S. Army Special Forces

15 February 1972

To my dear son Ron (or my grandson):

The book you have in your hand right now is the journal of my grandfather, Charles Dawson, who served valiantly with the 1st Volunteer Cavalry in Cuba in the Spanish-American War of 1898. Yes, he was a Rough Rider, and if you know anything about them, you know they were a hell of an outfit, which contributed greatly to our nation's victory in that conflict and the liberation of the Cuban people.

I write this to you on the eve of my departure for South Vietnam. It is my fourth and final tour. God willing, I will return safely in six months' time, and then I will be able to tear this letter up and talk to you personally, someday, about this journal, as my father did for me. But in the event I do not return, this letter will have to do.

You have seen, Ronnie, that I added "or my grandson" to the salutation. This is in the event you do not join the U.S. military. Under the terms of my grandfather's will, this journal is to pass to his oldest direct descendant and from there down the line to succeeding descendants, provided those men choose to put on their nation's uniform. Ronnie, you are just past your fifth birthday, and so for this tour I am entrusting this journal, along with this letter and the other letters within, to my younger brother John, your uncle. My grandfather's original instructions were to have his diary passed down to the eldest son of each generation who serves in uniform. My father had two sons, and he convinced his father to amend the restriction to allow all Dawson sons to read it. But your uncle will not give it to you if you do not join the military. Hopefully, if you make that choice, you will serve in other, honorable ways, for there are many ways of service. But my grandfather was specific, and so in that event, your uncle John will pass the journal to your oldest child who chooses to put on the uniform. If that happens, you will never even read this letter. It is impossible for the person who never serves to understand what it means to wear his country's uniform. My grandfather's intention was to make sure all Dawson men who make that choice know what they are getting into, what it really means.

It's possible you will not have sons but will have a daughter or two, and if so, it may go to her if she serves. Anything is possible, and I see women doing great work in the Army all the time, but frankly I hope they never are allowed into the combat arms. That is difficult work, hard work. Man's work. It is not for women. Your mother might disagree with me, but that's how I feel. I have seen many of my buddies, America's sons, sent home in body bags. I don't ever want to see America's daughters sent home that way.

I read Charles Dawson's journal right after I finished boot camp in '65. He was five years in his grave by then, but I remember him well to this day. I was 14 when he died, he was 84. He was a quiet sort of guy, and no matter how many times I prodded him, he would not talk about his time in the service. He would look off in the distance, and his chin would start to quiver, and his eyes would tear up. (When you read his journal, you will understand.) He would never say anything, except once when he said that in all his years afterwards, he never met a finer group of men. And he always spoke with the highest regard for his commanding officer, Theodore Roosevelt, who went on to become President of the United States.

He said he knew Roosevelt personally and saw him at Rough Rider reunions, even campaigned with him when elections would come around. His greatest regret in life, he said, was not jumping in front of Roosevelt that day in 1912 in Milwaukee, when an assassin put a bullet in Roosevelt's chest at close range. My grandfather had helped Roosevelt into the car outside the hotel and was walking around to the other side when the shot rang out. As you should know by the time you read this, Roosevelt survived. In fact, he insisted on going to the meeting hall that night and giving his speech before he went to the hospital. My granddad said it was the greatest example of guts he'd ever seen, and he'd seen more than a few. The only president since then who came close, he said, was Eisenhower.

Perhaps it was fate that Roosevelt took that bullet and not my grandfather. If he had, he might've died, and my father would never have been born. Neither would I, nor you. The Lord moves in mysterious ways, my grandmother sometimes said. Roosevelt lived another six years or so after taking that bullet. My grandfather lived another 48 and because of that, the Dawson line went on to this day and beyond.

Although my grandfather never really talked to me about his service, my own dad certainly did. They called him "Two-Fist" in the Marine Corps because he was handy with both of them, and he talked like he fought, with what can delicately be called great enthusiasm and confidence. He is still a young man today, only 52, and Ronnie, I carry a picture of you sitting on his lap. I hope you get to know him well as you get older, and that he lives long enough to know your own kids. He wrote many letters home to my mother during his years overseas and some to me, but I have included only two with this journal. Both are from his time in Korea, although he also served in WWII.

I will warn you right now that your grandfather was a man who did not mince words, in person or in writing. You will see some of that in his letters. Do not be shocked by what he writes of his time in the Pacific and Korea. If you put on the uniform you may see things just as bad, even though the main reason we all put that uniform on is to work so that our own sons never have to do it, and so never have to see those things. I myself have seen things I cannot talk to you about now. I have done some things I'm not proud of, except I did them to save a buddy's life, or the lives of defenseless civilians. Maybe someday I will speak of them to you. But not for a while.

You are my only child, Ronnie, a situation I plan to rectify once I get back from this tour. Your mother will take good care of you while I am gone, and if I do not return, she will make sure you grow into a fine young man who will be a credit to his family and his country. Your mom is the love of my life and my greatest fear is not being able to grow old together with her.

I'm sorry those last words are kind of shaky. That happens when I think about your mom. Sometimes I wonder why she married a rough Green Beret sergeant back in '67. She was a real catch and I'm sure a lot of men were after her on her college campus. But when we met at that Christmas party in '65, when I was home on leave before going to 'Nam for my first tour, it was love at first sight for me and I think for her, too. Believe you me, she took a lot of grief from her so-called friends when she went back to school and told them she was dating a soldier. She told me once a guy on campus spat on her when she told him about me. (I looked that guy up when I got home and I don't think he's spat on anybody since.) But she hung tough, and we got engaged in '66 when I got back and married after my second tour. She has been the best thing that ever happened to me.

Sorry, there I go again. I better never let my men see me like this. But I think they would understand. I see them looking at pictures of their wives and kids and I know exactly what they're thinking. Every night I pray to God that He will see me through this deployment so that I can get back to her, and to you. I trust He will help me through one last tour.

But if He has something else in mind for me, I will accept His will. I likely will not have time to think about it when it happens. It quite probably will be hard for you to understand, too. All I can tell you is what my mother, your grandmother, told me, and that is you have to keep the faith and believe that God knows what He's doing, even if we don't. Keep that faith, my son, and someday you and I and your mother will be reunited in Heaven for all eternity.

I hope someday that you wear your country's uniform with pride, as four generations of Dawson men have done all the way back to the Civil War, when Charles Dawson's father fought at Gettysburg and Antietam with the Iron Brigade. Read about them someday. They were tough young fellows from Wisconsin who left their homes and farms and went far away to free a whole race of people from bondage. Every Dawson man since then has done the same thing. All of us have made it through, so far. Someday it might be your turn. I know you will serve with pride and uphold the honor of the Dawson name.

Your proud father,
Dennis Dawson, SgtMaj, 5th SFG, USA

I had to take a deep breath before I folded the letter gently and put it back in the diary. Uncle John had managed to talk me into going down to Madison to see my dad, but there was no way my dad would ever see this letter. It would tear him up inside. My father had been bitter about the war for forty years, had allowed it to come between him and his only child. This letter would not make that bitterness go away.

CHAPTER FOUR

Madison, Wisconsin
October 2013

There had been a time when I walked through the University of Wisconsin campus and students would wave and say hello, maybe wish me good luck for an upcoming meet. Of course I'd been wearing my wrestling jacket in those days. Today, wearing my Army Combat Uniform, almost everybody ignored me as I headed up Bascom Hill. I saw a few other people in uniform, some from the other services, and if they were coming toward me I'd zero in on the rank insignia tab and render a salute, or receive one. There were just enough of those to make the deliberate snubs by the civilians tolerable. But at least there were no one-fingered salutes by the civvies. None I saw, anyway.

It wasn't as bad as what my grandfather had encountered, if what he hinted at in his letter was true, and I was glad of that. Times had changed, even on campuses, but I wondered whether that would change back if we didn't wrap things up overseas sometime soon.

My father's building was North Hall, the first one ever built on the campus, I'd heard. Sometime before the Civil War. Not much to look at now, a rectangular brick box with four stories. I took a deep breath and entered, removing my patrol cap. In a few years, if I stayed the course, I'd earn a green beret. It would be a helluva challenge to get it, but I'd never shied away from a challenge in my life. Which was why, when you got right down to it, I was here right now.

My great-uncle had challenged me, in an uncharacteristically subtle way, to see my father. It was just about the last thing in the world I wanted to do, for more reasons than one. Samantha Peterson was still up in Minocqua, for one thing, and if I'd stayed in town one more night we might've been able to get together again. I could feel a grin splitting my face as I stopped to look over the directory on the wall. Sam had stuck around the party long enough for me to suggest we go somewhere else, and she said her place would be just fine, her roommate was away visiting her parents in Oshkosh and so we had her apartment all to ourselves. We'd made the most of it. I got to explore every inch of those gorgeous legs and beyond.

But it turned into more than a one-night stand for old time's sake. The next day, when I was storing Mom's deck furniture, I was squaring the garage away and found our old tent, still in good shape. On a whim, I called Sam and asked if she'd like to go camping up in the state forest north of Minocqua, and she agreed. I picked her up after she got off work Tuesday and a couple hours later we were sitting in front of a campfire, toasting marshmallows and talking about our high school days. The next day had been one of the best I'd had in some time, hiking with Sam through the forest and taking a brief but exhilarating skinny-dip in Big Lake. Before packing up the tent to come home, we spent one last hour together inside, and this time our lovemaking was exactly that. In fact, that was the first time I could ever recall thinking of sex that way. Not that I'd had a lot of women—there were only four before Sam, in fact, starting with Angie—but even though they'd been fun, I had never felt like we were making love. To do that, you actually have to be in love, don't you?

Sam was everything I had dreamed she'd be, and more. Athletic, energetic, passionate. That last time, when she reached her peak, she shuddered and gasped like she had before, but then she held me tight as I finished, and then she cried. When I dropped her off at her apartment, I promised to write when I could, and she cried again. I almost did, too. Damn, was I falling for her?

I forced himself to snap out of it. Ronald Dawson, Professor of Political Science, was on the third floor. I ignored the elevator and took the stairs two at a time, anxious to get this over with. I wanted to stop by the wrestling complex over at Camp Randall, see if Coach Davis was around. I'd enjoyed my two years competing for the Badgers, especially my sophomore year, when the team finished fourth in the nation and I was named All-American. Big 10 champ in my weight class, then third place in the NCAAs and people were talking about me winning it all the next year, then going for two in a row and maybe the London Olympics. But the call of the service had been too strong. I made it through the rest of the academic year and was off to boot camp in the summer of 2010.

I'd been so busy since then I hadn't had much time to reflect on my two years here, but now that I was back on campus, I couldn't help wondering what might've happened had I stayed. Would I have been good enough to win a national title, to get on the Olympic team? I'd followed the London Games as close as I could online. A guy from Azerbaijan had won gold at 84 kilograms, which would've been my weight class. In the quarterfinals that guy had beaten America's best, Jake Herbert of Northwestern. Herbert had pinned me in the Big Ten tournament to end my freshman season. So, maybe my Olympic dream would've died on a mat somewhere in the Trials. Well, what the hell. I had no regrets.

My father's office was one of several in the department, and as I stepped into the reception area I saw that there was just one secretary, probably serving all four of the offices in this section. It had to be a huge comedown for my dad, after six years in Congress. I'd visited his office in Washington once, during the first term, and even though it was just a freshman congressman's deep inside the creaking old Cannon Building, it was sure as hell more impressive than this setup.

The young guy behind the front desk appeared well-organized and competent. He looked up at me, did a brief double-take, and asked, "Can I help you?" He peered at my rank insignia, obviously puzzled by the single gold bar. "I'm sorry, I'm not up on Marine stuff," he said.

"It's the Army," I said. "I'm Lieutenant Dawson."

"Oh." The kid's eyes went wide. "Are you related to Professor Dawson?"

"Yes, he's my father. Is he in? I'm sorry, I don't have an appointment."

The kid looked at his computer screen. "Uh, he's with a student right now, but I don't see him scheduled for anything else until his next class at one."

I glanced at the clock on the wall. Eleven-fifteen. "Is it all right if I wait for him?"

"Sure." The kid gestured toward a small cluster of chairs in the corner, with a coffee table dominating the floor. "Right over there would be fine. When he's done with his meeting, I'll let him know you're here."

"No need for that," I said. I nodded toward a door that had my father's name on a wall plate at eye level. "I'll surprise him."

I was glad there was a *National Geographic* on the coffee table, because otherwise it would've been *Rolling Stone* or *Mother Jones* or a couple of scholarly journals that looked about as interesting as toe fungus. I kept one eye on my father's office door as I leafed through the magazine. An article about Afghanistan caught my eye and I made a mental note to find it online, assuming I had time. The next few days—months, actually—were going to be pretty busy, without a lot of downtime for casual reading. Still, I wanted to find out everything I could about what I'd encounter downrange. This next deployment would be somewhere with more action than my first tour over there had provided, that was for sure, although some guys would have considered that tour in Wasit to have more than enough action. But somehow I found myself wanting more, and Afghanistan sounded like it would provide as much as I wanted. So, the fewer surprises when I got there, the better.

The door opened and a waiflike, purple-haired coed stepped out, clutching a textbook and her phone. She started texting before she'd taken two steps out of the office and kept at it as she turned past the secretary, never making eye contact with either me or the kid behind the desk. She stared at the screen with a distraught expression, thumbs flying, nearly walking right into the doorjamb on her way out.

I stood, nodded at the kid, and walked over to my father's office. The door was still open. I glanced inside. A tall but stooped man was standing at a file cabinet, stuffing a thin manila folder inside. I rapped on the door.

"Yes?" Ronald Dawson said, eyes still on the files.

"Hello, Dad."

The graying head whipped around. I saw the hair was receding but still stylish. No ponytail, thank God. The clothing was business casual: long-sleeved cotton shirt open at the neck, khaki pants, and I didn't have to see his feet to know he was wearing Birkenstocks. Ronald Dawson pulled his wire-rimmed glasses away and his eyes blinked. "Jake? My God."

I couldn't resist. "Shouldn't it be, 'My science,' or 'My Mother Earth'?" But I also couldn't resist showing a small grin. My heart, to my great surprise, was almost racing. It had been three and a half years since I'd seen my father.

Dad pushed the file cabinet shut and walked over to me. He stopped at arm's length, looked me up and down, and reached out. I accepted the embrace, even returned it, sort of. I was surprised at how frail my father seemed to be. This was not a guy who had ever been a weightlifter, by any means, but at least he'd had a little more meat on the bones at one time.

Dad pulled away, eyes blinking. "It's good to see you, son," he said at last.

In spite of myself, I felt tears forming. "Same here, Dad. How have you been?"

It was unseasonably warm in Madison and it was lunchtime anyway, so I said sure when my father suggested we pick up a couple sandwiches from a coffee shop in the building next door and "hang out" in the sunshine. He asked what he could get for me, and I said whatever he thought was good, except I wanted water, nothing with caffeine. The cappuccino I'd had on the drive down was my daily limit. My dad, the professor; it was still hard for me to think of him in that context, and I couldn't help wondering what it would be like to sit in his classroom and listen to him lecture. Not that I hadn't heard a lot of lectures from him before, but in his classroom they'd be different. I found a seat at a patio table, surprised they hadn't been brought in for the upcoming winter. A hundred yards or so to the north, the azure-blue waters of Lake Mendota glistened. Here and there a sailboat cut through the small waves. Pretty late for sailing, I thought, but the sight of the lake brought back more pleasant memories. To the northwest I saw the green of Picnic Point, where I'd enjoyed some nice days with my wrestling teammates and our dates. And thinking of those girls made me think of Sam again, and how they all measured up to her. It was no contest. Sam was—

"Here you go," Dad said, setting a tray down on the Formica-topped table. "Chicken BLT salad for you, on wheat, and a bottle of water. Sure you wouldn't rather have a cappuccino?"

"Water's good, Dad. Thanks."

"No problem." He sat and unwrapped his own sandwich. "Italian-style ham and spicy salami," he said. "A weakness of mine." He took a big bite.

I was having a hard time understanding what was going on. My father hadn't seen me in three and a half years, since that ugly scene at his campaign headquarters in Fond du Lac, when I had come up from Madison to tell him of my plans to quit school and join up. In the midst of a tough re-election fight, Dad hadn't been in the best of moods anyway, and what started out as a frosty exchange got colder fast. Since then, not a word from him. Not one letter, not one email. To be fair, I hadn't exactly been busy writing to him. And now here we were, acting just like...well, like a father and son should act.

"So," my dad said, "your enlistment should be done pretty soon, right? What are your plans?"

I took a bite of the sandwich. It was pretty good, I had to admit, and I was surprisingly hungry. I washed it down with a swig of water. "Ah, well, Dad, I signed up for four years, but I...I'm going to make it my career." Why was I so nervous?

Dad seemed to chew his next bite more slowly. He swallowed, then said, "I see. You're an officer, so I suppose that's...reasonable."

"Yeah."

"I heard that officers must have a degree before being commissioned. You left here with two years to go."

"I squeezed the next two years in doing night classes and online," I said, a tinge of pride in his voice. "Finished up last spring, just in time for the next OCS class." It was the toughest grind of my life, but I made it. More than once I'd thought about chucking it, just staying in as enlisted, getting up to E-7 maybe, or even higher. Master Sergeant Dawson had a ring to it, I'd once thought, but Colonel Dawson sounded a lot better, and besides, O-6 paid a lot more. Not that I was in it for the money, but it was something to consider.

I felt compelled to explain myself. "Dad, I can retire after twenty years of active duty. I'd be only forty years old. If I go another five years, the bennies are even better. Retiring at forty-five doesn't sound too bad to me."

It was a subtle dig at my father, I knew; Dad was how old now, forty-six?

He put the rest of his sandwich down on his plate, took a sip from his coffee, and said, "Assuming you survive, of course."

"Don't worry, I will."

"Don't they all say that?" he asked, and I heard a new timbre in the voice, a tension. "Didn't all the four thousand-plus men who died in Iraq think that? And the two thousand-plus and counting who died in Afghanistan?"

"Dad—"

"You're not invulnerable, son. The American soldier is not some superhero who can leap tall buildings at a single bound and watch bullets bounce off his chest."

"No, but we have body armor that helps with that part," I said, my anger suddenly rising. "You know about body armor, right? Takes money to buy the good stuff, but if we get enough money, we can outfit every soldier with the best. Reduces casualties. Believe me, I've seen it." My last memory of Chet invaded my mind. The body armor hadn't saved Chet from that haji's knife. I shoved the memory aside. "But first we have to get it, and that means Congress has to vote us the funds. For some strange reason, there are a few people in D.C. who don't think we should have money for body armor."

My father cleared his throat. He stared at me, and there it was: The Look. How many times had I gotten one of those over the years? Almost always followed by some high-and-mighty Official Dad Pronouncement. "Wrestling is beneath you, son. It's violent. You should focus on your studies." Or, "She's a nice girl, Jake, but, well, what are her college prospects?" Or, "You intend to major in Athletic Training? Really?"

Not this time. I decided to beat him to the punch. I'd never had the guts to do that before, even when I was the best wrestler in the state in my weight class, with the strength and skill to tie my father almost literally in knots if I chose to. More than once, I'd come close to doing just that. And now, when I knew much more efficient ways to hurt, to maim, even to kill….I took a deep breath to compose myself, and said, "I followed your votes, Dad. Every one of them. And every time an appropriation came up for the military, you voted against it. I've always wanted to ask you why you did that. So now I'm asking."

My father looked past me, back toward the campus, as if to draw strength from it, as if the state's largest bastion of liberalism could send waves of invisible courage to its children when they were facing off with the barbarians. He cleared his throat, took a sip of coffee and said, "War is wrong, son. War never solves anything. I've believed that all my life, and so when I was elected I decided to make a stand. And I was always honest with my constituents about it."

I picked up my cap from the table, feeling its worn fabric. That cap had been with me a long time. A lot of my sweat went into it, training and marching and everything else I did to get ready to defend my country, to defend my fellow citizens' right to speak their minds, even if I didn't agree with them. If my dad could draw strength from something, well, two could play that game. "You're wrong about war, Dad. It's dirty and nasty and people die, but sometimes it does solve something. The Germans didn't vote Hitler out of office. Hirohito didn't call up FDR and ask to be friends. And your great-grandfather didn't exactly find a bastion of liberty when he went to Cuba."

"All of those issues could have been resolved peacefully. Economic sanctions. Political pressure. It does work, you know."

"Dad, when I was in Iraq we intercepted a weapons cache bound for the hajis, the insurgents. If those guns and explosives had gotten through, American lives might've been lost, and sure as shit a lot of innocent Iraqi lives. And guess where those guns and explosives came from? I'll tell you: Iran. And you voted for sanctions against Iran. How's that working out?"

"Look, Jake, you're a grown man, and you can make your own decisions."

"Damn right, and I have. Let me tell you about another decision I've made. Tomorrow I fly down to Fort Benning to start Ranger School. It's the toughest school in the Army short of Special Forces, and that's where I'll be headed once I get that Ranger tab on my shoulder and another deployment under my belt."

That brought a surprised look from my father. "Special Forces?"

"Yes. The Green Berets. If I work hard and keep my nose clean, I'll have mine in three years, maybe less."

A different look came across my father's face, one I couldn't recognize. When he spoke, his voice was different, more emotional. A father's voice, not a professor's. "Why would you want to do that?"

I had been waiting for a long time to tell him exactly why, and now I found no pleasure in it. But it had to be done. "I started reading up on them when I was in middle school, ever since I learned Grampa Dennis was a Green Beret."

Dad responded by taking another sip from his cappuccino, then licking his lips. He wasn't buying it, so I had to press my case. "I'd think you'd be pleased with this, Dad. SF does a lot of work with the locals. Medical care. Engineering projects, like wells for villages that don't have fresh water, or even a school. It's not like Big Army. Big Army does a really great job of blowing things up, taking ground and

THE HEIGHTS OF VALOR   49

holding it. If the politicians in Washington let us hold it, anyway," I couldn't resist adding.

"Humanitarian work can be done without carrying a gun, you know."

"Humanitarian work can be done as long as there's security," I countered, "and you can't have that unless you have men with guns. When I'm in SF, I'll be helping to make sure your precious NGOs get to where they need to go and can do their work without worrying about getting their heads cut off." I knew my father was a big booster of non-government organizations, the civilian outfits that went overseas to teach, to help the locals build, to provide medical treatment and lots of other useful and needed work. But no NGO would go anywhere in Afghanistan without a military escort, or at least knowing there was help close by. I knew that from experience.

Dad shook his head. "I'm sorry, Jake, but I cannot agree with your choice."

I pushed my plate away, took a final swig from the water bottle and put my cap on. "I'm not asking for your blessing. I'm going to go for Special Forces. I may not make it. A lot of very good soldiers don't. It's the toughest training in the Army."

"Well, then, go ahead. I will be back here in the real world."

I laughed, and swept an arm back from the lake to the buildings next door. "You call this the real world? All of you here in your own little cocoon, where the most threatening thing you ever face is Ohio State coming to Camp Randall for a football game. Or maybe the campus Republicans trying to bring in a guest speaker. And then you picket or shout him down."

Dad's ears were turning red, a sure sign that I was getting to him. When he spoke, the professor was back. "If that happens, those who protest are merely exercising their Constitutional rights."

"Yes," I said, "the very rights me and my buddies risk our lives to protect. Because trust me, Dad, if we don't stop those bastards over there, this is where they're coming next."

"Oh, spare me the sanctimonious neocon bullshit!"

I stood, shaking my head. "You know, Uncle John persuaded me to come down here. He and I had a long talk about it the other night, when he gave me the book."

"What book?"

"Your great-grandfather's Rough Rider diary. There's a letter from your grandfather in it, and one from your father, too." As soon as I said the words, I knew I should've kept my mouth shut. In the heat of the moment, I'd forgotten the decision I'd made just a few hours before.

Dad sat up straight. "From my father? Do you have it with you?"

"It's with my gear in the car."

He stood up, his eyes watering. "Can you get it for me? Please."

I shook my head, and it was one of the hardest things I'd ever done. "Sorry, Dad. Uncle John was clear: Charles Dawson specified that the diary could only go to a descendant who serves in uniform. And that goes for the letters, too."

He reached out and clutched my arm. "Jake…I barely remember my father. Vietnam took him. It took over fifty thousand other young Americans and what the hell did we gain for it?"

"Look, Dad, I'm not going to debate history. I've gotta go." But I didn't pull my arm away from his grasp.

Which promptly became firmer. "That war took my father away from me! Forever, Jake. I never got to know him, never got to play catch or have him teach me how to ride a bike or drive a car. War killed my dad, and I don't want it to kill my son. That's why I worked so hard against it in Congress. I was serving my country too, you know."

This time, I put my hand on my father's and moved it away. The hand was trembling. A tear rolled down my dad's cheek. I had to turn away. I took a deep breath, then grasped his hand in both of mine for a second, then two, before releasing it. "I know you were, Dad. I just wish you had done what you could to help your son and his buddies. Listen, I'll…I'll drop you a line when I can. Goodbye."

I made it three steps before my father's voice stopped him. It wasn't the professor this time, it was…well, it was a dad who was trying to get through to his son. "Jake, I know you think…well, you can think what you want."

I turned around and saw Dad standing there, his half-eaten sandwich lying on the table, forgotten. The man looked like he'd aged a year in only minutes. But he still had pride. He was standing as tall as he could, his chin tilted upward slightly, but even though his pose was defiant, his eyes were sad. "You're wrong about the body armor, Jake. The last bill I ever co-sponsored, just after the election. It was a special appropriation. Money to up-armor your vehicles, and money for body armor for the troops."

I blinked. This was news to me. "What happened to it?"

My father sighed. "It never got out of committee. I'm sorry." He spread his hands. "I tried, Jake. Maybe it was too little, too late, but I tried to…" His chin trembled, no longer defiant. "Tried to help you."

I covered the distance between us in only two steps. The physical distance was easy; the emotional distance, that would take a lot more time. I gave him a hug, then turned and walked away with a steady stride. Only after I'd gotten twenty paces away did I reach up and brush away the tears.

CHAPTER FIVE

Camp James E. Rudder, Florida
December 2013

Two months. When I stepped into Gator Lounge, I realized it had been two whole months since I'd felt this clean. I would've felt better about it if I hadn't been so damn tired.

Every muscle in my body ached. In the past two months, I'd patrolled over two hundred miles through the forests and mountains of Georgia and the swampland of the Florida panhandle, most of the time while carrying a ruck with eighty or ninety pounds of gear. The scale they'd conveniently positioned next to the shower bay in the barracks told me I'd lost fifteen pounds, and I'd considered myself lean and in shape when I left Wisconsin. I had no idea then what "lean" really meant. Now I knew.

But at least I was clean now. For two months, the only bathing I'd done was with Handi-Wipes in the field, and that wasn't allowed too often. I was lucky to get one or two hours of sleep a night. Maybe two meals a day, always MREs, and though everybody thought they sucked at first, by halfway through the course they were like delicacies at a gourmet restaurant. There was little time for eating, even less for hygiene. My feet were clean, though, by God. "Take care of your feet!" How often had the instructors told us that? Well, how many days had we been in the field? Sixty-plus, and we heard it every day, usually more than once.

Soldiers were filling up the lounge, enjoying the luxury of a real chair or a couch. There were several large TVs, some tuned to music videos, most to ESPN. There was a bank of corded phones on the far wall and they were all in use, with men lined up for each of them. At one time I would've laughed at the sight of those antiques. Now, with my cell phone a distant memory, the phones looked like the greatest invention of all time, next to the hot shower. I'd have to get in line at one of them or it might be some time before my chance came. We were allowed two calls, and I knew where mine would be going.

My mother got the first one. What day was this? I had to ask, found out it was Tuesday. Mom would be at her desk in the office at the technical college in Rhinelander, where she was the assistant administrator. She picked up on the first ring and gasped when she heard my voice, then she broke down crying. I had to tell her three times that I was all right. Yes, I'd lost some weight, but nothing too drastic. That was a bit of a fib, but by the time she saw me at graduation three days from now up at Benning, I'd have four or five of those fifteen put back on. Even as the thought hit me, the smell of fresh pizza surged out of the kitchen, leading to shouts and a general stampede to the serving line. My stomach roiled in protest at being denied such perfectly reasonable and way overdue sustenance.

"Listen, Mom, I gotta go," I said. "You'll be at graduation, right?" I gave her the details again, although she'd already booked her flight two months ago, confident in her son's ability to survive Ranger School. She was more confident than I'd been. "There's one more thing, Mom," I said, and then told her what I had in mind. I waited for her response, a little worried about what she'd say.

"That sounds like a fine idea, Jake," she said. Did her voice catch a little bit?

"You sure?"

"Yes, of course. John will be as proud as all get out."

I felt my shoulders sag with relief. "Okay, Mom, I gotta call him next. See you soon. 'Bye."

The second call was to my great-uncle, and I was taking a chance because it was even money the old Marine was out on the lake somewhere, ice fishing, but he picked up on the second ring. "Uncle John?"

"Jake! Where are you, son?"

"Florida. I made it, Uncle John. I–" It hit me right there. My knees almost buckled. I had to lean against the wall, clutching the phone's handset, feeling it shake in my hand. I tried to suppress a sob, gave in. "I made it. I'm gonna have my Ranger Tab."

On the other end of the line, I heard Uncle John clear his throat. "I knew you would, Jake. I knew you had it in you. I'm proud of you."

"Thanks, Uncle John. Having you in my corner sure helped."

The wave of emotion had passed, but I'd have to get some pizza and whatever beer they had here, and damn fast, or I might pass out. There was one last thing, though. "Uncle John, can you come down to Benning for graduation with Mom? She booked an extra seat on the flight."

"I wouldn't miss it for the world, son."

"And…and there's one thing I'd like for you to do for me, when you're here."

It was just the bottom bunk of a two-bunk rack in a long line against one wall of the otherwise featureless barracks, with another line of bunks on the opposite wall, but tonight to me and ninety-five other soldiers they all looked like king-sized beds in a five-star hotel. We'd seen the barracks earlier in the day, of course, but hadn't taken much notice of the racks except to choose one for ourselves, dump our gear, strip and head to the shower, which proved to be every bit as luxurious as I'd dreamed a shower could be.

I ate too much pizza, and adding three bottles of beer to that wasn't exactly a smart move. My head felt like it was about to twist off of my neck and fly away. Maybe just a few minutes of rest….

"Jake! Wake up, Ranger buddy."

The hand shaking my shoulder belonged to Travis Taylor, one of the three Marines who had started Ranger School with me and my fellow soldiers. All three of the jarheads had finished the course, which they'd made clear to everyone, loudly, at the Gator Lounge. Taylor had been the odd Marine out, forced to pair up with a lower life form as his Ranger Buddy. We'd hit it off and became close friends during the brutal weeks of the course, constantly pushing each other to drive on.

I struggled to wake up, finally elbowing myself up to a sitting position on the rack. "What's up, Trav?"

"The CSM wants to see you."

Those initials served to bring me fully awake. "The Command Sergeant Major? What for?"

"Hell if I know, buddy. He sent one of the cadre over to the Lounge to find you."

"All right." I managed to stand, staggering a bit on my still-recovering legs, and reached for my cap. I almost lost my balance, but Travis pulled me back upright. The Marine had been one of the strongest candidates on the obstacle courses, and I'd never seen him flinch once on any of the long ruck marches we'd endured. "I'm okay," I said, upset with myself that I'd once more fallen short of the standard my Marine friend had set. "I gotta hit the latrine, then I'll see what CSM wants."

"This might be your lucky day, bro. They might want to kick you out of the Army so you can join the Corps and get toughened up."

Travis laughed about it, and I knew it was a joke, but as I stood there getting rid of some of the beer, I knew how seriously Ranger School had kicked my ass. This was the first time Army training had done that to me. When I got to OSUT, I was still in great shape from wrestling season. Wrestlers never let themselves fall out of shape, not if you want to be successful, and there hadn't been a day since eighth grade that I hadn't worked out for at least an hour. So what boot camp threw at me was nothing I couldn't handle. OCS hadn't been a breeze, but the mental grind was worse than the physical.

I'd never thought that the Army could beat me, physically, but now I was starting to wonder. Yes, I'd made it through Ranger School, but Special Forces training would be a lot tougher. As I washed my hands, I looked in the mirror and saw the hollow-eyed guy looking back at me. Would that guy ever wear a green beret? For the first time in my life, I had a flicker of doubt.

I had to ask for directions twice, but I found my way to the headquarters of 6th Ranger Training Battalion, which oversaw the

Florida phase of Ranger School. On the way, I wondered whether Travis had meant the 6th RTB sergeant major, or the actual CSM of ARTB, the Airborne and Ranger Training Brigade, which was based up at Fort Benning. The graduating Rangers–no, we were now Ranger Qualified, not actual Rangers–would be heading back up there in a few days for the formal ceremony.

The corporal manning the reception desk looked up at me like he saw gaunt, nervous soldiers every day, which he probably did. "Lieutenant Dawson," I said. "I'm here to see the Command Sergeant Major." The corporal's reaction would tell me whether Travis was on the money or not.

"Yes, sir," the corporal said, pointing down a hall. "First door on the left."

"Thank you." It was eight steps to the doorway, where I paused to straighten my utility jacket. Like all the candidates at Ranger School, I wore no rank insignia. My patrol cap was still on; was I supposed to uncover indoors? Hell, I'd completely forgotten. It had to be the fatigue, causing me to blank out on simple things I'd learned months, years ago. Wait, that was it: uncover indoors unless under arms. I removed the cap, took another few seconds to make sure my uniform was as squared-away as possible, and stepped to the doorway.

The olive-skinned, well-built man sitting at the desk had three stripes up and three down on the insignia tab at the front of his ACU blouse, with a star in the middle. He was the real CSM, all right, and he also had a Ranger Tab on his left shoulder. My single knock on the doorjamb caught his attention. "Enter."

I stepped inside, stopped three feet in front of the desk and stood at attention, but didn't render a salute. "Second Lieutenant Jacob Dawson, reporting to the Command Sergeant Major as ordered, sir."

The CSM stood and offered his hand. "We're still under Ranger School regs, Lieutenant, so no need to stick to formalities like standing at attention or saluting."

I took the hand gratefully and almost regretted it. The sergeant's grip nearly crushed mine, and I'd always taken pride in my firm handshake, something Uncle John had taught me when I was fifteen. The CSM gestured to one of the two empty chairs. "Have a seat. I'd imagine it's nice to be in a real chair right about now."

"You've got that right, Sergeant Major." I had to force himself to sit normally; my legs were about to turn to rubber again. "But I'm sure you've been through this yourself."

"Yes indeed," the man said. "I'm Command Sergeant Major Mendez, and I'm down here from Benning to talk to selected members of this class. You're one of them."

My nerves started to spasm. Had I screwed up? Had my peer reviews been subpar?

Mendez saw the reaction in my face and smiled. "Relax, Lieutenant. You'll be going to graduation with the rest of the class. In fact, your performance in this school has been outstanding, especially your leadership skills. Because of that, I'm authorized to tell you that you'll be receiving the Ralph Puckett Award as the Officer Honor Graduate. Congratulations."

It took me a moment to process what the CSM had said. What little reserves of adrenalin I'd had left were used up when Travis told me of the summons. Now I felt almost dizzy. Ranger School had been the toughest thing I'd ever done in my life, and I was sure it had beaten me. "I'm sorry, Sergeant Major," I managed to say, "but I'm not sure I heard you right."

Mendez leaned back in his chair and smiled. "Named after Colonel Ralph Puckett. He was awarded the Distinguished Service Cross in Korea for an action with 8th Army Rangers. Puckett led his men on a mission against a numerically superior force, captured the objective and then they held off five Chinese counterattacks before he was wounded and evacuated. Against his wishes, I might add."

I had heard that somewhere, but my foggy brain was still having a little trouble getting organized. "Holy…"

Mendez nodded. "My thoughts exactly. He got another DSC in Vietnam for a similar action. He's pushing ninety now but he'll be at your graduation. I would imagine he'll want to present the award to you personally."

I had to blink more than once as that sank in. "I'll, ah, try not to embarrass the class in front of the colonel," I finally said. Before I could stop myself, I said, "I have to be honest with you, Sergeant Major, I felt that Ranger School…well, it kicked my ass, sir."

The CSM smiled. "It kicks everybody's ass, Lieutenant. It's designed to. Even those cocky Marines got theirs handed to them, I guarantee it." When he saw my expression, he laughed. "Yeah, I heard all about them. Happens every time we have our brothers from the Corps come through this training. As for embarrassing Colonel Puckett, I'm sure you won't have any problems." He gestured to the open file on his desk. "Needless to say, the RIs had a lot of good things to say about you, and your peer reviews were outstanding. The men enjoyed working with you, especially when you were in charge of a squad during an evolution."

"Thank you, Sergeant Major." Inside, I felt pride welling up. The Ranger Instructors had been tough on everyone in the class, but they'd also been compassionate. I'd trained under some terrific cadres in my time in the Army but I had to say, the cadre at Ranger School were the best I'd seen so far.

"What are your goals in the Army, Lieutenant?"

I thought a few seconds, wondering where the CSM was going, then said, "I'll be returning to my unit, I'm sure. Fourth Infantry Brigade Combat Team, First Infantry Division. We're deploying to Afghanistan in about two months."

"And after your deployment?"

I sat up a little straighter. "I'd like to apply for Special Forces, Sergeant. My grandfather was a Green Beret."

Mendez nodded. "An exemplary goal." He tapped the file. "Your performance here has caught the attention of some important people," he said. "That's another reason I'm down here. Would you be interested in joining the Regiment?"

That one didn't take more than a few milliseconds for my tired brain to evaluate. "The 75th?"

"The one and only Ranger regiment in this man's Army," Mendez said with pride. "We think you've got what it takes to be one of us, Lieutenant. What do *you* think?"

I thought of the men I'd trained with during the ordeal we had just finished. About thirty of the graduates were already in the Regiment and had earned the right to call themselves Rangers. The rest of us were just Ranger-qualified. Aside from SF, the 75th was well-known as one of the toughest outfits in the Army. If you wanted to spend time in the field, and lots of it, being a Ranger was the way to go.

"What would I have to do, Sergeant Major?"

"Even though you'll already have your Ranger Tab, you'll have to cycle through RASP like everyone else who wants to be one of us," Mendez said. Ranger Assessment and Training Program was notorious for its difficulty, but if the squared-away soldiers I'd observed during Ranger School were the caliber of men serving in the 75th, I knew immediately that was where I wanted to be. But my ultimate goal, the one the CSM had called "exemplary," was still out there.

"Would I still be able to try for SF later on?"

Mendez nodded again. "There are more than a few Ranger officers and enlisted who move on to SF eventually," he said. "Colonel Puckett himself served with 10th Group before he went to Vietnam with 101st Airborne. So yes, certainly, you could go SF later, although I think you'll like soldiering with us." He closed the file and sat back. "So, what should I tell my colonel back at Benning, Lieutenant? Do you want to be a Ranger?"

It took me only a few seconds to make up my mind. "I'm pretty sure I'll still want to get my green beret, Sergeant Major, but until then, I think a tan beret will do nicely. Thank you for the opportunity."

"No need to thank me, Lieutenant," the CSM said as he rose. He held out his hand again. "You've earned it."

The racks were starting to fill up when I got back to the barracks. On the way over, my thoughts were all over the place, careening back and forth between berets tan and green and the inviting comfort of the bunk. It wasn't yet dark but the Florida evening was starting to get chilly. I barely had enough energy to grab my shaving kit and brush my teeth before falling into the rack. It took my last ounces of energy, but I managed to unlace my boots and get them off before collapsing.

I was asleep almost instantly, oblivious to the near-constant snoring from several racks and the gaseous rip of an occasional fart. And sometime during the night I dreamed.

I saw my grandfather, his green beret at a jaunty angle, smiling at me, then marching off into a jungle that came alive with Viet Cong. I waited for him to come out, but he didn't. Instead, a man who looked vaguely like Grampa Dennis appeared at my side, wearing a long-sleeved blue shirt, khaki pants, a slouch hat. He had a thin mustache, and a commanding voice as he pointed at me. "Did you read it yet?" the man said. "Read it, and learn.
You will need it. Soon."

I jerked myself awake, the dream disappearing in wisps of imagery. My watch said 0437. Reveille was at 0600. There would be PT, then a day of cleaning my gear, checking it in, and getting ready for the next day's bus trip up to Benning. We wouldn't be parachuting in like we had when we arrived at Camp Rudder.

The dream stayed with me, just enough so that I knew what had to be done. Trying not to make a sound, I hit the head, then padded back to the rack, rummaging in my gear. I found the flashlight first, and then the book.

CHAPTER SIX

The Journal of Charles J. Dawson, Sergeant, 1ˢᵗ U.S. Volunteer Cavalry, U.S. Army

May the 2d, 1898 -- The headline in to-day's Wisconsin State Journal once again screamed of War! The city of Madison and the University campus are in a dither. The Congress declared formal hostilities against Spain 5 days ago, and I have not seen the campus in such an uproar since the return of the foot-ball team from its triumph at Minnesota last autumn. Indeed, Pat O'Dea, who will captain our eleven next season, announced at a rally last evening that he is thinking of enlisting. As he is Australian by birth, it was pointed out to him that such an action may not be possible. I offered that it would be; Father told me that many enlisted men in the Union Army were Irish and German immigrants. In my opinion, though, O'Dea was merely spouting off for the crowd of admirers. He will, I believe, take the field again with the lads come September.

Where shall I be then? Probably not at the Randall Field grounds watching O'Dea and the lads. The war is now officially commenced. The newspapers are full of rumors. A Spanish naval squadron was said to have been sighted off the coast of Florida, then farther north off Cape Hatteras. A boy burst into the commons today and declared that Spanish gunboats were sailing up the Chesapeake to shell the capital! A crowd gathered around the Western Union office, hungry for news, dispersing only when the telegrapher emerged to declare the rumor utterly false.

But there was news from the far side of the world that was indeed true. Our navy, under the command of Admiral Dewey, has engaged the Spaniards in Manila Bay and has defeated them utterly. The first triumph of the conflict belongs to America!

Dewey's great victory was the topic of much discussion in the commons, which led to yet another spirited debate about the sinking of the Maine, more than 2 mos. past. The brave sailors were barely in their watery graves when the news of Spanish treachery dominated the headlines. It was a torpedo, some said. Or saboteurs who boarded under dark of night and threw a bomb into the armory. I think we shall not know the true cause until the hulk can be raised and examined. But now it lies in Havana harbor still, and I fear our navy will not be able to reclaim it for some time.

As I write this, I have not yet heard from Father or from the War Department regarding my application for enlistment in the 1st U.S. Volunteer Cavalry. I will soon commence my classes for the day. Two companies of militia are now holding daily drills on the grounds of Camp Randall, but I have declined their invitations to participate. Even though it was where my father and his comrades drilled before seeing action in the late Rebellion, I will wait to hear if my request has been granted. If not, I shall join the Regulars. I have heard that the enlistment office in Milwaukee would offer a prospective recruit the best chance of joining up.

Later, same day ~ I returned to my rooms after my final afternoon class, intending to change clothes and go to the gymnasium for some sparring, and it was in my mail-slot that a telegram awaited me. I tore it from the envelope and could hardly believe my eyes. I have been accepted into the Regiment! It was from Theodore Roosevelt himself, at the navy department in Washington City. I am to report to San Antonio, Texas, no later than one week from to-day, May the 9th. Without delay I went to the Milwaukee Road depot to enquire about ticketing for the journey. I informed the clerk that I absolutely had to arrive in San Antonio no later than 6 o'clock p.m. on the 9th. He said, "Two days at the best, and it is $45 one-way." I nearly fainted. I knew that my account held no more than $40, perhaps less.

But once again Father was there for me. I have just returned from the office of my Professor of Economics, Dr. Block, who has taken quite a shine to me since I took his first course as a freshman. He has a telephone, and for the first time in my life I placed a long-distance call. Fortunately I found Father in his office. (The telephone came to Platteville when I was a child and I remember gazing at the amazing device as it sat on his desk. He could speak into it and converse with someone as far away as Milwaukee!) I found it hard to catch my breath as I spoke to Father of my conundrum. He promised to wire me the funds for the ticket to-morrow. It was the first time we had spoken since I sat in his office to plead my case for joining the Regiment. Upon disconnecting, I had to fight hard to avoid bursting into tears. How I love that dear old fellow, and how desperately I want to make him proud of me on the battlefield! And now, thanks once again to him, I will have that chance.

I repaired to the gymnasium for one last round of sparring with the lads. My thoughts were on the Regiment and the great adventure ahead, and not on the task immediately at hand. Thus it was I foolishly agreed to spar against John Richards, the great lineman of the foot-ball team and a renowned boxer as well. O'Dea and several of his mates were also in the gymnasium. Richards is a stout fellow and must outweigh me by 20 pounds, yet I consented to the match. I had seen Richards fight in the famous Music Hall match a month past and should have known better. I acquitted myself honorably for the first round and much of the second, but then Richards, perhaps enraged by the harassment his mates were now giving him, drove me into a corner and attacked me with great vigor. Only the bell saved me from a pummeling that might very well have resulted in injury, enough to keep me from the Regiment. Knowing the truth of the matter, I conceded the bout to him and left the gymnasium, humiliated, the laughter of O'Dea and the foot-ballers ringing in my ears.

Back in my rooms, I treated my bruises as best as possible. My bruised ego, I fear, will need more extensive treatment.

May the 8th, 1898 ~ I am aboard the Rock Island Line. We pulled out of La Salle St. Station in Chicago yesterday at noon and are southward bound, due to arrive in Dallas sometime early to-morrow morning, whereupon we will transfer to another line for our final leg to San Antonio and the Regiment. According to the schedule we will arrive in that city by 12 o'clock noon to-morrow, and so I shall easily meet my deadline to report for duty.

I had intended this diary to be a daily record of the events carrying me through what is already being called the Spanish War. But after my initial entry, my time was so consumed with the busyness of preparing for the great adventure that I scarcely had time to sleep, much less write. I spent the last few days after reception of the blessed telegram in finalizing my affairs on-campus. To my great regret, I was not able to take a day and go to Platteville to see Father and my sister. As the day of my departure grew ever nearer, the gravity of my decision began to weigh on me, and I desperately wanted to see Father one last time and to hug little Margaret. But there was too much yet to do in Madison.

The word had spread on campus and I was the object of many congratulatory handshakes. Two nights before I left for Chicago, I saw Richards, O'Dea and the other foot-ballers once more at the gymnasium. To my great surprise, they greeted me as they would an old comrade and treated me to dinner at a gentlemen's club. One of them told me that my acceptance into the Regiment, not to mention my willingness to challenge the great Richards in the ring, had gained their respect.

Our host, a local businessman and supporter of the team who shall remain nameless, had hired several young ladies to act as "hostesses" for the diners. One of them, a girl named Leona, with blonde locks and a rather impressive figure, appeared to take a fancy to me. When she heard I was bound for Roosevelt's Rough Riders, she was positively giddy. I offered to walk her home after the soiree. Upon reaching her boarding house, I asked if I might kiss her good-night. She said I could have a lot more than that, and for only $5. "I always have a soldier-boy discount," she declared, batting her lashes at me.

There was a momentary tussle within my breast as I considered her offer. Two things prevented me: firstly, I did not have a French letter upon my person and did not want to risk catching the clap. And second, I had only $20 to my name after purchasing essentials for the trip. It seemed unwise to deplete my funds by one-fourth with the journey to Texas yet to begin.

The conductor who took my ticket upon boarding in Chicago saw the destination and inquired if I was one of the Rough Riders. My chest must have visibly expanded as I said, "Yes, indeed, sir." "Well," he declared, "there are a dozen young men from New York who are aboard as well, destined to be your comrades-in-arms." He led me to the appropriate car and made a rather big show of announcing my presence. The gentlemen in question eyed me with some measure of suspicion, except for one of their number, who bounded up from his seat and pumped my hand. He gave his name as J. Ogden Wells, of Harvard and New York City, and proceeded to introduce me to his colleagues, all Harvard men. One of them, Dudley Dean, is the quarter-back of the Harvard eleven. Upon hearing I was from Wisconsin, he asked if I knew Pat O'Dea, who I gathered has gained some notice in Eastern gridiron circles. When I said I had just dined with O'Dea and his teammates two nights previous, Dean slapped me on the back and declared, "Boys, we have here a genuine Badger who knows his foot-ball!"

All in all they are a fine bunch of fellows, and I gather they are not at a shortage of funds, as they have frequently bought treats and souvenirs at our various stops on the journey. My own family is one of the most prominent in Platteville and quite comfortable, thanks to Father's efforts, but I assume each of these Harvard lads is heir to an estate with a few more zeros in front of the decimal point than the one I might one day inherit.

May the 9th, 1898 ~ We have arrived in San Antonio, and a weary bunch we are. The time aboard the train was spent in conversation, playing cards and dozing in our seats. Some of the Harvard men have fine voices and led us in song, their favorite being "A Hot Time in the Old Town." A family from Indiana with a banjo taught us "On the Banks of the Wabash, Far Away."

I joined the fellows in the dining car for supper last evening, but our other meals were taken from vendors at the stations we stopped at along the route. At each stop one or more of the lads would purchase newspapers as we were hungry for information about the war. Each edition brought aboard the train spurred vigorous debate. Without exception, the Hearst papers trumpeted atrocities allegedly committed by the Spaniards against their Cuban subjects. Some papers, among them the Chicago Daily News, were more temperate in their reporting, often denouncing Hearst's stories as half-truths or entirely fictional. I tend toward the latter view. Father had always cautioned me against believing everything I might read. He often told me stories of his encounters with reporters during the Rebellion and how frequently their articles misrepresented what was actually happening at the front. "More than once we declared that certain reporters should be tried for treason and shot," he told me, "and there would have been no shortage of men volunteering for the firing squad, myself included."

This morning our arrival in Dallas and change of trains allowed us to breakfast in a restaurant across the street. This being my first-ever visit to Texas, I was surprised at the number of sombreros worn by men and boys. Several of the New Yorkers purchased hats of the Stetson brand from a nearby store. I declined, staying with the reliable derby that was a Christmas gift from Aunt Florence in '96. Part of my reasoning was that we will be issued campaign hats with our uniforms. Also factoring in, as per usual, was my chronic shortage of funds, having lost $5 at cards during the journey. (Had I used that money for the favors of the lovely Leona back in Madison, the memory of its loss might have been more pleasant.)

Upon arrival in San Antonio, we enquired as to the location of the

Rough Riders' camp and was told it was at the International Fairgrounds on the outskirts of town. Wells insisted we must have one last "civilized" meal, so we repaired to the town's finest hotel, the Menger, near the Alamo, for luncheon. Another dollar of my dwindling funds went for this endeavor, but it was a fine repast. Finally we thirteen, toting our bags, prepared to board the electric trolley for the short ride to our camp.

Whilst waiting for the trolley near Alamo Plaza, I was approached by a rough-looking codger of indeterminate years. He wore a graying, droopy mustache of the kind favored by Wyatt Earp, from what I saw in photographs of the famous Arizona lawman. His sombrero was weather-beaten and dusty, his clothes of similar state, and he wore an actual six-gun holstered in a belt 'round his waist. With a drawl as thick as molasses, he asked me, "Y'all come to join up with Roosey's bunch?"

"Indeed we have," I replied. The old-timer was half a head shorter than I, but possessed something of an air of coiled strength about him.

Dean, the Harvard quarter-back, came over to meet the Texan. "We aim to go to Cuba and teach the Spaniards a thing or two," he said.

The old cow-boy squinted at us, then spat a long stream of tobacco juice onto the dusty street. "Well, you boys might learn a thing or two yourselves," he said. He doffed his sombrero, revealing an ugly scar along the right side of his head above what remained of his ear; the top half was gone. "See this, boys?" he said, pointing to the scar. "Yankee sword damn near cut my head off at Antietam."

Dean was visibly taken aback by the sight. I was sobered by it, but not shocked; I had seen similar wounds, and in fact some more grievous, among Father's comrades in the Platteville Guards. I cleared my throat and said, "My father fought at Antietam, with the Iron Brigade."

The old Reb squinted up at me, then grinned, showing yellowed teeth. "Well, G-d damn, son," he declared, "maybe it was your daddy's pig-sticker that did this." He cackled as he replaced his sombrero, covering the hideous scar. Then he turned serious, looking both me and Dean up and down. "You boys think it's gonna be fun down there in Cuba?

Adventure, glory, all that hogwash? Shit." He spat another stream that nearly splashed on Dean's calfskin shoes. "Want my advice? Go home. Now, while you're still in one piece." He turned and walked away, with a limp almost exactly like my father's.

CHAPTER SEVEN

Fort Benning, Georgia
December 2013

Georgia on the cusp of winter wasn't half bad. I was waiting in formation with the other Ranger School graduates, feeling the breeze blowing off Victory Pond to our right. It must've been about sixty degrees. In the grandstand, we could tell who was down here from the Upper Midwest; they were the ones in shorts and tee shirts.

The weather had been a topic of conversation on the bus ride up from Florida two days before. One of my classmates, a tall drink of Georgia water who was even more slender now than he had been two months before, said that sometimes in January it actually got cold at night. "Below zero one time, I remember," he said. "Damn, that was cold." The northerners on the bus hooted with laughter. I remembered winters up in Wisconsin where zero would've been considered a heat wave.

I was in the back row of Class 01-14, ninety-six men strong standing at parade rest. Of that total, I was one of thirty-seven who had gutted out the class from start to finish, with the rest being recycles, soldiers who had been in the previous class but dropped out due to medical problems or, in a couple cases, family emergencies. To our left were shaded bleachers for the civilians, friends and family of the graduates, probably close to two hundred in attendance. I was surprised to see quite a few senior citizens who had to be veterans among them, probably grandparents of the graduates. Most of the old guys were wearing caps from their service branch or unit, and when the colors were presented on the small, sand-covered parade ground in front of us, many of the old vets struggled to stand, some relying on canes or the helping hands of younger family members. But they all made it.

A chaplain gave the invocation, and the public address announcer welcomed the guests to the graduation ceremony. The guest speaker was a major general whose own class had graduated thirty years before, and his speech lasted several minutes. It was good, even inspiring, but I couldn't keep my eyes from wandering over the bleachers. I thought I'd spotted my mother before, when the graduates were sitting in our own bleachers on the far side during the "Rangers in Action" demonstration, but now I wasn't sure. Holy cripes, had they not been able to make it? Did they miss their flight? She'd told me they were coming down the day before, flying into Atlanta through Chicago. Anything could've happened. I gave up looking, focusing my gaze straight ahead over the shoulders of the men in front of me, trying to concentrate on the general's closing words. A trickle of sweat dribbled down my spine. A fly landed on the right ear of the soldier in front of me. It was Glaser, the kid from Minnesota who had looked a little chubby at the start of the course, the guy nobody thought would make it, but by God he had, and he never flinched now. The fly buzzed away.

The general concluded with "Rangers lead the way!" and got a round of applause, many of the civilians standing as he worked the front row, shaking the hands of the vets. Thirty years ago, that guy had been right here, in the same formation. He must've seen some combat in those years. I could hardly imagine myself being back here thirty years down the road. Right now I couldn't think any further ahead than the next ten minutes. The back row would be the first men up on the sand, and that included me.

The crowd had been revved up by the showcase of Rangers displaying their skills: rappelling down a wall, leaping into Victory Pond from hovering helicopters, racing down a zip line from the tower into the drink. The show was impressive and reflected many of the skills Rangers of the 75th learned and perfected during their training. Not all of them had been taught during Ranger School, but as I watched the show and listened to the Rangers describing the action over the PA system, I felt better about deciding to try for a billet in the Regiment. I had to admit, the Rangers in their rakish tan berets sure as hell looked good, and they backed it up, too.

About a dozen men in the class had already earned the tan beret, and I picked their brains about RASP during the bus trip to Benning. It was tough, they all said, in some cases even more intense than Ranger School, because you had to pass RASP to get into the Regiment. If you failed Ranger School, well, you just went back to your old unit and soldiered on as infantry or a tanker or a cook, whatever. But if you passed RASP, you were an honest to God Army Ranger and there was nothing like it in the world. You'd be a member of the best light infantry unit on the whole damn planet.

That gave me a lot to think about. The pull of the Green Beret was still strong. I'd never met my grandfather, but I felt a sense of legacy. And now, after reading the first entry of the old Rough Rider's diary, I felt it even more. Dawson men had been members of elite military units for over a hundred and fifty years. Hell, the Rough Rider's old man himself was in the Iron Brigade, and I'd picked up a book on that outfit at the Benning bookstore just yesterday. They were a damn tough bunch in their own right, seeing some of the worst combat the Civil War could offer, and that was saying something. My ancestor was in the thick of it, had been wounded, in fact. Did Charles make it back from Cuba unscathed? I'd have to read the rest of the diary to find out, although I had to admit, it was hard to get excited about the diary, legacy or not. College kids going off to a great adventure. Yeah, right.

But really, I realized now, as I stood in formation, hadn't that been myself just a few years ago?

It was worth thinking about, but not right now. The PA announcer said it was time for the honor graduates to step forward. The class leader called the formation to attention and summoned our group of eight men forward onto the sand.

I was fifth in the line. The first three were Ranger Instructors, one from each battalion, who had distinguished themselves during the phases of Ranger School. I'd met some tough non-coms during my time in the Army, and none came tougher than these three. But what impressed me the most was not just their physical and mental toughness, but their self-discipline. I had always considered myself a highly disciplined individual, starting with wrestling in high school. Wrestling is not for the faint of heart, but that was nothing compared to what these guys did.

The brass led the way in the group coming onto the sand to greet the honorees. There was the general who'd been the guest speaker, of course, but also the colonel in command of the 75th. I had a feeling that guy wasn't present at every Ranger School graduation, scoping out possible recruits for his outfit. An old man in civilian clothes was next, followed by a sergeant carrying a stack of books, and a couple more officers, whose names I didn't catch over the PA; I was focused on stepping up onto the sand without stumbling.

We came to attention facing the crowd, and the three RIs were the first to be recognized, each receiving a plaque and handshakes from the officers. The old civilian gave each of them a book. The first member of the class after the RIs was a staff sergeant from Montana, a guy named Kessler who'd been a cowboy, he said, before joining the Army. Kessler got the William O. Darby Award as Distinguished Honor Graduate. He was already wearing the tan beret and I hoped that one day I'd have the pleasure of Kessler's presence in my own platoon. He was good, and I knew that I'd need good men around me down the line.

The crowd's applause for Kessler had barely diminished when the PA announcer said, "Receiving the Ralph Puckett Award as the Officer Honor Graduate, Second Lieutenant Jacob Dawson." I had to steady myself. Somewhere back in the depths of my mind, a voice had been telling me that I wasn't really good enough to get the award, it would be a mistake and they'd recognize it at the last second. But here it was.

The general was the first to present the plaque and shake my hand. "Well done, soldier." The general's eyes drilled into me and his grip was like iron.

"Thank you, sir."

The colonel was next, with eyes even more intense than the general's. "Dawson, I'm told you'll be joining us, is that right?"

"Yes, sir," I said in a voice that I hoped sounded full of confidence, although I suspected it didn't.

But if my reply was weak, the colonel didn't seem to notice. "Glad to hear it. Come see me after the ceremony is dismissed, we'll get you squared away for the next step."

"Yes, sir."

Puckett himself was next. The guy might've been pushing ninety but he still carried himself like a soldier. "Congratulations, Lieutenant," he said with a smile that was thin but still meaningful.

"Thank you, sir. It's an honor."

"The honor is mine," the old colonel said, and I could tell he wasn't faking it. My pride meter kicked up a couple notches. "Please accept this as a token of my respect." He took a book from the dwindling stack carried by the trailing sergeant and handed it to me. "A few things I've picked up over the years. Hopefully they'll help you out."

I glanced down at the cover. *Words for Warriors–A Professional Soldier's Notebook.* When would I ever find the time to read this? But I knew instinctively that I would have to. What was inside might save my life over there, so it would be worth the time. As for the old Rough Rider's diary, maybe that would have to wait in line. After all, what could I learn from a few firefights in Cuba that happened over a century ago?

After the last honoree was introduced, the announcer invited our families down from the grandstand. It was a Ranger School tradition to have a family member pin the coveted Ranger Tab on their soldier, and I finally saw my mother and Uncle John, descending the stairs from the upper rows of seats. And who was that with them? My God, it was–

Next to me, Kessler looked over with a grin. "Hey, Jake, who's the babe?"

"That's my mother, you dumb cowboy."

"No, the other one."

I was about to answer when Kessler's family came up behind him, an older couple along with a younger Native American woman holding a toddler. And then my family was there.

"Mom," I said, and I almost broke down, surprising myself with the depth of the emotions that plowed through me. How often during those hellacious two months in the field had I thought of her? At times I could almost smell the chocolate chip cookies she'd baked for me so many times.

"Oh, Jake, I'm so proud of you," she said, tears glistening her eyes as she hugged me.

My great-uncle stuck out his weathered hand. "I knew you could do it, Jake," the old Marine said. "You boys look pretty good, for a bunch of Army pussies."

I gathered him in a fierce embrace. "We even had some jarheads who made it," I said. "I'll have to introduce you to them."

"You do that. But in the meantime, we brought someone with us. Last-minute thing, you know, but, well, she asked your mom, and…"

I released him and turned to the gorgeous young woman in a Wisconsin Badger tee shirt and jeans. "Sam," I croaked, barely able to get the word out. How often had I thought of her during the long ruck marches, the rain, the time in my sleeping bag when I was desperately in need of shuteye but unable to nod off? Always wondering if what we'd started up in Minocqua was real, could it last? And here she was.

"Jake," she said, her lower lip trembling, eyes welling up. "I missed you so much, I had to come."

Later, after all the graduates received our Tabs and the assembly was dismissed, after I had introduced my great-uncle and mother and Sam to the Marines in the class and the RIs and just about anybody else I could find, the fatigue finally started to overwhelm me. I had to sit down on the now-empty bleachers as the crowd and their soldiers started filing out, heading for private celebrations. I reached up and felt the Ranger Tab on my left shoulder. It had been one of the proudest moments of my life when Uncle John pinned it on, and it was still there.

"Jake, you coming?" Taylor asked as he passed by.

"Yeah, Trav, we'll be there," I said, giving him a weary grin. How did these Marines do it? I'd considered myself in top shape going into Ranger School, but now I knew my fitness level would have to be ramped up even higher if I was going to get the job done in the Regiment.

"Okay. Homer's Lounge on Victory Drive, don't forget."

"Got it, buddy."

Uncle John came over and sat down next to me. A few yards away, Mom and Sam were talking to CSM Mendez. The sergeant looked pleased, and why wouldn't he be? Two of the best-looking women in the crowd were with him. I had to smile at that.

"Feeling good, son?"

"Yeah," I said. "Tired, but good. It's all over."

"I doubt that," Uncle John said. "If you're going into the 75th, it's barely begun."

I nodded and sighed. "Yeah, I know. The colonel filled me in. RASP is next, then my battalion will be deployed, and I'll be back in the fight."

We were quiet for a moment, and then my great-uncle asked, "Started the old Rough Rider's diary yet?"

"Yeah." I hesitated, then said, "You know, I'm not so sure that's going to be high on my reading list, Uncle John. I mean, hey, college kids playing soldier? Come on."

"Yeah, I know," Uncle John said with a wry glance at me. "Imagine a guy leaving college to join the Army." He clapped me on the shoulder. "It looks that way at first, but stay with it. Tell you what, read your great-grandfather's first letter next. It's in there with a couple pictures of him."

"That was Ernie, your father, right?"

"Yes," Uncle John said, and his eyes blinked. "Taught me and my brother a lot about how to be good men, good soldiers. He wanted both of us to be Marines, but he was okay with Dennis going into SF. Just wanted us to be the best we could be."

"I remember him, a little," I said. "I was fourteen when he died, but I never saw him much. I was up in Wisconsin, he was out in California. He seemed like a grouchy old fart to me." I smiled, then looked down at the ground, suddenly somber. "I'm not sure my father taught me much of anything," I said, barely above a whisper.

The old Marine put his hand on my shoulder. "I'm sure he's proud of you."

"Well, he's not here, is he?"

Uncle John didn't have anything to say about that, but after a moment, he said, "I suppose we'd best be moving on to that party."

"Okay," I said, "but this Rough Rider thing…"

"You know, I remember him," Uncle John said. "I was thirteen when he died. About like you and my dad. Grampa Charles, he was a guy who led by example. No lectures, no long letters full of advice. I remember wishing he would talk to me about his time in the Army, his time in Cuba, but he only did it once, that was it, except to say how much he thought of Roosevelt. Then I read the diary, and I found out some other things about his life after Cuba. There's letters about that, too, in there." The old gunnery sergeant stood, his knees cracking like rifle shots. "Damn, maybe it's time I got these hinges replaced."

I stood, and even though my legs still felt weak, at least the knees didn't sound off. "I suppose we should be getting to that party," I said.

"Son, my own dad was a Marine," Uncle John said, "but he had to have an example to show him the way, and who do you suppose that was?" He slapped me on the back. "Come on, those three young jarheads are waiting for us. They think they're gonna show the old Gunny how to celebrate. We'll see about that."

CHAPTER EIGHT

The first letter of Ernest Dawson, Captain, U.S. Marine Corps Aviation
23 November 1950

Dear sons of mine,

You guys aren't really old enough to understand any of this crap, but a buddy of mine says I should write a letter to you because, hell, I might not get to see you again. I will tell you what I can, some of it may not get past the censors. ██████████ my squadron has a mission and every time I climb into that cockpit, I fear I might not be climbing back out of it. We try not to think about that but it's true. Every pilot who ever flew into combat knows that and pretending we don't think about it is bullshit. But we signed up for this job and that's part of the risk.

I'm your old man and damn proud of you boys. Denny, you're only 6 years old now, and I know you were tearing through those Dick & Jane books before I shipped out, but I am going to ask your Mom to hold this letter until you are at least 13. So sometime in 1957 you will be reading about your dear old Dad in the Marincs. I hope I'll be there to give you the letter.

It'll be a couple or three years after that for your brother. Here in 1950, Johnny is only 3, or is it 4? Hell, I forget sometimes. I try to remember your birthdays but I have to tell you, it's a lot easier to remember the times when your Mom and I got things rolling in that direction! New Year's Eve 1943 for Denny, I was home on leave before shipping out to Italy and there was a party at the Corner Bar in downtown Potosi and before midnight we couldn't stand it anymore and ran down the block to the little yellow house your Mom grew up in. Thank God her folks, your grandparents, were visiting your Mom's auntie down in Dubuque because we sure broke some furniture that night.

You can see now why I don't want you reading this till you're 13. A boy at that age should have some idea of what goes on between guys and gals, you ask me. I knew the score when I was 13, but it wasn't till I was 15 that I first got honey on my stinger. It's a humdinger of a story but that'll have to wait.

Up until I joined the Marines in '41, that was about the most exciting thing that ever happened to me. When I was born in 1920, my old man, your granddad, was 44 years old. My ma was his 2nd wife, his first having passed on years before I was born. It was important to the old guy to have a son, I was told, and after my ma gave him three girls in five years' time, I came along, the first and only son of Charles Dawson, the best damn lawyer in Grant County, Wisconsin, and a Rough Rider before that.

Well, when I graduated high school in '38, I told him there was no way I was gonna be a lawyer. Truth be told, I wanted to be a fighter. I had my share of scraps when I was a kid, because some of the boys didn't like it that my old man was a bigshot in town and they said that we were loaded with dough, although that was news to me. My old man threw nickels around like manhole covers. Mind you, we never missed a meal and lived in a nice house on Main Street across from the Mining School, but I never thought we were too terribly flush. I had to go to work when I was 13, hustling newspapers, selling extra vegetables from my ma's garden, anything to make a buck. My old man insisted. Learn how to work, he said. You'll be working all your life, start now. So I did.

My best job was cleaning the gym at the college. The old duffer who was my boss let me train there when I was done with work, and that's when I found I had a knack with my fists, and that got me the moniker Two-Fist. In high school I played football because I liked the blocking and tackling, and even though I was maybe 170 dripping wet, the ball-carriers found out that when I hit them, they stayed hit. When I was 16 I started going around to the bars when they had boxing smokers and making a name for myself in the ring. I had listened on the radio in the summer of '35 when James J. Braddock won the heavyweight title in the big upset of Max Baer, and it was damn near the most exciting night of my life. Well, second-most, it wasn't as good as that night with Henrietta a few weeks later.

Let me tell you that the fight game is not an easy one to get into and even tougher to make a living once you do get in. I fought as a light heavyweight. Won more than I lost, made a few bucks, managed not to get my face rearranged. There was one fight that I remember especially.

Summer of '38 it was, and I was booked at a roadhouse near Dodgeville when I met your Mom. She was there with another guy, some schmuck from her hometown that I remembered from football. I was running late because my car had a flat on the drive over from Platteville. The first thing I noticed when I walked in was a guy standing at the bar, bare-ass naked. It was Tim Schwab, a guy from Potosi who was a fan of mine. What the hell, I said, and the barkeep told me a local guy had bet Tim that I wouldn't show and a half-hour went by, so old Tim had to have a beer in his birthday suit. The hometown fighter was a tough hombre name of Ralphie something-or-other, Golden

Gloves champ, they said. Well, I said, I'm here, tell Tim to get dressed, 'cause the next guy to get undressed will be Ralphie boy when he gets in the ring with me. The next thing I noticed is your Mom. Bright red dress, long blonde hair, and curves where you like 'em. Great legs, too. I've always been a leg man, tell you the truth, and she had the gams. Still does.

I noticed her watching me as I climbed into the ring. I'd loosened up outside and had a good lather going and she liked my muscles, she told me later. I'd been training hard at the gym on campus back home, sparring against college guys. I was in pretty good shape, but old Ralphie had a pot on him and if he'd ever won Golden Gloves, it had to have been back when Coolidge was president. I took care of him in the third round, left jab got through his guard and then I unloaded on him with a right cross and that was it. I got dressed and collected my purse from the barkeep—it was $25, I remember, not bad money for a night's work in the Depression. The schmuck had gone to the john or something 'cause your Mom was all alone and I bought her a beer. He came out and saw me with her and walked out the door. Too bad for him. Your Mom and I, we've been together ever since.

Another guy who talked to me that night was John J. Walsh, who was the boxing coach at the University of Wisconsin. He was at the bar to scout me, he said. Let me tell you they had a powerhouse team in those days. Every kid boxer in the state knew about them, and he said he wanted me to come to the UW and box for him. Well, I hadn't thought much about college but when he told me I could get a scholarship and fight the best college fighters in the country, I was seriously interested. So that fall I went to Madison, where my old man had gone before he joined the Rough Riders and where he finished up after coming home from the war. He'd boxed in college too, although that was before they had an actual team, so he came to a lot of my bouts, saw me win the national light-heavyweight title at Penn State in '41.

I had a great time at school. I wasn't much in the classroom, just enough to stay eligible. For me it was all about the team, and boy, we had some terrific boxers. Omar Crocker at 145, lost only one decision in four years and that was because the judge got the scorecards mixed up. Woodie Swancutt, national champ at 155 in '39 and '40, later on he flew bombers in the war and dropped an A-bomb from his B-29 in the tests at Bikini Atoll in '46. Both good buddies of mine, great fighters.

But by the summer of '41 it was pretty obvious we were going to get into the war eventually, so I told my old man that I wanted to quit school and join the Marines. He could hardly say no because he'd done the same thing when he joined the Rough Riders. He had never talked to me too much about his time in Cuba but that night he told me a few stories, and I gotta be honest, I was close to shitting bricks by the time he was finished. But then he said, "Son, I would be proud to have you serve your country. Dawson men have served whenever their country called, and now it's your turn." He shook my hand and said, "I'm proud of you." That was the first time he'd ever said that to me. And I started to cry. Don't mind telling you. Here I was, the national champion boxer, tears coming down my face.

So off I went to Parris Island and then to flight school. Didn't want to be a grunt storming the beach, I wanted to be the guy up above. After Pearl Harbor, things got serious pretty fast. I found out that I really liked flying. Just me, up there in the cockpit, me and my aircraft. I had a knack for it. You have to use your hands in the cockpit and I knew how to use mine, that's for sure. When you get up there and the enemy is coming at you, it's like being in the ring only about a million times better. Just me and him, just like in the ring, and the better man gets to fly back to his base. I loved every minute of it and still do.

I'll write more later, it's time to hit the hay, we take off at ▮▮▮ ▮▮▮▮▮. We're up here in ▮▮▮▮▮▮ and it's cold as a bitch, but there's word that something's going on up at the ▮▮▮▮ and the boys on the ground need our help. Remember that no matter what you hear, your old man loves you boys.

Love, Your Dad

CHAPTER NINE

Fort Benning, Georgia
January 2014

"Keep both eyes open, Dawson. Why do we keep both eyes open?"

"Situational awareness, Sergeant."

"That is correct. You're in a gunfight. The enemy may be all around you. Your life, and the lives of your Rangers, depend on you putting rounds on target with your secondary weapon. It's part of your shooting mechanics, and it's all about your shooting mechanics. If they're bad, you lose the fight and you die. If they're good, you win and get to see your family again."

With one fluid motion, the instructor drew his nine-millimeter Beretta pistol, aimed and fired fifteen rounds in less than three seconds. Every one of the rounds impacted the target center mass, from five meters away. I had never seen such shooting, but there were a lot of things I'd never seen before that were now being shown to me in RASP 2.

Thirty-five soldiers had made it out of RASP 1, and now there were twenty-six men left in the class. Four had dropped out this week, and one more had been dismissed after his second safety violation on the range, just the day before. There were eight days left. Physically, I felt pretty good. But mentally, emotionally, this was far tougher than Ranger School. I couldn't allow myself to just go through the motions. I had to be focused every waking moment, and my sleep, such that it was, had been fitful. The psychological evaluations were like nothing I'd ever been through before.

I found myself relying on three things to get through it: prayer and the 23rd Psalm, which I'd been re-introduced to by my Ranger School buddy Travis, and reciting the Ranger Creed. The psalm had become my mantra, and the creed was never far away, always ready to be summoned when needed.

I focused on the first target silhouette. *Recognizing that I volunteered as a Ranger, fully knowing the hazards of my profession, I will always endeavor to uphold the prestige, honor and high esprit de corps of my Ranger Regiment.*

"All right, Dawson, show me what you can do."

I accept the fact that as a Ranger, my country expects me to move further, faster, and fight harder than any other soldier. The first target was at fifteen meters. It was all muscle memory by now. I drew my weapon, aimed and fired. Four of my five rounds were center mass.

"Twelve seconds," the instructor said, looking at his stopwatch. "Next target, ten meters. You have eleven seconds."

Stance, posture, draw, aim, extend, press. *Never shall I ever fail my comrades. I will always keep myself mentally alert, physically strong, and morally straight...*

"Not bad. Five on center mass, ten seconds. Next target, seven meters. Reload and shoot."

I released the empty magazine and inserted another without a thought. The gun felt good in my hand. *Gallantly will I show the world that I am a specially selected and well-trained soldier...*

"Getting better, Dawson. Five on center mass, six seconds. Five meters."

The weapon was a part of me now, an extension of my will, my determination to complete the mission. *Energetically will I meet the enemies of my country. I shall defeat them on the field of battle for I am better trained and will fight them with all my might. Surrender is not a Ranger word...*

"Five on center mass, four seconds. Good shooting. Final target, three meters. Reload and shoot."

It loomed before me, but the weapon and I were one now. *Readily will I display the intestinal fortitude required to fight on to the Ranger objective and complete the mission, though I be the lone survivor.*

The instructor clicked the stopwatch. "Two and a half seconds, and all on center mass. Well done, Ranger."

I felt a surge of relief and pride. I secured my weapon and slipped it back into the holster on my hip. A few weeks ago, I never would have believed that being called "Ranger" would mean that much to me. The next two drills went by quickly, climaxing with the "El Presidente," where I began with my back to a pair of targets at seven meters. From hands raised in "I surrender" mode, I had to turn, draw, sight and fire, a double-tap to the center mass of each silhouette. After a hot reload, I re-engaged the targets again with two more double-taps. To pass, three of the four rounds from each target had to be in the kill zone. I made three of four in the left target, all four in the right. When I holstered my Beretta, I felt as good as I had since starting the course. Maybe, I thought, just maybe, I was finding my groove.

"Mighty fine shooting, Dawson," the senior cadre sergeant said.

"Thank you, Sergeant."

"Just got word before we started, you have to report to the colonel."

My good mood evaporated. "Something wrong, Sergeant?"

The instructor shook his head. "Don't know, son. Everything's squared away for you as far as I'm concerned. Better head on over there and find out."

Whatever good mood I had been in evaporated quickly as I made my way to the C.O.'s office. The night before I'd read my great-grandfather's letter and enjoyed it immensely. Old "Two-Fist" was almost the exact opposite of his old man, the Rough Rider, and I wondered how that had gone over in the Dawson household while Ernie was growing up. There were a couple more letters from Ernie in the diary and I was looking forward to reading them. Too bad the whole thing wasn't about that swashbuckling Marine pilot. But I'd promised Uncle John I'd read everything, so tonight I'd make an effort to get back to the Rough Rider's story, if I had time.

And if I wasn't packing my duffel and heading out the door.

Was it possible I was being booted from RASP? No, it didn't work like that. My record was clean as a whistle. The psych evals had started but the word was they wouldn't be discussed until I went before the board, and that was next week. I had to get a grip. Everything about the training told me it was going well. The cadre had complimented me on more than one occasion, just a few minutes ago on the range, for God's sake. Had I missed something? The leadership lessons they'd been hammering at us had something to say about this type of situation. Don't be worrying all the time. Plan your work and then work your plan. Mistakes would be made, but recognize them, make corrections and drive on. The last thing in the world the Rangers of the 75th wanted was for one of their lieutenants to be overcome with worry about every last damn thing that was going on.

By the time I got to the colonel's office, I had managed to calm myself down. The reason the boss wanted to see me would be revealed in due time. I held that thought until I entered the office and saw the colonel behind his desk. Seated in one of the chairs facing the colonel was an African-American soldier I knew very well, only this time the soldier was wearing the three-up and three-down stripes of a Master Sergeant, not the three-and-two of Sergeant First Class. I forced my eyes away from the man in front of the desk to the officer behind it. Snapping to attention, I rendered my best salute. "Lieutenant Dawson, reporting as ordered, sir."

"At ease, Lieutenant," the colonel said. "I believe you know the Master Sergeant here."

Boudreau stood up, favoring one leg slightly, and extended a hand, backed by a big smile. "Good to see you again, Jake. If I might call you that, sir."

I took the hand gladly, although the pleasure at seeing my old SFC from my Iraq tour didn't exactly clear up the confusion about the colonel's summons. "Anytime, Sarge. Good to see you, too. How's the leg?"

"Just about back to full strength," Boudreau said, sitting down again. "Itchin' to get back to the Sandbox, or maybe the 'Stan."

"Have a seat, Jake," the colonel said, relieving some of my anxiety.

The C.O. wouldn't use my first name if he was going to give me an ass-chewing, would he?

The colonel must have seen something in my face, because he smiled, rather tightly, but it was there. "Relax, Jake. I hear you're doing well in RASP. I asked for you to see if we could get some intel about the firefight, the one where you saved Sergeant Boudreau's life."

"Well, sir, I don't know if I saved his life, really."

"For sure you did, son," Boudreau said. "The hajis were gonna make gumbo out of me, just like they did those IAs, the poor bastards. You got me back to that compound and I wouldn't be here now if you hadn't, there's no two ways about it."

A part of me noticed that Boudreau's Cajun accent wasn't as strong as I'd remembered from three years ago. Wherever he'd been serving since then, somehow it had smoothed off some of his rougher edges, but this was still a formidable man, a man I was damn glad to have on our side. Right now, though, all I could do was nod my assent. The Bronze Star citation had credited me with saving Boudreau's life, all right, but I hadn't been able to save Chet's. It was going on three years and it still ate at me, and despite what the colonel had said, I knew it was holding me back in the training. Today, in fact, had been the first day I'd started out feeling good about how things were going, right up until the order to report to the colonel. Somehow I'd known it wouldn't last.

"During his convalescence," the colonel said, "the sergeant here was helping out MI, digging into that firefight a little more, looking into some other things that were going on in Wasit back then, tying them to things that are currently going on in both theaters."

I would never have guessed that a gung-ho infantryman like Boudreau would have wound up in Military Intelligence, but maybe I didn't know as much about the old non-com as I thought. And he wasn't that "old," really, was he? Boudreau had to be in his late thirties, and I'd known plenty of soldiers in that age group who were still able to keep up with, and usually surpass, the younger men in their commands. Like the training cadre, for instance, both at Ranger School and RASP. They were the most squared-away soldiers I had ever met.

I addressed the colonel. "How can I help, sir?"

"I understand you were able to see one of the enemy up close at the end of the firefight."

I took an involuntary deep breath as the memory flooded back. "Yes, sir, that's right."

The colonel nodded. He reached into a file on the desk in front of him and withdrew an eight-by-ten photo. "Is this the man you saw?"

The black-and-white picture showed a man in a uniform I didn't recognize. A military dress uniform of some sort, as he was wearing white gloves, carrying a rifle at port arms. He wore a baseball cap sporting a rounded logo, a symbol of some kind bordered with what appeared to be a wreath. The symbol included an upraised hand holding an AK-47, but I didn't recognize the script. "The writing on the logo, is that Arabic?"

"It's Farsi," the colonel said. "Do you recognize the face?"

I looked at it again, compared it with the image burned forever in my memory of the dead haji on the ground in the ditch two feet away from Chet, with my buddy's KA-BAR buried to the hilt in the haji's solar plexus. Chet had done that, with his last ounces of strength. I'd been too late to do anything. "Yes," I said, "that's him. That's the guy who killed Chet…before I could get to him." I handed the photo back to the colonel, anxious to let go of it, as if that would somehow soften the image I carried with me everywhere.

"We believe his name was Jahandar," Boudreau said, "and he was in the Quds Force. That's the Special Forces branch of the Iranian Revolutionary Guard Corps, known over there as the Pasdaran. He held the rank of First Warrior, which is roughly equivalent to Sergeant First Class."

I took a moment to process that. "When we were over there, in Wasit, there was talk the Iranians were infiltrating," I said.

"The IRGC has been in Iraq since shortly after the invasion in '03," the colonel said. "They supplied the insurgency with IED materials in great quantities, especially EFPs. I believe you've been briefed on them, haven't you?"

"Yes, sir," I answered. "Explosively formed penetrators, a shaped charge designed to penetrate armor."

"Those IEDs were responsible for about twenty percent of our KIAs in Iraq," Boudreau said. "Lots of soldiers went down from those damn things. Some of them were buddies of mine." The sergeant looked very grim indeed, and one glance told me that anybody on the other end of Boudreau's rifle when he had that look would be dead in very short order.

"When President Bush ordered the surge early in '07, he also signed a Presidential Finding," the colonel said. "That finding directed our military and intelligence agencies to go after the IRGC inside Iran itself, staging raids primarily from Iraq and Afghanistan, but also a few from the other nations on Iran's northern and northwestern borders. The Master Sergeant here knows about how those went down."

Boudreau nodded. "I was on three missions," he said. "Two from Iraq, one from Armenia."

I was stunned. I had no idea Boudreau had ever been in any kind of SF unit. Boudreau saw my expression and chuckled. "Yeah, I had my Green Beret for a while, Jake. I was in 5th Group, '07 to '09. I guess I must've gotten to know the Sandbox pretty well, because then I got assigned to the training unit that you joined in '11."

The colonel took another photo out of the file. "One of the things that Sergeant Boudreau's MI unit has found out is that the unit that engaged your platoon that day in Wasit was commanded by this guy," he said, handing the photo to me. This one was in color, showing a fierce-looking man in an officer's uniform, with the same patches that Jahandar guy had sported on his. "We think his name is Mazdaki. At the time, he held the rank of Guardian Major in the Pasdaran. He's now at Guardian Lieutenant Colonel, and he's been involved in all sorts of activities targeting our Iraqi and Afghan allies."

"One of the Pasdaran's main targets has been the Kurds," Boudreau said. "There are ethnic Kurds in Iran, Iraq and Turkey, for the most part, and they want their own independent nation, carved out of all three of those countries. They've been fighting against all three for years. The

Iranians have been pretty effective in tamping them down in their country, and now the Pasdaran is moving against the Kurds in Iraq."

"The Kurds are fighting ISIS now, too, right?" I asked.

The colonel offered a grim smile. "Sometimes it seems everybody's fighting everybody over there," he said, "and it's not easy for our government to decide who to back, or if we should back anybody at all."

"Just let 'em fight it out. That's what I think sometimes," Boudreau said.

"I might agree, to a certain extent," the colonel said, "but things are not always that easy. The Kurds supported us during the '03 invasion, and they've been virtually autonomous in their region of Iraq since then. The Turks don't like them, because there are a lot of ethnic Kurds in eastern Turkey and the Turks don't have any intention of giving them autonomy."

"And Turkey is one of our NATO allies," I said.

"One of the most important, right now," the colonel said, "because of the fight against ISIS in Iraq and Syria."

I shook my head. "How do you people keep it all straight?"

The colonel sat back in his chair. "It's not an easy job, Jake, but if you have ideas about making the Army a career and rising in rank, then you'll be getting more and more involved in this, because that's where the action is now and where it's likely to be for several years. We don't make policy, but we're the ones who are ordered to carry it out, so we have a responsibility to understand what's going on."

I nodded, unsure whether I wanted to even approach that level of involvement. International politics had never been one of my strong suits, to say the least. For a moment, I wished I'd stayed in college to study it more. "How can I help?" I finally asked.

"SOCOM is very concerned about the Pasdaran's involvement in Iraq right now," the colonel said. SOCOM was Special Operations Command, and the 75th Ranger Regiment was a part of it. So were the Green Berets, I knew. "This is going to be an important year. ISIS is on the march over there and they've got to be stopped. The Iranians are aligning with the Iraqi government to fight them, but we also think they'll be using that to cover their efforts to go after the Kurds in northern Iraq, with the tacit approval of some important people in Baghdad, who'd like to see the Kurds taken down a notch or two. We're going to be deploying more Special Forces troops in the theater, starting very soon. Master Sergeant Boudreau here is in a specialized unit that is looking for good young officers."

"I heard about you getting the Puckett Award at Ranger School," Boudreau said. "I asked around, heard you were in RASP, and convinced my C.O. we could use a guy like you in the outfit. So I came to see the colonel here."

"If you pass RASP, and I have every confidence you will," the colonel said, "I can see my way clear to get you a shot at that unit. It's part of the 75th, Special Troops Battalion."

I had heard about that battalion. I turned to Boudreau. "Sarge, would your outfit be the Regimental Reconnaissance Company?" The word was that RRC was one of the Rangers' most elite units, and that was saying something. It was open not only to Army soldiers, but Navy SEALs and Force Recon Marines. I also knew it would require more advanced training.

"Sort of," Boudreau said. "I helped organize the outfit about a year ago. We were working on something pretty important through MI and got some actionable intel about a prime target. We didn't have any assets available except what I could cobble together on short notice, but we got the job done. After that, my C.O. got permission to keep the unit going. Officially we're under the RRC command structure, part of the 75th overall."

"They're short-handed right now, Jake," the colonel said. "That's why the sergeant came looking for you."

I nodded again, searching for something to say. I sure as hell felt proud that Boudreau had thought of me when he was in a jam for officers, but that also meant extra pressure to perform. I had dealt with that since I was in middle school, though. This would be a lot bigger challenge, but I was starting to like challenges. One thing about the Army I had noticed quickly was that its soldiers were challenged every day. Sometimes, I thought they were getting the better of me, but maybe, just maybe, I was worrying about that too much. Thinking too much about what my grandfather had gone through in Vietnam, and his father in Korea, and his in Cuba. Dawson men had been taking on the big challenges for a long time. Now, it was my turn.

In a way, I wanted nothing to do with that. I wanted to carve my own path, in the Army and then later. But there was something about destiny at play here, I thought. Maybe I didn't have a choice. A long line of honorable men–a line that took a leap over my own father, I thought, but then corrected that; my father had chosen a path of service that was honorable, hadn't he? The line started with Jeremiah, a hundred and fifty years ago, and now it was touching me, pushing me forward, despite my own questions about whether I could wear the Dawson mantle. And that's what it came down to, wasn't it?

I had to stall a little bit as I figured this out. "They say the first requirement is RSLC, sir," I said.

The colonel smiled. "Ordinarily, for someone wanting a billet in RRC, Reconnaissance Surveillance Leaders Course is a prerequisite, yes. I think you'd do very well there, but Sergeant Boudreau is working with a time crunch."

"The word I get is that my outfit will eventually be absorbed into RRC," Boudreau said. "I can see that happening, but right now we have a couple things on our plate that have to be dealt with before we can consider that move. Everybody from the outfit going into RRC will have to go through the regular training for that unit, and as you probably have heard, that's an entire year."

I had indeed heard that. "I think I might want to get back into the fight a little sooner than that, Sarge."

"That's what we thought you might like to do," the colonel said. He tapped another file on his desk, one that I recognized as my service jacket. "Special operations seems to be in your blood, Jake. Your grandfather was a Green Beret, and his grandfather was a Rough Rider."

Boudreau picked it up from there. "If you're half the man those SF guys in 'Nam were, and those Rough Riders down in Cuba, you're the kind of man we need." He leaned toward me, giving me that hard stare I remembered so well from that deployment. "So, how about it, Jake? You think you got what it takes to be in my outfit? You want to go after the bastards who killed Chet?"

I felt my emotions surge, and had to force myself to remain calm. Destiny. Maybe it was time to stop shying away from it, time to meet it head on. Like I had met challenges on the mat: overpower them, pin them, make them mine. I looked at the colonel, then back at Boudreau, and said, "Hell, yes."

The colonel stood, along with Boudreau, and I was right behind them. The Master Sergeant held out his hand. "Hooah, Lieutenant. Welcome to the Wolverines."

CHAPTER TEN

The journal of Charles J. Dawson, con't.

May the 16th, 1898 – I have been in Camp for one week and can truthfully say, this has been a momentous experience. Words sometimes fail me as I contemplate it, but for the sake of this record, I will make an attempt to describe it.

Our arrival at the Camp on the Monday past caused a sensation that would only be eclipsed six days later (yesterday) by the arrival of Lt. Col. Roosevelt himself. But I must build up appropriately to that moment.

Accompanying the Harvard men, many of whom had changed into blue flannel shirts and were wearing their new sombreros, we stepped down from the trolley onto the Fairgrounds on the 9th and were almost immediately surrounded by newspapermen as well as troopers whose arrival had preceded ours. (Being in my rather drab suit jacket and derby, I was, thankfully, largely ignored by the reporters.) At the Menger we had met William Tiffany, who is an executive with a New York railroad firm and the grand-nephew of Commodore Matthew Perry of Lake Erie fame. He was badgered by a reporter who wanted a photograph of him with his New York mates (and myself), but Tiffany refused. "We came here to fight," he said, "and we don't want all this nonsense." Tiffany has by his example become a leader in the Camp and it is said he will be named an officer, and rightly so. A San Antonio paper, the Daily Express, retaliated the next day by declaring that Tiffany had complained about food here at the Camp and the lack of a hot bath. Nothing could be further from the truth, and the boys were outraged when the paper made the rounds. I related my father's advice about newspapermen from his time fighting the Rebellion and we all agreed to henceforth be wary around the reporters.

I am pleased to report that, for the most part, our comrades from the West have accepted us heartily. They are tough and hardy men through and through, but we have demonstrated we are not dandies by pitching in with the work to be done, and they have come to respect us. One cowboy from New Mexico territory with a splendid mustache and swarthy complexion, bespeaking perhaps Spanish or Indian heritage, called me "a right plucky fellow" after I displayed my horsemanship skills. Some of the Easterners, polo players back home like myself, are even better than me in the saddle. (Many of the Westerners, though, are true artists.) We have not shirked on the chores necessary to care for the horses, and two cousins from Boston, who worked in their family's restaurant since childhood, have volunteered to assist in the Camp's kitchen, such that it is, quickly improving the quality of the victuals.

Regarding the Western men and their willingness to embrace us in comradeship, there has been one notable exception. A fellow named McGee, from Denver, is a rather surly sort who appeared to be suspicious of us. One of the other Coloradans informed us that McGee had been involved in some shady activity back home and was in the Regiment only due to the influence of his uncle upon the Governor. As I myself benefited from my father's patronage to obtain my billet, I could hardly fault the man for that. But the first time he saw me he insulted my derby, implying that anyone who would wear such a "prissy lid" is not worthy of being a Rough Rider. The derby, as mentioned, was a gift from my favorite aunt, so I was ready to seek satisfaction right there, but Wells and Dean calmed me down, and I walked away with them, McGee's laughter burning my ears. We would soon meet again.

Of victuals there is no shortage, although there is of every other commodity necessary for the proper operation of a military camp. Upon arrival we learned that what few tents were available from Fort Sam Houston were being reserved for the officers, and the rest of us were to be housed in the Exposition Building here at the Fairgrounds until our own dog-tents arrived. Some even had to sleep under the adjacent grandstand, but I have been indoors. We had not even blankets until the 13th, and even then not nearly enough to go around, and so I have shared with Dean, the Harvard quarter-back. On the second night a ruckus commenced when a shoe was tossed and struck one of the New Mexicans, who retaliated by lobbing the shoe back in the direction from whence it came. Within seconds shoes and other articles were flying every which way, and it took the arrival of two officers to calm the scene.

Uniforms came in two days ago, the Model 1884 fatigue trousers of brown canvas, dastardly hot at times but hardy and easily worn. Our blouses, which just arrived to-day, are of regulation dark blue wool and of the pullover style. I can only imagine how oppressive these will be in Cuba, but nothing is to be done about it. Also issued, per trooper: a khaki canvas coat (doubtless never to be worn, where we are bound), canvas leggings, a pair of socks and of shoes (most of the Westerners prefer their own boots), and the Model 1889 campaign hat. The uniforms were issued in this way: we formed lines and presented ourselves singly to an officer, who would guess our size and hand us a bundle. Fortunately, mine was mostly correct in measure, although some fellows' were not, and later there was much exchanging taking place. To my surprise, in a pocket of my shirt I found a note, written in flowery hand by a woman from Cincinnati, offering marriage to whomever received the shirt. Not being interested, I was able to exchange it with an Arizona trooper for his newly-purchased bandanna, a hot item among the Easterners who saw quickly how much the Western men preferred such affectation. Mine is of dark red in color with small white polka-dots, and when I first apprised myself in a mirror in my new duds, I was quite proud. If Father could see me now! I must have a photograph taken.

Typically, the men of each state stick together. I have heard there are one or two other Wisconsinites in the Camp, but have been unable to find them, so I remain with the Harvard men. As there is not much to do before our weapons and horses arrive, not to mention the full complement of officers, we have been trying to stay busy. Some of the state contingents have already elected their officers and have been performing marching drills and so forth. The Arizona men have brought a mascot, a young mountain lion named Josephine, and she is quite popular with the townsfolk who infest the Camp. Privately, we began to grumble about the necessity to actually begin learning to be soldiers.

That all changed yesterday with the arrival of Theodore Roosevelt himself. It was a spectacle of the most amazing sort.

He entered the Camp in the morning, fresh from the train depot, wearing a khaki uniform with bright yellow collars. Word spread that he had ordered it specially tailored from Brooks Brothers. With him was a Negro man, whom we found out was his valet. They were escorted into the Camp by Col. Wood, our commanding officer, and Maj. Dunn, whom Tiffany informed us was master of the hounds at Chevy Chase Hunt Club. As we happened to be walking past the headquarters tents when the retinue arrived, I was able to get a close look at the man responsible for raising this regiment.

Roosevelt was shorter than I anticipated, perhaps two inches shy of my six feet, and rather stockily built, but a man of immense personal charisma and energy. He was wearing pince-nez spectacles, sported a brushy brown mustache and a wide, somewhat toothy grin. Many of the troopers had followed his party as they arrived, but we were the first ones to approach him as he dismounted the phaeton that had conveyed the quartet from town. Tiffany had taught us all how to properly salute, and we snapped our heels together and offered Roosevelt one that brought a wide grin to his face. "Well, that's bully indeed!" he said, as he approached us. "And who do we have here?"

Tiffany introduced himself first, and Roosevelt seemed especially pleased to hear that most of us were Harvard men like himself. He offered each man a hearty handshake as he came down the line. When my turn came, my heart was near to burst through my blouse. His grip was like iron. "And you, sir?" he asked me.

"Charles Dawson, Colonel, from Wisconsin."

"Wisconsin, you say? Dee-lighted!" He slapped me on the shoulder and moved on to the last man, Dean.

Roosevelt then repaired to his wall tent, and we went on our way. The Camp teemed with visitors, thousands of them, and I must confess we troopers lapped it all up like thirsty dogs, especially the attention from the many young ladies. Late in the afternoon, we heard the sound of a band, and quickly discovered that musicians were marching through the Camp toward the headquarters tents. Once again we were fortunate as we were already in the vicinity. A local informed us that the troupe was Professor Carl Beck's Military Band, which performs a regular Sunday afternoon concert in the city. After their performance they had come to the Camp, where they formed a circle around Roosevelt's tent and began playing a rousing series of patriotic tunes. The maestro finished the final number with a flourish, and the crowd, now in the hundreds including both troopers and civilians, gave them thunderous applause, many of the Westerners tossing their hats skyward and whooping with delight. Then someone called for Lt. Col. Roosevelt to speak.

Over the course of the past few years I have heard many speeches from prominent men, including President Cleveland himself when Father took me to the opening of the Columbian Exposition in Chicago in '93, but this one by Roosevelt, impromptu as it was, topped them all by a wide margin. He began by reminding us that "the eyes of the entire civilized world" are upon us. He concluded thusly: "I expect you to acquit yourselves creditably, and I know I will not be disappointed. When we get to Cuba and get at the Spaniards, I want your watchword, my men, to be 'Remember the Maine,' and you shall avenge the Maine." With his teeth flashing, he pointed at us and shouted, "We are expected to fight, and that we must do!"

I had never heard such a cheer as went up from the troopers. Hats flew in the air, including my own. Nearby, a young woman swooned, overcome with excitement, and two troopers gallantly caught her before she could hit the ground. The band began to play "Yankee Doodle," bringing another loud cheer. Roosevelt waved to the crowd and withdrew to his tent, and eventually the crowd began to break up.

After supper, which I have learned to call "evening chow" in the Army way, we began to set up our dog-tents, clustered together by state. My Harvard friends insisted I remain in their company, as we have not yet been assigned to any specific Troop. To my dismay, the Coloradans were located next to us, including my nemesis McGee, who had not let up with his vitriol toward me, making remarks every time he found himself in my presence over the past few days since our initial encounter. This time, we were finishing our chow when he sauntered over, accompanied by two comrades. This I regarded as a bad sign, as it indicated he had obtained allies.

"Hey, Badger boy," he called out.

"What do you want, McGee?" I answered.

"I see you have got yourself a proper hat at last," he said. I again noted something about his speech, perhaps a southern drawl, although not as pronounced as that of the many Dixie lads we have among the troopers. He continued: "Tell you what, if you don't want that other lid of yours anymore, I could use it myself. Might need something to piss in when we're in Cuba."

Next to me, Dean shook his head slightly. "Ignore him, Charles. He's not worth our trouble."

McGee was close enough now to have overheard my friend. He laughed, then said to his comrades, "Y'see there, boys, we have us some typical Yankees here."

"What do you mean by that?" I said, rising to my feet as my temper also elevated.

Wells stood up and took a step toward the Coloradans. "Why don't you fellows just go on your way?" he said. "We have no quarrel with you. We're all on the same side, after all. Before long we'll be in Cuba and then the Spaniards will provide us with all the fighting we want."

McGee laughed. "It'll be a sight, you Yankee boys, when the lead starts flyin'. You'll be crappin' those new drawers of yours right quick."

These words aroused a few more of the Harvard men. Dean stood up beside me. "Our fathers didn't flinch when they saw combat, and neither will we," he declared. "Dawson's father won the Medal of Honor with the Iron Brigade, in fact."

Although I am intensely proud of Father's service, my heart sank when Dean uttered those words. I knew they would provoke more insults from McGee, and that's exactly what happened. He laughed again and then slurred Father and his regiment, casting their manhood into serious question with a foul epithet which I refuse to print here.

It was at that point I had no choice but to demand satisfaction. My family's honor was at stake and I could not back down in front of my comrades, nor McGee in front of his. It was determined that we would settle the matter fifteen minutes' hence, at a location near the fringe of the Camp, well away from the officers' tents.

The sun was lowering as we gathered at the appointed spot. It was to be bare-knuckle boxing, although Dean cautioned me that McGee, if pressed, would doubtless resort to tactics well outside Marquess of Queensberry rules, which we were violating anyway because of the lack of proper gloves. I entered the "ring" with some trepidation; should I become injured, my time in the Regiment would surely be over. But to submit to McGee after verbal insults of his kind would be humiliating. Father would have told me to walk away, but the die had been cast.

A neutral third party, a trooper from Arizona, volunteered to be the referee. The bout would end when one man submitted to the other, or was ruled unable to continue. There would be no timed rounds. I had not engaged in such fisticuffs since my teenage days in Platteville, but felt confident that my training at the gym in Madison would carry me through. McGee and I stripped our blouses and began.

He was cocksure by more than half, leading him to make a mistake with a wild right, which I easily ducked and countered with a left to his exposed ribcage. That staggered him, and I pressed my early advantage with a jab and then a right cross, which caught him flush on his left cheek. Down he went, and I danced back, with the cheers of my mates ringing happily in my ears. Before the referee could begin a count, McGee's fellow Coloradans pulled him back to his feet. He shook his head, wiped blood away from his mouth, and came at me hard.

But he was under control, I had to give him that, and he unleashed a flurry of punches that I caught on my arms as I covered up, then clinched. With a roar he pushed me away, but the moment's respite had refreshed me, and my confidence soared as I knew I had taken his best shot. He must have known it, too, as he was more cautious now. As he backed away, I was distracted by a movement to my left, outside the group of troopers surrounding the fighting space. A now-familiar figure was standing on a slight rise, watching. Turning my attention back to the contest, I pressed my advantage, controlling the space as I had been taught, cutting off his angles, and when his back was to his mates at the edge of the "ring," I faked a jab that caused him to bring his guard up, and then I caught him with a right uppercut into the solar plexus, giving it everything I had. He expelled his breath with a loud "oof!" and went down like a sack of potatoes.

I backed away as the referee moved in and began the count, having warned the Coloradans not to intervene. McGee tried to regain his feet but failed. The count had reached seven when a loud voice from outside the ring interrupted the proceedings.

"See here! What is going on?"

Theodore Roosevelt shouldered his way through the crowd of troopers, which had now grown to about fifty. When the men recognized him, they stepped back. The Arizonan stopped his count, and two Coloradans pulled McGee upright, although still bent over and gasping.

Wells stepped forward and saluted. "A matter of honor was being settled, Colonel. Dawson, here, had been grievously insulted by-"

Roosevelt cut him off. "I don't want to hear any of it. We don't have time for this foolishness, men. We start our training to-morrow in earnest. Soon we shall ship out for Cuba, where all of us will engage in real fighting. Lives will be at stake, and I need every man jack of you to fight together as one. If you are fighting each other, the Spaniards will carry the day and those poor Cubans will remain in bondage. Now get back to your tents and bed down. To-morrow we start bright and early!"

The troopers began to disperse. Roosevelt went over to McGee and spoke to him, quietly enough so that I could not hear, but I saw the transplanted Southerner say a few words in reply, then nod his head. He stepped past Roosevelt and approached me, his hand held out. "I apologize, Dawson," he said. "I was out of line."

I took his hand gratefully. "It's all in the past now," I said.

"My daddy was in the 15th Alabama," he said. "Took a Yankee ball in his shoulder at Little Round Top. Took to drink when he got home, they said, died drunk when I was six. I guess I..."

Suddenly touched, I clapped his shoulder. "It's all right," I said. "My father was at Gettysburg, too. Took a Reb round to the leg on Seminary Ridge." I did not add that Father recovered from his wound with much more success than McGee's unfortunate sire had experienced.

"Well, he must have taught you how to fight," McGee said. "Tell you what, Yank, I'll have your back in Cuba."

"And I yours," I said. We shook hands again and he went off with his mates.

Roosevelt now approached me. "It's all settled, then?" he asked.

"Yes, sir," I said. "Thank you for intervening when you did, Colonel." I knew he had done so to save McGee the humiliation of official defeat, although his loss was evident to everyone present.

"You acquitted yourself well, Dawson," Roosevelt said. "I've had some experience in the ring myself, at Harvard."

By now my erstwhile Harvard mates had gathered round. "We've all heard the story of your lightweight bout in '79, Colonel," Dean said. "Is it true you excused Hanks for hitting you after the bell?"

Roosevelt grinned. "Oh, I never excused him for it," he said, "I merely suggested to the referee that Hanks may not have heard the bell." That drew laughter from all of us. "The point is," the colonel continued, "he and I became fast friends after that match. Dawson, you will need a friend when you find yourself in battle in Cuba, and thanks to your comportment this evening, I dare say McGee could be that friend for you."

"I hope so, Colonel," I said.

He clapped me on my shoulder. "Again, well done. Now, I have a daunting stack of letters waiting for me at my tent, so you will excuse me, gentlemen. Carry on." He touched the brim of his hat in salute and departed our company.

"You know, fellows," Wells said, "we are fortunate to have that man to lead us in battle."

"Indeed we are," I said, reflecting on the lesson in leadership we had all just learned.

CHAPTER ELEVEN

Erbil Governorate, Iraq
March 2014

I hurt everywhere. Top to bottom, from the scalp wound that had stopped bleeding only when I bandaged it with a strip of cloth torn from my dirty shirt, all the way down to the soles of my feet. What had they hit me with there, anyway? Batons of some sort, but what? Bamboo? Oak? And exactly what difference did it make? They hurt.

Five weeks in the Wolverines, third mission. It hadn't taken long to go to shit, had it?

It started out pretty well. I had a week's leave after graduating RASP 2, enough time for a quick visit back home. It was great to see my mother and Uncle John, of course, and I got to spend a full day with Sam before heading back to Benning. That gave me three days to get my stuff together before leaving to join up with my new outfit in Turkey.

The Wolverines' base was in eastern Hakkâri Province, in the corner of the country right on the Iraqi and Iranian borders. It was mountainous territory, dominated by ethnic Kurds, and a perfect place from which the unit could stage its missions. But that didn't mean it was easy to get to.

My travel path to the outfit wasn't the worst I'd ever experienced, but it was close. The first two legs weren't bad, Andrews Air Force Base to Ramstein in Germany, an eight-hour layover and then to Incirlik in Turkey. But then came the hop aboard a Vietnam-era C-130 to a Turkish base in Diyarbakir, and from there on an even older bird to another base in the city of Hakkâri, the provincial capital. The Chinook helicopter scheduled to take us to the Wolverine base had mechanical problems, so we hopped aboard a Turkish Army deuce and a half for the seven-hour haul through the mountains over roads that would be an American driver's worst nightmare.

The only thing making it bearable at all was meeting up in Ramstein with a soldier heading back to the outfit after two weeks' leave back home. Ellis Burns was a sergeant first class who had been with the Wolverines for a year, and he was happy to give me the lay of the land during the long haul to Incirlik. Burns was from Idaho and loved mountains, American or otherwise, and seemed to know everything there was to know about this corner of the planet.

The Turks had been here in force since the Ottoman days, and had been persuaded to turn an old facility over to the Americans. Anything to keep the Kurds in line, Burns told me. Ethnic tensions here went back a long ways, to the Assyrian Genocide of 1915 and earlier. The Kurds, he said, weren't too sure about which side the Americans were on. No wonder I had been warned to keep a low profile while in transit.

But the Wolverines welcomed me to the outfit in as much style as they could muster. The C.O., a major named Kulinski, was a graduate of the University of Michigan, hence the outfit's nickname. He introduced me to the rest of the team: two dozen men, all of them enlisted except for Kulinski and me. Like a Special Forces ODA team, none of the enlisted were below the rank of sergeant. Boudreau was the senior man. Three of the guys were Force Recon Marines, two were Air Force Special Ops. Burns was the chief commo tech, in charge of the radios.

I barely had time to settle into my hooch when Kulinski started prepping the team for the next mission. Every day was full, and at night I usually had just enough energy left to send an email or two home before hitting the rack. A week after my arrival, we went into northern Iraq by truck, waved through the border checkpoint by the Turkish guards without so much as a question. Kulinski led the team, composed of me, Boudreau and six other operators, in a snatch-and-grab of a suspected ISIS recruiter near the northern Iraqi town of Welati Jori. Kulinski and Boudreau took three of the men into the compound, leaving me in command of the backup force. We weren't needed. I never even heard any shots fired. The Wolverines all used suppressed weapons, of course, but they were in and out so quickly that the enemy didn't even have time to return fire with their noisy AKs. I got the message: this was a first-rate outfit.

Back at the base in Turkey, I observed Kulinski and Boudreau questioning the prisoner, who turned out to be a Syrian who knew a fair amount about what his gang was up to in the neighborhood. The CIA turned up the next day and whisked him away. Black site, one of the Marines told me, somewhere in Armenia. The Armenians, and the folks next door in Azerbaijan, weren't quite as sensitive about things like prisoners' rights as they were in NATO countries.

A couple weeks later, I had a more active role in the second op, a recon into northern Iran, where we observed a Pasdaran unit prepping for an incursion into Iraq. I had one of the Air Force operators along with me, and we tracked the Iranians through the mountains on horseback. The hours I'd spent in the saddle riding through the forests of northern Wisconsin came in handy. Once the Pasdaran squad crossed the border, I gave the word for the airman to call in a strike. It felt good, seeing those Iranian vehicles lit up by the F-16s, flying from Incirlik out of the west. It pays to have friends in high places.

Three weeks into my new assignment, I was feeling pretty good about things. This was a good bunch of men, and every day the good-natured insults and one-upmanship served to relieve some of the inevitable tedium. Word had gotten around about my SF ancestors, and not for the first time I started to feel a little pressure about living up to their legacy. There was training every day, and I almost went into information overload a few times, but there was a hell of a lot to learn from these operators and I soaked it all up. When I got the word from Kulinski that I was going to lead the next op, I thought I was ready.

I wasn't.

It was another move into Iraq, this time to recon a suspected ISIS unit that was said to be on the move against the Kurds. By this time, I was starting to get a sense of the complicated politics of the region. The

Kurds had been virtually autonomous in northern Iraq since the fall of Saddam in '03, but their military forces, the Peshmerga, were fighting on two fronts: against ISIS coming from the west, and Iraqi Shiite militias, backed by the Iranians, from the south. With the Turks at the border on the north and Iran to the east, the Kurds were surrounded. It was up to us, the Americans, to keep them from being overrun, although the Turks weren't exactly happy about that, as I'd learned during Boudreau's original recruiting pitch back at Benning.

Maybe that's why things had gone tits-up on this mission. The intel about the ISIS unit hadn't come through CIA or Army Intelligence, but from the Turks. *Millî İstihbarat Teşkilati,* their National Intelligence Organization, ostensibly wanted to help Turkey's American allies, but Kulinski said he had a bad feeling about the intel package when it came in. He had to go with it, though, when he kicked his reservation up the chain and it was kicked back to him. Now, I knew that my C.O.'s bad feeling had been right on the money.

The village where ISIS was said to have set up shop turned out to be just a village, a few dozen families and no weapons beyond the few obligatory AKs that were everywhere in Iraq these days. The country was the world's largest ammo dump. My team of six picked up a Kurdish interpreter near the border and after twenty-four hours of overwatch from a nearby hill turned up nothing irregular, I decided to take Burns, the radio telephone operator for the mission, and the 'terp down into the village to talk to the chief. Kulinski cleared the recon, and shortly after first light we started down out of our hide spots on the hill.

The vill's location bothered me right from the start. Tucked into a small, narrow valley, the cluster of buildings was served by only one road, snaking east-west through the mountains. Granted, these mountains were minor-league compared to what I'd seen in Afghanistan, but they were serious mountains nonetheless, and that meant it was impossible to get a line on what was around the bend unless you had a drone up above. I'd asked for one, in fact, but Kulinski radioed back that none were available. Air cover was sparse in this neck of the country. The Turks could've staged one out of Diyarbakir, but

Kulinski's request had been refused outright by MİS.

The first sign of trouble was a warning on the radio from Boudreau, up in the hide spot, telling Burns they heard vehicles coming in from the west. The only ones in the village were a few tired old Toyota pickups and a twenty-year-old Geo Tracker, of all things, that belonged to the chief. Burns and I were letting the chief show off his little rig when the radio call came in, and seconds later I heard the engines myself.

The chief's attitude turned on a dime, from easy-going to fearful. He spoke rapidly to the 'terp. "It is Kata'ib Hezbollah," the wide-eyed interpreter said. "They were here one week ago. Drove out Peshmerga. Now they come for you."

I remembered now that the 'terp hadn't said "us." I also remembered the 'terp vanishing as we high-tailed it for the hill where the rest of the team nervously waited. But we were on the south side of the village and the team was halfway up a hill to the north. We'd barely made it to the edge of the vill when the first Hezbollah vehicles rolled in. They were U.S. Army-issued Humvees that the militia unit had no doubt stolen from the Iraqis, and the convoy of four deployed like they knew what they were doing, flanking the vill with one vehicle on each side and two more roaring down the middle. The guy on the .50-caliber machine gun knew what he was doing, too, firing a burst that pinned us against the side of the last building. There was no way we could make it across the fifty meters of empty space that separated us from the trees on the hillside. If that gunner had anything on the ball, his .50 would cut us to pieces. I didn't want to tell Boudreau to provide covering fire; that would've given away their position, inviting return fire, maybe more friendly casualties. Boudreau offered, but I turned him down, told him to bug out with the rest of the team and come back later in strength.

Even as Burns radioed up to Boudreau, I knew we were done for. There weren't enough Americans here to take on the militia force, the Peshmerga was nowhere to be found, and even if we had air support on the way, there was no way any U.S. commander would authorize a strike on a populated village.

I struggled to hear Boudreau on the radio over the roar of the .50-cal and the crunch of rounds impacting the building we were hiding behind. The master sergeant said something about Kulinski being on the horn to Higher right now, calling for help, but there was no quick reaction force available for this mission. "We're pretty much on our own out here," Kulinski had told me on my first day with the outfit.

Well, that's for damn sure, I thought now, sitting in the dark hut, twelve hours or so after we were captured. I had no idea where my RTO was, or whether he was even still alive.

The beating came during my first hour in custody. I didn't expect them to care much about the Geneva Convention, and they didn't. They put a hood on me, took my boots and socks off and started in with feet and fists to the body and sticks to the soles of my feet. I wanted to fight back, but some instinct told me to hold off, that if I tried to defend myself it would only get worse. So I swallowed what was left of my pride and took it, trying as best I could to protect my head.

Two things that got me through the pain and humiliation. One was thinking of Sam back home, waiting for me. I'd almost popped the question during my leave, and now I wished I had. It would've strengthened our bond, given me something more to hang onto. Yeah, we'd only been back together for six months, had only seen each other a few times, but I thought about it a lot on the flight over and realized I was in love with her. I was pretty sure she felt the same way about me.

Engaged or not, if I was going to marry Sam, I'd have to get out of this rat hole first. I had not yet been through SERE training, although I'd certainly heard of it. Survival, Evasion, Resistance and Escape. Sounded good, and I was sure the training would be helpful, but that wouldn't come until I got to Special Forces. If I got there, and right now that was a pretty big if. But something my great-uncle had told me came back now. "Adapt, improvise, overcome." It was when I was training for the wrestling sectional my junior year in high school, preparing for a match against a kid who'd beaten me two years in a row. "Use what you have, find a way around the problem, get it done," Uncle John said. It worked back then; I won the match on the way to my first state title. But this new challenge was several degrees of magnitude tougher.

I peered through the gloom of the dank, empty room. There didn't seem to be a lot here to improvise with, but there had to be something. I might only have one chance, so I'd damn well better be prepared to take it. I took stock of what was available. To my surprise, they hadn't tied me up or used cuffs. My boots were gone, but they'd allowed me to put my socks back on. Whoever these guys were, they were playing low-minors ball with me. Wherever they would take me, though, that would be the major leagues. That had to be prevented at all costs.

I thought again about the second thing that had gotten me through the beating, the thing that might just wind up saving my ass. On the transatlantic flight I'd read another letter from the Rough Rider's kid Ernie, my great-grandfather. Two-Fist had gotten himself into the same kind of jam in Korea that I was in now, and he'd come through. He'd made it home alive, and now, sixty-some years later, it was my turn.

Time went by. They'd taken my wristwatch, so I had no idea what time it was. Maybe ten, twelve hours since the capture. That meant it was dark outside. The room's only light was from a low-watt bulb hanging from the ceiling. There was no furniture, although there must've been before they brought me in here, from the indentations in the dirt floor. They hadn't put a piss pot in here and there sure as hell wasn't a bathroom, so I whizzed once in the far corner, adding to the aroma of the room. I was just starting to think about being really thirsty when the door opened and an armed fighter stepped in.

I stood up, trying to calm my breathing. One chance.

CHAPTER TWELVE

The second letter of Ernest Dawson, Captain, U.S. Marine Corps Aviation

22 December 1950

Dear Denny and Johnny,

I am writing this letter to you at your Mom's request. We can't talk on the telephone so she wants me to explain to you what happened to me, in my own words. I don't want to screw around with the censors so I am having a buddy of mine take this back to the States, he's flying out tomorrow and will put this in the mail when he gets to Honolulu.

You mom has told you that I was shot down over North Korea and captured. It is true. I am very sorry you had to hear about that but your old man is alive and well. I am writing this from the hospital in Japan. I was sent here to recover from my injuries after I was rescued.

The mail takes a long time to get back and forth from here to the States. By the time you get this it will be after Christmas. I sure wish I could've been there to celebrate with you boys. At one time I thought I'd be home for it. That's what we all thought over here. We had the North Koreans on the run and everybody thought it was pretty much over. That's certainly what the brass thought, all the way up to MacArthur. But then the Chinese came over the Yalu and now it's anybody's guess how long it'll take. I am beginning to think this won't be like the last war at all.

I got a letter from your Grampa Leibfried in Potosi. He told me how when your Mom got the telegram about me being shot down she almost died from the worry. It was so bad for her that Grampa and Grandma had her and you boys come stay with them in Potosi for the duration. The telegram said I was missing in action.

It was a week before the Marines finally tracked her down. An officer and a chaplain came to the house in Potosi with more news. They said my wingman saw my chute opening after I bailed out and he was sure I made it down in one piece because he came back around and buzzed me at about 500 feet and I waved up at him. But he couldn't stick around because he had to provide air support for some Marines on the ground who were retreating. By the time they got a helicopter to where I'd landed, the Chinese were all over the place. They had me, although the chopper guys didn't know that. All they could report was that there was no sign of me or my chute. Just a lot of Chinese.

But I made it out. There is more to tell you and that is in another letter I have enclosed with this one. Your Mom will hold that for a few years till you are old enough to understand it. It is like the first letter I wrote to you, just before I took off on the flight when I was shot down. Only it is different in some important ways. That will be obvious to you when you read it a few years from now.

I hope to God that I am there in 1957 to hand it to you, Denny, but just in case I am not, I am sending it to your Mom to hang onto. They have talked about sending me home after I get better but I aim to get back to Korea and back into the cockpit. Plenty of my Marine buddies are still fighting up there and they will need my help. I also aim to get some payback from those Chink bastards for what they did to me.

So I will close this part now. Be good boys and mind your Mom and your grandparents. I will see you when this is all over.

I love you boys with all my heart. I always knew that. For damn sure it became clear to me when I was a prisoner. One reason I mean to go back up there is to do what I can to make sure neither of you boys ever has to fight these guys again. They are mean sonsabitches and we have to take care of them once and for all.

Your dad

22 December 1950

Dear Denny and Johnny,

This is the story of my capture and my brief time as a POW and my escape. They are telling me I am one of the first Americans to escape in this war. There were quite a few guys taken prisoner in the first few months after the Commies invaded. (Commies are Communists. The North Koreans and their Chinese and Russian allies are all Communists. Maybe by now your schools have taught you what that means but the short version is, they are the ones who intend to take over America and our friends someday. Your old man and his buddies are fighting to stop them.) But thankfully, our troops liberated those guys when our counteroffensive began.

I saw my first action in the war to support the landing at Inchon. We hammered the hell out of the North Koreans behind the lines and our troops began to advance pretty quickly. I am proud to say I helped liberate Seoul and was able to spend some time there after we drove the Commies out. It is a big city, biggest I've ever been in, and the North's troops had trashed the place during their occupation. They treated the South Korean civilians worse than dogs. A lot of them were shot or jailed during the occupation, which lasted 3 months. But I heard that a lot of prominent ROKs, that's South Koreans, collaborated with the North. That's how it goes, happened with the French and others in the last war. Last I heard, they were now being the ones rounded up and jailed. It is a real mess. It will be a long time before these people get their shit together. In the meantime, guess who will be protecting them? That's right, good old Uncle Sam.

But MacArthur had the right idea, and that was to land at Inchon and cut off the Commie supply lines from their bases in the North. The word we got was the candy asses back in Washington didn't like his plan, some of them even wanted us to bail out and let the North win. But Mac had other ideas and in we went, and by God it worked like a charm. The Marines showed once again we know how to do this, just as we had showed in the Pacific during WW2. I saw plenty of action during that war, shot down six Jap planes and chopped up a lot of their troops on the ground. And here I am in Tokyo, in a hospital with Japs cleaning the toilets and serving us the meals. I'd say turnabout is fair play.

But I've also got to say, the Jap people are very friendly to us here. I've talked to a lot of guys who were here on occupation duty and they all say they were treated well by the civilians, no problems at all. So who knows, maybe they'll turn into friends of ours, even allies, by the time you boys are grown. Hope so. I am really getting tired of fighting these people all the time. Seems like that's almost all I've been doing, or training to do, for ten years or so now. One thing's for sure, the Japs are great fighters. They gave us a hell of a time in the last war and it would sure be better to have them on our side for the next one, although with

Korea, they're sitting this one out. Koreans hate Japs, and you can't blame them, they were treated pretty shitty by the Japs during their occupation.

But back to my story. I was with Marine Aircraft Group 33 at the time, VMF-214, the Black Sheep. That was the outfit I spent most of WW2 with. I served under Maj. Pappy Boyington, one of the best fighter pilots and greatest leaders I've ever known. We lost 23 pilots in the war, and I knew most of them and called them friend and comrade. We lost 32 men from the squadron when USS Franklin was hit off Honshu, the main Jap island. I was in the air, had just taken off from the carrier when a Jap bomber came in hard and dropped two big ones on the deck. Ken Linder and I got the bastard but it was too late to save our boys on the ship. Nearly 800 good men died that day.

But I survived that war and stayed in the service after the Jap surrender. Served as a pilot instructor between the wars and then the squadron was activated again after the North invaded, summer of 1950. I flew the F-4U Corsair, like I did in the Pacific. I was in my Corsair when I was shot down, a lucky hit from some AAA on the ground. Knocked out my hydraulics and hit the engine, too. So I had no choice but to bail out, first time that ever happened to me in I don't know how many combat missions, both wars combined.

I knew my wingman had seen me get down safely under my chute and would radio my location. I just had to stay alive and out of Commie hands until then. But I could hear artillery fire in the distance and knew I had to get out of there. My best bet was to head south. That's what they told us, if we were shot down just head south and stay low. Us and the ROKs controlled damn near the whole country by then but we had just gotten word that the Chinese were coming over the Yalu by the thousands. The brass didn't believe it at first but they damn sure did when we got back to base and told them what we'd seen from the air, and they saw the recon photos. Masses of troops, too many to count. No armor, and we'd knocked out all the North's aircraft by then, but the Chinese were like ants, waves of them without end. Some of the guys here in the hospital who were on the ground told me they fired on the Chinese till they ran out of ammo, killed hundreds, and still they kept coming, blowing their bugles. The infantry guys hated those bugles, said it was something that will haunt them forever and having heard the damn things I believe them.

It was getting dark and it was getting cold. The brass hadn't seen fit to fix too many of us up in winter gear. We'd all be home by Christmas, they said. But the guys on the ground were in tough shape. Us pilots had heavy coats because for sure it's cold up there and only the bomber pilots get heated cockpits, but still I got cold when I was on the ground. I kept moving. Had a compass, kept going south.

But there were troops all around me, none of them Americans or other friendlies. I had to avoid the roads because that's where the enemy would be. It was rough country and I had a hard time. Finally it was near dawn. I'd been on the ground about twelve hours by then. Tired, hungry, thirsty, and colder than I'd ever been in my life. Only my .45 for a weapon, which wouldn't do much good against an infantry platoon. But I said to myself, they're not taking me alive, and I'll take down as many of the bastards as I can before they get me.

I had no idea where I was. Had a small map with me up in the cockpit but when my aircraft was hit it was all I could do to keep it level so I could bail out, and I lost the map somewhere. So I was pretty much blind as far as where to go. The infantry guys here tell me it was chaos up there for a few days around that time, nobody knew what the hell was going on and the Chinese were everywhere. And the infantry had maps and radios and even some vehicles. I had nothing except my compass and my .45. I knew enough to head south.

They finally got me just as dawn was breaking. I heard some movement on a road nearby and headed up a hill, trying to find cover. But I slipped on some loose rocks and they saw me. I had my .45 out when I was climbing but lost it in the rocks.

I was surrounded by guys in these strange, padded uniforms, all of them jabbering their lingo. They grabbed me, hit me a couple times with the butts of their rifles, and hauled me down to the road. An officer came over and yelled something at me. I started giving him my name, rank and serial number, like they told us in training, and that got me more rifle butts.

The officer detailed a squad to take me to the rear. I knew if I ever got back there, it was all over for me. I'd wind up in China somewhere and never get home. But I couldn't make a break for it, the sergeant in charge of the squad knew his stuff. After about an hour or so we came to some sort of field headquarters. They had put together a ramshackle pen for the prisoners, just a spot on the ground about thirty feet square, with bobwire to keep us from getting any ideas.

There were two other Americans and an Australian in there, plus three ROK soldiers who were scared as hell. We were all scared, but those guys were petrified. For good reason, because I hadn't been there two hours when a squad came in and separated the ROKs from us, forced them to their knees and shot them in the back of the head. They left the bodies lying there.

The other Americans and the Aussie were all pilots, like me. The two Americans were Air Force, the Aussie was RAAF. All of them captured after being shot down. The Aussie said he was flying a Gloster Meteor, that's the Brit-made two-engine jet, and was knocked down by a Russian MiG. He swore to God the pilot was a Russkie, said the guy flew like no NK or Chink he'd ever seen. I have since heard the Russians have a lot of pilots in the war, flying MiGs with Chinese markings.

Well, we were all pretty sure the Chinese would shoot us next. They brought in some food, some bread and hot soup, but even with that we were all damn near frozen to death. Later in the afternoon three soldiers came inside the wire and took me to see an officer. They shoved me inside a tent and thank God there was a heater going in there, a coal stove of some sort. They let me sit there for a while and then an officer and two guards came in.

The officer was Chinese but he spoke some English. Started asking me questions, like my unit designation, where my base was. I didn't give him anything. Name, rank and serial number. The guy slapped me. My hands were tied behind my back and I couldn't fight back. Even as cold as I still was, if I'd had my hands free I would've taken out that Commie bastard for sure.

After about an hour of this, the officer said something to the guards and they came over and pinned my arms down. The officer took something out of a pack. I could see it was a bamboo stick, about two feet long, sharpened at one end. He stuck the sharp end in the stove. I knew what was coming next.

I will spare you boys the details, but it hurt like nothing

I'd ever felt before. You will see the scars on my chest and stomach. That's what caused them. There is one other scar. Only your mother will see that one.

I must've passed out because when I woke up it was getting dark and I was back inside the wire. One of the Americans had cleaned my wounds with a strip of cloth ripped from his shirt, dipping it in what little water they'd been given. The other American had been taken away by the guards after they brought me back. We never saw him again. Fred Olson was his name, from Minnesota. I sure hope he makes it out. When I got to the rear I told them about Fred, but I haven't heard anything about him since.

The guards threw us some blankets when it got dark. We got one more meal, if you could call it that. The Aussie, Niles Chambers was his name, from Adelaide, was in pain, he'd twisted an ankle pretty bad when he came down, and it was swollen. The only good thing about the cold was that it kept the swelling down. But he was really hurting. All we could do was try to keep him warm by sandwiching him between the two of us. The other American was Bill Nolan, from downstate Illinois. He said he'd been shot down over Germany in the last war and was six months in a POW camp there before being liberated, and by God here he was again, new war, new enemy, same POW shit as last time. But he said the Germans treated him fairly decent in their camp. He was pretty sure the Chinese were gonna be different.

They told us in training that if you're captured, you have to keep your spirits up. Well, that's easier said than done, I can tell you. We all thought we were goners. Nobody really knew what the Chinese were doing with their POWs, but it wasn't gonna be good, that was for damn sure. That night was a rough one, boys, I'll shit you not.

Right after first light the next morning, we saw a couple planes coming over. They were ours. They took some fire from the camp and high-tailed it. Bill said, "Hell, that was our only chance, they didn't have time to see us." But they must've, because an hour later a flight of F-84 Thunderjets came in through the valley and started strafing the camp. Three of them, the most beautiful sight you could imagine. They were tearing hell out of the camp and we just huddled together, trying to stay low. But when I saw some rounds take out the guards, I said, "This is our chance, boys, let's go." Bill and I helped Niles up and we got to the gate and one of the guards was still alive, but not for long with both legs pretty much gone. I took his rifle and handed the dead guy's to Bill. They were bolt-action rifles I later learned were Soviet-made. But they weren't too much different than the M-1s I'd trained on with the Corps and pretty soon I proved I could use it just as well.

The strafing runs by the jets had the whole camp in an uproar. Guys were running everywhere and diving for cover, shooting up in the air without a prayer of hitting any of those Thunderjets. The camp had no appreciable anti-aircraft guns that I could see or hear. The scout planes must've seen that, too, so when the jets came in it was ducks on a pond for them. But we didn't want to be three more ducks for them, so we had to high-tail it.

About fifty yards away there were a couple vehicles parked. The jets hadn't gotten to them yet and there were two Chinese behind them, taking cover. The first guy I took out with my rifle. The next guy brought his rifle around. I pushed Bill and Niles toward the nearest vehicle and yelled at them to get in and fire it up. I shot at the second Chinese and missed. He couldn't get his weapon to fire. Lucky for me, tough for him. I jumped him and clocked him a couple good ones in the face. There was a knife in a sheath on his belt, I got hold of it and jammed it right into his throat from the side. I'm not proud of that, boys, I took two men's lives that day and they might've been no more than teenagers, it was hard to tell with those Chinese, but it was them or me, and if they got me then they'd probably get my buddies, too. So it had to be them.

Bill had the jeep fired up. It wasn't a real Jeep like we use, but the Russian equivalent. No roof on it. The Aussie was in the back seat with Bill's rifle and he was firing at some soldiers who'd seen us. He yelled, "Got 'em both! Floor this bitch and let's go for it, mate!" Bill hit the gas and we took off. Bill knew where to go, he'd looked the camp over best he could when they brought him in, he told me later, just in case. Well, that was major points for Bill, because I had been too scared to pay attention, I have to tell you.

It was the scariest damn ride of my life, I'll shit you not, boys. Bill clipped a couple or three guys with the front bumper. One of them flew up and over us, head over heels like a rag doll. We took fire from a couple guys but none of us got hit. The Chinese were still hunkering down from the jets. We made it out the front of the camp and Bill put the pedal to the floor. The road ran through a valley along a small river. If you want to call it a road, anyway. Bill kept the speed as high as he could but had to slow down some because of the chuckholes and rocks. We were about a mile out of the camp and heading south when the jets finished their last run and peeled off. Two of them gained altitude pretty quick, I was keeping an eye on them and thinking, Boy, if I get out of here alive I want to fly one of those babies. The third one started down the valley after us. Holy shit, I thought, he'll get us, thinks we're Chinese. I tossed my rifle to Niles, took my coat and shirt off and then my dirty white tee shirt. I told Bill to hold her as steady as he could and I stood up and started waving the white shirt at the jet. He came screaming down low over that river, and instead of firing on us he waggled his wings and then headed upstairs. "He saw us!" I yelled. Bill let out a whoop and so did Niles.

We decided to keep going as far as we could, and if we saw any enemy troops up ahead we'd double back and try to get some cover, get to higher ground and maybe signal another plane. We had gone maybe ten miles when we saw troops in the distance, heading in our direction. Bill hit the brakes and we sat there. We had some elevation on them and we could see a couple tanks with the infantry. I'd had pretty extensive training on tanks as to which were ours and which weren't, and pretty damn quickly I could see they were M24 Chaffees. "They're ours!" I yelled. Bill slumped over the wheel and started crying. Niles was clapping me on the back. I got my tee shirt off again and started yelling and waving it for all I was worth. Bill gunned the engine and we took off to meet them. Turns out they were vectored to us by the Thunderjet pilot who'd seen us escape.

It was an Army recon patrol. I'll tell you, in the Marines we didn't have too high an opinion of the Army, but my opinion of those boys changed right then and there. And I'll tell you this, too. They were all colored troops, 24th Regimental Combat Team. We were with those boys the next couple days till we finally got back to U.S. lines. They were real pros, never gave us any shit because we were white, and when we got into a couple firefights they were just as good as any white troops I ever saw, and that includes the Marines, I'll say that right now. Bill and Niles and I helped them out some in the fights but we just mostly stayed out of their way, because they knew what they were doing and we pretty much didn't. So I am here to tell you, boys, that the colored man is just as good as the white man is when it comes to combat, and that should mean he'll be just as good at a civilian job, too, because serving in a combat unit is the toughest job there is. Not too many colored in the part of Wisconsin where we're from but eventually you boys will meet some and work with them and I will tell you this, you will treat them with the same respect any man deserves. Your old man owes his life to men like that, never forget it because I never will.

They got us to the rear as fast as they could. We got some hot food and Niles got his ankle treated. Bad sprain, as it turned out. A few days later I made it to the hospital here in Tokyo.

So that's the story of my capture and escape. My wounds are healing nicely. There was an infection but the docs took care of it. I am getting my strength back and today an officer stopped by and said based on the reports by Bill and Niles, they are putting me in for a Silver Star. He also said they will be rotating me back home for convalescent leave. I don't care about the medal but I do care about seeing you boys and your Mom again. I'm not sure if your Mom and I will ever be able to have another kid, after what those Chink bastards did to me, but I know your Mom, she is a saint and it will be all right.

But I will tell you this, after I get rested up I will be coming back here to get back in the fight. I have some unfinished business to take care of in Korea. A Dawson man might be down, boys, but he's never out. Remember that.

Your dad

CHAPTER THIRTEEN

Erbil Governorate, Iraq
March 2014

The man stared at me, hard eyes peering through the gloom. The rest of his face was covered by his *keffiyeh.* His finger was outside the trigger guard of his AK-47. There wasn't much light coming in from outside the door, so I couldn't tell if it led outdoors or into another room inside the building.

The stare seemed to last several minutes, but I knew it was only seconds, long enough for me to size the guy up. Not very big, probably not very skilled in hand-to-hand. I decided to take him if nobody else showed up at the door and this guy came over to lead me out. But the guy took only one step into the room and then motioned toward the doorway. My heart sank, expecting another fighter, but it was a woman, dressed head-to-toe in a burqa, carrying a small covered pot in one hand, a jar in the other.

She approached cautiously as the guard watched, his AK held loosely. An American guard would've had his weapon in combat carry position, ready to bring it to bear on the prisoner within a second of being alerted to possible trouble. This guy's was at something approximating port arms. I filed that one away and focused on the woman.

She knelt three feet away, set the pot on the floor and took off the lid. Steam rose into the air and the aroma of chicken wafted up. My stomach growled as I stared at the soup. The jar was next, and I could see water near the rim. It took every bit of my discipline to tear my attention away from it and focus on the woman. She sat back on her haunches and pulled a wooden spoon from inside a sleeve.

When she held the spoon out, she looked up at me, and for the first time I saw her eyes. They were wide with fright, and they were blue.

I held the flimsy paper up to the light one more time. The words scribbled there hadn't changed from the first four times I'd read them: *I am American. Please help me. Be ready.*

To say that I was surprised would be a serious understatement.

Was it a trick? Some sick joke, just to mess with my head? But her eyes hadn't been joking. She'd slipped the rolled-up paper from the sleeve of her robe as she gathered up the pot and jar after I'd emptied them both. I quickly palmed the paper as she got to her feet. "Thank you," I said, and was rewarded with a slight nod, and one more glance from those pleading baby blues.

In the hours after she and the guard left, I paced the room, stretched and punched out a couple dozen pushups, just to stay loose and burn some energy. The soup had been surprisingly good, with chunks of meat I assumed was goat or mutton. The water was the best I'd ever tasted, even though it was tepid. My feet were still sore as hell, but I forced myself to walk. From what I'd heard about the torture practice known as "bastinado," I'd gotten off lightly. No toes had been broken. I'd taken my socks off to examine my feet, and now the cool dirt against my bare soles seemed oddly calming. I didn't relish the idea of running for the hills virtually barefoot, but the thought of captivity was even less appealing, so I'd make do.

If she was going to come for me, how could she get past the guard? There'd be at least one outside the door. If the situation had been reversed, I'd have put two men out there, in two-hour shifts. But maybe these guys didn't have that kind of manpower, or the smarts to play it that way. If there were two guards, there was no way that girl could get back in here, even trying to bluff her way in. She'd–

Something thumped against the door, and I was instantly alert. I moved quickly and hugged the wall next to the doorway, on the hinged side. Anybody opening it wouldn't be able to see me until they came around the edge of the opened door, and then I'd have a momentary advantage.

The door swung inward and a keffieyeh'd head bounced off the hard dirt floor. A dark shape stepped over the fallen guard into the dim light of the bulb. It was the girl in the burqa, and she was holding a bloody knife in one hand.

I quickly pulled the body into the room and shut the door, but not before glancing outside, long enough to take in the stars overhead and the dim shapes of other buildings. Nothing moved.

The guard had a gaping slash on his throat and another wound in his stomach. A search of his pockets yielded an extra magazine for the AK. I slipped the mag into one of my thigh pockets and checked the rifle, thanking my instructors back at RASP 2 for including training on the weapon. Having a loaded rifle in my hands again gave me a sense of power I'd rarely felt before. After checking the weapon, I thought of one more thing. I pulled the guard's boots off the body, compared the sole of one boot with my foot and decided it would be a tight fit but better than nothing. In thirty seconds I had them on, trying not to think of what might've been crawling on those dead feet.

I looked at the girl, who had dropped the knife. "Who are you?" I asked.

"My name is...is..."

I stepped closer and put one arm around her. "It's okay to be scared. Now, what's your name?"

"Kristi," she said. "Kristi Amundson."

"Where are you from, Kristi?"

"Sioux Falls. Can you get me out of here?"

How in the hell had a teenage girl from South Dakota gotten herself mixed up with these jokers? The answers would have to wait. I squeezed her shoulder. "We're gonna give it our best shot, how about that? Now, do you know where my buddy is, the other American?"

The burqa moved in a semblance of a nod.

"Okay," I said. "Pick up that knife, you might need it again."

I tried to remember the layout of the village as I'd observed it from the hillside. One thing that had struck me was that the village was not as haphazardly plotted as an American might presume, especially an American used to the tidy small towns of Wisconsin. What passed for the business district was actually the town marketplace, in the center of the village around a communal well. Electricity flowed in from power lines down through the valley, but indoor plumbing was something that these people could only see in bigger cities. I figured that I was on the south side of the vill. The hillside where my team had their hide spots was beyond the northern edge. Maybe about six blocks away, give or take.

Would the team still be there? That would depend on whether the militiamen had spread out into the hills. Capturing two Americans in the vill had to tell them there were others lurking up there in the timber, and from what I had seen of the convoy coming in, they had the manpower to scout a klick or two out from the vill, just to secure their position. Boudreau would certainly have led the men deeper into the wilderness, trying to avoid contact and keep the militia leader guessing.

And if that guy had any brains at all, and by now I was pretty sure he did, the militia would be pulling out at first light, with their prisoners. They wouldn't want to risk a confrontation with a larger American rescue force, and there was no guarantee U.S. aircraft wouldn't be coming over the mountains to hose down the town.

We crept from one shadow to the next. The town seemed quiet, but whenever we paused to hunker down, I could hear noises: a goat bleating, a man snoring. The militia leader would have set up a security perimeter on the outskirts of the vill, just in case the Americans would try for a night rescue. The moment that thought occurred to me, as we crouched behind a garbage pile outside a house a hundred meters from my cell, I saw movement on the street around the corner. A single man, armed, and he was heading back toward the cell. The guard's relief?

We didn't have much time. "How much farther to my friend?" I whispered to the girl.

"Two more doors," she said. A trembling hand emerged from the burqa, pointing north.

I hoped she was right. I couldn't afford to take a lot of time searching for Burns, especially now that I was responsible for a civilian. If we were caught, what the militia would do to her was something I didn't want to contemplate. What they'd probably already done was something I didn't want to think about, either.

Another twenty meters brought us to the back of another nameless hut. The girl pointed toward the corner. "The door's on the front side," she said.

"Okay." We'd have one chance at this. I'd need a diversion. I leaned closer to the girl. "Listen up, Kristi. You've been very brave tonight. I need you to be brave one more time."

"O–okay."

I explained what I needed her to do. She nodded, but I could feel her trembling as I put my arm around her shoulder. "Good girl," I said. "We get my buddy and head for the hills. My friends are waiting. We'll have you back in South Dakota in a couple days."

She handed me the knife. "Are…are you gonna kill these guys?"

The question surprised me. I hesitated, then asked, "The ones who took you captive?"

"Yeah."

"I can't get them all tonight, but…"

She clasped my arm with a desperate grip. "Promise me you'll come back and kill them all," she said.

"Yeah," I whispered, "I'll get them."

She released me, stood up, shuffled around the corner toward the front and was gone.

CHAPTER FOURTEEN

Hakkâri Province, Turkey
March 2014

"Honest to God, Major, I'm good to go."

Kulinski shook his head. "You might think you are, but you need a couple or three days to decompress."

I looked around the major's hooch. Tacked onto the wall were pictures of his wife and two kids back in Saginaw, but those were the only signs that the C.O. of the outfit had any kind of thoughts outside the mission. Kulinski was just a hair under six feet, kept his brown hair high and tight and his black horn-rims gave him an owlish look. Give him a pair of wire-rims, put him in a shirt and tie, Kulinski could've passed for a manager at any office in America. But here he was a warrior. I had developed a healthy respect for the major since joining the Wolverines, but right now Kulinski was treating me like a candy-ass kid.

"With respect, sir, I think you're wrong," I said. "I'm ready to get back in the fight."

Kulinski leaned back in his rickety chair and pointed a pencil at me. "What you want to do is go back down to that village and kick some militia ass," he said. "It's been two days since you got out of there. They're long gone by now, trust me."

"If they are, it's because they figured we'd be coming back after them hard," I said, my temper rising. Even as it did, my training and experience tried tamping it down. I knew the logistics as well as Kulinski did. Holding onto that village wouldn't be smart for the militia unless they had more men coming into the province, and there was no intel to suggest that was happening. At least, nothing I had heard. But they might still be hanging around, and if they were, I wanted to go back there and take them out.

"Look, Jake, if I get orders to take the vill, we'll do it, but I sent my report up the line twenty-four hours ago and I haven't heard a thing. So I figure it's not going to happen. If it was, I'd have been told to prep for another recon of the vill, because our outfit sure as hell wouldn't be assaulting a fortified target like that." He started tapping the pencil on the metal desk, very lightly, a sign that he was running out of patience. "Boudreau tells me there were about fifty fighters in that unit that took you and Burns. I wouldn't go in there at less than company strength myself, and we don't have the resources up here to put together that kind of assault on short notice. The Peshmerga might be planning something, but I haven't heard anything. If they want our assistance, they'll get it. But until then, we stay put and think about our next mission." He put down the pencil and leaned forward, elbows on the table. "Jake, I know you want some payback. I'd feel the same way if it had been me. You did a hell of a job getting Burns and the girl out of there. You'll have your chance at them, trust me."

I forced myself to dial it back a couple notches. I knew the major was right. I also knew that I wouldn't be satisfied until I was able to strike back. It was eating at me, and something had to be done. But what? We didn't have the manpower here to assault that village. Any C.O. who would order an assault like that would be cashiered, if he survived. I nodded, then sighed. "You're right, sir," I said. "It's…well, it's pretty tough."

"Nothing about this job is easy," Kulinski said. The hardness that had seeped into his voice a minute ago had softened. He was less the commander now, more the comrade. "Let me offer you some advice, Jake."

I hesitated, then said, "Of course, sir."

"I know part of what makes you want to go back is the Iran connection with that militia unit."

I sat up straighter, about to object, when Kulinski raised his hand. "Boudreau said you mentioned it to him on the way back here. But you didn't say anything about it when I debriefed you yesterday."

"Kata'ib Hezbollah is trained by Quds Force," I said. "There might've been a couple of Iranian officers in the unit that took the village."

"Maybe," Kulinski said. "Or maybe not." The major was silent for a moment. Then he said, "Jake, you've got a bug up your ass about the Iranians and that might turn into a problem for you. As much as you might want to, you can't make this personal. We have a job to do up here. We have to support the Peshmerga, and take out any high value targets we're told to intercept if they're wandering around up in these mountains."

"There might've been one or two HVT's in the vill, sir," I blurted out.

"Then if we get orders to take them, we will," Kulinski said, and the commander's voice was back. "I'll say this again: don't make this personal, Jake."

"Major, those bastards–"

"That's enough, Lieutenant!" Kulinski stared at me hard for two seconds, three, then said, "I'm gonna chalk that up to the stress you've been under. You're officially off duty for twenty-four hours. I don't want to have to write you up for PTSD, that'd get you sent back to Incirlik on the next bird. As it is, I should give you forty-eight hours, but we've got too much to do here and not enough people to do it. Go back to your hooch and get some shuteye. Read a book, write a letter home, relax. Read that diary you've got, maybe the old Rough Rider has some advice for you." A grin tucked at his lips, then it was gone. "At 1400 hours tomorrow you're back in the saddle. I'm told to expect a mission package from Higher by then. You and I and Boudreau will meet in the DFAC to go over it. Until then, I don't want to see much of you. Are we clear?"

"Yes, sir."

Outside Kulinski's hooch, the sun glared down from a brilliant blue sky, trying to dispel the chill. I wasn't used to living in the mountains and felt cold almost all the time here, although the altitude hadn't been a problem. A few of the guys, hailing from western states, felt pretty much at home here, occasionally using some down time to go hunting nearby, fortifying the camp's kitchen with venison. Burns had brought in a huge buck just a week or so ago, in fact.

Burns. I felt a sudden urge to check on the soldier from Idaho. When we'd made it back, there'd been talk Burns would be airlifted back to Incirlik for treatment of his injuries, but he'd raised enough hell with Boudreau that the master sergeant had promised to get him treated here. The Wolverines' medics must've been able to do the job, because the only helo that had come in since our return had left with the girl from South Dakota as its only passenger. Her last act before climbing aboard had been to toss her burqa into the burn barrel, where it went up along with the latest deposit from the latrine.

Burns shared a hooch with two other soldiers, who were out at the shooting range with the rest of the enlisted. I knocked on the plywood door. A voice from inside answered, "It's open."

The first thing I noticed when I opened the door was the large rack of antlers mounted on the wall. The young first sergeant was lying on his cot and tried to get to his feet when I stepped in. "As you were," I said. Burns flopped back down on the cot with relief. "How are you doing, Ellis?"

The question was more for politeness than anything, because I could clearly see Burns wasn't doing too well. One arm was in a sling, one eye was closed and surrounded by the nastiest shiner I'd ever seen, and both feet were bandaged. This guy should've been at the base hospital in Incirlik, but that wasn't my call. Kulinski must've signed off on that, and I would have to trust my C.O.'s judgment on that one, like everything else.

"I'm doing all right, sir," Burns said, offering a brave but weak smile. He gestured toward a nearby chair. "Have a seat, LT. I'd offer you something, but I haven't been able to get to the supermarket lately. And my buddies, well…" He tried to shrug his shoulders, but the effort brought a wince of pain.

I pulled up the chair and sat. "Take it easy, Ellis," I said. Burns nodded and slumped back onto the cot. I could see beads of sweat on the soldier's forehead. "Listen, you should be in a hospital. I'll go talk to the major."

Burns's eyes snapped open. "No! I mean, please don't, sir. I just need another good night's sleep and I'll be ready for duty."

I understood exactly where Burns was coming from, but I'd definitely have a word with Kulinski if Burns hadn't shown any improvement by morning. "They must've worked you over pretty good," I said.

"They took their shots at me. Might've gone better for me if I hadn't tried to fight back. That seemed to piss them off, you might say." He laughed, then winced again.

What he said got to me. I'd wanted to fight back, very badly. Maybe my decision not to had allowed me to be walking around right now, while Burns had taken the other path and paid the price. Even so, I couldn't prevent a tinge of guilt from creeping in.

Burns looked at me with his good eye. "But I'll tell you what, LT, if you hadn't come got me when you did, I wouldn't be here right now."

"How's that, Ellis?"

"'Cause I was gonna kill that guard and make a break for it. At least, that's what my intention was." He propped himself up on his good elbow, paused for a couple breaths, then swung his legs off the cot. When his stockinged feet hit the wood floor, he winced again. "Shit, that hurts. Pardon my language, sir."

"Don't worry about it. Ellis, I don't think you'd have been in any kind of shape to take out an armed man." I regretted it almost as soon as I said it, but it brought only a nod from the young comms sergeant.

"I think you're probably right about that, LT. I was gonna try, though. They were gonna take me in the morning, take both of us. God knows where to, but it wouldn't have been good for us, that's for sure."

That got my attention. "How do you know that?"

"Heard the guard talking with an officer who came in to check on me. They thought I was passed out, but I'd come to just before I heard the door open. This would've been about an hour after they fed me. Or tried to feed me, I couldn't keep anything down."

I struggled to keep my anger from taking over. I took a breath, then managed to say, "I didn't know that you could understand Arabic."

"Learned it at DLIFLC, just before my first tour," Burns said. I hadn't known that Burns had attended the Foreign Language Center at the Defense Language Institute in California. All four branches sent people there to get some of the best language training in the world. "My grandmother was Mexican, taught me Spanish as a kid. Picked up French in high school. I guess my lieutenant at boot camp thought I might have a flair for languages, so they sent me there. But you know, nobody has a flair for languages. What you got to have is a flair for studying, because that's what it takes." He tried to laugh, but it came out as more of a cough. After taking a swig of water from a canteen, he said, "I'm pretty good in Arabic, but it wasn't Arabic. It was Farsi. Picked up some of that before I got deployed here, just in case. Guess it paid off."

Farsi. So, the officer was an Iranian. The guard likely was, too, if he could converse in that language with the officer. "What did they say?" I asked.

"I couldn't catch all of it, but the officer said they were gonna ship us out at first light. Didn't catch where to, but my guess is across the border into Iran. We'd have been in a world of hurt over there, LT, so you really saved our asses. They knew who we were."

"Did you tell all this to the major?"

Burns shook his head. "Haven't been debriefed yet. The drugs the doc gave me when we got back here made me pretty fuzzy. The major stopped in this morning, said he'd do my debrief tomorrow."

I nodded. If the Iranians knew about the Wolverines, that might be a game-changer. Maybe they knew about the unit, but not where our base was. Even though we were across the line in Turkey, I had a feeling that might not prove much of a hindrance if the Iranians decided to come after us. And using an anti-American, anti-Kurdish militia unit would be the perfect way to do the mission. The Iranians would call the shots, the Iraqi Shiites would do the dirty work. If they were captured by the Turks, it would cause far less of a diplomatic crisis. But I had seen how light the Turkish military presence was in these parts. There wouldn't be much in the militia's way if the Iranians told them to cross the border for a quick strike.

"Listen, Ellis, what you heard is pretty important intel," I said. "I'm not sure we should wait till tomorrow. You feel up to talking to the major tonight?"

Ellis gave me a worried look. "Yeah, I think so, LT. You think there might be some trouble from those guys? Even though we're across the border?"

"Well, we cross the border all the time, so I'd imagine they might be willing to do it, too." I stood up. "I'll get some chow sent over here, how's that sound? Then I'll go see the major."

"Okay."

I stepped to the door, then stopped. "One more thing. Did you hear any names mentioned, when you overheard the Iranians?"

Burns shook his head. "Not really. Not our names, anyway. The guard was just leaving when the officer showed up in the doorway. The guard addressed him as 'Guardian Lieutenant.' Then the officer said something about 'the colonel' wanting to know what kind of shape I was in. The guard told him something like 'not good,' and then the officer said the colonel wanted to move us in the morning."

"Did the officer mention the colonel's name?"

Burns frowned, then said, "I think he said it was Madazki, Mazdaki, something like that."

"Okay. Get some rest, Ellis. I'll get some hot chow in here for you."

"Thank you, sir. And, thanks again for getting me out of there."

I nodded, then glanced up at the antlers. "Pretty nice rack you got there, Ellis. Gonna try and get it home?"

The young man's good eye lit up. "Better believe it, sir. That's a Caspian red deer, and that rack's gotta be a good twenty-five points, maybe thirty. The boys back in Pocatello will shit bricks when they see this one."

I gave him a grin that I tried to make genuine, then left the hootch. Outside, I looked to the south. Down there, over the border, was the village, and maybe the militia unit was still there. I'd promised the girl to go back there and take care of the men who'd kept her as a slave, and I'd been sure I could convince the major to let me do just that. But that hadn't gone very far, had it?

And now it was worse. I recognized the name Burns had heard: Mazdaki. I hadn't heard it since that day back at Benning, when Boudreau recruited me into the Wolverines. We'd gone over the firefight in Wasit, when I hadn't been able to save my best friend. Mazdaki was the name of the officer in command of the Iraqi insurgents that day.

The man responsible for Chet's death was just over that border. And I couldn't do a damn thing about it.

CHAPTER FIFTEEN

Hakkâri Province, Turkey
March 2014

The computer screen stuttered and skewed, then cleared as if by magic. Uncle John was there, six thousand miles away in northern Wisconsin. Despite my mood, I had to smile at my great-uncle's puzzled expression.

"Is this first time you've Skyped, Uncle John?"

"Hello, Jake? Is that really you?" The old Marine's eyes squinted at the screen, peering at the corner.

"Yes, it's me. And don't look at the small window, the one with you in it, just look straight at the main screen."

"Okay." The eyes warmed, the old familiar smile reappeared. "By God, Jake, it's good to see you. I wish to hell they'd had this thing when I was overseas."

"I'm not sure how long we'll be able to talk," I said. "Internet's pretty spotty out here."

Uncle John gave me a look I'd seen many times, starting with that day when I was twelve and he caught me looking through his *Playboy* magazine stash. "You okay, Jake? What's going on?"

I had to think about this one. I couldn't tell Uncle John what was actually happening. So much of the Wolverines' work was classified, I could hardly say anything at all. I didn't like being vague with my great-uncle, but he'd understand. "I can't talk about specifics, but...well, I had a target in my sights, you might say, and couldn't pull the trigger."

Uncle John nodded. He'd been in that kind of situation before. "Couldn't, or they wouldn't let you?"

I hesitated, then said, "The second one. I understand the situation, but..."

"Yeah, I know. It's a bitch, ain't it?"

We talked for a few more minutes. We didn't seem to be getting any-where, so I changed the subject, asking about the weather, if the fish were biting. Still cold and not much, Uncle John said. The Badgers were kicking ass in the basketball playoffs, and the Final Four was a definite possibility. The wrestlers had finished a pretty decent season. The Brewers were looking good, but it was still spring training.

It was the usual stuff men talked about, and I wanted to talk more, but then the screen started jumping again. "I think we'll lose the connection pretty soon, Uncle John," I said.

"Okay, Jake. Keep your head down over there. Listen to your sergeants. Remember that your C.O. has to answer to Higher and he's probably not always pleased with that."

"Yeah, I'm pretty sure you're right."

"And one more thing. That problem you mentioned at the start? The old Rough Rider had something like that happen, too. You been reading the diary?"

I reluctantly shook my head. "No, not really, sorry."

Uncle John's face dissolved into large pixels, then came back. "Get at it, boy. Let him help you."

I managed a wave just before the screen went blank. After a moment, I turned off the tablet, set on the small table beside my rack, and reached into my duffel for the diary. I missed Uncle John, more than I thought I would, and when I opened the diary again, it was like the old man was still with me.

The journal of Charles J. Dawson, con't.

June the 22d, 1898 – We stand on the deck of the SS Yucatan, and the excitement of the Regiment is palpable. Each man awaits the moment we shall finally step onto the soil of Cuba. Our journey is nearly over. Our baptism in combat awaits us ashore.

Each of us carries upon our backs a pack with all the belongings we have brought with us. We learned to compose these packs from a Regular infantryman who visited our temporary camp in Tampa. I carry half of a dog-tent, with the other half going to my tent-mate, Lee W. Burdwell, a young cow-boy from Texas. Also within my pack is my blanket, poncho, change of underwear, two pairs of socks, my razor, and quinine pills. It is rolled up with the loop on my left shoulder and the ends tied under my right arm. I have a cartridge belt with 125 rounds of ammunition. From it hangs my tin drinking cup along with my canvas-covered canteen. My haversack, slung over my right shoulder, contains my mess kit and rations.

My rifle is the Model 1896 Krag-Jorgensen carbine, which fires a .30-40 round that employs smokeless powder. Back in Camp we had been issued Colt revolvers, but we were told to leave these aboard the ship, as they were deemed to add too much extra weight, as we shall fight as dismounted cavalry. Essentially, infantrymen. Most of the Regiment's horses were left behind in Tampa. Only some of the officers had their mounts brought along. The officers are also allowed their side-arms. There has been some grousing about this among the fellows, but nothing is to be done about it.

The six-day voyage from the Gulf coast of Florida allowed me time to organize my notes. Since my last entry, the busyness of becoming a soldier has been so all-consuming, I have barely had time to jot down a page or two of notes per day. Even on board the transport ship, I have not had much time alone to devote to this diary. I have used most of what little solitude I had to write letters home to Father and Margaret, and also to O'Dea back in Madison, as he wanted me to keep the foot-ballers posted of my exploits. So I will use this time to update my tale as we await the order to board the boats and head to shore.

From the date of my boxing match with McGee to our departure for Tampa by train was exactly two weeks. In that time we were issued our arms and our horses and organized into Troops. There were 12 Troops, each composed of some 100 men, including officers. I was placed in

Troop K. To my dismay, my erstwhile mates from Harvard, Wells and Dean, were assigned to different Troops: Dean to B, Wells to D. We began to learn how to be cavalrymen. At that time we had no idea we would fight as foot soldiers. But on the day of the assignment I met Burdwell, who was next to me as the dog-tents were passed out, and we have become fast friends. The Troop is a good mix of Eastern and Western men, although we have been saddled with the nickname of "The Silk-Stocking Troop," likely due to the presence of some prominent Easterners in our midst.

The training was arduous as the officers worked us relentlessly. Our commanding officer is 1st Lt. Woodbury Kane of New York City, a yachtsman who attended Harvard with Lt. Col. Roosevelt. His sisters purchased one of the Regiment's two machine-guns, manufactured by Colt. They fire an astounding 500 rounds per minute and have a range of some 3,000 yards. A truly terrifying weapon. I was able to witness a demonstration of their abilities when they arrived on the 20th. Roosevelt was most impressed by them. We have both guns in our Troop. Apparently, one New Yorker noted, only troopers with silk stockings can be trusted with these ferocious weapons.

When we were issued our horses, they were not as ready as the Army had apparently promised. Almost all needed "busting," as the Westerners called it. Some of the Easterners were unable to tame their mounts and hired Western men to do it for them. I, fortunately, had a mount that required only a little encouragement to accept me as his partner. The first few times we fired our rifles while in formation caused a stampede, with many riders dragged by the stirrups. But once accustomed to gunfire, the horses began to get used to the sounds, and to us.

Within a couple of days we were thundering along in more or less acceptable formation, dust rising, hooves pounding, men shouting. We formed columns of four, six hundred men and their mounts in all, and the dust was like fog. The heat was oppressive. By the end of the day, men and horses were exhausted, and we barely had energy enough to get our mounts properly corralled, groomed and fed before trudging off to our tents. Many times we went directly to the river to bathe before repairing to the mess tents for chow call. One time, though, our squadron, which is composed of four Troops, was led by Roosevelt himself, who is a fine horseman. Before returning to the Camp he ordered us to dismount at a beer garden. "The men can go in and drink all the beer they want, and I will pay for it," he shouted, eliciting hearty cheers from our parched throats. The next day we learned Roosevelt had been chided by Col. Wood for having officers drinking with enlisted men.

One of our first days of real training was marked by tragedy. A young man from New Mexico, Irad Cochran Jr., was thrown from his horse and landed on his head. He died in the San Antonio hospital on the 26th. We were all most chastened at this news. I did not know Cochran personally but his death hit us all hard. Many troopers were thrown by their mounts, some were injured, but he was the only fatality. The entire Regiment attended the funeral.

Three times during this period I obtained a pass to go to town that evening. I wasted little time in having a photograph taken and mailed home to Father and Margaret. One occasion saw us bathing in the indoor pool at Scholz's Natatorium. On another I happily rejoined my Harvard friends, Dean and Wells, for an evening of socializing at some of the town's many saloons. Knowing my luck with cards was unlikely to change, I avoided the gambling halls. Several of the troopers reported they were cleaned out of their funds quickly, although a few of the sharper cardsmiths, after getting tips from some of our Western fellows, were able to do quite well. These dens were in the Sporting District, which the city had set aside for the location of some of its more nefarious enterprises, including houses of ill repute. The most popular of these was Fannie Porter's Sporting House. I avoided this place, but some of my comrades from Troop K took Burdwell there one evening to "get his ashes hauled," and upon their return they swore they had seen the outlaws Kid Curry and Butch Cassidy in attendance.

But I digress. On the 28th of May we were told to break Camp and prepare to entrain for Tampa, where the Army was assembling to take ship to Cuba. Some troopers still lacked accoutrements such as unit insignia for their hats, but others, unbelievably, lacked their weapons. Lt. Kane explained that the colonels, Wood and Roosevelt, were raising Cain, such as it were, with the War Department. It is suspected that the Regiment's popularity in the newspapers is causing friction with the Regulars, who may be diverting our arms to their own units.

The embarkation was an enormous undertaking. Nearly 1,000 horses along with some 200 pack mules were to be transported along with the entire Regiment of men and our supplies. But the Southern Pacific Railroad came through for us. On a blazingly hot day we mounted up and rode the hour from the Fairgrounds to the Union Stock Yards, where the trains awaited us. Many of us glanced back at our Camp site and wondered if what we had learned there would keep us alive in Cuba.

It took seven trains to carry the entire Regiment. The enlisted men filled three passenger coaches per train, while the officers had a Pullman car. The coaches were packed with men and the heat was oppressive. There was not enough water in the coolers. But our spirits were high regardless. There was much singing, especially of the Regiment's unofficial anthem, "A Hot Time in the Old Town." There were the inevitable card games, and much writing of letters home. Our last bags of incoming mail had been received on the morning of our departure from the Camp. To my great surprise there was a letter from the fair Leona, she of the $5 "soldier-boy special" back in Madison, who had obtained my address from one of the foot-ballers. She enclosed a lock of her hair, and declared her desire to see me when I return to campus, and made no mention of a fee this time.

To our astonishment and delight, our route was lined with crowds of cheering citizens all the way. We stopped frequently and were recipients of many treats from the crowds, food of all kinds and souvenirs, including ribbons and locks of hair from young ladies. Many of the troopers gave out brass buttons from their coats. Occasionally a trooper would receive a sealed envelope from a lady and open it to reveal a photograph of the sender in scandalous night-dress. These were quite popular, as one might expect. There were flags aplenty, and we saw many veterans of the Rebellion alongside the tracks, wearing their old grays, some with missing limbs. They all saluted us and we returned the salutes with pride. For many of our Southern lads, it was quite emotional. On one such occasion I saw McGee with tears running down his cheeks as he saluted a group of old Johnny Rebs.

Tampa was a madhouse. We arrived late on the evening of May the 2d, and it took all night to unload the horses and equipment. Trains were arriving every hour or so, adding to the confusion. By dawn on the 3d we were mounted up and on the move to our temporary Camp. It was on a sand flat but at least it was somewhat breezy, which helped keep the flies who swarmed about our horses at bay. It cooled off some at night and we were relieved not to have the dust we'd dealt with in Texas. Our Troop was lucky; Troop H, one of the last to arrive, was sidetracked for some 18 hours.

We spent our days in drill and fending off the curious townspeople, who eventually had to be restricted from entry, especially the women. There was talk that some "soiled doves" from the town had found their way to the Camp and were doing brisk business until being rousted by an officer. What the men had paid them with was another question, as our pay has been held up because, unbelievably, the quartermaster ran out of money before he could pay our Regiment. We were finally paid the night before our departure. One woman who was allowed to visit was Edith Roosevelt, the wife of the Lt. Col. A most impressive lady, and very friendly.

The newspaper-men are thick as the horse-flies. Among them are many photographers, including a man from the Edison Kinetoscope Company, who is said to be making "moving pictures" with his device. I shall be curious to see the result. I was able to meet the artist Frederick

Remington. He was astonished that we did not all resemble desperadoes and gunslingers. "You are nothing but a lot of cavalrymen," he said. On the 6th, we drilled with our mounts before military attachés from several countries, including an officer from Germany wearing a spiked helmet and one from Japan who had a large plume of feathers on his cap.

A few of the Easterners actually stayed at the Tampa Bay Hotel, where the officers were quartered, and this did not go over well with the rest of the troopers. Among the former is Robert Wrenn, the national tennis champion, who joined the Regiment in New Orleans. The majority of the Ivy League men, I must say, have worked hard from the get-go to quash any impression that they are dandies and deserving of any special treatment. I myself was well-received by my mates in Troop K. I have run into McGee a few times; he is in Troop B, with Dean, who has told me that McGee seems a changed man since our little encounter in Texas. He told Dean that nobody had ever before bested him in fisticuffs, "and then that Badger boy cleaned my clock right good." Certainly he has seemed happy to see me since then. Hopefully we will both survive Cuba and can remain friends after the war.

To our great dismay, four of our twelve Troops had to stay behind in Tampa for lack of space on board the ships. They must wait for the next flotilla, and it is anybody's guess when that will be. Thank the Lord that my Troop was one of the lucky 8 to be chosen for this first voyage. It was only through the inspired exertions of Roosevelt himself that we were able to get the rest of the Regiment aboard the Yucatan. After boarding on the 8th, we sat idly in the harbor for nearly a week before setting sail. It was said the delay was due to the sighting of a pair of Spanish warships north of Cuba, ready to intercept us. Boredom was our biggest enemy. The ship was so crammed with soldiers that it was impossible to do any physical training on the deck. Conditions below decks were unbearable. As many men as possible slept topside. We swam twice a day but had to beware of sharks, and once or twice the beasts were spotted by lookouts and driven off by carbine fire. It was certainly different than swimming in the Mississippi back home.

But at last we sailed, and by then some Regulars had been moved from the Yucatan to other vessels, so conditions aboard improved. No Spaniards were sighted on the voyage. Some sailboats with Cuban rebels aboard welcomed us when we caught sight of the island at last. They are known as "insurrectos." Our path took us eastward around to the Caribbean side. The Marines had landed and took the fortified port of Guantanamo Bay after a four-day fight, clearing the way for our squadron to proceed without fear of attack from our rear. Finally, we arrived off the coast not far from the entrance to Santiago harbor, where an enemy naval squadron is said to be waiting. We were assured that our Navy had the Spaniards bottled up there and they could not escape to attack our transports. Certainly the U.S. warships amidst our convoy were an impressive lot indeed. It was hard to imagine any foreign power would have the fortitude to challenge them, although a few of the Easterners said they had been to Europe and saw British and German dreadnaughts that were even more formidable.

Fortunately, we are not facing Europe's varsity team in this conflict. Although some of the men boast of being able to take on the Kaiser's finest, I shall settle for facing those of Queen Maria Christina. This is not cowardice, but honesty. We are a long way from being capable of standing against elite European regiments. The subject was raised one evening aboard ship. An Eastern fellow, who shall remain nameless, declared that the Regiment could hold its own against the best European armies. He said, with some justification, that the Continent's most formidable power, Germany, had not been tested since defeating the French some 17 years ago. The British, meanwhile, had recently been humiliated by the Boers in South Africa. I said that our fathers' generation, which fought in the Rebellion, had by the time of Appomattox assembled the greatest army in history. But it had now been 33 years since that time and our soldiers had not been tested in battle since, other than some skirmishes against the Red Indians in the West. "And look what happened at the Little Big Horn," I added. This did not sit well with my debate opponent and we nearly came to blows. I found out later he claimed to have had a cousin under Custer's command on that tragic day 22 years past. My attempt to apologize was rejected.

The word had spread that General Shafter, who commands the Army's 5th Corps, was originally planning to land us at Mariel to march on Havana, but we have been diverted here to assault the city of Santiago. The goal is to put pressure on the Spanish squadron in the harbor to either surrender or make a run for the open ocean and into the teeth of our fleet lying in wait. One officer told us the Spaniards could ravage the East Coast all the way to New York if they escape the harbor. Another man said with great confidence that Spanish gunboats could sail up the Potomac all the way to Washington and shell the capital. That was disputed by another, a yachtsman from Baltimore, who said the river is too shallow for warships, else the Confederates would have mounted such an attack during the Rebellion. In any event, it is clear we must stop the enemy here. Sgt. Ronalds, from the Knickerbocker Club in New York, said that if we can seize or destroy the Spanish fleet here, the war will be over, as our Navy will rule the seas and the Spaniards will then have no way to resupply or reinforce their army in Cuba.

As the hour of our landing drew near, the men became more reserved. The band ceased its twice-daily concerts on the deck. It rained hard yesterday and a waterspout was spotted, an ominous sight. Some took it for a bad omen. But the rain ceased overnight and when reveille was signaled at 3:30 a.m., it was already steaming hot. By dawn most of us were topside, and at 8 we heard the sound of naval gunfire to the west. A feint, we were told, to deceive the Spaniards about our intended landing site. At 9:40, nearby warships began to shell the town of Daiquiri before us. The reports of the massive guns were deafening, reverberating back from the mountainsides ashore. Great gouges of earth were thrown up. Buildings were demolished and set ablaze. I had never seen anything like it and neither had anyone else. "By God, it's a hot time for those

Spaniards," somebody yelled. Another trooper started whistling "A Hot Time in the Old Town," and we all joined in.

Some boats from another ship, carrying Regulars from the 8th Infantry, have begun to row toward shore. And now there are mounted "insurrectos" on the shore, waving a large Cuban flag. Have the Spaniards fled? Have they surrendered already? Have they moved inland to lie in wait for us?

Lt. Devereaux has just made his way through the ranks and announced our departure is imminent. Below us the sea is heaving. The ship is making its way closer to the single, decrepit-looking dock. I will write more when I can.

I closed the old diary and rubbed my eyes. My watch said it was nearly midnight. How long had I been reading? Before the Skype call, I'd read a long email from my mother and pecked out a reply. While doing that, one came in from Sam, with an attached photo showing her in a bikini. "Something to keep you focused," she said. I had to laugh at that. How could I focus on my job when that picture was staring at me? But I didn't delete it.

I hit the latrine one last time before returning to my hootch and turning out the light. Even though Kulinski had told me I was off-duty till the next afternoon, he'd heard me out earlier in the evening about Burns's intel, but hadn't invited me to sit in on the debrief. That bothered me. Was the captain trying to ease me out? No, come on, I told myself, Kulinski was just being serious about forcing me to take some downtime.

It was the middle of the night up here in the mountains at the ass-end of Turkey, and the temperature might get down to freezing. I pulled off my boots and jacket but kept my pants and tee shirt on, slipped into my sleeping bag, and with one last glance at the decrepit little electric space heater that probably wouldn't stay on all night, I clicked the light off. I forced myself to avoid thinking about the Iranians down in that Iraqi village. It had been just about 116 years ago that my ancestor had found himself in another vill, this one on an island coast in steaming hot weather. What was old Charles going to find out when he experienced combat? I tried to remember the history. Had the Rough Riders fought an engagement before San Juan Heights? No, they…wait. Yes, by God, they had. A firefight in the jungle. No wonder Uncle John was excited about it, he'd had plenty of his own in Vietnam. Something was in there, he'd said, that could help me out now.

What the hell could that be? So far, the Rough Rider stuff had been interesting, but come on, only three weeks of training and they're going into combat? Today they'd get cut up like tissue paper against the Taliban or even those ISIS yahoos. And back in 1898 those cowboys and football players would be going up against veteran Spanish infantry that had been fighting Cuban guerillas for years. It's a wonder any of the Rough Riders had survived.

But my great-great-grandfather had, so in the morning I'd have to find out how.

CHAPTER SIXTEEN

The journal of Charles J. Dawson, con't.

June the 24th, 1898 – We have seen the elephant.

This morning we encountered the Spaniards and had ourselves a big fight. For the first time in my life I was both frightened and thrilled at the same time. It was like nothing else I had ever experienced. In some ways I cannot wait to once more join with the enemy in battle. In other ways I hope never to experience it again.

We were not fired upon as we came ashore at Daiquiri, although it was hazardous enough to deal with the churning sea and the rickety pier which we had to reach from the boats. Two Negro soldiers from the 10th Cavalry slipped on the dock, fell into the sea and drowned, despite the gallant efforts of the Captain of Troop A, Bucky O'Neill of Arizona, and the Regiment's best swimmer, Troop E's Charles Knoblauch, to save them. Their bodies were later recovered and a somber funeral service was held. Our first casualties in Cuba had been felled by the Caribbean, not by Spanish lead.

After a night spent in the open, following Col. Wood's orders to sleep on our packs with our carbines ready in case of enemy attack, we awoke on the 23rd rather refreshed, in spite of the large sand crabs which skittered over us during the night. Our rations of beans, hardtack and coffee were supplemented by coco-nuts, prepared for us by our new Cuban comrades. The "insurrectos" are a motley crew, emaciated and many wearing clothing resembling more a set of rags than a uniform. But they have been fighting the Spaniards for years and so deserve our respect. Most of the Arizona and New Mexico troopers know their lingo and eagerly served as interpreters. The rest of our army came ashore that morning without incident, except for the loss of one of Lt. Col. Roosevelt's horses, which drowned after being lowered into the water from the ship. The other, Little Texas, was able to swim ashore successfully. Some men claimed to hear Roosevelt's curses all the way into our campsite behind the village. I am glad I was not there, having witnessed a similar tragedy when I was eight years old. I saw a horse fall off a ferry whilst crossing the Wisconsin River near Muscoda and the poor beast was caught in the current and swept away. I shall never forget its terrified screams.

We marched overland some eight and one-half miles to Siboney, which had been secured by Regulars. Word spread that the Cubans had been in a fight that morning with the retreating Spaniards. The sun was boiling hot and the jungle was a furnace. The trail was so narrow we could not go even two men abreast for much of it. The heat and humidity were oppressive to the point where many men tossed their packs aside. I retained mine and thanked myself for it later. Roosevelt started out mounted on Little Texas but soon joined us afoot, a gesture we much appreciated.

By the time we reached Siboney we were soaked in sweat. No sooner had we built fires to cook supper and dry our clothes than a rainstorm struck, and it poured for an hour. Fortunately, Burdwell and I had both retained our packs and had pitched our dog-tent first thing. Other men were not as fortunate. As we turned in we did not know that the officers were then deciding that we would march on the Spaniards in the morning.

Reveille sounded before dawn. Word came down from Col. Wood that we would "smell the powder" today, and the Regiment was much excited. All fatigue from the previous day's march was forgotten. By 6 a.m. we were moving out, those of us still with packs having left them behind.

We climbed over limestone rocks as we ascended a steep ridge behind the campsite. Some of the lads could not make the summit, as the heat was already rising. At the top we met some Regulars stationed there as pickets, and they bade us Godspeed as we advanced to meet the enemy. The vegetation alternated between thick brush that crowded the trail to open glades. To our right was a valley about a mile distant. After another four miles we came to a pass through the hills. Word came back that this place was called Las Guasimas, named after a type of tree much in evidence in the dense foliage. We came to a halt as Col. Wood ordered silence in the ranks. Then came the words we had longed to hear: "Load chambers and magazines." The magazine of my Krag-Jorgensen held five cartridges. I filled it and chambered a round, feeling a powerful urge to relieve myself, which I did along the trail, along with many other men. Some tried to hold out unsuccessfully, based on the stains on the front of their trousers. Then we waited, some men sitting down. Many were nervous, including myself, but others calmly began discussing matters far afield from battle. Burdwell, next to me, engaged a fellow Texan in conversation about cow-punching.

A barbed-wire fence flanked the trail at this point. Up ahead, I could see Roosevelt examining one strand of wire and gesticulating at it with determination. He was showing it to one of the journalists who was accompanying the column. "Burdwell, what is going on with that wire?" I asked. My friend peered at them, some 50 yards away, then said, "I think he's pointing to where it's been cut." The other Texan chimed in, "Damn right he is. Look, he's holding one end up. Stay sharp, boys, the Spaniards have been through here not long ago, I think."

I knew with a certainty that they were up ahead, over the knoll some 100 yards before us. Sure enough, within a few minutes gunfire rang out, a single shot we recognized as from one of our Krags, and then a fusillade of fire from what could only be Spanish Mausers.

"On the double-quick, men!" Lt. Kane ordered. Troop L had been in the lead of our column, and we were fifth. Wood and Roosevelt were splitting the troops into two columns, directing ours, right behind Troop G, to the right through a break in the wire. Wood was calm as a cucumber but Roosevelt was much excited, gesturing frantically and hopping up and down as he shouted encouragement to the lads. Once we had all passed through the wire he ran to the front of the column, ordering us to scatter out into skirmish lines. "Look alive! Look alive!" he yelled. Mauser rounds whizzed past us. Ahead of us I could see the Spaniards in their distinctive white sombrero hats. They appeared to be dug in to a trench, forming a V, with the point away from us. Just beyond the point of the V were a pair of machine-guns, elevated to fire over the heads of the Spaniards.

The officers formed us into another V, with the open end toward the enemy, and ordered us to advance. Bullets tore into the leaves overhead, cutting them like a scythe cuts wheat. We would advance a few yards, then crouch or lie down and fire in the direction of the Spaniards. The trees afforded little protection. I saw one trooper from Troop G, twenty yards to my left, take a round in the throat that had passed entirely through the foot-thick trunk of the tree he had knelt behind. As the round tore through him, his eyes bugged out and he began the most horrible coughing. He tried stanching the blood from the wound but it was mortal. As his mates rushed to his side, I heard him croak, "Mother! Mother!" Another trooper cried, "Hang on, Marcus!"

I was mortified, but could not take a moment to contemplate it as Burdwell, next to me, shouted, "Get down!" and shoved me on the back, into the grass. A torrent of machine-gun rounds ripped through the air where we had been moments earlier. My comrade peeked up above the grass and exclaimed, "I see the bastard! Can you see him, Charlie? At the machine-gun!"

I rose up, trying to control my breathing as Father had cautioned me in one of his letters. Indeed, I saw the Spaniard, some 75 yards ahead, right behind their line. He was sitting behind the weapon with a comrade feeding the ammunition belt into it. The gun had ceased firing and the Spaniard began working its mechanism furiously. A jam! Lee had seen it too. "Shit fire!" he yelled, rising to one knee and raising his Krag to his shoulder. He sighted and fired. The man feeding the machine-gun dropped, but the gunner remained cool. He cleared the jam and crouched back down, swinging the barrel around in an arc right toward us. I got up on one knee, aimed at him and fired. His sombrero flew away as did the upper part of his head. I had scored a direct hit. "G-d damn! You got him, Charlie!" Burdwell yelled, clapping me on the back. I had indeed, but I felt no joy. I felt nothing except the need to find more targets and fire. I squeezed off two more shots and we were ordered forward as the Spanish line buckled and the enemy retreated through a glade.

To our right we saw Troop A, and beyond them, Regulars coming from the ravine that had paralleled our line of march. They were Negro troops from the 10th, forcing the Spanish left to collapse and fall back. Not too far from us, one of our corporals, Fredrik Lie, took our Troop K guidon and climbed up into a tree to signal the men of the 10th. He drew fire from the enemy but kept signaling. Within moments his signal was answered. The Regulars linked up with Troop A and we began to advance as the Spanish fire decreased.

Roosevelt had been with us but then went around to the left. We often saw Col. Wood, leading his horse, walking calmly among the men. Miraculously, neither he nor his horse were so much as scratched in the battle, but there was one disturbing scene. As we were advancing, a man went down. Near us was Lt. Hall, the regimental adjutant, the bane of our existence back in San Antonio for his nit-picking rules and imperious attitude. He yelled, "Colonel Wood is down! He's down!" Without bothering to go to the aid of the fallen man, Hall bolted from the field and ran to the rear. Several of the troopers who saw him run cursed his name. No sooner had Hall fled than Wood arrived, very much alive.

The fighting went on. We would fire, then creep forward a few yards and fire again. The Mauser rounds of the Spaniards made a peculiar buzzing sound as they passed by us. One came so close I could feel it whisk across the crown of my hat. Three inches lower and I would have been sent to my mother's side for eternity. The enemy moved from one trench line to another, but always yielding ground. Eventually we emerged into a large clearing, perhaps a half-mile across. It seemed to be filled with Spaniards. Many were crouching and returning our fire, others were fleeing in the direction of Santiago. In the midst of the clearing was a cluster of buildings, tiled in red. A rum distillery, we later learned. Enemy fire came from its doors and windows. From behind us, Col. Wood ordered the charge, and the bugle sounded. We rushed forward out of the trees, yelling at the tops of our lungs. To my left I saw Roosevelt leading another group of troopers toward the buildings. They stopped a hundred yards away and poured rifle fire into them, with Roosevelt working his Krag furiously. Within minutes, a few Spaniards rushed out the rear and ran for their lives after their fleeing comrades.

Some of the lads began running in pursuit, but Roosevelt ordered the bugler to sound recall. The battle was over. I was stunned to discover that some two hours had gone by during the fight. It was not yet noon and hot as blazes. I emptied my canteen almost in one gulp. The rest of the afternoon was spent making camp in the shade of the trees, replenishing our water and taking whatever food we could find.

I assisted in finding the wounded men who could not move, and the bodies of the dead. The vultures helped us locate them. I had helped bring two wounded men to the hospital tent when I saw Roosevelt and Capt. O'Neill standing near the body of a man, whom I later found to be from Troop A. The birds had ravaged the boy's face. It was an awful sight. I heard O'Neill quoting Walt Whitman, something about vultures plucking the eyes of princes. Roosevelt said it wasn't Whitman, but from the book of Ezekiel.

Another was that of Hamilton Fish, a sergeant in Troop L, which had led the column into Las Guasimas. Fish's grandfather and namesake had been Secretary of State under Grant. The Troop's captain, Allyn Capron, had also fallen. Capron had been a lieutenant in the 7th Cavalry, guarding Geronimo's Apaches at Fort Sill in Oklahoma Territory before joining the Regiment, and was well-liked in his Troop. Several of his men were near the body. Many were weeping unashamedly. I had heard that his father and namesake commands an artillery battery.

After leaving the hospital tent, Burdwell and I were making our way back to our Troop's campsite when we saw Lt. Hall being upbraided by none other than Lt. Gen. Wheeler, the bandy-legged old Confederate cavalryman who is the commander of the Corps of Cavalry. He railed against Hall for displaying cowardice in the field, calling for him to be tried and shot. Wood stepped in to intercede, and whatever he said I could not hear, but it calmed Wheeler somewhat. I could not help but contrast Hall's appalling behavior with the heroism and leadership shown by Wood and Roosevelt, who had repeatedly exposed themselves to Spanish bullets as they led the Regiment forward.

"I heard Hall is a West Pointer," Burdwell said to me.

"I heard that, too," I agreed.

"Well, that don't mean squat when the lead starts flying," my comrade said, squirting a stream of tobacco to the ground as we walked past the officers. "That's when the men stand up and the kids run for it."

Later on, as the sun began to set and the temperature dropped a few degrees, I walked through the Regiment's camp, looking for Dean and Wells and the rest of my Harvard mates. I found them unharmed and our reunion was joyous. We spent some time talking of our respective roles in the battle. We spoke of the officers who had shown the way, such as Wood and Roosevelt and Capron, and those like Hall who had performed shamefully. To be fair, several of the troopers had also caved under the pressure and spent more time hunkering down or even running back than advancing to engage the enemy. But the officers, we all agreed, are the ones who are counted on to keep that from happening. They gratefully assumed positions of leadership in the Regiment upon its founding and during training, and when the chips are down, that's when the men must see them at the front, leading the way. Otherwise, all will be lost.

Making my way back to my Troop, I was hailed from a nearby campfire. "Dawson! Hey, the Badger boy is all right!" It was McGee, my old boxing opponent. He waved me over and bade me share coffee with him and his mates. The brew was strong and had a kick to it. One of the Coloradans had slipped a little whiskey into the pot, I assumed. I accepted gratefully.

We swapped stories from the battle. McGee had taken a wound to his right arm, but had been treated and was still fit for duty. "Only a scratch," he told me. "We were taking hell from one of their machine-guns, and then bang-bang, those two boys went down. I wonder who got them? It was a hell of a shot on that gunner, right between the eyes."

The whiskey must have had an effect on me, for I did not hesitate. "My tent-mate got the ammunition feeder," I declared, "but it was my round that took the gunner." I immediately regretted claiming the kill, not wanting to boast, but McGee responded with wide-eyed amazement, and then he and his mates whooped and clapped me on the back. I received another healthy offering of their brew and they raised their cups in a toast to my marksmanship.

Several minutes later I knew I had to leave or I would be in no shape for the march in the morning. I rose and bade them good-night. McGee walked with me to the edge of the firelight. He offered his hand gingerly, as it was on the arm that had been wounded. "You saved a lot of men today, Dawson. I am grateful. We all are. That was some piece of shooting. As good as any Western man could shoot and better than most, and that's a fact." He asked where I had learned to shoot, and I responded that Father had taught me, feeling it was an important thing for a young man to learn to handle a firearm competently. I had begun hunting rabbits and squirrels with him at the age of seven. Some of my fondest memories, I said, were of hunting with my father amongst the hills of Grant County back in Wisconsin. McGee nodded, saying he did the same as a lad in northern Alabama, only in his case it was with his grandfather. And now here we are in the jungles of Cuba, on the hunt again.

This time, though, our quarry has the ability to shoot back.

By then I was starting to feel a strange emotion. I did not revel in the death of the Spaniard as the other men seemed to do. I had taken a man's life. As Father had warned me in one of his letters, it is a terrible thing, the only justification for doing so being that it was him or me and my comrades. Still, I took no pleasure in the act. But I accepted McGee's gratitude as genuine, for I knew it to be true. Another trooper might well have killed that gunner and ended his murderous fire, but maybe not till others of us had fallen.

I finish this entry by the faltering light of the fire. Burdwell is already snoring in our tent. I shall join him shortly. No one knows what the morrow will bring, except perhaps the officers. Undoubtedly we will maintain our advance toward Santiago. Other troops have joined us, Regulars who set out from Siboney after us. They are upset that they missed the fight. Well, there will be plenty more fighting for them and for all of us, of that I have no doubt.

There are four other troopers sharing the fire, each pair with their own tent. The heat seems to have let up, and the fire would not be necessary except for the brewing of our coffee, and of course for light. From one tent are Creighton Marshall of Washington, D.C., and Frank Kania of North Dakota. I was much surprised and pleased to find that one of the other men is William J. McKoy from Oshkosh, Wisconsin. His tent-mate, George L. Smith, is from Michigan. McKoy is with the Colt machine-gun crews, but related that he fought with his Krag because the mules carrying the machine-guns were spooked by the Spanish guns and their packs, containing the priceless weapons, were dumped on the ground, and the crews had no time to assemble them.

Everyone wanted to know how many men we had lost. Marshall said he'd heard of 30 to 40 dead, McKoy thought more than that. Each of the other men said they'd seen a comrade fall. I related an account of the Troop G man who had taken a Spanish round in the throat. Marshall asked if I knew the man's name. "Someone called out the name of

Marcus," I said.

Marshall breathed in sharply. "My God," he said. "Marcus Russell? From New York? I tented with him until we were assigned to different Troops." He hung his head, his chest heaving, then stood and excused himself. For a long minute there was silence around the fire, then the remaining men said their good-nights and retired.

I stayed there by myself, the image of Russell's life draining out of him refusing to leave me. I had never seen a man die before today, much less taken one's life. Not for the first time since leaving Wisconsin, I questioned my reasons for joining this crusade. But I remembered what Father had told me about fighting during the Rebellion, and how he justified risking his own life. "Every man must decide what it is he is willing to stand for," he said. "For me, it was to preserve the Union and free men from bondage. I meant to have my children grow up in a unified country, where all men and women enjoy liberty."

And now, here I am, risking my own life for these Cubans. It is not America and may never be part of our nation, but does that mean these people are any less worthy of the gift of liberty? Jefferson wrote in the Declaration that all are created equal. He did not differentiate between people of one land versus another, between white men and those who are black or red. For several minutes I pondered on this. When we were in Camp, I overheard some troopers speaking disparagingly of Negroes and Mexicans and certainly Indians, even though we have several men of Mexican descent and some Indians among our number. And we have witnessed Negro troops fighting as valiantly as white men. Certainly O'Neill and Knoblauch, two white men who dove into the surf to attempt rescue of the two drowning men of the 10th, did not hesitate because the imperiled soldiers were Negroes.

Lt. Kane just appeared, asking if I was all right, if I needed anything. I said no, and thanked him for his concern. I asked him how many casualties we had taken.

"We lost 17," he said. "About 50 wounded." He was silent for a moment, then said, "You fought well today, Dawson. I've been told you and Burdwell silenced that machine-gun."

I admitted that it was true. "Well done," Kane said. "You had best get some shut-eye now. To-morrow there will be more work for us all." He touched the brim of his hat, and I returned the salute. He went off to his tent.

What I saw today has made me respect Father even more. As an officer, his duty was to lead his men, accomplish the mission and bring as many of them home as possible. His commendations, secure in his display case back in his Platteville office, attest to his leadership. Without the leadership of men like Wood, Roosevelt, Capron and Kane today, I dare say there would have been many more bodies back there at the hospital tent. I shall conclude my prayers tonight with a thanks to God for allowing me to serve under such men. I shall also ask Him for His divine protection in the days to come. I am sure I shall need it.

CHAPTER SEVENTEEN

Hakkâri Province, Turkey
May 2014

The mission brief was scheduled for 1300 hours and Kulinski, surprisingly, was late. As the men settled in their seats, I took a look outside and saw the major emerge from the command hootch. Kulinski double-timed the twenty meters and motioned me over.

"What's up, sir?"

"Just took a message from Higher. They've thrown us a curveball. I'll mention it at the end of the brief, then you and I can get together to discuss it."

"Sure thing," I said, but I was worried. You never knew what was going to come down the pipeline. Most of the time the orders were clear, but sometimes you had to wonder if somebody had slipped something into a general's morning coffee.

I forced myself to focus on the brief as Kulinski laid out the mission. At the end, though, I was just as stunned as everybody else.

The brief had sounded pretty routine up to that point. Cross the border, join up with a Peshmerga platoon near the Rubar Shakiu River and assist in scouting a string of three villages along the main road that wound its way through the mountains to the town of Chama. ISIS units had been reported in the area, although Chama itself, garrisoned by a Peshmerga force of twenty men, was said to be quiet. By now I knew things could change quickly in that area of Kurdistan. A mission said to have a strong likelihood of encountering the enemy often turned out to be a dry hole, and it could be the other way around, too.

The squad would be gone about four days. I was up to lead this one; in the last few weeks, our operations had all been small enough so that

Kulinski only needed to send half his force, so he and I alternated as the mission commanders. The vills we were going to visit probably didn't have a lot in the way of amenities, so we would prepare for nights in the open and not much in the way of food or water beyond what we could carry. Generally, though, the Peshmerga guys came through on that last score. Still, I was already thinking ahead about loading our two Humvees when Kulinski's final words caught my attention.

"Okay, guys, one last item," the major said. He hesitated, took a breath and then looked over the heads of the seated men. He seemed to be considering something. I didn't like the look on his face. It was not Kulinski's usual all-business expression. His eyes, in particular, seemed to be focusing on something far away for a moment, then they came back and scanned each of us. "This will be our last operation."

I was as stunned as everybody else, but I had to say something. "Then we'll have to make it a good one," I said, hoping it didn't sound like something out of an old movie.

The major nodded. "We will." He looked back at the gathered soldiers. "Look, gentlemen, we've been operating here for about nine months now. You all know as well as I do that nothing lasts forever in this man's Army."

"Politics," Boudreau muttered. "Has to be."

Kulinski nodded. "I have to agree with you, Master Sergeant." I was surprised at that. I'd never talked politics with Kulinski, had no idea how the major had voted in the last election. Since joining up, I had heard every political opinion under the sun, although the troops appeared to lean more to the right than in the other direction. In 2008, my first presidential election, I had voted for McCain, following Uncle John's lead–and to make a dig at my father, I had to admit–but in 2012, I hadn't voted at all.

"Major, the word is the hajis are moving on Mosul," Burns said. "This doesn't seem to be the best time for us to be pulling out." I knew from the latest intel package that Burns was right. Mosul, the largest city in northern Iraq, was only about seventy-five miles from our base camp. The Kurds were getting pretty nervous. What would they be thinking now, with their nearest American support unit about to leave them in the lurch?

"We could be here all night debating this, but it's not our decision," Kulinski said. "As of oh-one June, we strike our unit colors here and start packing to go home. If any of you want to talk about it later, my door's open. But for now, guys, we have a mission, so let's get to it. Dismissed."

The mood of the men was subdued, and the brief concluded without the wisecracks and associated off-color remarks that usually peppered the conversation among the men. I had quickly found out that being an officer meant you were usually excluded from that, even at a small outpost like this one, and I missed it. Today, I missed it more than ever. I knew the men were troubled by Kulinski's news. That meant I'd have even more work to do in prepping my team for the mission.

But, I was an officer in the United States Army, and I had a job to do. Tomorrow was Memorial Day. We'd be moving out at 0700 the next day, May twenty-seventh, and rolling back in here on the thirtieth. As always, I had a lot to do and not a lot of time to do it in. That was par for the course, but I was reminded of something I'd heard the Navy SEALs often said: The only easy day was yesterday.

I made one last visit to the latrine before turning in. On the way back to my hootch, I stopped to take in the night sky. It was just after nine, local time. Sunset had been two hours earlier, and the stars above were spectacular. Every now and then I forced himself to take a few minutes in the evening to appreciate where I was. Even in northern Wisconsin, there wasn't a view quite like this.

Was Sam looking at the same stars back home? Well, no, she wouldn't be; Turkey was nine hours ahead of Wisconsin. Or was it ten? Did they have Daylight Saving Time here? Was Wisconsin on it yet? I shook my head and chuckled.

"Private joke, LT?"

It was Boudreau. The master sergeant was heading back from the latrine as well. I hadn't even heard him coming, but that was the way it was when it came to Boudreau.

"No, Sarge, I was just thinking about my girl looking at these stars, but it's afternoon there. I'm pretty sure it is, anyway."

Boudreau joined me in gazing skyward. After a moment, he pointed upward. "Orion is out tonight."

I recognized the constellation, too. "I didn't know you were into astronomy, Sarge."

"Took a course in it back at Tulane," Boudreau said. "You?"

"Boy Scout merit badge."

Boudreau grunted, then said, "We're all disappointed the unit is standing down, Lieutenant, but we're glad you're leading us on this last mission."

I was surprised. Boudreau occasionally would let me know how the other men were thinking, but it wasn't like him to reveal much about his own feelings. "Thanks, Sarge, I appreciate it. I hope I won't let you down."

"You won't. The guys appreciate a good leader. You and the major, you're getting the job done. I've served under some who didn't, and there's a big difference."

That tickled something from my memory. What was it? Yes, the diary. I hadn't read any more of it since that night several weeks before. Too damn busy. But I remembered now what my ancestor had written. "'Otherwise, all will be lost,'" I said.

"How's that?"

I looked up at the stars in Orion's belt. "Something my great-great-granddad wrote after his first firefight in Cuba." I sketched out the old Rough Rider's impressions of the officers at Las Guásimas.

Boudreau grunted again when I finished the story. "Some things don't change," he said. "Your granddad, he got home from Cuba okay?"

"I haven't finished it yet, but yeah, he did, in one piece, as far as I know." I'd have to get back to the diary. Well, after we broke down the camp and headed back to Incirlik or wherever the hell we were going, there'd be plenty of time.

After a moment, Boudreau said, "My great-great-granddad was a slave."

Startled, I looked over at the sergeant major. In the dim starlight, his ebony face was even more unreadable than in daylight. "I didn't know that," I said.

Boudreau nodded. "That's the family story, anyway. Something right out of *Roots*. He was on a plantation upriver, near White Castle. Nottoway, they called it. The massa was a big shot, one of the biggest slaveholders in Louisiana. Grew sugar cane, some cotton. Old Silas Randolph, that was my ancestor. Took the massa's last name, like lots of them did. Just a boy during the Civil War, stayed on afterward as a hired hand."

"I heard a lot of those plantations were burned during the war."

"Not this one. Worst that happened, took a few hits of grapeshot from a Yankee gunboat on the river. I went there when I was in college. Still had one of those holes in the big column. Tour guide said the ball didn't fall out till 1971."

I had known a lot of African-Americans in the Army, but none of them had ever said anything about being a descendant of slaves. I said, "The Rough Rider's father fought for the Union. He was an officer, wounded at Gettysburg."

Boudreau said nothing. Maybe that hadn't been the right thing to say. "I didn't mean that to sound defensive, Sarge. Like I'm trying to make up for something."

"No problem, LT. It was a helluva long time ago. And none of that's gonna mean squat when we move out on Tuesday. The hajis out there don't give a shit about who our ancestors were. All they want is to send us to join 'em."

"Roger that, Master Sergeant." After a moment, Boudreau said his good night and headed off into the darkness. I took one last look up at the stars, thinking about what the tough old Louisianan had said about the enemy. He was damn right about them. It would be my job to make sure they'd be disappointed.

CHAPTER EIGHTEEN

Erbil Governate, Iraq
May 2014

I had been getting better with my Arabic, but this man was speaking Kurdish. I'd learned there were three different dialects of Kurdish, but so far I'd only picked up a few phrases in Kurmanji, the dialect used by the people in this region. I had to rely on the interpreter. "Tell him to slow down," I ordered.

The Peshmerga spoke to the man, and got a response. The elderly Kurd nodded, then looked at me and said, *"Şeytan li gundê din in."*

The 'terp licked his lips nervously, then translated. "He say, 'The devils are in the next village.'"

"Who does he mean by 'devils'?"

"Şeytan kî ne?"

The Kurd looked at the 'terp as if he was an imbecile, then glowered at him and rattled off a long sentence. The 'terp nodded, looking even more nervous than before. Next to me, Sergeant Burns, the commo sergeant on this operation, shook his head. "Going too fast for me, too, Lieutenant," he said.

"Well?" I asked the 'terp, "what did he say?"

"He says it is Da'esh, Lieutenant. Da'esh took his granddaughter. They will make slaves of her and the other girls. He demands you go there and free them."

There it was. "Da'esh" was the acronym for the Arabic name for ISIS, *al-Dawla al-Islamiya al-Iraq al-Sham,* the Islamic State of Iraq and the Levant. "How many?" I asked.

More jabbering and gesturing. "Twenty, maybe thirty," the 'terp said. The Kurd looked at me, squinted, then spoke, appearing to ask him a question.

"I'm sorry," I said, and looked at the 'terp.

The young man grinned. "He asks, 'Are you the American they call the...*Dargiran Siwar?*'"

"What the hell does that mean?"

"It means, 'tough horseman.' The man who escaped the Pasdaran."

Burns cleared his throat. "Uh, LT, I think he means 'Rough Rider.'"

"What the..." I glared at him, then turned back to the interpreter. "Ask him what kind of vehicles they have."

The exchange went on for another five minutes before I'd heard enough. I thanked the old man, assured him that the Americans would do whatever we could to free his granddaughter, and headed back to my men. The 'terp stayed behind to talk to more of the refugees.

When we were out of earshot, I stopped and said, "All right, Burns, what's with this 'Rough Rider' shit?"

"Sir, they know about our escape from that village when the Iranians had us. The Peshmerga must've gotten the word from those villagers, and, well, like back home, word travels fast, even here."

"All right, but the other thing?"

"Ah, well," Burns averted his gaze. "Some of the guys might've said something to the Peshmerga about your ancestor. Respectfully, I'm sure. Sir." He was fighting against letting a grin loose, and he was losing the fight.

"Christ almighty, Burns! As if we don't have enough problems, now they expect Teddy fucking Roosevelt to ride to their rescue?"

Burns lost the grin. "Sir, you have to understand with these people, symbolism is big for them. Religious, historical, you name it. They've been fighting against damn near everyone around here for centuries and sometimes it's like their traditions and myths, it's all that keeps them going. You better believe one of the Peshmerga heard about your Rough Rider connection and he got on the internet and there you have it. Your ancestor fought alongside Roosevelt, who was a great warrior. Back home we'd call it street cred. Well, you got it in spades with these people."

"Terrific." I was still pissed, but in a way, proud. So, what would TR have done in this situation? I knew the answer to that one. He'd saddle up and ride toward the sound of guns.

"What's the story, LT?" Boudreau asked, when we had joined the rest of the team at my Humvee.

"That worst-case scenario we talked about just bit us in the ass," I said. "Let's see the map."

The sergeant spread the map out on the hood of the Humvee. He pointed to a dot about twenty klicks to the west. "If they're in the next village, that would be here," Boudreau said. "The middle village of the three we're scouting south of Chama."

The road, such that it was, snaked through the mountains, rarely giving us a stretch of a kilometer before making a turn, and sometimes the turns were wicked hairpins that almost doubled back on themselves. The prospects for an ambush anywhere along the way were pretty damn high.

"How far is it to Mosul?" Burns asked.

"Not that far as the crow flies, but on this road, maybe three hours," Boudreau said. "And this is the only road from here to there."

I pointed at the road leading south from our present position. At the village of Shanidar it hooked west, then eventually to the southwest toward Mosul. "If they're north of Shanidar, they're a hell of a lot farther from Mosul than we thought. Our last intel package had them west of Mosul but closing in."

"Could be a long-range scout team." Boudreau touched another road that ran along the Great Zab River from extreme northeastern Syria through northern Iraq. "If they came along this road, their goal might be to see what defenses the Iraqis have way up here. If they don't find much, they could open up another approach to Mosul from the north. Their main units are coming up from Anbar, in the south and west."

"Might be a good idea to find out," I said. "Burns, get on the horn to base, I need to talk to the major."

A few minutes later, I gave the radio handset back to Burns. "We're cleared to advance," I said, "but only the next vill. Recon and see what the enemy's up to."

"Do we engage?" Boudreau asked.

"The major says it's my call." I gazed down the road. The next village, where the old Kurd's granddaughter and the others were taken, was about ten kilometers away. "What do you think, Master Sergeant?"

"The enemy's likely cleared out by now," Boudreau said. "The old guy and the rest of 'em walked here. Their vill got hit around nine this morning. Time we get there, it's comin' on dusk."

"If they're a long-range scout team, like we think, then they probably won't be taking hostages with them, at least no more than a few," Burns said.

"But we don't know where they're going," I said. "They could be advancing toward us right now, hoping to take this village before nightfall."

"If that's the case, I'd just as soon we advance," Boudreau said. He pointed down the road, toward the looming mountains. "Good ambush spots in there. We hear them comin', we can set something up, hit 'em when they come around a bend, give the Peshmerga mortar teams a chance to open up on 'em. With the fifties on our Humvees plus the mortars, we can handle whatever they've got. At the very least, we get ourselves a firefight without risking the people here in this vill."

I needed to make a decision, and make it quickly. Every minute we waited let the enemy get a half-mile closer, or half a mile farther away, if they were on the move. For damn sure every minute we stood around here brought nightfall closer. With the possibility of civilians in the mix, I didn't want to be taking on these jokers in the dark, even with my unit's advantage in night-vision gear.

I turned back to Burns. "Ellis, go get Staff Sergeant Bakken. He's had contact with these guys before, he might have some insight."

Less than a minute later, the hulking Marine Corps intelligence specialist joined us at the Humvee. I had always felt a type of kinship with Bakken. For one thing, he was a fellow Wisconsinite, from the small town of Cambridge down near Madison. For another, he was the best hand-to-hand combatives guy in the unit, and that reminded me of my own great-grandfather, another Marine who'd been pretty good in a scrap. Bakken had been talking to the refugee Kurds.

He was probably the toughest guy in the outfit, and certainly the tallest, at six-four. When he played on UW-Whitewater's national championship football team in '07 as an offensive tackle, he'd weighed in at three hundred pounds. He'd lost about fifty of them since then, but what remained was pretty much all muscle and bone. If there was one guy besides Boudreau that I wanted around if a firefight devolved into hand-to-hand, it was Bakken. "What'd you get from them, Staff Sergeant?" I asked.

"They're pretty clear on the numbers, Lieutenant. Maybe three dozen tops. Four vehicles, Toyota pickups with heavy machine guns, probably Russian DshK, like our fifty-cals. The standard technicals."

"We're thinking they're a scout unit," Boudreau said.

Bakken nodded as he took off his sunglasses. He kept his helmet on, as all the men did. I thought it was the biggest helmet I'd ever seen. "I'd go along with that," Bakken said. "We know ISIS has a lot of Humvees they captured from the Iraqis, but these Toyotas get a lot better mileage, and out here you never know where you'll find the next gas station."

"What will they do with the women from that village?" I asked.

"It won't be good, LT, of that you can be sure. They might take two or three along, but the intel we have on these guys says they only take a lot of hostages when they move into a region in battalion strength with the intention of settling in."

"They've been in that village all day," Boudreau said. "Them girls…"

The master sergeant's words were left hanging. There was no need to finish the sentence.

"Our orders still stand, gentlemen," I said. "We're on recon, not a rescue mission." Even as I said it, I knew that if we encountered civilian prisoners, I would do everything I could to save them. I wouldn't be able to live with myself otherwise.

"Mount up."

CHAPTER NINETEEN

Erbil Governate, Iraq
May 2014

I was tempted to send one of my vehicles ahead as a scout, but the bends in this road were too sharp. If the scout came around a turn and encountered the full enemy force, they might not be able to retreat, and the rest of the platoon might not have time to get up there before the scout was overwhelmed.

I leaned forward and tried to see the top of the hill through the Humvee's windshield. No dice, we were too close. The gunners in all the vehicles were keeping an eye out for movement on the hillsides. I would've loved drone cover right now, but we hadn't had a drone for a mission in two weeks and weren't going to get one now. Calling in an air strike out of Incirlik was tempting, but I couldn't risk it with the possibility the hajis would have civilians with them. Maybe a gunship; an AC-130 could direct fire away from potential civilians. It would be just like those ISIS bastards to use young girls as human shields. Yes, that's what they'd do, they'd rape the hell out of them and then–

"LT, the major's on the horn."

Burns, in the back, handed me the handset. Glad to have something snap me back to the job at hand, I said, "Wolverine actual, this is Cowboy One, over."

Kulinski's voice crackled with static. *"Cowboy One, be advised, Big Eye reports enemy units in Barzan, being engaged by local Peshmerga. Possible battalion strength."* I found the town on the map. It was along the east-west road we'd suspected this nearby unit was using to infiltrate from Syria. "Big Eye" was the Army Intelligence unit keeping an eye on Kurdistan with a combination of ground, air and space assets. During

THE HEIGHTS OF VALOR   171

my time in the Wolverines, I had come to trust Big Eye implicitly. They'd been on the money every time.

"Wolverine actual, that confirms the unit we're heading toward is a recon team. I make their main force about fifty klicks from my location by road." I was still hesitant about giving our location over the air, but Burns had assured me comms were scrambled, and we hadn't gotten any intel about the enemy using any kind of decryption.

"Concur, Cowboy One. We have confirmation from 4th ID in Baghdad, an official request from Peshmerga Command in Erbil to stop the enemy's advance toward Chama. You're up, Cowboy One. Clear to engage. Air assets available upon request, over."

There it was. The 4th Infantry Division was in charge of U.S. Division North, part of U.S. Forces-Iraq, and nominally the Wolverines' parent division. It wasn't often that 4th ID actually gave Kulinski a mission; most of his taskings came directly from Special Operations Command. The Peshmerga brass in Erbil must have made a quick call to Baghdad for help.

"Wolverine actual, I confirm, Cowboy Team is clear to engage. Request Spooky cover, over."

"Roger that, Cowboy One, I will pass that along to Incirlik and will advise. Good hunting. Wolverine actual, out."

I gave the handset back to Burns and allowed myself a sigh of relief. Having a gunship overhead would dramatically change the dynamics of the coming firefight. Air power was the coalition's major advantage in its war with ISIS, and I had no doubt that it would be the deciding factor and lead to ultimate victory. If, of course, the troops on the ground and in the air were allowed to achieve it. For some reason, a picture of my father flashed through my mind. I put it aside; I had to focus my entire attention on what was to come. The enemy could be right around that corner up there, half a klick ahead.

But even then, my thoughts drifted slightly away from the road, back to the Rough Rider's diary. I'd started reading it again last night, but couldn't focus after a few pages and turned in, fatigue finally winning the night. The officers old Charles had served under, they were a pretty squared-away bunch, even the newbies like Roosevelt. They'd looked after their men and led the advance toward the enemy, every time. I wondered if any of my men now were keeping a diary. What would they say about my leadership? And especially now, when the Peshmerga thought I was some kind of holy warrior?

I shook my head. Stay sharp. Corner's coming up. The Humvee rounded the bend and the soldier up in the turret shouted, just as I saw them myself.

"Contact! Three hundred meters!"

One of the first things I had learned in the Army was that no plan survived first contact with the enemy. Not completely, anyway. There were always variables to be considered, unexpected complications. Shit would happen. But I'd also learned that while no plan was perfect, Patton was right when he said something about a good plan executed violently now was better than a perfect plan next week. So when my Humvee rounded the bend and I saw the pickup trucks less than half a kilometer ahead, I didn't hesitate. I snapped an order over my shoulder to Burns. "Execute! Execute! Execute!"

Before heading out from the village, we'd come up with contingencies for a possible confrontation with the enemy. Ideally, I would've wanted to set up an ambush, but the terrain, and lack of a drone to provide overwatch, put that option down the list. Far more likely was a situation just like this one. As Burns shouted the order over the radio, I threw open the Humvee door and ran for cover along the side of the road. There were about forty meters of open ground on this side before the terrain started a sharp rise. The driver and gunner would stay with the Humvee, and before I hit the dirt I heard the .50-cal opening up. Burns hustled over and crouched low.

Over the roar of the fifty, I heard the growling engines of the next two Humvees as they maneuvered off the road, left and right. Without looking, I knew my soldiers were dismounting and running to firing positions. Bringing up the rear were the two Peshmerga vehicles, one of which carried the mortar team. I'd designated my most experienced

THE HEIGHTS OF VALOR   173

mortar man, a wiry Mexican immigrant named Gonzalez, to advise the Kurds as they set up their twin M224 tubes. All told, I had three .50-cals, the two mortar tubes and twenty soldiers to engage the enemy.

Against how many? I took my binoculars from their case and scanned the ISIS formation. They were already scattering in the face of the Humvee's fire, and they weren't doing it very efficiently. About two dozen fighters, and four technicals, like the old Kurd had said. My first scan of the enemy line didn't reveal any non-combatants, but you never knew who might be hunkered down inside those pickup cabs, or in the boxes behind them.

Using my MBITR tactical radio, I directed my soldiers, although I hardly have to give orders to a veteran like Boudreau, who was fanning his squad out to the left of the road. From the rear, I heard the unmistakable thump-thump of mortar rounds being launched. The Peshmerga dropped their first two rounds twenty meters in front of the lead technical, just as we'd planned. Stop any advance, then box them in as the dismounted infantry closed in from the flanks. Having two mortars would make the difference here. Gonzalez would be helping one of the teams to drop rounds behind the enemy formation, while the other team focused on its front.

Ordinarily, I would've had the mortars take out the vehicles, but not here, not with the possibility of civilians inside. That would make this a lot harder, but I couldn't gamble with innocent lives. The enemy, of course, would have no such qualms if the situation was reversed. But that's what separates us from them, I thought, just before a mortar round exploded behind the rearmost technical. "Gonzalez, you have the range, fire for effect," I ordered over the MBITR.

Next to me, Burns spoke up. "Contact from the Spooky, LT. They're overhead and ready to assist. Call sign is Condor One."

"Tell them to target the individuals on the west side of the road but avoid the vehicles."

Burns acknowledged and relayed the order up to the gunship. I was tempted to look up and try to spot the bird, but kept my attention where it was needed. I clicked my tac radio. "Cowboy One to all units, hold in place, Condor One is upstairs and about to engage. Squad leaders, acknowledge."

"Cowboy Four, holding place," Boudreau said from my left. From behind me and to the right, Bakken checked in an instant later. The Marine had three men with him as they scrambled up the hillside, giving them the advantage of the high ground. One of the two snipers in my platoon was in that squad.

There was a sound like a heavy cloth being ripped. Three hundred meters away, on the opposite side of the road, a half-dozen enemy fighters vanished in a rolling torrent of dust, rocks and pink mist. Condor One's chain gun in action. With the gunship closing off the enemy's right flank and our own mortars preventing a retreat, I signaled the men on my side of the road to advance.

The Spooky could've taken out the entire ISIS unit in minutes. Ordinarily I would've been happy to sit back and watch the show, but I still didn't know whether those technicals were filled with civilians. Our rules of engagement had always been clear: avoid collateral damage and civilian casualties if at all possible. Until I knew the trucks were clear of friendlies, this would have to be done the hard way. That meant advancing on foot as we kept the enemy pinned down. But I'd respect the ROE only to a point. If my men were in danger of being overrun, I wouldn't hesitate to order Condor One to cut loose.

The dust kicked up by the mortar rounds hung in the air. The temperature had gone up a half-dozen degrees in just minutes. The breeze that had been with us since leaving the village was gone. A part of my brain registered the sweat inside my BDU and the grime on my face and neck, but I ignored it all. I ran from one piece of minimal cover to the next as my men leapfrogged their way forward. AK rounds snapped overhead and dug into the dirt around me. I fired a few rounds, making sure my own gun was in the fight, but I focused on watching the enemy and directing the men.

If the hajis had any rocket-propelled grenades, this would be about the time to use them, when their leader realized their only chance of escape was to take out the American Humvees and their deadly fifties.

I saw a man in a black turban, standing in the box of the lead technical and waving his arms back toward the second vehicle. So that was the alpha dog of the pack, and he was smart enough to realize he and his men were in a world of shit. Sure enough, two men jumped down from the box of the second truck, each carrying a loaded RPG tube. They crouched and ran ahead to their leader. They were at the very edge of their weapons' effective range, but once a rocket was launched it was going to hit something, and I didn't want to take any chances.

I thumbed my MBITR switch. "Bakken, the RPG gunners are all yours," I said. The Marine sergeant acknowledged, and without looking up the hillside, I knew Bakken was ordering his sniper into action.

Sergeant Dale Dailey was on his fourth tour and had already proven himself to be one of the best snipers I had ever worked with. Today was his twenty-fifth birthday, and instead of hunting rabbits back in Maine, he was here in Iraq, looking through the scope of his M24 rifle at bigger targets. Three hundred meters was nothing for a well-trained sniper, and Dailey proved it by dropping the nearer RPG gunner with his first shot. The gunner on the other side of the lead technical hung in there, though, ignoring his comrade's fate as he crouched down and aimed his weapon. I had to give him props for guts, but not for tactical smarts. Instead of using the truck for cover, he'd come out ahead of it by about a meter. That was all the room Dailey needed. I heard the distinctive bark of the M24. An instant later, the supersonic round popped the gunner's head like a balloon. The launcher fell to the ground, its rocket still in the tube.

Panic swept through the ISIS ranks when they saw their heaviest weapons neutralized. Several men broke and fled back down the road. They made it thirty meters from the rear technical before they were vaporized by Condor One's chain gun.

Now was when the fighters would be the most dangerous. Half their number had evaporated in minutes. One sniper had taken out the RPGs, and now the other sniper, with Boudreau's group across the road, began picking off the machine-gunners in the technicals, starting with the rear-most. In the box of the lead truck, the black-turbaned officer must have realized he and his men were toast, and I knew what he would do next.

Surrender was not in their vocabulary. He shouted orders, waving his men to charge. The engine of his truck roared as the wheels dug into the dirt and gravel.

I clicked my radio. "All units, hold in place. Here they come."

CHAPTER TWENTY

Northern Wisconsin
June 2014

"Need some help, Jake?"

"No, Mom, I'll make it."

I didn't. Trying to swing my legs out of the car, my undamaged right leg made it, but the toe of my left shoe caught the edge of the doorway, the leg twisted and a bolt of pain shot through my knee. I gasped and slumped back in the seat. The stitches on my left shoulder stretched, producing another groan.

"Jake! Are you okay?"

I forced himself to calm down. "Fucking piece of shit brace," I muttered. Then I glanced at my mother. "Sorry."

She placed a gentle hand on my shoulder. How many times had she done that over the years? It felt good, reassuring. Things would be all right. I was home, with Mom. "It's okay, honey," she said. "Let's try it a different way."

This time, sliding myself ass-first out the door, I was able to hop up on my good leg and get my crutches positioned. The shoulder had calmed down. I'd never used crutches before, and even now, with six days of practice under my belt since the surgery in Germany, I was still having a hard time.

It was all mental, I knew that. Before, overcoming mental blocks had never been a problem for me. The discipline I'd known all my life, on the wrestling mat and during basic training and Ranger School and RASP, all seemed to have vanished. And the hell of it was, I still couldn't remember how it had happened.

My mother had said we'd have my favorite dinner, brats on the grill with sweet potato fries, and Monica Dawson always kept her word. I couldn't muster much enthusiasm for it, though. Still, I put myself through the paces. Taking the cover off the grill, turning on the gas, getting the heat just right, putting on the potatoes wrapped in tin foil, turning the brats. The same routine I'd done a hundred times before, although not so much in recent years. In fact, I remembered the last time with near-perfect clarity: home from college, just before the start of basic training, four years ago almost to the day. Uncle John had been there, along with a couple of my buddies from high school. Mom had fussed over all of us, and we'd gone through quite a few brats and a few beers besides. A fine time was had by all.

Routine usually provided me with some comfort. It was one of the things I liked best about the Army. There was a job to do and you did it, no questions asked, not really. Sure, there was bitching and moaning, but that was par for the course, part of the routine, really. The structure.

Turning the brats today, though, it was different. I didn't draw anything from it, much less comfort. I thought of the last time I'd done this. Was it just three weeks ago? Yes, just before the final mission. A Memorial Day cookout, almost like back home. Burns had gotten one last deer, and the venison was sizzling on our makeshift grill. We went through our last case of non-alcoholic beer and everybody ate till we were stuffed. If the hajis had come across the border that night, they might've added a few Wolverines to the fire. Thinking back on it, my breath caught, and I loosed a sob. I was shocked. That never happened, ever. Even when I lost my NCAA semifinal match sophomore year, ending my quest for the national title, I hadn't cried. I was wiping my eyes with the barbeque mitt when Mom came back onto the deck with plates and silverware.

"You okay, honey?"

"Yeah, Mom. Knee hurts, is all."

She paused, smiling, and touched me on the arm. "It'll get better. It all will."

Mom had kept my room just the way it was when I left for college. There was the poster of Dan Gable on the wall. Next to that, the one of Cael Sanderson, who'd broken Gable's record of collegiate wrestling victories. The two greatest wrestlers in history, men I had thought to emulate. I'd given it my best shot, but by the end of that sophomore season with the Badgers, I knew I'd never get close to them. Maybe that's why leaving college for the Army had been so easy.

What about now? The house was quiet around me. Out on the lake, a loon called. It was a haunting sound, tempting. If I stayed here, I could hear the loons every night, at least until the snow fell. But they'd be back in the spring. They always came back. The lake was eternal. In middle school my science teacher told the class that the lakes of Wisconsin had been formed by the receding glacier, thousands of years ago. If anything would last, it was the lake, the one I'd fished on and swam in since I was a boy. Those were the days, when summer vacation rolled around and the only decisions I had to make were what fun things I was going to do that day.

If I stayed…I hadn't really thought about it, until now. Could it even be done, resignation? Well, sure, but when? I had to stop and think about it. Once I'd accepted my commission as a second lieutenant, I was in for a while. How many years….Finally I remembered: eight. There were some exceptions, I thought, that might allow me to get out early, but they likely weren't easy. I'd have to look it up.

I sat up, thinking I had to get online, check it out. Did Mom still have a PC in the third bedroom, the room that had always been her office and library? I was about to get up and hobble down the hall when I stopped myself.

If I did leave the Army, what would I do? My mother just wouldn't let me move back here and hang out indefinitely. No, Monica Dawson was not the kind of person who tolerated slackers, and I had never been a slacker. So, why was I even contemplating it now? I cursed myself for being such a candy-ass. I'd been given two weeks of convalescent leave to come home after the surgery, and it wasn't as a prelude to getting out of the Army. It was to relax, let the shoulder heal and start rehabbing the knee, get recharged, then get back in the fight, somehow. The Wolverines were done, but the Army would send me somewhere else, and there was always SF training waiting down the road.

That had been the plan, anyway. The shoulder, where it had been hit by that haji AK round, would be fine. The knee was messed up, but not too badly. Torn meniscus, partially torn anterior cruciate ligament. With therapy and exercise, it would come around. Never be the same, of course, and I'd have to wear a brace or a sleeve most of the time in the field, but it could be done. I'd have to demonstrate to the Ranger brass that I could handle myself with the knee never again at full strength, but damn it, it could be done. Would be done. That had been the plan.

I lay back on the bed and stared at the ceiling. I'd run into soldiers who claimed they had mirrors on their bedroom ceilings back home. They were bullshitting, I was pretty sure, but the thought of it made me think of Sam. I hadn't called her since before the firefight in the Kurdish mountains. I owed her that, at least, especially now that I was home. Then I shook my head. I had to think of sex before I thought of her? I cursed myself again, out loud this time, then looked at the door with alarm. Had Mom heard me?

I sat up again, looking at Gable and Sanderson. What would they think of me right now? On the dresser were photos of my grandfather and great-uncle from their Vietnam days. I had never known Grandpa Dennis, but I knew what Uncle John would think if he heard I was considering throwing in the towel. And what about the Rough Rider?

I had to pull my eyes away from the photos, and back to the posters. They were more abstract. One of those guys, I had never met. That was Sanderson, undefeated in four years at Iowa State, four-time national champion, '04 Olympic gold medalist, and now one of the best coaches in the country. The other, I'd gotten to know, if only a little. That was Gable. The summer after my sophomore year in high school, I had traveled down to Iowa City to attend one of the legendary coach's camps. Gable won two national championships in college, losing only one match in three varsity seasons, then he destroyed the field at the Munich Olympics. After that he'd gone on to be one of the greatest

THE HEIGHTS OF VALOR   181

coaches in the history of college athletics. Twenty-one years at Iowa, twenty-one Big Ten titles, fifteen national titles. When Gable talked, young wrestlers listened.

I'd learned more about wrestling in those two weeks in Iowa back in the summer of '06 than I'd learned in the ten years I'd been on the mat. And it was more than just technique. It was about training, about sacrifice, about setting goals and doing everything possible to achieve them, and once you did, you moved on to the next goal. There was one thing Gable had said that weekend that had stuck with me: "Pain is nothing compared to what it feels like to quit."

The pain in my knee was nothing compared to the pain I felt in my gut. I'd wanted to end my last mission with the Wolverines in glory, leading my men to victory over the enemy. I'd wanted to free those Kurds in the village from their ISIS oppressors. That would be my springboard to Special Forces. Their motto was *De Oppresso Liber,* "To Free the Oppressed." Instead, I'd–

But could I quit, over that? A fucking *accident?* I could still see the face of the girl in the window of the ISIS pickup as it charged toward my Humvees. I could still hear the bullets whizzing past me as I got up from cover and charged toward the truck. I could feel the stock of my rifle as I pulled it to my shoulder and prepared to fire at the tires, hoping to slow the truck down so I could deal with the driver and rescue the girl. But I didn't see the round that hit my other shoulder, knocking me off-balance, and I didn't see the rut in the road I'd tripped on.

Could I let a goddamn rut in an Iraqi mountain road make me quit? What would Gable have to say about that? And more than that, what would Charles Dawson think?

"I'll bet the Rough Rider had tougher jams than that to get out of," I said aloud, "and he made it." I felt a rush of hope. Yes, dammit, I'd finish reading the diary. That would give me the juice I needed to get going again. I couldn't very well call Gable on the phone for a pep talk, but I could sure as hell read more about what my own ancestor had done in Cuba. That guy, and his own dad before him, had set the standard that Dawson men still had to meet. And even though I had grown a little tired of hearing about the Rough Rider back in Turkey, right now I needed him.

I got to my feet, felt pain shoot through the repaired knee, took a moment to steady myself with a hand on the back of the chair at my desk, and then hobbled over to my duffel bag. I heaved it onto the bed, ignoring the shoulder's protest, opened the duffel and dumped everything out. Clothes, papers, books, toiletries, a framed photo of Sam, more stuff than I realized I'd taken to Turkey in the first place. I tossed things aside, one after the other.

But the diary was gone.

CHAPTER TWENTY-ONE

Northern Wisconsin
June 2014

The drive to Tomah wasn't the longest one I had ever done, but it was the toughest. The VA Medical Center there was only three hours from Minocqua, but I made it three and a half, including a stop in Wisconsin Rapids to fortify myself at a coffee shop. Adding caffeine to the mix on this hot morning probably wasn't a good idea, but it was better than adding alcohol, that much I knew.

I had a lot to think about on the way. The day before I'd gotten an email, notifying me that I was being promoted to first lieutenant. That was the good news. The other news was that I was to report to Fort Benning no later than 30 June. I hadn't decided yet whether that was good news or bad. Then there was my great-uncle's condition.

On the ride home from the airport in Green Bay, my mother had told me that Uncle John was having some heart problems and was down in Tomah for bypass surgery. It had come on suddenly, as these things sometimes did. Out fishing on the lake one day, some chest pains, a visit to the local ER and then a ride down to Tomah with a buddy, another Vietnam vet who was going there for some tests of his own. That's where the extent of the trouble had been discovered. I'd talked to him a couple times on the phone since arriving home, but hadn't mentioned the missing diary, hadn't talked at all about what I was going through, in fact. But Uncle John didn't miss much, and one day when I was in town, he'd called and talked to Mom. She told him about my depression. When I got home, she laid it out to me.

"Uncle John called, and he's worried about you," she said. "You need to go see him, Jake. He's due to come home tomorrow. You can go down there and bring him back."

"I don't know, Mom, my leg…"

She took two steps and stood in front of me. "I don't want to hear any more of this leg bullshit, Jake. You'll be behind the wheel at seven o'clock in the morning, tomorrow. Do you hear me, Lieutenant?" She looked up at me intently, and I could see she wasn't kidding.

Shocked that my mother would use anything close to profanity, I said the only thing I could. "Yes, ma'am."

It was easy to find the medical center's campus, and I was impressed as I drove up to the main building, a stately facility proudly flying the American flag. I couldn't help wondering if I'd wind up here myself someday. Walking in, I found the registration desk and was directed to the fourth floor. I'd left my crutches in the car and knew the knee wasn't quite ready for all those stairs, so I took the elevator.

I took a right when the doors opened and saw a nurses' station ahead. "I'm here to see John Dawson," I said to the smiling young redhead behind the desk.

"That's right, Mr. Dawson is going home today," she said. "We're going to miss him. Such a funny guy!" She looked up at me. "Are you his grandson?"

"Almost. Grand-nephew."

"Sure. He's in 4020, down the hall and take a right. In fact, you can follow Mr. Anderson, he's right next door." She gestured toward a tall, gray-haired man on crutches who was passing the station. "Larry, could you show Mr. Dawson's grand-nephew to his room, please?"

The old veteran stopped, looked me up and down, and then winked at the woman. "Okay, Julie, but that means you owe me a date."

She laughed. "Larry, you know I've got a boyfriend!"

"Who said he's got to find out?" He nodded to me. "All right, son, see if you can keep up."

It was only when I fell into step that I noticed the left leg of Anderson's sweat pants had no foot extending from it. Anderson must have seen me notice. "Vietnam, 'sixty-nine," he said.

Holy Christ, this guy had been without a leg for, what, forty-five years? "Sorry about that," I said.

"Nothing to be sorry about," the old vet said. "I served under a damn fine officer, Jim Webb. If the people in this country had half a brain, they'd elect him president." He was moving at a pretty good clip. "Have to come here every few years to get my prosthetic adjusted. Every now and then they get me a new one. I'll get one now, just had surgery to fix some of the plumbing in there."

I had read a few things about Webb. "Marines?"

"Damn right," Anderson said. "Have you served, son?"

"Yes, sir," I said. "Army."

"Still in? What's your unit?"

"A special outfit within 75th Rangers, but we just got disbanded, and I'm home on convalescent leave. Got winged in my shoulder and hurt my knee in a firefight."

Anderson stopped and looked down at my legs. "I can tell," he said. "I've seen enough of 'em."

"It's coming along," I said. There was still some pain when I walked, and it must've showed.

"When are you going back?"

"Well, I…"

Anderson squinted at me through his glasses. "Don't tell me you're thinking of hanging it up, are you? Shit fire, boy, we need strapping young bucks like you. Even if you're a candy-ass dogface." He said that last with a grin, showing teeth that were so perfect I assumed they were dentures.

We resumed walking. "Where were you wounded?" the old Marine asked.

"Northern Iraq. Kurdistan," I said.

Anderson grunted as they turned the corner. "My grandson was in Iraq with the Corps."

"How's he doing?"

"He's dead," Anderson said. "Second Fallujah, 'oh-four."

I didn't really have anything to say about that, except another apology, and regretted it as soon I said it. How many times had this fellow heard that about his grandson in the past ten years?

"He died saving his buddies," Anderson said. "Fell on a grenade to protect them. Not much left of him to send home."

We reached Anderson's room, and the old veteran paused at the door. "I go to see him when I can," he said softly, "in the cemetery down in Richland Center."

I struggled to figure out something to say, then blurted out, "When you're there, please say a prayer for him. From me."

Anderson nodded. Behind the glasses, his eyes blinked. Then, he straightened up and extended his hand. "'Preciate it," he said. "I'd ask you to go back over there and take care of the gomers who got him, but his brother Marines finished them off." He gripped my hand. "There's still more of them to take care of, from what I hear."

"Yes," I said, "there are."

"Well, you got to make your own decision about that, son. This is a tough one we're in, over there. Hard work, to be sure. If you're a relation to John, then you're probably not a guy to shy away from hard work." He nodded, then cripped a step over to the next door. It was open, and Anderson didn't bother to knock. "Hey, John, get outta the rack, goddammit, somebody here to see you. Army guy, but I wouldn't hold that against him."

Uncle John had lost some weight since I had deployed. Ten, fifteen pounds, which wasn't a bad thing. But he looked drawn and tired. Well, hell, the man was in his seventies and had just undergone heart surgery a week before. Not major surgery, sure, but it wasn't a simple knee arthroscopy, either.

The old Marine used a cane, although it was clear he didn't like it. My knee was acting up and I caught myself wishing I had a cane of my own right about now, but kept quiet about it. I was honestly glad to see my great-uncle, but the fear of what he'd say when told about the lost diary was never far from my thoughts.

An hour away from Tomah, we'd gone over everything about my

deployment. He wanted to know every detail, and now, with the unit disbanded, I figured to hell with security restrictions and laid it all out for him, including my last firefight. I told him how that had left me, physically, but kept quiet about the emotional side. I could wait on that, because I figured it was time to tell him about the diary. Get it over with, deal with it. I was about to speak when Uncle John asked, "What's new with Sam?"

A reprieve, although not a pleasant one. "I, uh, I haven't seen her," I said.

"Why not? Everything okay?"

"She's in Milwaukee, bridesmaid for a girlfriend's wedding. I've talked to her a couple times since I got back, but she's been pretty busy."

"When's the wedding?"

"Tomorrow."

"She'll be coming home the next day, then?"

"Yeah." I didn't add that Sam had asked me to come down for the weekend. Escort her to the wedding on Saturday, stay the night, head back to Minocqua on Sunday. I'd declined, citing my knee.

John grunted, shifting in his seat. "You still thinking of popping the question?"

"Yeah, I think so. Maybe."

"Well, that sounds just like the decisive young officer the Green Berets are looking for."

I glanced at him. He was gazing serenely out the windshield. "It's complicated, Uncle John," I said.

"Always is. Trust me, I've done it enough times to know."

John Dawson had been married twice, I knew, but neither marriage had lasted beyond five years. The first was when he was in the Marines, post-Vietnam, the second after he left the service. Neither marriage had produced children, something I knew Uncle John deeply regretted. Without ever having to ask, I had always known that was why John had always treated me more like a son than a nephew, grand or otherwise.

We were nearing Wausau, and now I'd swung over again toward delaying the diary revelation, yet another big emotional swing. I wasn't used to those, and I didn't like them, not a damn bit. But I was thinking that we had only an hour or so to go, maybe we could get through the hour without the subject of the diary coming up. Maybe tomorrow would be a better day. Uncle John would be home, he'd be rested, I could go over to his place and we'd talk. Maybe I could tell him about how uncertain I felt about continuing in the Army, much less going for SF. If I had to admit it, I was wavering about that, hour by hour, sometimes almost minute by minute. That wasn't like me at all, and it bothered me. Maybe the firefight and the injury were affecting me a lot more than I thought. Was this what PTSD was like? I shook my head.

"You okay?"

I snapped out of it. "Yeah, fine. Still a little disoriented. Just a couple weeks ago I was in Turkey, prepping for our last mission. Now I'm here."

"Yeah, back in The World," Uncle John said. "I remember the feeling well. My dad, when he came home from Korea, he was on a ship, took him a couple weeks just to get to the West Coast, then a day or so on a train to get home. Lots of time to depressurize for those guys."

"Doesn't sound too bad, really."

"Had its benefits. Say, I'm kind of hungry, what say we stop for a burger? I'll bet you haven't had a real honest-to-God cheeseburger since you got home, hey?"

I grinned, more relieved than amused. "No, I have not. I don't know Wausau, where should we stop?"

"Pick the first place you see. Not a Mickey D's or crap like that. Something authentic."

"Got it." I pointed to a billboard. "Rib Mountain Tap House, how about that one?"

"Looks like a winner," Uncle John said. "Things are looking up, boy. Say, I meant to ask you, did you finish the Rough Rider diary over there?"

"Uh, no. I meant to, but we got pretty busy, and then I got hurt…"

"No problem. You'll have time while you're home, even if Monica puts you to work."

I was silent a moment. It was still five miles to the exit for the restaurant. No way to avoid it. "Say, Uncle John, about the diary…"

"Yeah?"

"I, uh…well, I don't know what happened to it." I risked a glance over at my great-uncle. John was staring straight ahead, but he wasn't smiling anymore. "I didn't get a chance to pack my duffel after getting hurt. Some of the guys did it for me. But the diary…I'm really sorry, Uncle John."

The old Marine was silent for a moment, then he sighed deeply. "Well, shit," he said.

CHAPTER TWENTY-TWO

Northern Wisconsin
June 2014

My mother put me to work, just like Uncle John predicted. Monica Dawson was warm and loving and all the good things I remembered her to be, but I'd forgotten that she could also be a taskmaster. The day after bringing Uncle John home from Tomah, a Saturday, she reminded me.

I had slept in and was pouring milk on my Wheaties when Mom came in, wearing a yellow Packer tee shirt and black yoga pants. "I'm heading into town for class," she said. "I'll ride my bike so you can have the car if you need it. What's on your schedule for today?"

"Well, I was thinking I might go over to the school, see if the weight room's open. The orthopedist told me I could start doing some basic exercises with the knee, and the shoulder feels pretty good."

"That won't take all day, will it?"

"Uh, no..."

"Good!" I knew what was coming, and she was entirely too chipper about it. I desperately needed some coffee. "The lawn could use mowing," she said.

I wondered if the weight room would be any different than it was during my days as a Thunderbird wrestler. Well, hell, it wasn't that long ago. School had been out for a couple weeks, and if I remembered right, the football players wouldn't start drifting in for pre-season lifting till after the Fourth of July. The office was open, just like it always had been on Saturday mornings in my days as a student. Uncle John had once called Lakeland Union a "gung-ho school," and it still was, with office staff frequently coming in Saturday mornings to finish up the week's work and get a head start on next week's. I was told the weight room was open to current students and staff. "How about alumni?" I asked. The secretary was about to say something when a man came out of the office behind her.

"Jake! Hey, welcome back." Tom Welch, the principal, extended a hand. He was a little stockier than I remembered; the golf shirt he wore tucked in didn't help matters. But Welch had been a wrestler in his younger days, so he and I had always gotten along.

"Thanks, Mr. Welch. I'm home for a couple weeks, rehabbing a knee."

"I heard. Well, the weight room's open. Remember the way?"

"Sure do," I said. After another handshake, I hefted my old black T-birds gym bag, rescued from my closet, and headed down the hall. When I realized I was still grinning, it occurred to me that this was the best I'd felt since before the last mission.

Two girls were using the room. They looked awful young, but were probably at least seventeen. They were also pretty toned, in halter tops and short shorts, and they knew what they were doing with the weights. Athletes, obviously. I tried to remember the schedule of spring sports for the girls. Everything was done by now, wasn't it? I hadn't heard anything about Lakeland's softball and soccer teams advancing too far in the playoffs, and the track and field season was ending today at the state meet down in La Crosse.

I pulled off my sweat pants and started stretching. Regular PT with the Wolverines had been pretty old-school, with lots of runs through the mountains and lifting with the basic weights that might have been some of Joe Weider's originals from sixty years before. With nothing much else to do in down time, every one of us had gotten after it, and I was certainly no exception. I hadn't really thought much about it until I noticed the girls glancing at me and whispering. I was finishing a set of goblet squats, using a thirty-pound dumbbell just to take it easy on the knee, when they approached me.

"Hi," the taller one said. She was blonde, with a dusting of freckles around the nose. Her friend was perhaps half-Native, with darker skin and jet-black hair.

"Hello," I said, setting the dumbbell down and grabbing my towel. I was already starting to sweat through my dark green tank-top, which, I now remembered, bore the word ARMY in black across the front.

"We were just wondering," the shorter one said, "if you were the guy from overseas."

"She means, the guy who's from here and just got back," the blonde said, getting a dig in the side from her friend's elbow.

"Word travels fast," I said, extending a hand. "Jake Dawson."

The girls giggled, but gave it their best with the handshakes. They gave their names as Beth and Shania. "Like the singer," the brunette said.

"We're joining up," the blonde said. "The Army, that is."

The bright eyes, the enthusiasm. I remembered it well, although the guys who'd been in my recruiter's group had tried to mask it with typical I'm-too-cool indifference. The women I'd served with displayed it a different way. "Glad to hear it," I said. "The Army's always looking for good people."

"We go to Basic after we graduate next year," Beth said, "and our recruiter said now's the time to start preparing."

"He's right about that," I said, forcing myself not to stare at the sheen of perspiration across Shania's chest. One drop was sliding down between her breasts, in fact. I had to remind myself that I was supposed to be an officer and a gentleman, not to mention that these girls were still minors.

"Well, we're just finishing up," Beth said. "Nice to meet you."

"Any advice?" Shania asked, looking up at me with smoldering green eyes.

I had to focus on the fact that these two young ladies were future soldiers. Someday I might find myself commanding their unit. I had to think like an officer, not like a guy who hadn't slept with his girlfriend in months. Pulling back my shoulders just a bit, I said, "It's going to be the biggest challenge of your lives, but if you hang in there, you'll make it."

"Awesome!" Beth said. There was another round of handshakes, then the girls headed for the door. Shania stopped and gave me one last look, but it wasn't one of seduction. I saw something else there. Admiration, maybe? Certainly her smile wasn't hard to decipher. I'd seen it on teenage girls before, at rock concerts when the singer looked at them from the stage.

I moved on to the bench press, putting a pair of forty-five-pound weights on the bar. Before the wound, I had benched as high as three hundred pounds, but I was going to take it easy now. As the plates clanked into place, I thought of those girls. Could it be that they'd been inspired by me? Was that why they were going in? I settled onto the bench. Had word gotten out about my combat experiences? Well, hell, it was a small town, and my mother had mentioned there'd been a write-up or two in the local paper. And of course there was that Fox News special about my original unit three years ago. But the publicity was one thing. Being an inspiration for somebody, that was something else entirely. In a way, it made me feel good. And as I pushed the barbell up for my first rep, I realized that it felt good to be feeling good about something again.

A blast of cold water at the end of my shower and then two cups of strong coffee were required the next morning before I accompanied Mom to church. I'd been out till midnight, getting together with Nate Fisher, my best buddy from high school. It had been even better than the old days; to the local cinema for the latest Tom Cruise movie, then a pizza joint, and finally capping the night with a stop at a watering hole, something we hadn't been able to do as teenagers. I had watched my alcohol input but was still feeling it as I slipped behind the wheel of Mom's Mazda SUV. "Let's swing by and pick up Uncle John," she said.

"He's going to church?" I asked, surprised and then a little worried. I hadn't spoken to the old Marine since bringing him home from Tomah, two days before.

"He showed up when you started your deployment. Said he needed to put a word in for you, then he just kept showing up."

Uncle John was still a little drawn, but looked better than he had on the drive from the VA hospital. The subject of the Rough Rider diary didn't come up, and that was fine by me; I hadn't yet mustered the courage to tell my mother.

The service was uplifting. I wasn't much of a church-goer as a kid and even less so as an adult, although I'd taken to praying more often. Today, the Gospel lesson had given me a moment when Pastor Mary read from the book of John: "Greater love has no one than this, that he lay down his life for his friends." I choked up as I thought of Chet, lying in that ditch in Iraq, his life draining out into the muddy water as I held him. My mother's hand on my arm gave me the strength to keep it together.

We were enjoying the fellowship hour after the service when my phone buzzed with a text from Sam: *Heading home, c u at 3?*

Taking a deep breath, I tapped out a reply: *Your place or mine?*

Her response was immediate: *Mine! Cant wait!*

I was nervous. I'd thought about this moment for months, wondering what she'd look like, what she'd be wearing, even what she'd smell like. The answers were terrific, a Packer tee and short shorts, and a scent I liked a lot but couldn't place.

But it wasn't just her scent. It was everything about her. All those months overseas, waiting for her emails, her pictures…it was just too much, too quickly. We kissed, we hugged, standing there in her apartment doorway, enjoying the moment. My heart was pounding.

There was so much I wanted to say to her, questions I wanted to ask, answers I might be afraid to hear. But all I could say was, "You smell good."

"It's lavender. Part of my gift package from the bride. Special soaps. You like it?"

I'd never much cared one way or another about things like scented soaps, or perfume on a woman, or cologne on me, for that matter, but now I realized that I might want to change my thinking. After so many months of odors that were, well, definitely not lavender, this was a nice change of pace. Even better than my mom's house, which by itself was a vast improvement over Turkey. "Yeah," I finally said. "I like it. A lot."

She looked up at me with her head tilted in that just-so way that had first tugged at me, back in freshman year study hall. She was the new girl, just moved to town from Eagle River, and she'd been wearing a–

"You want to talk soap, or you want to go to bed?" she asked.

The afternoon sun streamed through the window. From the bed, I couldn't get a full view, just a part of the field beyond the building, a stand of trees at the edge. Down the hall, the toilet flushed. Sam padded barefoot back to the bedroom, leaving the door open, and slid into the bed alongside me. Her fingertips flicked through my chest hairs. "You've got more," she said.

"More what?"

"This," she said, pulling on a hair. "But I'm not sure I like how they curl around your nipples now." She shifted her head, dipping her tongue onto my left nipple, sending a jolt all the way down my leg. "Oh boy," she said, noticing, then reaching lower. "Might be a little hairier, but they're still your 'on' switch." She flicked the tongue again, then lowered her mouth, taking the nipple lightly in her teeth.

"Sam…"

She looked up, tongue still working. "Yeth?"

"Can we just…talk?" I surprised himself just by saying it. Saying no to a second time at bat? That had never happened, and Sam noticed.

"Wow. Okay. In fact, there's something I wanted to talk about, too."

Whatever thoughts I might've had about another go-round vanished. "Uh, you first," I said.

She smiled, shaking her head. "Nope. You started it, soldier boy, so talk."

I turned onto my side, facing her, as much to give myself a few extra seconds to think as to get a better view of her. All during my time overseas, I'd wondered if I was truly in love with Sam. Sometimes it seemed to change by the day. And there were some days, I had to admit, when I was so busy that I barely thought of her. Was that how it should be, if I was in love? Shouldn't I be thinking of her all the time? It was so damn confusing, up until the moment she opened her door, and then I knew. It had hit me like nothing I'd ever felt. And now I was with her, in our own private little cocoon. Even more private than before; Sam's roommate had moved back home to Oshkosh. No upcoming mission to worry about, no Iranian commandos to obsess over. No burden of a family legacy to shoulder. There was, however, a future out there, and whether Sam would be in mine or not was the question. It was time to face that.

But I needed time to get the words just right, so I decided to stall. "How's work going?"

She blinked, surprised. Sam was director of human resources for one of the county's largest employers, on the fast track to upper management. Her talents went way beyond the bedroom, one of the many things I admired about her. She'd kicked ass on the softball diamond in high school and then in college at St. Norbert, now she was kicking ass in business.

"Good," she said. "I got a raise last month. But do you really want to talk shop? Out with it, Lieutenant."

She knew me too well. No way to avoid it now. "I, uh…well, I'm thinking of getting out of the Army."

She gave me another look. Surprise, again? Pleasure? Both? After a moment, she asked, "Can you even do that?"

"Not right away," I said. "Once I graduated OCS, I committed to at least three years, plus another three or four in the Reserves." I was pretty sure about that, anyway, but I'd have to do some more checking. Even as I said it, though, I felt a surge of emotions. Confusing, even troubling. I'd always enjoyed being in the Army, yet here I was, thinking of getting out, and I couldn't really put a finger on the reason. I'd gone so far as to talk to my mother about it the day before. She'd told me to follow my heart, but make sure that whatever path I chose, to go forward and not look back.

"I've been thinking about the future," I blurted out, "and I want you in it. But I don't know if I can make it work…if *we* can make it work, if

I stay in. Especially if I go Special Forces. I'd be deployed a lot. It'd be a hard life for you."

She was gliding a hand over my arm, but not looking at me. She was blinking. Holding back tears? A flash of panic shot through me.

"I worried about you all the time when you were gone," she said softly. A tear drifted down her cheek and onto the pillow. "I talked to your mom a lot. She was dealing with it better than I was. There were a lot of nights I was over at your house, just the two of us. We went through a few bottles of wine." She smiled, finally looking up at me, eyes wet. "A lot of tears. I couldn't have gotten through it without her." She reached over and touched my face. "I love you, Jake. I want to be with you, but I just...I just don't know if I can take it if you're gone so much. I don't know if I'm that strong." Another pause, a sob, and the tears came faster. "You're a warrior, Jake. You always have been. And a warrior needs a strong woman beside him."

I felt like I was having a heart attack. This was another side of Sam, one I hadn't really seen before. Or maybe I just hadn't recognized it. "Hey," I said, tipping her chin up, using a thumb to wipe away a tear. "You're stronger than you think, babe."

"You...you think so?"

"Yeah. That's one big reason why I love you."

She smiled, and my world lit up. She squeezed me tightly, and I held her, never wanting to let her go.

CHAPTER TWENTY-THREE

Northern Wisconsin
June 2014

I was making my bed when the thought hit me: This could be the last time I'll ever do this. Well, this particular bed, at least. Tomorrow morning, Mom would have me strip the sheets and take them to the laundry room. A few hours after that and Uncle John would come by to pick me up for the drive to the airport in Green Bay. And from there, it was back to the Army, and who knew what would happen?

Special Forces seemed a long way away. After coming home from Sam's the night before, I'd tossed and turned till nearly midnight. Stay in and go for SF, or just go back and get out as soon as possible? I hadn't told Sam I was leaning one way or another. In the end, I decided to just let things play out. Keep an open mind. But I had to admit, deep down inside, that I was leaning away from the Green Beret route. As much as I loved the Army, and I had long ago realized that I did love it, something told me that making SF a career would be too tough on Sam, too hard for our future. It would be hard enough as it was, especially now that I'd made a decision about that future. At least I'd been able to make up my mind about that. Of course, there was always the possibility she would turn me down…

But I shrugged that thought away. This was my last day at home, and I wanted to make it a good one. Mom had the day off. Sam would be coming over later that afternoon, and we'd grill some steaks and enjoy the evening with my mother and my great-uncle. My family. Yes, Sam was a part of that now. I intended to make that official, which was why I wanted to get the bed taken care of. It was already seven o'clock, and I needed to get in a run. The knee was really coming around, and I wanted to push it more today, give it a real workout, see where it was.

The jewelry store opened at nine. I'd be too antsy to have breakfast at home, so I'd head downtown early, stop by the coffee shop for a bite, and wait for that door to open.

My orders were sending me back to the 75th Ranger Regiment at Fort Benning, and I had a slot in the next Reconnaissance Surveillance Leaders Course. If I passed that, next up was a billet in Task Force Red. Maybe not as good as Special Forces, but the next best thing. And if I decided not to go for SF, I could serve out my contract, maybe have one or two more deployments before it was done, and that would be it. Sam and I could move back to Wisconsin and I could start enjoying civilian life. Exactly what I'd wind up doing was a question that would have to be answered eventually, but not now.

I puffed the pillow one last time and stood back to admire my handiwork. Not bad. Bed-making hadn't been my strong suit as a kid, but the Army had changed that, as it had so many things. Make your bed every morning, I'd heard somewhere, and even if you wind up having a shitty day, at least you will have done one thing right. There was a lot of truth in that.

My eyes flicked to the night stand, and there was the book, pages yellowed and dog-eared. *The Green Berets.* Whenever I'd read it, I imagined myself wearing the beret. The moment I would put it on, that would be something. I'd be one of the elite warriors of my nation, like my grandfather. I hadn't really known about the Rough Rider back then. Grandpa Dennis' legacy was enough for me. Now, put Two-Fist and the Rough Rider in the line, and it was very heavy indeed. I felt a small sense of relief. Goodbye to all that. Too bad about the diary, but that was the breaks.

Something tingled, deep inside me. A sixth sense, like I'd had a few times in the field. Something was *there.* From the corner of my eye, I caught movement near the door. A flash of dark blue, a slouch hat…

I whirled around. Nothing. I sat down on the bed. Holy Christ, was I starting to crack up? Was it PTSD? I fought to control my breathing. No, it had to be the stress of the day, what I was planning. A big step, the biggest…

The house phone rang and Mom answered, but I couldn't hear the conversation. A minute later I padded barefoot out to the kitchen, just as she was hanging up. "Anybody I know?" I asked.

She had a wry smile, a look I'd never really seen before from her. "Yes," she said. "We'll have an extra guest for dinner."

"Who?"

"Can't say, it's supposed to be a surprise."

People recognized me on my run. I'd been noticing that since the first one, a week ago. They waved, said hello, shouted encouragement. This morning I turned a corner a half-mile from home and there was Mrs. Brunner, waiting for me with a glass of lemonade.

"How'd you know I was coming?" I asked before taking that first delicious sip.

"Laurie Passard called me, said she saw you run past her house, and I had a pitcher ready to go in the fridge." Mrs. Brunner had gotten a little thicker since my high school days, but she had the same merry smile she'd displayed when handing out chocolate-chip cookies to her son Mike and his friends, including me.

"How's Mike doing?" I asked, after downing half the glass.

"Just fine. Loves the Navy. Got an email from him last night, said he's sorry he missed you. Also said to remind you that Navy will kick Army's butt in the game this year, again."

I laughed, drained the glass and handed it back. "Tell him we'll see about that. Thanks for the lemonade."

She placed a hand on my arm. "God be with you when you go back over there, Jake. You're helping keep us safe. We'll be praying for you back here. Never forget that."

Stunned, my eyes misted. I blinked a couple times, then said, "Thanks, Mrs. B. I really appreciate it." I gave her a hug, then loped away. My God, these people were counting on me. If I got out early, would I be letting them down?

Sam arrived around one, resplendent in a yellow sun dress that emphasized her shoulders and her shapely legs. One of the things I had always liked about Sam was her commitment to fitness. She'd started serious training in her high school volleyball and softball days and that continued through her time in college, where she led the St. Norbert softball team to a conference title as a senior. And now she was back in her hometown. Sam had truly blossomed from the somewhat gawky sixteen-year-old I'd first dated. My heart damn near leaped out of my chest when I saw her get out of her car in the driveway.

We hugged. "You look great," I said.

"Thank you." She pinched my bicep. "And you ain't so bad yourself, soldier boy."

My heart was racing for more reasons than just the sight of her. The lump in the pocket of my shorts was an ever-present reminder of what I wanted to do. Best to get it over with before losing my nerve. "Let's say hello to Mom, then I need to show you something down at the lake," I said.

A few minutes later, we were digging our bare toes into the sand. My mother had about a hundred feet of lakefront at this end of the lot, not bad for around here. When we'd moved in ten years before, I had cleaned away the scrub and landscaped the frontage for her. It still wasn't much of a beach, but it was ours, by God, and I'd always loved coming down here. Our small dock extended twenty feet out into the water, and our canoe bobbed alongside it. I'd wondered if it would be a good idea to paddle Sam out onto the lake for the big moment, but had decided to do it here. The last thing I wanted was to stumble in the canoe and tip us over.

"I've always loved the lake," she said, gazing outward. "So peaceful."

"Yeah." It came out as a croak. I cleared my throat, reaching into the pocket. It was now or never. "Uh, Sam, there's something I wanted to ask you."

She turned to me, eyes focused on mine. "Yes?"

"Hold that thought," I said. Taking a deep breath, I took her hand. "I, uh…before I ship out tomorrow, I wanted to give you something."

She blinked. Oh God, she knew. I pulled the little box out. I'd rehearsed this, but not out loud. Suddenly I felt an immense pressure. My entire life was focused right here, right now, with this woman. If she said no, I didn't know what I'd do. But that was a risk I was willing to take.

I started to get down on one knee, but it zinged, reminding me to use the healthy knee. "Ouch! Dammit," I said, and Sam giggled. I made it safely down to the other knee, regained my balance and what I hoped was some semblance of dignity befitting the occasion. I cleared my throat again. "What you said yesterday, about me needing a strong woman beside me, you were absolutely right. And I…I want you to be that woman. I need you, Sam. I love you." I flipped open the box and held it up for her. "Will you marry me?"

My first big surprise that day was that she actually said yes. From the moment I walked into the jewelry store that morning, I feared she might very well say no. Or at the least, "Not yet." But she cried and shouted her acceptance to the sky, and we hugged and kissed, and then she insisted we go back to the house so she could show my mom. And there were more tears and hugs all around.

The second surprise came later when I was on the deck, firing up the grill for the day's meal. Bison steaks, a little pricey but damn tasty and healthy besides. I was feeling good, maybe better than I'd ever felt. Mom and Sam were in the kitchen, getting the potatoes and dessert ready and undoubtedly making wedding plans. The sky was filled with puffy white clouds. Were the Brewers playing today? Maybe I should set up the radio. I was actually whistling, so I didn't hear the sound of the car pulling up to the front of the house, or the knock on the front door. But I heard the whoosh of the sliding glass door leading onto the deck, and thought it might be Uncle John. I'd forgotten all about what my mother had said earlier that morning. So when I turned to see, it took a moment before my brain could actually believe what my eyes were seeing.

"Hello, Jake," my father said.

"Dad."

It had been a year since I'd seen my father, and it might as well have been five years ago, by the way he looked. Dad was thinner than ever, the hair had more gray, but at least he'd cut it shorter. His eyes looked a little hollow, but they glistened. "I'm so glad to see you, son," he said.

Impulsively, I walked over and embraced him. "Dad," I said again, and in spite of myself, I felt the tears coming, and I didn't want to stop them this time. Through the doorway, I saw my mother and Sam, and they were wiping their eyes, too.

When I stepped back, I said, "Well, this must be the surprise Mom talked about."

"Yeah, I suppose it is. I heard you were shipping out tomorrow, and I wanted to see you."

Everything I had always felt about my father, all the negative crap, it all seemed to melt away. It was like a weight was lifting off my shoulders. "I'm glad you came," I said, and I meant every word.

"And, I have something to give you." He reached for an envelope, sticking up from the pocket of his shirt. I hadn't noticed it. "This came in my mail the other day. I called Monica, she said you were home and invited me up."

The return address was from Cut Bank, Montana. "'The Murphys,'" I read. "Chet's parents?"

Dad shrugged. "I remember you mentioning a Murphy you served with, in one of your letters from Iraq." What he didn't say was that it had to have been one of the very few I'd bothered to write him back then. That brought a momentary pang of guilt, but it passed quickly. I hadn't made it to Chet's funeral, but I'd written one letter to the family. They sent me a nice note back. How long ago, now? Three years?

I tore the envelope open. Inside was a single sheet of paper, hand-written on both sides.

Dear Jake,

I hope this letter gets to you. I'm sending it to your father. I remember Chet mentioning that your dad was a professor at the

University of Wisconsin, so I looked him up. I'm sorry that I no longer have your letter that you wrote after Chet's death.

Chet's mother passed away last year, and things have been pretty rough for me since then. She had breast cancer and it caught fire pretty quickly. Not much could be done. I have been pretty lost since then, we were married 35 years. I'm trying to put my life back together. Chet's brother and sister have been a big help. Jerry has moved back here to the ranch to help me and Jill comes up from Butte when she can. She's given me two grandkids and they're pretty special to me.

I am very proud of Chet's service, and he wrote often about his friendship with you and how much it meant to him, how you met in boot camp and how you helped him along the way. From what I'm told, you tried to save his life. Knowing that there is a man out there willing to risk his life to save my son means a lot to me. Tells me what kind of man you are and how you were raised.

He said that your goal was to be a Green Beret. I hope you realize that goal. My older brother was a Green Beret and he's twice the man I'll ever be. He's helped people all over the world fight for their freedom and that's about the best any man could hope to do for his fellow man. God knows we need men like that now more than ever.

Good luck and if you ever get up to this part of Montana, come visit us, you're always welcome.

Sid Murphy

I sat quietly for a few minutes after finishing the letter. My father had gone inside, giving me some solitude. I looked out at the lake. A fish leaped up, then splashed back down. I thought of Chet, how we met, how we helped each other out during OSUT, the good times we shared. And I thought about Chet's last mission. Its outcome had been driving me for three years, pushing me to stay in the fight, finish the job. But would it ever be finished? Yes, it would, someday. It had to end, and I knew how I wanted it to end, my part of it, anyway. What it all came down to, I knew, was what kind of a role I was going to play in it. I could let someone else do the heavy lifting, take the biggest risks.

Or, I could get in there and do the job myself.

The loons were starting their evening calls when my father and I cleaned up the grill. Inside, the women were putting the dishes in the washer and Uncle John was making another visit to the head. I was pleased that my great-uncle had downed only one beer, but this one seemed to pass through more quickly than they used to. "Just renting it," Uncle John had said with a wry grin.

We rolled the grill back to its spot under the eave and put the cover back on. "Well, that's that," I said. "I wonder how long it'll be before I'm uncovering it."

"There'll be a next time," Dad said. He turned and faced the lake. "It's so different up here from down there."

"In Madison? Hey, you've got a couple of pretty nice lakes there."

"Yeah, but it's not the same as up here." He looked at me with a grin. "Not that I'll be moving up here, you understand."

"You could visit more often, maybe," I offered. "Your uncle isn't getting any younger."

"No, he isn't," Dad said, looking back at the lake. "Neither am I."

The conversation over dinner had been light and friendly. Dad and John had embraced when the old Marine arrived, and there was another round of misty eyes for all. I enjoyed it all immensely, especially the way my father had carried on with Sam. They'd met only once before, in the summer of '06, when I took her to one of Dad's campaign events in Sheboygan. He hadn't thought very much of her then, as I recalled, but neither of them seemed to remember that now. Sam had come up to me when Dad went inside for a minute. "Your dad is so cool," she said.

And now here I was with the dad I'd never thought of as cool. But something had changed about him, something I couldn't put my finger on. We stood next to each other at the edge of the deck, looking at the lake. After a minute of silence, Dad looked at his watch. "Wow, it's getting late. I'd better hit the road, long drive ahead."

"You could stay," I said. "Take my room. I'll bunk on the couch."

Dad turned to face me. "That's okay, son." He looked away, then back at me. "You're leaving tomorrow, right?"

"Yeah, Dad, I am. Back to the Rangers."

"And what about Special Forces? That comes later?"

I couldn't look my father in the eye. Instead, I turned back to the lake, leaning on the rail. "I might be able to get into the class that starts in October. I don't know. I might just get out when my contract is up. I'm kind of pushing my luck as it is."

Silence. Then, a hand on my shoulder. "Jake, look at me."

My father's eyes were sharp. There was something in there, something I had never seen, a force of some kind. It surprised me.

"My father…" Dad blinked, turned away, turned back. "He was proud to be a Green Beret. I know he was, my mother told me. He always wanted his sons to follow him. Well, John went to the Marines, he didn't have the aptitude for the Green Berets, and I went…" He chuffed what could have been a bitter laugh. "I went into politics."

"But, Dad…you served your country, too. Just in a different way." Where had I heard that before? Oh, yeah…but back then, on that summer day in Madison, I had written it off. Now, I didn't.

Dad nodded, sniffed, then rubbed his nose with the back of his hand, a gesture I had seen from Uncle John many times. "Yeah, for what it was worth. I did what I could. Did what I thought was right." He looked back at me. "After you came to see me in Madison, I did something I should've done a long time ago. I went and talked to some people, men who had been Green Berets. I actually found a few guys my own dad served with, can you believe it? They were fine men, all of them. Proud of their service. Proud to have…" His voice choked. "To have served with my father."

I didn't know what to say. Maybe because I was afraid to say anything.

Dad smiled, and I could see him mustering up his courage. I had never thought of my father as a courageous man, and in fact, I had sometimes thought he was exactly the opposite. As those memories ripped through me, I felt a sudden weight of shame.

He took a deep breath. "Son, one reason I came up here was to see you before you left. But, I also wanted to tell you that I'm proud of you. My son is a soldier. And when he puts on that Green Beret, he'll be fighting to free the oppressed, just like his grandfather."

I hesitated, then said, "I don't know if Sam wants me to, Dad." I looked away, toward the lake, down at the little beach. "It would be hard on her."

"She's tougher than you think, Jake. Don't sell her short." Dad stepped back and offered his hand. "Do they have a graduation ceremony for Special Forces?"

I couldn't remember the last time my father and I had shaken hands. I was surprised at the strength of his grip. "Yes, they do," I said.

"Good. Make sure to let me know. I'll be there."

CHAPTER TWENTY-FOUR

Camp Mackall, N.C.
December 2014

"You are lower than dog shit! Even the filthy swine would shit on you!" The hand rocketed toward my face, but I was helpless to stop it, could barely turn my head to reduce the impact. It was just an open palm, thank God, a fist would've broken my jaw. Be thankful for small favors, a part of my brain whispered, because this was a place with damn few favors of any kind.

"Take this pig back to the other pigs! Bring me the next one!"

Blood flowed down into my eyes. The whisperer said it was just a forehead cut, they bled but didn't disable, I'd make it. My hands were tied behind me, so I couldn't wipe the blood away. The guy must've been wearing a ring. His West Point ring, maybe? No, not here. Wasn't a West Pointer anyway. No West Point over in Afghanistan, or Iran, wherever the hell he was from. His madrassa ring? I laughed. Did they give out rings? Did they have football teams? "U rah rah," I mumbled, "Tehran U…"

"Quiet, pig! Back in with the other swine!" I was hurled into a dark space, banging my head against the wooden wall. I slumped to the scabby floor, fighting to stay conscious. It was so hard, I was so hungry. Thirst clutched at me like a cobra. It was cold, damp, they couldn't have made it any more miserable, but they would try. This was worse than that village in Kurdistan, and I had thought that couldn't be possible.

The box was maybe four feet on each side. I had to sit cross-legged, could never get comfortable. How long had I been here? Two days, three? I tried to focus, to remember. Three days out in the forest, on the run. Hunger was a constant threat. Thank God I'd paid attention during the opening days of SERE training—survival, evasion, resistance, escape. My buddy proved adept with a snare and we caught a rabbit. I dispatched it with a chop to the back of its neck. Billy found a sharp rock and we used it to hack the rabbit up, skin it, then roast the meat over a fire. That sustained us for the next twenty hours, until we were caught and brought here, to this camp.

I shook my head, trying to think clearly. I was starting to lose track of time. No calendars here, no wristwatches, sure as hell no smart phones. I tried to focus on something concrete, something I could remember with clarity. It was a struggle, but I found it: the day I proposed to Sam. The lake, Sam kissing me. It was so warm that day, so peaceful. The lake, the house, the barbecue. My family. My father, with his stunning plea for me to try for Special Forces, regardless of my doubts. How long ago? Six months. So much had happened since then, all of it bringing me right here, to this goddamn box in this goddamn camp with these SOB guards…

We were given two meals a day, if you could call them that. Rice, some bits of what might've been meat, might've been grubs for all I knew. There were a dozen other men here besides me and Billy. Two of them had come down with some form of dysentery. One of them was three boxes down and he must've just shit himself again. The smell was awful. The guy was sobbing.

Somebody pounded on the top of my box. "American pig! You, the officer. You must tend to your man. Get out here!"

The door to my box was lifted open. I crawled out, stood on shaky legs, remembered to bow. That was the toughest part for me, bowing to these bastards. Two of them stood there, swaddled up in their scarves, holding AKs. Just like I'd seen in Iraq. One of them, the taller one, was the guy who'd been giving me the most grief. He motioned with his rifle. "Down there. Take him out and clean him up."

The other guard pulled open the box three doors down. The smell was even more intense. The man crawled out, sniffling. It was Carson, the sergeant from St. Louis. Football star, I remembered hearing, some big school, but grades washed him out. He found his calling in the

Army, put in for SF training. He'd done well, up till now. There were other officers among the prisoners, weren't there? Where the hell were they? Why had I gotten stuck with this duty?

At gunpoint, I helped Carson over to the latrine. Another guard stood there with a garden hose. Carson was sobbing again. I struggled to help him along, finally snugging an arm around the guy's waist. "It's okay, buddy, we'll take care of it. No problem."

"I'm…I'm sorry, LT."

"Don't worry about it."

The butt of a rifle slammed into my shoulder. "No talking, pig!" I dropped to one knee, struggled to shake off the pain. He'd hit it right on the wound, of course. Drive on, my instructors had told me over and over. I had to drive on now. Carson was depending on me. Nobody else was stepping up to help. It was my responsibility now. Drive on.

I got Carson to the latrine, helped him pull his pants down, used the hose to wash him as best I could. The guy's pants were a mess, but everybody else's were, too, although maybe not this bad. Our uniforms and boots had been taken from us when we got to the camp, replaced with baggy pants and shirts. No boots anymore, just the most uncomfortable sandals I had ever worn, way too small. Nobody had been given their correct size, another mind game from the guards.

We left the latrine but were told by one of the guards to stand in place. The rest of the prisoners were being rousted up and mustered. The sun was low in the afternoon sky and it was getting colder. We were shivering, drawing laughter from the guards. The other guy with dysentery was struggling to stand, failed and sank to his knees, crying as an ugly ripping sound came from behind him. This was inhumane, it was beyond comprehension. I was an officer in the greatest army the world had ever seen, and by Christ I was not going to stand for this anymore.

"I want to see the commanding officer," I said to the tall guard.

The man looked at me, incongruous blue eyes staring through the gap in his scarf. "What for, pig?"

"My men need medical attention. You are duty bound to provide it."

The guards looked at each other and laughed. The tall one motioned to the next guard. "Bring Mullah Akeem. The filthy American swine wants to talk to him."

"It is close to *Maghrib,*" the guard said. "He will not be pleased."

"Then he can take that out on the American." The second guard nodded and walked off, across the yard toward a low building I knew to be the camp headquarters. I also knew *Maghrib* was the time for sunset prayers, when all these ragheads would be pulling out their rugs and facing Mecca. The prisoners had been forced to watch the guards pray five times a day. Enough guards abstained from the prayers to keep an eye on us. But when a few of the Americans had taken a moment at a meal to pray, we were cuffed around by the guards.

I had to force myself to think clearly, as clearly as it was possible to do for a guy desperately hungry and thirsty. I'd lost weight in recent weeks, and the conditions here weren't exactly conducive to working out, even if I'd had the strength. I saw the guard knock at the commandant's door. I glanced behind me. The other prisoners were watching. One of them caught my eye, then looked away. He was a captain, senior in rank to me, but he'd bailed on taking any sort of command from the moment he'd been thrown into his box. The other guy? No sign of him. There was a retching sound from one of the boxes. Maybe that was him.

So, I was on my own. The men were counting on me. I tried to remember training, the stories we'd heard from Vietnam War POWs. What had one of them said? Ellis, that was the guy's name, Lee Ellis. It snapped into my mind with perfect clarity.

"Leading with honor is about doing the right thing," I whispered, "even when it entails personal sacrifice."

A memory came back. My grandfather had sacrificed, he damn sure had. He'd been a leader, and he sacrificed his life for his men. The least I could do now was speak up for mine, even if it meant a beating, even if it meant that goddamn box. My grandfather wore the Green Beret. At one time, I doubted if I had what it would take to earn one of my own. It was time to find out.

The door opened and the commandant stepped out. Average height, average build. I knew I could take him hand-to-hand, even in my current condition, but that's not what this would be about. The officer walked briskly toward me. A breeze caught one end of his *keffiyeh* scarf, pulling it away from the bottom of his face, and I saw the smile.

The commandant stopped four feet away, carefully out of my reach, and he was flanked by two guards. "You are the officer pig?"

"First Lieutenant Jacob Dawson, United States Army. Sir…" I had to pause, my mouth was so dry. I tried to work up some saliva, got a smidgen. "Under Article 29 of the Geneva Convention, I request that my men be afforded conveniences which conform to the rules of hygiene. Also, under Article 30, you are required to provide prisoners with adequate medical treatment. Two of my men are suffering from dysentery. I request that they be immediately transported to a medical facility for prop–"

The commandant stepped forward and slapped me across the face. "I will tell you what I will do for your men, pig. I will get for them copies of the Geneva Convention and let them wipe their asses with it. Will that be all, Lieutenant?" He stepped back and sneered. "Or do you have any other requests? I can relay them to my superiors in Tehran."

That last slap was the hardest yet. I shook my head to clear the fog, then stared at the commandant. *Tehran.* Part of the mind-fuck games they played here, and they knew my service jacket backwards and forwards. They knew what my buttons were and how to push them. Well, by Christ, he wasn't the only one who knew how to push a button. "Yes," I said. "Would the commandant be so kind as to tell his mother that I really enjoyed our time together? In Tehran. She has big nipples, doesn't she? But maybe you don't remember."

The tall guard rammed the butt of his AK into my gut. Even though I saw it coming, I couldn't absorb the blow. I collapsed with a loud grunt and my head bounced off the hard ground. I saw stars. Through the haze of pain I heard the commandant scream at the guards, felt myself lifted up and frog-marched back to the boxes. Just before they threw me inside, I saw one of the Americans looking at me. The man's eyes were tearing up, but his head was held high.

We were marching again. At least this time without bags over our heads, but the routine was the same. Single file, left hand on the shoulder of the man ahead, forced to march in step. Left, right, left, right. Every time our left feet hit the ground, we had to chant, "Boots!" Men who stumbled or failed to chant were taken out of the line, slapped around, insulted. One time the rest of us were forced to watch as the soldier singled out for special treatment knelt in front of us and repeated the vile epithets hurled at him by the guards.

We were supposed to figure out how to escape, but as I marched around the yard, looking out at the fence and the guard towers, each one sporting a menacing heavy machine gun, I knew escape was impossible. The guards watched us like hawks. The men were in no physical condition that would allow them to stage any kind of revolt. It would be suicide to try. The best thing was to just wait it out. But could we even begin to tolerate that?

The interrogations were the worst. Each of us was taken away to a small room, questioned relentlessly, slapped around, threatened with execution. "Sign this confession, pig, and you will have a much better cell. Better food. No work." I refused every time, but I wondered, had any of the other men broken? I hadn't noticed anyone taken away, separated from the group of POWs. So far, we had hung tough, but how long could that last?

I thought of Sam all the time, waiting for me back in Wisconsin. The wedding was set for next fall. In her last email, Sam had talked about honeymoon plans. How about going up to Isle Royale in Lake Superior? A week of hiking and camping and making love. Most women would've sneered at that kind of honeymoon, insisted on a luxury resort somewhere in the Caribbean, but not Sam. Her idea all the way. Even though I'd spent more than enough time out in the field, I told her sure, whatever she wanted. God, how I loved her. I was beginning to wonder when—if—I'd see her again. Christmas was coming up, wasn't it? Maybe we could move the wedding up. After the wedding came the wedding night. What I wouldn't give to feel her body next to mine right now…

A commotion burst out, up ahead in the line. Carson had gone down again. The toughest man in the group to start with, he'd had it the worst. It was the dysentery, I knew. Could've happened to any of us. The guards called a halt as Carson sagged to his knees, then onto his side in the dirt. Three men behind him, I broke ranks and went to my soldier's aid. A guard approached. "Back in line, pig!"

I ignored him and knelt next to Carson. "It's okay, buddy. We're all here for you."

Carson's brown eyes were wide with fear as he looked up at me. "LT, I can't do it no more. I'm done."

"Hang in there," I said. "Don't let the bastards get to you."

A hand grabbed me by the shoulder and shoved me away. "Leave him alone, pig American!" the guard sneered. "If he dies, he dies."

That was it. I'd had enough. "Fuck you!" I yelled. This particular guard, the tall one, had been in my face ever since we were hauled in. My grandfather wouldn't have taken this guy's bullshit and now I was done with him. I struggled to get up. I had hardly any strength left, but what I had was going to be used right goddamn now on this bastard.

The guard stepped back, leveling his rifle at me. "Back in line, pig!"

I got up to one knee. "No," I said. "I'm done taking your shit. Go ahead and shoot me, you son of a bitch. Or you can put down that chickenshit gun and we can settle this like men." That got to him. I stood up. "Or maybe you're not a man after all. Everybody here knows you got no balls." I took a step toward him. "Come on, tough guy. Let's get it on."

The guard raised his rifle to his shoulder and aimed. Behind me, I could hear some of the POWs gasping. "Don't do it, LT," one of them said. But another said, "Kick his ass!" And others chimed in.

The moment stretched out. The camp loudspeaker was blaring its usual bullshit, Islamist propaganda interspersed with the chants of American and European antiwar demonstrators. At night it was different: the loudspeaker brayed a constant refrain of crying children, women screaming and calling out the names of their loved ones, young girls begging for their daddies to come save them. It was all but impossible to get any sleep. I had the idea that I would take out this guard, the men would kill the others and we would be free, but before we left the camp I was going to destroy that goddamn loudspeaker.

The electronic chanting stopped, and after a tense moment it was replaced by a man's voice, speaking English, with an American accent. "Attention!"

Years of training snapped into place. I stepped back, put my heels together, threw my shoulders back. All of the soldiers were ramrod straight, even Carson, who had been helped up by two of his comrades. We faced the guards. They were staring back at us, but their expressions had changed. The hatred was gone.

"About face!"

I turned with the rest of the men. At the far end of the camp, next to the gate, a guard was at the flagpole. The black flag with the Arabic lettering was coming down. Another guard took it off the line, and my heart skipped a beat as a different flag replaced it. The first guard pulled hard on the line. Halfway up, a breeze caught the fabric, and the Stars and Stripes unfurled. Carson began to sob, and he wasn't alone. "Praise God," one of the men said.

"Present arms!"

I snapped into the best salute I could muster as tears streamed down my face.

"Secure from SERE training!"

CHAPTER TWENTY-FIVE

Camp Mackall, N.C.
January 2015

"Mail call, bro. Something for you today."

I sat back in the chair, rubbing my eyes. On my lap, the thick training folder started to slide toward the floor. I caught it just in time. It wouldn't do to have all those papers scattered all over the floor of our quarters. If a cadre sergeant ordered me to produce my folder and it was a mess, I'd be in trouble. Well, hell, it would only make my pile of shit a little higher, wouldn't it?

Blinking my vision clear, I looked at my roommate. Chuck Larson was as chipper as always. He probably smiled all day long when he was tossing hay bales on his dad's farm in Iowa. Nothing ever seemed to get him down. It was a trait I sometimes found annoying, but other times, like now, I thought it would be a pretty good attitude to have. We'd just gotten through some of the toughest training in the Q Course and Chuck looked like we'd just come back from a day at the beach.

"Another CARE package?"

"Nope." With a dramatic flair, Larson reached into a thigh pocket of his BDUs and pulled out a thick envelope. I reached for it, but he pulled the envelope away. "Just a sec," he said, putting it up to his nose and taking a deep sniff. "No perfume. My granddad said Grandma always put perfume on the envelope when she wrote to him in 'Nam." He handed it over. "Sorry, buddy."

I snatched the envelope, curiosity getting the better of annoyance. The return address was Madison. "It's from my dad," I said. "I've gotten some emails from him, but not a real letter."

"I'll leave you to it," Larson said. On his way out the door, he said,

"See you in the DFAC."

"Yeah, I'll be there. Don't want to miss evening chow." I put my folder aside carefully, then used my knife to slit the envelope open, trying to avoid slicing the letter inside. I couldn't remember the last time I'd actually opened an envelope, and never with a combat knife. I managed to get the job done and leave both the letter and my fingers intact.

One page, typed, and folded around another envelope, unmarked and sealed. I stared at it, then put it aside, unfolded my father's letter and began to read.

January 21, 2015

Dear Jake,

I'm going old-school on this letter because I'm sending along another one to you. Actually, it's a copy of a letter I received a couple weeks ago. Please finish this before opening the envelope.

When I came up to Minocqua that time before you shipped out, the day you and Sam became engaged, I mentioned that I'd gotten in touch with some old Green Berets, including one or two who were buddies of my father. The other day I received this letter, from a fellow in West Virginia named George Williams. One of the veterans I'd met before had met Williams, who was actually in my father's A-team on his final tour. My acquaintance recognized my dad's unit when Williams mentioned it, and asked if he might write me. I got an email from George and he offered to tell me about Dad's last mission. He wanted to put it in actual typewritten form, because he doesn't really like email. So, here it is.

Things are going well here, same old same old in class. I am starting to think seriously about getting back into politics. I've been approached about a position in the next administration. I've also been approached to write a book, believe it or not. One of the contacts I developed in my research about Green Beret veterans is an author himself, and he thinks the story of my search for Dad would be interesting, especially considering our family lineage.

Must close and grade some papers. It never seems to end, except for those few blessed months of summertime. By now you should be ready for Phase IV. Good luck, and keep me posted.
Your father

Well. I put down Dad's letter and picked up the sealed envelope. I was about to open it when I remembered it was just about chow time. I didn't really want to wait, but the letter would keep. I got up and stretched, wondering idly what would be on tonight's menu. Then I looked at the envelope again.

Screw dinner.

CHAPTER TWENTY-SIX

The letter of George Williams, Sergeant Major, U.S. Army (ret.)

January 10, 2015

Dear Mr. Dawson,

I was privileged to serve in the United States Army for 25 years. After graduating from high school in Rockford, Ill., in 1963, I enlisted and eventually qualified for Special Forces training. In 1967, I was assigned to 5th Special Forces Group (Airborne) and began my first tour in Vietnam in that year. It was during my second tour, 1969-70, that I met your father, Dennis Dawson. It was my great honor to serve with him during that tour and my last one, 1971-72. Some of the missions we performed were classified at the time and remain so, but I can tell you about his final one.

5th Group had been formally withdrawn back to Ft. Bragg by the spring of 1971, but some of us remained behind as a special attachment to MACV (Military Assistance Command-Vietnam). The war was winding down and everybody was confident that the North would come to Jesus, or at least to serious bargaining, and we could go home for good. By the spring of '72, we knew it was only a matter of time. The South Vietnamese (ARVN) troops were shouldering virtually all of the combat load by then and doing pretty well. Although the government itself left a lot to be desired, we felt pretty good about the South's chances once we pulled out. Nobody had any illusions about the North; we knew that as soon as we went home and they had a chance to regroup and rearm, they would make another push south of the DMZ. By then, we were hoping that with continued materiel and perhaps air support from the US, Saigon would be able to hang tough. As we know, that didn't happen. I have some strong opinions about that but they are for another time.

The special unit we comprised with MACV in '72 was not the usual SF A-team. There were no commissioned officers, just a Warrant Officer 2 who spent most of his time in his office. We didn't think much of him, to be honest. Orders would come down the chain through the warrant and out we'd go. Sometimes we would provide security for government big shots or ARVN generals if they ventured out into the field, which was rare. More often, we were tasked to advise ARVN and other South Viet units for training or on actual combat missions.

The Easter Offensive launched by the North at the end of March put a lot of pressure on the ARVN in the north of the country. By mid-May, the advance of the North Vietnamese Army (NVA) had been blunted and the line was being held. The word came down that we were to form a team to support a platoon of ARVN Special Forces, known by the acronym LLDB, to rescue a family of Montagnard tribesmen from Quang Tri Province. We had worked with the Yards many times and our assistance was requested. Dennis and I were convinced the "request" was a polite way of saying that MACV had leaned on someone in Saigon. The Yards were vital to the South's war effort but they were and still are a minority group in Vietnam, the People of the Highlands, as they were known, and weren't held in very high regard in some quarters. But we knew they were good fighters. When we found out this family was from the Bru tribe, Dennis and I were determined to help them. We'd worked with the Bru during our previous tours and we thought this group might be one we were familiar with. Sure enough, that turned out to be the case.

We staged out of Firebase Bastogne, which had been captured by the NVA and then liberated by ARVN troops two days before our arrival. The LLDB platoon numbered some thirty men, including two officers, a captain named Duong and his XO, a lieutenant. Our team was Dennis, myself and four other American SF troops. Dennis, as sergeant major, was the ranking non-com of our squad and in command. We also had an Air Force Joint Terminal Attack Coordinator (JTAC) along to call in air support if necessary.

We moved out from Bastogne by helicopter and were inserted about 15km west of the base, almost halfway to the Laotian border. Just a couple weeks before, a heavy NVA division had moved through the area toward Bastogne and the city of Hue to its east, and not a lot was left behind. Entire villages had been destroyed in their advance. For an army ostensibly trying to liberate the people of the South from their corrupt government, they had a strange way of going about it.

We went overland for another four or five klicks before we started encountering refugees. They were confused, didn't know where to go. Their villages were gone, their young men taken away, their women usually raped. Some told us that babies had been bayoneted in their mothers' arms. We didn't see that ourselves on this mission but I'd seen it before, so I didn't doubt their stories. They were Bru and told us that the family we were looking for was deep in the hills, hiding out, and there were still some NVA units in the area. It was near nightfall, so we made camp near an abandoned village. The terrain was very hilly and the foliage pretty thick. We'd all worked in this environment before so none of the Americans were spooked, but some of the ARVN troops were looking nervous. Whether it was because of the possibility of enemy attack or because of the Yards, we couldn't tell.

Dennis and I and the rest of the US team had a powwow before we bedded down. He didn't really trust Duong, and neither did I. The major problem with the ARVN officer corps throughout the war was that some were quite competent and brave and others couldn't be trusted, they'd gotten their rank through political patronage and connections and were poster boys for incompetence. Every army has incompetent officers, including ours, but the ARVN seemed to have more than its share. We were starting to think this guy Duong was in the latter group. He certainly didn't seem very enthused about the mission. But what we'd heard from these Bru convinced Dennis that the family we were seeking was indeed the one we'd worked with before. Back in '69, Dennis and I had been in an A-team that spent a month with the Yards not too far from where we were now, and we'd had a lot of success against the Viet Cong (VC) that were operating in the area during that time. The Bru chieftain we'd worked with, a guy named Tran, was one of the best fighters we'd ever seen over there. We figured now that if anybody could hold out with NVA all over the place, it would be him.

The night was hot and none of us slept well. Getting a good night's sleep in the field was almost impossible anyway; we stayed with SF procedure and rotated sentries on two-hour shifts. The LLDB had their own sentries but we didn't trust them completely. I pulled 0400 to first light.

Our commo sergeant, a guy from Arkansas named Nicholson, did a radio check with Bastogne and we were told there was intel indicating NVA were still in the area. An airstrike was going to hit a suspected enemy battalion about five klicks to our north at 0700. Dennis met with Duong and advised him we should move out then and use the airstrike as cover for our movement. The flyboys would keep the NVA occupied and should allow us to get to our objective, which we figured was about six klicks away. We would be close to the Laotian border by then. It was possible Tran and his people had bugged out across the border, but we wouldn't know till we got there. They'd still need exfil because the NVA operated freely in Laos. We weren't allowed to; if we'd had freedom of movement in Laos and Cambodia to match the enemy's, the war would've been won long before.

Duong didn't want to move. The abandoned farm we had bivouacked in was on some high ground and fairly secure. Dennis came back to us and he was pissed. I'll never forget what he told us: "That little prick wants to bag the mission, sit tight here till afternoon and then head back to base." I'd never seen him so mad. Dennis was a straight-arrow guy and the one thing that really frosted him was cowardice in the face of the enemy. That's sure as hell what we had here.

We couldn't afford to wait. Right on the dot of seven, we heard the sound of explosions to the north. Air power was our greatest advantage in the war, and its effective use allowed ground units a much better chance to achieve their objectives. But that would only happen if we actually moved to the target. Dennis went over to Duong again and I could hear them arguing. In a situation like that we would look to the XO for some support, but that guy was useless. We were about ten meters off and could hear their voices rising. Dennis was fluent in Vietnamese and I knew enough to understand it wasn't going well. When we saw a couple of their non-coms reaching for their side arms, I gave the order for our guys to get ready in case we had to go in and get Dennis out of that jam. But right then it broke off. Dennis came back to us and I could see he was still upset, but now he had that game face on I'd seen before. He said, "We're moving out. They're not." Nobody questioned him. We all knew the score. There was a family of Yards out there who needed our help.

CHAPTER TWENTY-SEVEN

Camp Mackall, N.C.
April 2015

I heard the tray sliding onto the table next to me. "Hey, bro, you're not eating," Larson said. "And they saved some meat loaf for you."

"Not much of an appetite tonight, Chuck." I poked at a piece of meat, finally deciding to stop playing with it and eat it.

"Good, that's good," Larson said. "Now take another one."

"Knock it off."

Larson was silent for at least fifteen seconds, which had to be some kind of record. Then he said, "Tapioca pudding for dessert. Pretty good." He scooped a spoonful, downed it, then said, "What's going on, Jake?"

The tone of his voice was different. Quieter, more caring, even. Highly unusual, which made me notice. I glanced at my friend, saw the concern in his eyes, then looked back at my tray. "The letter," I said.

"From your dad?"

"Yeah." I laid it all out. It took me a good minute. Then I said, "I don't know if I can finish it. They're going into the hills after that Montagnard family and the NVA is waiting for them and they're gonna grease my grandfather. I can't...I can't read that."

Larson ate another spoonful of the tapioca. "That's a tough one, for sure."

"I mean, how would you like to read about your granddad's death?" As I said it, I realized Larson had never told me about his grandfathers, either one of them. "Sorry," I said.

"It's okay. One's still alive. My mom's dad. He's eighty this year, lives in Texas. Don't get to see him much. My other one, my dad's dad,

I was there just after he died. Cancer. Got to his hospital room and there he was. My dad told me it happened just before I got there. I didn't get to say goodbye to him."

I looked up from his tray, saw my friend's eyes looking off into the distance. "Were you close to him?" I finally asked.

"Yeah. I was in high school. I knew he was in bad shape, knew it wouldn't be long. My dad called me, told me to get over there, but I was hanging out with some buddies, had to get in one more game of World of Warcraft. So I missed...I missed saying goodbye."

We ate in silence for a few minutes. Larson finished his dessert, using the tip of his spoon to play with the few specks left. I forced myself to polish off the meat loaf, then pushed the tray away. "I never knew my grandfather," I said. "Died in 'Nam when my dad was only five. But I always wanted to know more about him, and now when I have the chance to find out what he was like when the...when the chips were down, I just can't do it."

Larson leaned his elbows on the table. "Why not?"

I sat back in my chair, staring ahead. The men at the next table were finishing up, laughing at a joke. None of them looked worried about their peer reviews or psych evals, and they didn't seem concerned about whether they'd passed Phase III, either. I was worried about all of it. The first two phases had been tough, especially the SERE training at the end of Phase II, but I'd made it. The physical training I'd gone through back in RASP and with the 75th had sure as hell helped. A lot of soldiers had washed out because they couldn't handle the ruck marches, the land navigation course, the combatives, and everything else they threw at us.

After all that, I'd thought Phase III, our individual Military Occupational Specialty training, would be easy. Mine was 18A, Special Forces Detachment Officer, and it was a grind, challenging me like nothing I'd ever faced. It was like studying for a master's degree, but instead of nine months we had thirteen weeks.

I hadn't skated through my academic load back at UW, but my courses hadn't been too terribly taxing. Now, Phase III had it all: seven modules covering everything from mission analysis and planning to adaptive thinking and interpersonal skills, foreign internal defense and counterinsurgency doctrine, unconventional warfare, and the real kicker: cross-training in all the other MOSs that would be filled by the men of the ODA team I would be joining. Weapons, engineering, intelligence, medical, communications. We got maybe five hours of sleep a night, if we were lucky. Every day had physical training and there were plenty of days on the firing range and in field exercises.

I'd been told many times before starting the Q Course that it was the most challenging training in the Army, and they sure as hell weren't kidding. Although I hadn't ever seriously thought of going the VW route, to voluntarily withdraw, it had crossed my mind, a little bit more often lately. It crossed everybody's, and some of them did it. Our class of eighteen officers entering Phase III had lost four guys, and I was worried about becoming the fifth. And I had rarely worried about anything, not even wrestling in the NCAAs. It was all just a series of challenges, and challenges had to be met, overcome. You conquer it and keep moving, on to the next one.

What had changed? I was a combat-veteran infantry officer. I should be acing this course, showing the cadre the best damn soldier they'd ever seen. I'd been through Airborne School, Ranger School, RASP. The Q Course was tough, hell yes it was, but I should've been able to handle this better. This was what I'd always wanted. It was so close, everything I'd dreamed about since I was a kid. But now, because it was so close, it was getting real. And down deep, I knew why that scared me. What was waiting in the rest of that letter scared me.

"Same reason I couldn't finish the damn journal," I whispered.

"The Rough Rider's?" I'd told Larson about it, even admitted that I'd lost it. Despite that, the former Iowa farm boy had been seriously impressed. "Hell, man," he said, now, "I would've ripped through that in one day. Has to be a helluva story."

"It is," I said, "and I know he makes it home from Cuba. But I..." I sighed and looked up at the ceiling, cursing my reluctance, my goddamn fear. What the hell was going on? I'd made it through the prep course and SFAS, Special Forces Assessment and Selection, where a lot of eyes

were opened and a lot of guys chose to VW. Back to their old units, their
SF dreams dashed forever. Phase I was next, and I'd done okay there, a
few bumps along the way, nothing serious. Phase II was like SFAS on
steroids, especially because of SERE. I'd almost lost it there, getting
ready to throw down with that cadre. Saved by the flag. Now I was here
in Phase III, training for my specialty as an 18A. At the Military Free
Fall training in Arizona, I'd nearly VW'd before my first High Altitude,
Low Opening jump, out of a perfectly good airplane at thirty-five
thousand feet, falling and falling and falling until pulling the ripcord at
twenty-five hundred. I had to gut out that course like nothing I'd ever
gutted out before.

Hesitating in that doorway, the jumpmaster yelling at me…I'd almost
lost it. Yeah, I'd made it through the course, but they told me it was just
by the skin of my teeth. SF didn't want its officers afraid to jump out of
airplanes, no matter the altitude. MFF had shaken me, made me doubt
myself. Was it because I was so close to my goal, the one I'd been
thinking about since fifth grade? Was I afraid I just couldn't cut it as a
Green Beret? There was a lot more to being a Special Forces officer than
being in the infantry, or armor, or anything else. Only a special kind of
man could wear that beret. My grandfather was that kind of a man, and
he was up there somewhere, watching.

Watching…

This training was tough, but I'd been through tough training. The
Ranger Tab on my shoulder testified to that. But SF required a lot more
of its soldiers, especially its officers, than even the Rangers did. My
ancestors, going all the way back to the Rough Rider–hell, even the
Rough Rider's dad, the Civil War vet–had all made it through the
crucible, faced the ultimate challenge, met it, overcame it. Grandpa
Dennis hadn't made it home, no, but long before that last showdown
with the NVA, he'd earned the beret, proven he could cut it.

"Maybe that's what bugs me," I said. "The Rough Rider…what he
faced on San Juan Heights was like nothing he'd ever faced before, but
he made it. His kid survived being shot down in Korea. His grandkid,
my granddad, did all those tours in Vietnam before they finally got him.

The letter…well, I'm sure it doesn't show him turning and running."

"You afraid you won't measure up?" Larson said.

I sighed, then nodded, finally willing to admit the truth I'd known all along was somewhere inside me, building up all through the training, holding me back. "Yeah."

Larson nodded back. "Hell, I can see that," he said.

I was surprised. "You can?"

"Shit yes." Larson pushed his chair away, picked up his tray and stood. "A whole line of war heroes. Over a hundred years." He looked down at me. "You know, buddy, for a hotshot wrestler and a combat vet besides, Bronze Stars and all that shit, you can be a real pussy, you know that?"

"What the–"

Larson was angry now. I had never seen him like this. "Maybe you're peaked out, you know? You made the 75th, but maybe that's the end of the line. Maybe that's why your Q Course peers might look a little shaky. Maybe you just don't have it in you to wear that beret."

I stood up. The sound of my chair squealing on the cement floor attracted attention. Voices around us fell silent. "You'd better watch it."

"I am watching it," Larson said. "I'm watching a friend of mine go all candy-ass one day at a time. You kicked ass in SERE, everybody says so, but you can't read a letter about your grandfather? He was going in there to rescue those Yards and no goddamn NVA was gonna stop him. That's a real leader, bro. That's a Green Beret, you damn better believe it. Now it's time for you to figure out if you want to be one, too." He turned and walked toward the garbage cans. Around me, heads turned away, men began getting up and carrying their own trays. Pretty soon, I was alone.

CHAPTER TWENTY-EIGHT

The letter of George Williams, Sergeant Major, U.S. Army (ret.), continued.

We moved out, the six of us SF and the JTAC. Dennis had Nicholson get on the radio back to Bastogne to report our situation. The word came back that we were to hold in place while Higher figured out what to do. Dennis said, "I think that last part was garbled, don't you, Nicholson?" The commo sergeant said it sure sounded that way to him, and so we headed toward the target, leaving the LLDB platoon behind.

The terrain started to get pretty rough, like it always was back in those highlands. But we were all in great shape and didn't have any problems. At least it was pretty dry. In monsoon season it could be a bitch, especially when we operated down in the Delta, but up here it wasn't bad at all. Two hours out we spotted an NVA patrol up ahead and we went to ground. Dennis said he didn't want to take them out, didn't want to announce our presence this far in their rear. The idea was to get to the Yard family and get them out without contact with the enemy. The odds were against us, we all knew that, but we'd been in tight spots before and we all trusted each other's abilities, and especially we trusted Dennis. Our sergeant major was the best damn SF soldier I'd ever seen and he was proving it again on this mission. He seemed to have a sixth sense about what was up ahead.

By noon we'd made about three klicks from where we'd

left the LLDBs. Not much of a pace, but we had to take it slow, roundabout routes. We came to a small village, maybe ten huts, and most of the inhabitants were still there, just the women and children. The men were gone, they'd left earlier that morning to lead the NVA away, the women said. They were Bru, but not Tran's people. Their village was another klick or two to the west, we were told. It was a risk talking to these people; there was always the chance one of them could rat us out to the local VC cadre, but these Yards were tough and independent and Dennis trusted them. We were going with his instincts again and he was never wrong, not that I could ever remember.

We were just about to leave when one of the kids, a girl of about ten, came running into the hut, crying. The soldiers were coming, she said, and she didn't mean ARVN. She'd seen them just to the west, when she was chasing a pig that had gotten out of its pen. She didn't know how many. Dennis had a choice to make. We could leave and avoid the enemy patrol and keep on course for Tran's village, or we could stay and defend these people. If the NVA were coming back here, there was a good chance they weren't going to leave these people alone.

Of course, Dennis didn't hesitate. He moved us out into an ambush position a half-klick west of the vill and we waited. Only fifteen minutes after we got in position, the NVA appeared, coming down the trail, about a dozen troops. I was the best shot on our team and my job was to eliminate the officer with the first round of the firefight. He was in the front of the column, bold as brass, probably thinking about how many women he was going to rape when he got to the vill. When he got well into the kill box I took him out with one shot, center mass. The rest of the men opened up and it was over in five seconds. It took us another minute and a half to clean things up. This meant searching for any intel they might have on them and taking care of the wounded. Fortunately only two of them had survived the initial fire, so we only had to use two more rounds.

By then some of the male villagers had returned and they said they'd sanitize the ambush site. We knew they'd do a good job of it and let them get after it. The chief was profuse with his thanks. Other villages in the area, he said, hadn't been so lucky. We hoped their luck would hold.

We moved out, heading west. It was early afternoon and hot. We managed our water carefully. We'd filled up at the village well and had to use our purification tablets on it. That was always a hit or miss proposition but we wouldn't worry about that till later. At 1400 we checked in with Bastogne. They didn't say a word about their earlier transmission. Dennis reported our position and said we expected contact with the target very soon. The JTAC got on the horn and went over pre-selected exfil sites. It would depend on where the Yard family was, but there were three possibilities within a three-klick radius. We also were told that intel had come in about significant enemy movement in our vicinity. With about five hours till dusk, we knew that if we didn't get to Tran's people before then, we'd have to go to ground overnight and exfil at first light. None of us liked that idea but we'd done it before.

We came over a slight rise and saw the tops of about a dozen huts some 500 meters off. These were larger than the ones we'd seen before, made of bamboo and up on stilts as was the Yards' practice. Around the vill there were fields planted with rice and maize. Dennis glassed the area with binoculars and then I took a look. We always double-checked. Neither of us could see any movement. We proceeded cautiously, looking out for booby traps. At that pace it took us nearly a half-hour to get to the vill. It was deserted but there were signs people had been there within the past few hours.

The forest was fairly dense in this area. The farm fields had been cleared by the Yards years before, in their typical slash-and-burn method. We were in the middle of the vill but keeping toward the sides of huts for cover when Dennis stopped walking and cocked his head. "Did you hear that?" he asked. I hadn't, but then I did. A trilling sound, but repeated: down, down, then up-up quickly. I recognized it as a quail call, but not a natural one. Dennis answered in the opposite cadence. Within a minute, men came out of the forest into the vill. They were armed, darker-skinned than typical Vietnamese, and the one leading the way saw Dennis and smiled. It was Tran.

The reunion was short. Tran whistled to the rest of his people to join us, and when they had all made it out, I counted eight men, including Tran, four women and six children. The youngest was perhaps a year old. I didn't have to be told that the rest of the villagers had bugged out days before, but Tran and his family had stayed behind, maybe to delay the NVA, maybe just to make a stand if it came to that. Dennis ordered that we share some of our rations with the women and kids, then took me aside. "What do you think?" he asked.

Dennis was always a man who appreciated honesty from his people, and I was honest with him now. "This could mean trouble," I told him. "We have maybe four klicks to the nearest LZ. Who knows how many NVA are out there? With just the men, we could make it. But the women and kids will slow us down. I was thinking we might have one or two women, two or three kids. This is a lot, Dennis."

He looked at me with a stare that was chilling. "You're not suggesting we leave them behind, are you, Master Sergeant?"

"No," I said, "but you asked what I thought. We need to get moving. Three, maybe four hours to dusk." I gestured toward the forest. "Pretty thick canopy. Ordinarily I'd say we should lay up till full dark and then move out. Night exfils are tricky but we've done them before. With this cover, though, we can make some time right now. If we get to an LZ with some daylight, we can whistle up some tac air to cover the exfil."

His eyes were still intense, but now Dennis grinned. "I knew I could count on you for clear thinking, George," he said. "I'll talk to Tran. Pick the nearest LZ and tell the JTAC to get the bird ready to move, and have him find us some backup in case we need it."

"We'll need two birds," I said. The Huey's capacity was fourteen adults. We could squeeze all the Yards into one, but there was no way we'd all fit.

Dennis, of course, was reading my mind. "Then get two. If we can only get one, we send the Yards out and wait for the next one."

Within a few minutes, Tran had gotten his people organized and we pulled in our perimeter security to work out the details of the march. The JTAC showed us the LZ on the map, about 3½ klicks east and south from our position. We would have pretty decent cover all the way, which would certainly help. We didn't have to worry about any enemy air assets spotting us, but infantry patrols were another thing entirely. At 1600 on the nose we set out, with Dennis, Nicholson and the JTAC in front, Tran with his people, and the rest of the SF squad on the perimeter. I was at the six.

We got within a klick of the LZ before we saw sign of NVA in the area. Dennis and Tran hustled the civilians forward. Through a break in the trees we spotted the advance elements of an enemy patrol. They didn't appear to have spotted us but it wouldn't be long, especially when they heard the helo coming in, and it was right on schedule. A hundred meters from the clearing we formed a skirmish line to cover the exfil. Tran and Dennis met the helo and got the civilians aboard. The first contact with the enemy came when the bird was lifting off. The NVA weren't able to put any rounds on the helo and it got away clean.

It was a platoon-strength force, no doubt about it. The gathering dusk worked in our favor. Once the evac bird was clear, Dennis ordered us to retreat to the other side of the LZ and set up in ambush position. Tran and four of his men had stayed behind with us, so we had a pretty respectable force, if we could use the element of surprise. Fortunately, we were pretty good at that.

Whoever this NVA lieutenant was, he wasn't the sharpest knife in the drawer. He led his men straight into the clearing. The firefight was short. Maybe half of them were able to break contact and retreat, but we got the rest, probably 18-20. We didn't have time to search the bodies for intel; the JTAC had vectored the second Huey to the alternate LZ, three klicks away. We had to move.

The NVA regrouped quickly and we knew they were in pursuit. They'd be on the radio with any of their buddies in the area and there was a real possibility the new LZ would be compromised, or they'd close in on us before we got there. But we didn't have too many alternatives. The JTAC said there'd hopefully be some tac air soon to support us, but with the heavy canopy they'd be limited in what they could do. They could napalm the hell out of the area, of course, but we were too close to allow for that. It was not a good idea to be danger close to a napalm drop.

We double-timed it through the forest, Dennis in the lead, Tran in the middle, and me at the six again. Every fifty meters or so I'd stop, find cover and listen, then hustle back up to rejoin the line. We were about 1500 meters from the LZ when I heard the pursuit. There were a lot of them and they weren't being very subtle about it. Fortunately, it looked like it was just one group, nothing on our flanks. Yet, anyway. I ran back to the next man in line and had him pass the word up to the front.

I could hear the bird inbound, but that was it, no fast-movers, no tac air support for the exfil. If this NVA unit had mortars we were in deep shit, but the only thing to do was set up a security perimeter to cover the landing. Dennis came back with Tran and two other SF troopers. We set up just inside the clearing, which was roughly oval-shaped and about fifty meters wide. Dennis popped smoke, hoping to catch the last of the light and guide the helo in, also to signal that the LZ wasn't compromised.

We had caught a break in that the last 30 meters or so before the actual clearing was very light cover. Anybody emerging from the heavy cover would be in view well before they could get to the actual clearing. I later learned that Tran and his Yards had used this LZ in the past and had done the clearing work. Just as the bird was coming over the trees to our south, the first NVA entered the perimeter to the north.

We were prone, allowing the door gunner on the Huey to add his M60 machine gun to the fight. All of us had been in this situation before, so we knew what to do. When the bird landed, the men behind us quickly loaded and then the M60 opened up to cover us out near the perimeter. I was down to my last magazine for my M16 when it was just me, Dennis and Tran out there. The NVA were still coming out of the clearing but slower. If any of them had a rocket-propelled grenade, the bird would be toast, but an RPG gunner would have to clear the trees to fire, so we kept our eyes peeled as much as we could.

Dennis shouted at us to get to the bird. Tran went first, then I rose into a crouch and began running. Tran was just ahead of me but he looked back and yelled, "RPG!" I pushed him to keep him moving to the bird, but I turned and went to one knee. Dennis was still 20 meters from me, maybe 40 total from the bird, and he was engaging the NVA supporting the RPG gunner. He was staying there to buy time for the rest of us to get out.

The M60 zeroed in on the RPG team and pinned them down, but then one of their officers screamed a command and the gunner rose up to one knee. Dennis was just rising from his prone position. I saw him aim at the gunner and fire a three-round burst. The gunner went down. Dennis began to turn when I saw him stagger. He'd been hit, more than once.

I yelled to the M60 gunner to cover me and ran up to get Dennis. He was lying face-down, but still conscious. He told me to forget him, get to the bird. I told him to shut the hell up. NVA rounds were chewing up the ground around us and zipping past us toward the helo, snapping and cracking. I got Dennis to his feet and helped him back to the bird. I took a round in my left butt cheek and went down. Dennis rolled on top of me, trying to shield me from getting hit again. Tran and another American came out from the bird and pulled both of us along the ground and into the bird. Enemy rounds were pinging off the skin all around us. I felt myself being grabbed and tossed aboard as someone screamed at the pilot to take off. He didn't need any encouragement.

Dennis had been badly hit and lost consciousness just as we got over the trees. There was a medic in the helo crew and he came to me first. I told him to forget me, tend to Dennis. The guy did everything he could. Dennis had lost a lot of blood. When we came in for a landing at Bastogne, the doc was still doing chest compressions, but he was gone.

I hope this letter hasn't been too tough for you, Mr. Dawson. Your father was a great soldier and a fine man. A real hero. Without his leadership, those Yards probably wouldn't have made it. Tran was able to get his people to Thailand. Most of them eventually came to the States as refugees. Tran and his family live in California and we stay in touch. If you would like, I would be happy to give him your address.

In closing, I would like to wish you the best and also to your son. I'm sure his grandfather would be proud to see him wear the Green Beret. If he turns out to be half the soldier Dennis Dawson was, he'll be a credit to Special Forces.

Regards,
George Williams

I folded the letter and put it back in the envelope. From the rest of the barracks, I heard the sounds of men talking, some laughter, some snoring. I walked out into the night air. Chilly, but not bad. Up above, the stars were out. The same stars my grandfather had seen so many nights during his SF training, half a century ago.

Were they up there? My grandfather, Two-Fist, the old Rough Rider? Were they watching me? I had been raised a Christian, in spite of my father's indifference to religion. As far as I knew, all my ancestors were, too, so I had to believe they were in heaven. But if it was true, all of it, could they still see me? Communicate with me, even?

I had a pretty good idea what Ernie would say. "Two-Fist" never pulled any punches and he wouldn't have with his great-grandson. He would have told me to get my head out of my ass, that I was a Dawson and Dawson men didn't back down from a challenge.

Earlier tonight, when I'd started reading the letter, I was sure my grandfather was there with me. It was a feeling much more than you get when reading a story, identifying with the character. I'd read tons of Vietnam War novels and biographies, but I'd never had that same feeling with them. And there was that moment back home, on my last day, when I thought I saw someone in the hallway of my mom's house. Dark blue shirt, khaki slouch hat. The Rough Rider. Were they proud, or were they disappointed? I'd been thinking I wouldn't make it, that I couldn't measure up to what SF demanded of its soldiers. What Dennis and Ernie and Charles demanded from their graves.

They could've taken it easy, all of them. Charles could've stayed in school and read about Cuba in the papers. Ernie sure as hell could've sat out Korea, sticking with a training wing stateside. And Dennis? I knew plenty of Vietnam-era vets who'd served their time at a base in Germany or Japan or on a ship sailing far from the war zone. I didn't hold it against them; they'd all chosen to raise their hands, take the oath, put on the uniform. New orders could've come down for them anytime, sending them to the Land of Bad Things. The others, the ones who'd used deferment after deferment to stay out, those were the ones I had no respect for. And those who'd fled to Canada or Europe? They all said they went on principle, but I wondered about that. Maybe some did. Most, I felt, had not. They had quit before it even started. Not like Charles, or Ernie, or Dennis.

No, they had never quit, had they?

Reading the letter choked me up, but it made me proud, too. I was a Dawson, from a long line of warriors, and now I would not let them down. Reading about my grandfather's final hours, how he had sacrificed himself for those villagers, and for his men…. I took a deep breath and dropped to my knees. Without a thought to drive them, my hands clasped in front of me. From some distance away, I vaguely heard a door creak open, then slam shut. Footsteps, coming to a sudden stop. I ignored them and began to whisper the psalm, which had come back to me during RASP and SERE, as it had to so many of the men.

"'The Lord is my shepherd, I shall not want...'"

Something seemed to swell inside me, powerful, yet comforting. I finished the psalm, then said, "Grampa, wherever you are up there...I'll make you proud of me."

CHAPTER TWENTY-NINE

Somewhere in "Pineland"
May 2015

"The ears! We must take the ears! It is our right, as warriors and victors in battle. And you have fought beside us, so you must help!"

This guy was becoming more of a pain in the ass every day. I was tired, stressed, and in no mood for this kind of third-world bullshit, but I couldn't just stand here arguing with the colonel. We were five klicks from camp, night was about to fall and you never knew if another platoon of government troops might be close by, ready to avenge their buddies.

My mission, though, was to advise these men wearing the black uniforms and ball caps in how to overthrow their country's corrupt government. It was a war for the hearts and minds of the population, and how many hearts and minds would be won over if their sons' bodies were brought back missing ears, not to mention some of the other body parts I'd heard talked about?

But it was all a work in progress, and there would be another time when I could sit down with the colonel and explain why it was Americans didn't do these things and why we would prefer our allies didn't, either. For now, I said, "Colonel Smith, my men and I respect your traditions. However, I must ask you to respect ours, as well. It is against the values of our country to participate in such a thing. As soldiers in the United States Army, we must decline this honor." When I saw the colonel's eyes harden, I added, "Fighting beside you as brothers to take back your country is more than enough honor for us."

After what seemed like a very long moment, the tall man's eyes softened, and he smiled. "Very well. Maybe we will talk about this tonight, eh? You can tell me more about this strange concept of honor you Americans have."

"I'd be happy to. For now, though, I suggest we move out and return to our base camp. Your men won a victory here today, I'm sure they want to relax and celebrate."

"That they do, brother."

I made sure the men of my Operational Detachment Alpha were squared away when we returned to the camp, then joined the cadre sergeant for the after-action report. The fire pit was crackling, and pretty soon the Pineland guerillas, the Gs, would be sharing tonight's meal with the American advisors. Five days in, and walls were starting to break down. Trust was being established, and that was a primary goal of the Robin Sage exercise. With trust, my men and I could properly train the Gs to be effective insurgents.

Overall, I thought things were going pretty well. There'd been some curveballs thrown at us, like the first night after jumping in, when our scheduled linkup with the Gs had turned out to be a trap. We had to break contact and patrol five miles to an alternate linkup point, and do it all while enduring a cold rain. Since then, though, things had been looking up. I had to force myself to avoid thinking of how many days we had left in the field, but in the back of my mind I was starting to envision a calendar. With any luck at all, it would be pretty smooth sailing the rest of the way.

The cadre sergeant, though, had a slightly different take.

"You did a nice job helping guide your Gs in their ambush preparation," the sergeant said. Sergeant Major Pagos was a fifteen-year SF veteran with several deployments under his belt. Hearing praise from a veteran like that was always good. But the criticism could be withering sometimes, as I and the rest of his training class had found out throughout the Q Course. Right now, I was thinking there had to be a downside to this, and I was right.

"But I'm starting to see some things I don't like, Lieutenant," Pagos continued. "You're getting a little lax. Things are going well, but they won't always go well. When you're downrange things can go to hell in a rocket pretty damn fast, as you should know. Your G chief runs a pretty loose ship here. You need to do more to help him tighten things up. They'll get cocky after this ambush today. You need to maintain unit discipline with your own ODA and move the colonel in that direction for his men, too."

I nodded. "Roger that, Sergeant Major."

"Now, tell me about tomorrow's training schedule."

For the next ten minutes, I outlined what I had in mind. The cadre listened carefully, made a few suggestions and said, "Okay, that's it for tonight. Get some chow, maybe sit down with your colonel and talk about traditions, theirs and ours. Look for common ground. Don't bullshit him. We Americans have a tendency to think we're superior to everyone else. And why do we think that?"

I grinned, remembering a lecture from his training. "Because we have moon rocks, Sergeant Major, and nobody else has moon rocks."

"Exactly right. Gs can be difficult to work with sometimes but we're here at their invitation, and our government has decided it is in the national interest of the United States for you to be here. Otherwise we'd be sending you somewhere else."

"Thanks, Sergeant Major."

"All right, Lieutenant, drive on."

My team sergeant, Miguel Ortiz, was a tough-as-nails grandson of Cuban refugees, but he looked a little bleary-eyed the next morning, and it wasn't just because of the chronic lack of sleep all us SF candidates were enduring. Before we could even go over that day's training schedule, he asked, "Man, LT, what was in that shit they gave us last night?"

"I don't really know, Sergeant, but I was glad to see every one of us knock down a glass." Around the campfire, Ortiz and I, along with a handful of other members of the ODA, had engaged in a Pineland ritual with the G chief, Colonel Smith, and his men. After convincing the colonel of our sincerity in being willing to help the insurgents while still declining to participate in some of their more bizarre practices, I had agreed to do this one, as a sign of brotherhood and devotion to the cause. Whatever the brew was, it had a ferocious punch and a putrid stench. I didn't think I'd ever forget either of them. After that, dining on the plates of goat's eyes and brains served up by the grinning Gs was almost easy.

"Are we set for our training schedule today?"

"Absolutely, sir. We still have to work around this Rahaa shit, but we're starting to get things done." Smith had explained that Rahaa was a Pineland custom, a four-hour slice of the day beginning at 1100, when the natives could sleep, meditate, tend to personal needs or whatever else they wanted. Ortiz and I had discovered Rahaa during our first day in camp, when all of a sudden the guerillas had vanished in the middle of the day.

"All right," I said, "keep in mind that we have to maintain security during their down time, and we have to convince them to do it, too. There's no guarantee that the government troops will be respecting Rahaa like these guys do." My communications specialist, a tall first sergeant from Vermont, hustled over. "What's up, Swenson?"

"Lieutenant, I was showing my G commo team how our PSC-5 sat radio works when one of them gets a heads-up on his own field radio. The Condor Squadron has our base camp pinpointed and they're planning a night raid."

From my operations planning, I remembered that the Condor Squadron was the most feared unit in the Pineland Army. "All right, we're gonna have to strike camp and bug out. I'll go talk to the colonel, but proceed with the training schedule until I give the word."

The colonel was in a foul mood the next day, and I was starting to worry that things might be getting out of hand. The G chief had wanted to lay an ambush for the Condor unit, but I convinced him the prudent move was to strike camp and move out. The Condors were likely to have helicopter gunships, I said, remembering my briefing materials, and there was no way the Gs, even with help from my ODA, could hold up against a company of elite troops with night vision and air support. To me, evacuating the camp made perfect sense; the insurgents had to stay one or two steps ahead of the security forces. Ignoring this intel, or turning it into a suicidal stand, was senseless. I couldn't say that openly, of course, but I had the feeling the colonel saw right through me.

Almost in spite of Smith, the ODA and the rest of the Gs got the new camp in relatively shipshape order within a few hours of dawn's arrival. I was going over a scheduled airdrop of supplies with Ortiz when I noticed two strangers walking into the camp, bold as brass. Both wore the same black fatigues as the Gs, but while one had a ball cap without a logo, like the rest of the Pinelanders, the taller one had a patch on his. "What the hell's this?" I said to Ortiz. "How are these guys waltzing in here without any security escort?"

"They must've come through the perimeter where there's a G team stationed," Ortiz said. "I'll check on it." Without waiting for a reply, Ortiz hustled off. He knew I was pissed. Maintaining security in the field was preached over and over during the Q Course, and in Robin Sage, it was the ODA's responsibility to make sure the Gs were tight with their protocols.

I saw Smith coming out of his tent to greet the two newcomers, with broad smiles and handshakes all around. "Lieutenant Dawson, come meet my friends," the colonel said, waving me over.

It didn't register at first sight, but when I shook the tall newcomer's hand, I recognized the logo on the ball cap. It was the same one I'd seen when I was recruited into the Wolverines, and during my time in the outfit I'd learned enough Farsi to translate the words inscribed next to the upraised assault rifle: a portion of a verse from the Qur'an, translated as, "..and prepare for them what you can by way of power." It was the logo of the Iranian Revolutionary Guard Corps.

It was all I could do to ignore the cap and focus on the man. Tall, iron-gray eyes, and a firm grip indeed. "This is Colonel Santine," the G chief said, "and his aide, Captain Cousins. They have important intelligence for us."

"I'm always pleased to meet fellow freedom fighters," I said. In the back of my mind, I marked down this Santine guy as a potential security risk. The way Smith deferred to him said something about the political pecking order within the ranks of the insurgency. I knew that not only did an inserted ODA have to help the Gs with their efforts to topple the government, it had to start preparing the guerillas for life after victory. Who would be running the new government? What would happen to the triumphant guerillas? How would they get paid if the economy collapsed? It was all mind-boggling in its complexity, but I knew that if I was to wear the Green Beret, I'd have to handle it.

And right now, that damn Pasdaran logo was all I could think about.

Phase IV ended, but it wasn't over by a long shot. Not until you got through Phase V and had that beret on your head and the tab on your shoulder, and I had started worrying about that all the way through the post-op equipment inventory, overhaul and turn-in. How many times had I done that in the Q Course? Too many to count. And as the officer of my ODA, the 18 Alpha, I had even more work to do. About the only thing that made the whole process palatable was getting my first shower in two weeks and my first good night's sleep, indoors, in a bunk that most civilians would sneer at but which I now considered to be the most luxurious bed in the world.

My biggest worry was having to go before the Commander's Review Board. There were some soldiers who came through every phase shaky enough to be summoned before the Board, and many of those who came out would never wear the beret. A few were recycled back to the next class, a few were told they simply weren't SF material and were sent back to their old units. So far, I had made it through without getting the summons. I would have to sit down with Captain Schwab, the class's cadre officer, and his top sergeant, Master Sergeant Hansen, for my individual review. It would be those two who would make a determination about where I would be going next: the Board, or on to Phase V and then, hopefully, the graduation ceremony.

I was trying to kill time at the barracks by reading my last few emails from Sam, holding off on opening any of the photo attachments. Seeing her picture now would be too distracting, especially if she'd sent another set of the boudoir photos she'd grown so fond of lately. She'd gone to a photographer in Appleton for the layout and was sending them to me one at a time. Yeah, another one right now would be a major distraction. Even so, I was about to yield and had my finger on the download key when there was a knock at my door.

Ortiz stuck his head in. "You're up, LT."

I closed the laptop and put it aside, stood, couldn't stop myself from taking a deep breath. "How'd it go, Sarge?"

Ortiz tried to hold back his smile, finally turning it into a wry grin. "They cut me a new one, you might say, but my peers were strong. Thank you for that, sir."

I nodded. Every man in the ODA was subject to peer review from his teammates, regardless of rank, and the peers were vital parts of the candidate's evaluation. I had been through something similar in RASP, and found I rather liked it. Just one more way to hold yourself accountable, and in SF, I'd quickly found that accountability was everything. Downrange, it could save your life and the lives of your teammates.

"No problem," I said, "glad to help. Well, here we go." I adjusted my field cap. Ortiz stepped aside as I closed the door behind me.

"You're good to go, sir, no sweat." Ortiz offered his hand. "Lieutenant, it's been an honor to be on your team. I hope we can serve together again."

I was touched, and much to my surprise I felt a tear forming. I took the sergeant's hand gratefully. A line from some old movie came back to me. "The honor has been mine, Sergeant."

CHAPTER THIRTY

Fayetteville, N.C.
September 2015

The second-biggest day of my life was finally here.

In the back of the Crown Coliseum, I waited with a hundred and three fellow soldiers. We were in our ACUs, the combat uniforms we wore virtually everywhere these days, even when we weren't in garrison or downrange. Personally, I would've liked us to be in our Class-A's, like some earlier classes. But these would do. After all, we'd all be going to combat zones pretty damn quickly.

We had no headgear. Like my comrades, I would walk in bare-headed, and walk out wearing something I'd wanted since damn near forever, and it was something I had really begun to think I'd never get. Going back to the 75th Rangers and wearing their tan beret again wouldn't be bad, to be sure, but I wanted a different color. It wasn't until I got to the very end of Phase IV that I realized how badly I really wanted it.

The Robin Sage exercise concluded that phase, which was one of the roughest mental and emotional ordeals I'd ever been through. The cadre and all the role-players had poured it on. At one point I had to attend a meeting of the leaders of the "guerillas" and sit in front of Santine, wearing his damn Pasdaran cap. For two hours I was questioned and harangued and at one point Santine outright challenged me to a fistfight. Tempted as I was to throw down with that clown, I stayed calm, answered their questions as best I could, and afterwards, back at the camp, I had to sit quietly by myself, shaking with emotion. Was this how it was going to be downrange? The verbal abuse I'd taken in that meeting had been almost vicious. I was an officer in the United States

Army, and I had to ask myself, why should I put myself through this? I knew those guys were only playing roles, but I also knew that when I was deployed, something very much like that might happen. My first inclination would be to give them all the finger, walk out the door and call in an air strike to blow their asses to hell and gone, but that was not the job of a Special Forces officer. Did I want that job? In the end, I made up my mind that yes, I did, badly.

Phase V, the language training, flew by. At the end of that eighteen-week ordeal, I was conversational in Arabic and also had picked up some Farsi on my own time, of which there was damn little. Foreign language proficiency was required for graduation, and I was highly motivated.

I wasn't the only one. Every guy in here had wanted it as much as I did. We all had our reasons. And what I'd learned from talking to the guys the past couple days was that every damn one of us had our doubts, too, about whether we'd make it. One of those who had serious doubts tapped me on the shoulder now.

"Lieutenant, got a minute?"

It was Carson, the former football star from St. Louis. He'd recovered from the dysentery he suffered during SERE training and roared through the rest of the course. I'd never seen anyone so intense, so much so that the cadre occasionally had to tell him to ease off. But damn, what I would give to have that guy in my ODA downrange. Some of the guys had taken to calling him Captain America. "Sure, Sergeant," I said.

We took a couple steps outside the group of nervous soldiers. Carson offered his hand, and I could hardly see mine when I took it. The guy was made for football, but he had proven he was made to be a Green Beret, too. His dark face was solemn, and I could see his eyes misting. "I just wanted to thank you again for what you did for me during SERE," he said.

"It was my pleasure," I said automatically, then grinned. "Well, I'd have to say it wasn't the most pleasurable thing I've ever done. You know what I mean."

This time he returned the grin. "Roger that, sir. Anyway, I'd have

VW'd right then and there if you hadn't helped me. So, thank you."

"I'm glad you hung in there," I said, suddenly feeling emotional, even more so than I already was. "I sincerely hope to have you in my ODA sometime, Sergeant."

"That would be a real pleasure for me, sir." Carson stepped back and snapped a parade-ground-worthy salute. I returned it, then slapped him on the back as we rejoined the group.

I looked around the room. Tall men, short men. Men of almost every ethnicity. Three of them were foreign soldiers, from Poland, South Korea and Argentina. The Korean, Lieutenant Kang, had shown me a thing or two on the mat the past few days, as I matched my wrestling skills against his taekwondo. The rest were Americans, from every corner of the country. Big cities, small towns, farms, suburbs. There was Chuck Larson, who caught my eye and gave me one of his goofy grins and a wink. I'd gotten to know almost all of them, and I'd never served with a finer group of men.

Near the door to the arena, a voice shouted a command. "Graduates, fall in!"

At the front, a man in full Scottish kilt with bagpipes waited with a soldier holding a bass drum. We were lined up in five rows, about twenty men in each. The day before, we'd gone through a rehearsal. The arena was empty then, but now, hundreds waited for us. I could hear the hum of the crowd, reminding me of how it was back at the Kohl Center as I waited with the team, before a big match. The butterflies I had back then had returned, but they were different. Waiting in the tunnel in my red and white Badger wrestling singlet, I had been focused on my opponent in the upcoming match. The battle was before me then. Now, it had passed. This battle, anyway; far more important battles awaited me, awaited all of us, after we left this building with our new headgear.

From the arena, we heard an amplified voice boom, "Ladies and gentlemen, the U.S. Army John F. Kennedy Special Warfare Center and School is proud to present the graduates of the Special Forces Qualification Course."

The bagpiper fired up his instrument and it wailed the opening bars of "Scotland the Brave." The drummer began to thump on the big bass. We marched out into the arena. Cheers and applause greeted us. Flashes pulsed from cameras. I knew better than to look around for my family. Eyes front. Marching in step, each man was no doubt thinking of the difficult path he'd walked to get to this moment. For me, it had almost never happened. At the end of Phase IV, it was the Iranians who almost got me.

Camp Mackall, N.C.
May 2015

"Lieutenant, your peer reviews have been strong all the way through the course," Captain Dan Schwab said, giving me a stare I'd seen more than a few times during every phase. "But the cadre have some concerns. I have to tell you, we're on the bubble about whether to pass you through or send you before the Board." Schwab was around forty, haircut high and tight, wearing a uniform shirt that could've been painted on. The word was that he was a weight room stud, routinely out-lifting soldiers half his age.

I couldn't repress a swallow, hoping it wasn't that obvious, and tried to remain calm. What was the worst that could happen? I'd go before the Review Board, and if they washed me out of SF, I'd just go back to the 75th. A hell of an outfit that a lot of soldiers wanted to join, and I had been one of the few to make it. An outfit almost as exclusive, almost as renowned, as Special Forces.

But not quite. I had my Ranger Tab, and now I wanted that SF Tab on my shoulder, too. I wanted that beret, and as much doubt as I'd had in the past year, I had realized as I was waiting outside the door of this room that I wanted it more than almost anything else. Only Sam was higher on the list.

"I believe I've done my best, sir," I said. "I'm prepared to state my case before the Board if you gentlemen feel that would be necessary."

"Your performance in just about every aspect of every phase has been graded from good up to exemplary," Master Sergeant Paul Hansen said. Mid-forties with a graying buzz cut, Hansen looked more like a school teacher than a soldier, but he knew his stuff, like every member of the Q Course cadre. He glanced at a clipboard. "But every time something comes up that hints of a certain potential adversary you might face downrange, you have some problems."

There it was. I knew they'd get me on it eventually. "That would be Iran, wouldn't it, Master Sergeant?"

"That would be the one." Hansen sat back in his chair. "We were aware of your history with Iranians, Lieutenant. The firefight that killed your OSUT buddy. Your capture when you were with the Wolverines in Kurdistan. One or two other incidents."

"Individually, none of them would be considered serious," Schwab said. "Collectively, they make us wonder about your judgement. You've been downrange as regular infantry enlisted and as an officer, then as a Ranger officer. Now you want us to send you as a Special Forces officer. It's a lot different situation than what you've experienced."

"I'm aware of that, sir," I said, and immediately regretted it. That sounded defensive, but what the hell, wasn't I supposed to defend myself here? Or was I supposed to throw myself on the mercy of the court? If it came to the Board, that's what I would do, if it was my only chance.

For some reason, memories of the Rough Rider's diary flashed through my tensed-up mind. Each of my ancestors had gone through a gauntlet a lot worse than this. Charles in his first firefight, Ernie facing the Chinese in Korea, Dennis defending the Yards in Vietnam. As for me, I'd proven myself in combat more than once. Why were the cadre questioning my ability to be objective about any Iranians I might run into? I'd shown I could handle myself.

Yes, as an infantryman, and as a Ranger, but not as an SF officer. I'd heard all through the Q Course that this was a different ballgame. Maybe now it was finally sinking in.

"You've probably guessed that we took some opportunities to throw a few Iranian curveballs at you," Hansen said. "You were pretty shaky every time, but you did a good job recovering and driving on. This was training, though. As realistic as we make it, and it's pretty damn realistic, it's still just training, and every student knows that. Our concern, Lieutenant, is that if something trips your trigger in training, what will happen if that occurs when you're deployed?"

I tried to project more confidence than I felt, knowing all the while these guys could see right through that. They'd seen it all. Twenty-nine years combined in SF, dozens of deployments, who knows how many cadre assignments? There was no fooling these guys, but I didn't want to fool them. I wanted to convince them. I said, "I understand I have to deal with a few things about them, but–"

Schwab interrupted. "About who, Lieutenant?"

"About…those people."

"They have a name, do they, 'those people'?"

I took a deep breath. Images of Chet's death flashed before my eyes. I had to push them away. "Yes, sir. The Iranians. I have to be more objective about them."

"Not just *more* objective," Schwab said, boring in, "but *totally* objective. If you're downrange with an ODA and your mission is to help train an Afghan National Army company and you're in a province on the Iranian border, you can't be looking over your shoulder every day, hoping somebody infiltrates so you can go after them. If you're back in Kurdistan and another militia group comes around the bend, you can't advise your Peshmerga to tear them a new asshole just because they might have a Quds Force officer in one of their technicals. If your mission parameters call for it, you will be cleared to treat them as enemy combatants and engage them accordingly, but if not, they're not, and you don't. Do you understand that, Lieutenant?"

"Yes, sir, I do." I looked at Schwab first, then at Hansen. "You have my word, gentlemen."

Schwab stared at me, then nodded. "Very well." He stood, with Hansen and me immediately joining him. "My grandfather told me that a man's word is his bond," Schwab said. "If your grandfather had lived, I'm sure he would've told you the same thing."

My eyes were misting. I blinked once, twice. "I think that in a way, he has, Captain."

Schwab stuck out his hand. "It's on to Phase V for you, then. And I have every confidence that when that's done, we'll be welcoming you to Special Forces."

CHAPTER THIRTY-ONE

Fayetteville, N.C.
September 2015

It was Sam who got to me first, outside the building. It was a sunny, warm day and she looked absolutely splendid in her outfit, a cropped white top that left some–but not enough–of her toned midriff showing above the top of her skirt. Her smile flashed and her sunglasses weren't big enough to cover the tears streaming down her cheeks. She threw herself at me and I embraced her like I never wanted to let her go, and at that moment I didn't.

My parents and Uncle John weren't far behind. Sam let me go long enough for Mom to get in a long, teary hug, and then Dad shook my hand, his eyes misting. He was looking pretty good, had put on a little weight—visiting the gym regularly now, he'd told me—and his red polo shirt with the white Badger W made him look less like a professor and more like, well, a dad. I pulled him in from the handshake and we shared a hug. And speaking of looking good, my great-uncle was fairly svelte now, in a black polo with the Marine Corps logo on the left breast. Since his heart attack, he'd changed his lifestyle considerably, he'd told me in an email. Using email itself was a big change, and he described how he'd quit drinking entirely, went to the gym every day and the municipal pool three days a week. He was corresponding regularly with Dad, his nephew, and they'd challenged each other to get in shape. Uncle John had connected with other Marine veterans through a regional organization, and he was even dating again, a woman in her fifties whose husband had been lost at Fallujah and whose own son was now in the Corps. John had brought her along, a nice surprise.

Uncle John snapped a salute, touching the brim of his black and red

Marine ball cap, and I returned it, touching the edge of the new beret I had put on just minutes before. Then he gave me a bear hug. "I'm so damn proud of you, Jake," he said, his voice husky. Then he introduced his friend. "I want you to meet Jackie."

"Congratulations," she said, extending a hand. She was almost as tall as Sam, with flowing brown hair that had a hint of gray. A stunner, a woman who could give Monica Dawson a run for her money and even hold her own with Sam. I smiled, marveling that my crusty old great-uncle had been able to find a babe like this. Then I realized that the only woman I should ever refer to as a "babe" from now on was the tall, young one clutching my arm.

"Welcome to the family," I said, hoping that didn't sound premature. Jackie smiled, but didn't look embarrassed by it. Somehow I knew that before long, there'd be a ring on her finger.

"Jake, that beret looks awful good on you," Mom said.

Uncle John nodded with satisfaction. "Spitting image of your grand-father," he said. "When do you get your orders?"

"Any time now," I said. Graduates could state their preference for whichever of the five active duty Special Forces groups they wanted to serve in, but their proficiency in language training, not to mention all the other training they'd had and their previous Army experience, would be factored in. Right from the start I'd aimed for 5th Group, headquartered at Fort Campbell, Kentucky, and oriented toward service from the Horn of Africa to Central Asia. My grades in Phase V had been good, and I figured my previous deployments over there would stand me in good stead. But if they wanted to send me somewhere else, that would be fine with me. These days, every Group was eventually sending its men to either Afghanistan or Iraq. One way or another, I was going back.

A few months ago I would've thought that was fine because I had some old scores to settle over there, but things had changed. A lot of things, and there were more to come. One big change involved the woman on my left, the one who'd been wearing my ring for the past fourteen months, waiting very patiently. It was time to end that wait.

"But I've got a couple weeks' leave before I go anywhere," I said, "and so I'd like to come home."

"Of course, honey," Mom said, with a knowing smile. She glanced at Sam, unable to help herself.

"And I'd like to get married when I'm there," I said to Sam. "If, that is, my fiancée is in agreement...?"

Sam's eyes went wide behind the sunglasses. "Jake...I thought we were going to wait till after your first deployment?"

"That's six more months," I said. "I figured we might as well get it done now. How about it?"

"But, there's not enough time—"

"It's all been taken care of," Mom said with a big smile. "Invitations are already out, with a special note that mum's the word until they hear from you. Honey, all the planning we've been doing? I just kicked it into gear."

"Oh, my God..."

"Blame your husband-to-be," Mom said, with a laugh.

"One week from today," I said. "So you might want to be thinking about a dress."

Sam burst into tears, but they were happy ones, and Mom hugged her, and then Jackie. Kleenexes were deployed, eyes were dried, and the women moved smoothly into planning mode. I watched them happily. What a heck of a day this was turning out to be.

"Well, now I'll be able to try out that new suit I just bought," Uncle John said. "Jackie helped me pick it out."

"Forget the suit," I said. "Can you still fit into your dress blues? My best man has to look sharp up there."

Uncle John looked at me, surprised. "Best man?"

"Of course," I said, slapping him on the back. "And by the way you're looking at Jackie, I'm thinking that I might be returning the favor sometime soon." Standing with us, Dad was smiling, too. I'd tipped him off about the wedding and the difficult choice I'd made in selecting my great-uncle as my best man. Dad and I were making progress in fixing what had so long been broken in our relationship, but Uncle John had always been there for me, and deserved the honor. Dad made it easy by saying that he understood completely, a big relief for me. He'd be there, of course. Wild horses, and all that.

Uncle John was grinning as he looked at his lady friend. "I'll tell you what, boys, she's hell on wheels, and that's a fact."

Dad laughed. "I'll take your word for it," I said, just as two other men approached, both in ACUs, one a full bird colonel wearing a green beret, the other a master sergeant whose beret was Ranger tan. That guy I recognized immediately. They stopped a few feet away and I came to attention, offering the colonel a salute. It didn't even occur to me that the occasion wouldn't necessarily require it, but this was the man who I hoped would be my commanding officer very soon. "Colonel Hemple," I said.

"As you were, Lieutenant," the C.O. of 5th Group said. "I believe you know Master Sergeant Boudreau."

That wide Cajun grin was one I'd know anywhere. He offered a casual salute and then his hand. I pulled him into an embrace. To hell with protocol. "Sarge," I said, emotion rolling into my voice. "Thanks for coming."

"Wouldn't have missed it," Boudreau said. "Just so happened I was up from Benning on some other business for the 75th."

"I've been trying to get the Master Sergeant here to come back to Special Forces," Hemple said. "But the Rangers won't let him leave. I'm told I've already taken one of their best young officers, so I guess I'll have to be satisfied with that." He almost winked at me with that one. My chest expanded a little bit. Then I realized that there was something maybe more specific about what he'd said.

"Sir, I put in for 5th Group, and…"

"It won't be official until your orders come through, of course, but I have something for you." Hemple reached into his breast pocket and pulled out a patch. "I'm sure you'll wear this with pride, just as your grandfather did." He handed it to me.

It was the beret flash of 5th Group, shaped like a shield and solid black. Every group had its own flash. The 5th's was probably the plainest of the bunch, but to me it was beautiful. "My God," I said, barely able to breathe.

"I've got your first assignment ready to go," the colonel said. "Come see me at my office before you head for home, and we'll go over it."

"Where would that be, sir?" I asked, still in a bit of shock.

"Someplace you're familiar with," Hemple said. "You'll recognize the terrain, and the challenges you'll be up against."

Holy God. I realized he was sending me back to Kurdistan. Another shocker, but in the past year I'd learned a lot about self-discipline, so I didn't let my surprise show. Too much.

I introduced my family to Hemple and Boudreau, making sure to add, "Gunnery Sergeant, U.S. Marine Corps, retired," for Uncle John. My mother impulsively gave the colonel a hug. "Take care of my boy," I heard her say to him, her voice trembling. Hemple promised that he would.

From somewhere, a band began to play. It was "The Ballad of the Green Berets," by Barry Sadler, an SF staff sergeant in Vietnam. Sadler had co-written the song along with Robin Moore, the author of my all-time favorite book. Voices took up the lyrics, and I couldn't help myself. I had to join in.

"Fighting soldiers, from the skies, fearless men who jump and die,

"Men who mean just what they say, the brave men of the Green Beret."

Every one of us knew the words. The colonel and Boudreau were joining in. We sang with gusto, but our voices hushed as we came to the fifth verse.

"Back at home, a young wife waits, her Green Beret has met his fate,

"He has died for those oppressed, Leaving her his last request."

I looked at Sam. She'd taken off her sunglasses and her eyes were filling again, only this time it wasn't from joy or pride. I took her hand, squeezed it, trying to be reassuring. Our voices rose again as we rolled into the final verse: *"Put silver wings on my son's chest, make him one of America's best,*

"He'll be a man, he'll test one day, Have him win the Green Beret."

We roared as we finished the song. A few berets went into the air, but I kept mine in place. The band began a Sousa number, and I hugged Sam. Whispering into her ear, I said, "Nothing will keep me from coming back to you."

Boudreau cleared his throat. "Gotta be going, LT, but I wanted to give you this." He held out a small package. I hadn't noticed him carrying it. "Remember Burns, from the Wolverines? He found it in his gear when he went home on leave. Said he must've picked it up from your hootch back in Turkey when they were packing your own gear up to send home after you got wounded. I think there's a letter in there from him for you."

I opened the brown paper wrapping. I almost fainted.

"What is it, Jake?"

I handed it to Sam. She'd never seen it before. "It's the Rough Rider's diary," I said.

CHAPTER THIRTY-TWO

Qaszir, northern Iraq
November 8, 2015

In my twenty-five years, I had seen a grown man weep only twice. The first was my father, at his grandfather Ernie's funeral eleven years ago. The second time was today.

But, Captain Frank Jones had recovered quickly, at least on the outside, after I knocked at his door and he said to come in. He wiped his eyes and was now fiddling with his gear one last time, all the while running through a last-minute list of things for his second in command to do. Then he paused and looked off into the distance. That distance ended in the spare concrete wall just two meters away, but for those dark brown eyes, it was about ten thousand kilometers longer. The captain was a big guy, about six-five and built, but right now he looked like the weight of the world was on his shoulders, pressing down on him. He looked at me, the guy who was about to take over his beloved ODA team, and said, "Jake, I'm sorry to put you in this position, but I've just…" And then the tears started rolling down his dark cheeks again.

"It's okay, sir. We'll be good to go here till you get back." I wasn't sure if it was allowed, but I put a hand on his shoulder. I'd been told the captain was a straight-arrow West Pointer who went by the book so closely that some said he wrote the book, so I didn't know how he'd react. But Jones didn't shrug my hand off. He nodded, then stood up straight, allowing me to take my hand away with less awkwardness than I expected.

Only twelve or so hours had gone by since the word had arrived here from 5th Group headquarters in Fort Campbell. The word was not good for Captain Jones. In fact, it was about the worst damn kind of word any man could get. I was in the room, with the captain and two of the local Kurdish leaders, when Sergeant Darrel Bliese, the ODA's communications sergeant, came in to inform Jones that he had a flash radio call from the colonel.

"Which colonel is that?" Jones asked.

"The colonel back at Fort Campbell, sir. He's on the sat phone."

"Okay. Excuse me, gentlemen." Jones left the room with Bliese following. We were in what passed for City Hall here in this northern Iraqi town. Like virtually every building here, it had been shot up or at least looked as if it had. During my time with the Wolverines, I hadn't been to this town, our operations area having been farther north, but I had come to the conclusion that years of almost non-stop warfare would leave any town with more than a few scars. Its people had scars, too, lots of them, but that's why Jones and the ODA team were here in northern Iraq, to help the Kurds get squared away and start the healing.

Bliese came back into the room five minutes later. I had been continuing the meeting as best I could, using the 'terp to help out because my Kurmanji was still very rough and these guys either didn't know much Arabic or didn't care to speak it. I figured it was the latter, so the Arabic I'd learned in Phase V didn't do much good in these parts.

The sergeant gestured for me to step away from the Kurds. "Sorry, sir, but the cap'n asked if you could give his apologies and close the meeting."

"What's up, Bliese?"

"Bad news from home, sir."

"What happened?"

Bliese looked away, then back at me. "It's his son, sir. He's dead."

Karim Jones was seventeen years old, a star on the football field at his high school in a suburb of Milwaukee. An all-state running back last year and sure to be again in this, his senior season, he would be off to West Point when the school year ended. Considering that his dad was gone more often than not, the young man was doing pretty damn well, from what I had heard from his proud father. Preparing for his retirement, Jones had moved the family back to their native Milwaukee just over three years ago, before the boy started high school. Between the captain's extra hazardous duty pay and what his wife earned as a nurse, they'd been able to settle in Hales Corners, one of the metro's better suburbs. In fact, the captain was planning to take a well-deserved leave in another week, giving him a chance to see his son play in the state championship game at Camp Randall in Madison, if they won their semifinal. The young man had been doing well, indeed, making new friends, impressing college coaches.

But Karim kept in touch with some cousins in the 'hood, on Milwaukee's north side.

Bliese filled me in on what had happened just hours ago. The young man had gone to a party at a cousin's house after the football game, a victory in the quarterfinal round of the state playoffs. He'd lit up the scoreboard with four touchdowns, according to a proud post-game email from his mom to his faraway dad in Iraq. About midnight, some guys tried crashing the party and were told to leave. They did, but came back and sprayed the front of the house with gunfire. A round had come through the front window glass and into the temple of Karim Jones.

And now, Captain Jones had to go home to bury his son, the son he thought he'd be watching carrying the ball at West Point in another year, then graduating with the Long Gray Line three years later. The captain had been planning on retiring after this tour in March, so he could at least spend a few months with his son before the boy left for his plebe year. I had a feeling that retirement would now be very lonely. Karim had been their only child.

I also had a feeling that Jones would not be coming back to Iraq. That led to the question of who would ultimately be given command of ODA-5237, Charlie Company, 2nd Battalion, 5th SFG. I'd been in country only six weeks, and had arrived here just a few days ago as a replacement for the warrant officer who'd been Jones's second-in-command. The warrant had taken the brunt of an IED, losing a leg, and the orders from Battalion had sent 1st Lieutenant Jake Dawson, two months out of the Q Course, up here from Baghdad.

My initial weeks in Iraq were spent in the capital, working with a Special Forces planning platoon headquartered in the Green Zone. I was confident I'd get another combat assignment, but not this way. I wanted to earn it, not come in as somebody's replacement, especially the replacement for a wounded warrant officer who was pretty well-respected by the men, from what I'd found out. I would've had temporary command of the ODA during Jones's leave, but then he'd come back and spend the next few months showing me the ropes. Now, I'd have to earn the respect of the ODA, and earn it fast. ISIS was on the march in northern Iraq. The enemy had taken Mosul a year and a half before, something we saw coming when I was in the Wolverines, and since then had resisted major pushes by the Iraqi Army and Peshmerga to drive them out. Mosul was only a hundred kilometers from the town of Bujal, smooth sailing along Highway 3. We were in a smaller village, about ten klicks north in the mountains, but we were at the end of the road. The Kurds were ready to defend Bujal, but things didn't look good and we'd been ordered to move north into this vill, as the Peshmerga made plans to escape into the mountains if they couldn't hold the town on the highway.

The helo was touching down on the makeshift pad behind the compound the ODA was using as our headquarters and barracks. Jones made the rounds of the men, shaking hands solemnly with each one. Tough sergeants, all eight of them. The toughest was probably the 18Z, Master Sergeant Wilson, who had been with Jones in Afghanistan, riding horses through the mountains as part of Task Force Dagger right after 9/11. There were tears in the old sergeant's eyes now as he was the last man to shake his captain's hand.

"We'll all be praying for you and your family, sir," Wilson said.

"I appreciate that, Rob. Take good care of my new lieutenant, here, will you?"

Wilson glanced quickly at me, then looked back at his departing C.O. "Don't worry, sir, he'll do all right."

Jones led the way out to the pad, shook hands one last time with me, and tossed his gear into the helo. He turned one last time to face his men.

"Ten-HUT!" I barked, and with nine crisp salutes the ODA said goodbye.

It was time for evening chow call. We'd hired a couple of the locals to prepare evening meals when the ODA wasn't in the field, and the Kurds had been working hard on American cuisine. So far they'd managed to get hamburgers and fried chicken down pretty well, although the beef was different from what we remembered from back home and the chicken was tougher. But it all beat MREs to hell and gone so nobody complained. When I got to what passed for a DFAC, our dining facility, I fell in line behind Wilson.

"Say, Sergeant, I wanted to thank you for what you said back there," I said, when we were out of earshot of the other men.

"How's that, sir?"

"About me doing all right. I appreciate it."

Without benefit of a cover indoors, the old veteran's buzz cut was iron gray with some scalp showing at the crown. Unlike a lot of SF personnel, Wilson apparently disdained letting his hair grow out while on deployment. One more indication that he was an old-school guy. That word "old" kept coming to mind when I thought of Wilson, and yet he was younger than my father. I'd have to change my thinking about that. Wilson had to be forty if he was a day. Maybe a couple or three years younger than Jones. "No problem, sir," he said. "It always takes some time to get squared away when you get downrange. Let's grab a seat."

Six other members of the team had taken chairs around two of the rickety tables, pretending not to be paying attention. I was pretty sure they were; one thing I'd learned damn fast on this deployment was that SF guys definitely had a sixth sense about their surroundings. It helped keep them alive.

Wilson led the way to the lone remaining open table, and I sat down across from him. "Let me ask you something, sir," Wilson said. "This isn't your first tour in the Sandbox, is that right?"

"That'd be right, Sarge, but I'm sure the captain read you in on my record when he found out I was coming up here as Mr. Severson's replacement."

"He said you had two here, plus one over in the Stan."

"Yep." I dug in to my chicken breast, wondering where Wilson might be going with this, and also wondering if I was now eating one of the scrawny birds I'd seen wandering around this morning.

"There's one main similarity between the enemy there and here, as I see it," I said, chewing on a forkful of chicken. It wasn't bad; whatever spices these guys put on it were okay. "They both like to kill people."

"That would be true, sir," Wilson said. He took a swig from his water bottle. "But they like to kill Americans a lot more than they like to kill anybody else."

"Roger that, Master Sergeant."

Wilson took a couple bites of his bird, seemed to contemplate something, then said, "We haven't had a lot of action here, ROE and all that, but in case you haven't picked up on it by now, this group of Peshmerga fighters will be in real trouble if the hajis attack this village in force. I don't know if the captain shared that with you, but that's what he and I talked about. Bujal has a garrison of only about fifty men. The rest are here, waiting to see what happens. All told, about eighty men. At any given time we have about seventy effectives, the rest being in the infirmary for one reason or another."

"That's what they were telling me in Baghdad," I said. I hadn't been here long enough to get a good read on the situation, and then Jones had gotten that phone call. I was playing catch-up ball on a lot of things, and I knew I'd have to rely on Wilson, a lot. SOP in the Army, of course, where good sergeants were worth their weight in gold, and if said sergeant was in Special Forces, you could make that platinum.

As for our rules of engagement, I knew we were very limited when it came to aiding the Kurdish fighters, and in fact Jones had brought me up to speed on that problem within an hour of my arrival. Up till now, with the fighting many miles to the west, the ODA's duties had mainly been confined to training the Kurds. So far that had been going pretty well, as far as I could see, although the ODA was understaffed. In addition to the warrant's WIA evacuation, Jones had told me the team was down two enlisted men, one medical sergeant and one intelligence sergeant. Fort Campbell had replacements in the pipeline, but they might not get here for another two to four weeks. I was getting the feeling from Wilson that it maybe wasn't going pretty well. "The captain did tell me he had some concerns," I said, honestly. "The Peshmerga I worked with last year when I was with my previous unit seemed to be in pretty decent shape. What about these guys?"

Wilson chewed thoughtfully, maybe thinking of how to break the news. He swallowed, chased it with a slug from his water bottle, and then said, "Well, as I'm sure you've seen by now, they're eager to learn and they're motivated, but they're not battle-tested. Like I said, if ISIS advances on us in company strength or better, we're gonna have real trouble holding this town. And we've got nowhere to go. We're at the end of the road, and when you're at the end of the road up here, you're well and truly fucked, if you'll pardon my French, sir."

I couldn't suppress a small grin. "No problem."

"Anyway, the skipper argued against moving the Peshmerga company headquarters here. He said that if we have to go anywhere, we should go east, along the highway to the next town, where at least we would have an open avenue of retreat if it came to that. But the Kurds can be stubborn, and the colonel running the show with this unit was adamant."

"The captain told me the colonel's rationale was that if he didn't defend this vill, the enemy would come up this way and slaughter everyone."

Wilson nodded sadly. "Well, he's got a point. At the very least they'd come up here looking for any rear-echelon guys the Peshmerga might leave behind. They'd have to cover their six and they're not stupid enough to overlook that. And once they got here, they'd do what they always do when they take a vill. Whoever couldn't escape into the mountains would be at their mercy, and that's one thing they don't seem to have."

Another swig of water. "When the hajis came into Iraq from Syria last year, they caught the locals by surprise. The IA and the Kurds took their lumps. Losing Mosul was huge, a real blow to their morale." He looked at me for a moment, then said, "Some people back home seem to think these guys down the road are just a junior varsity team. Trust me, they're not. Without our air support keeping the locals in the game, they would've taken Baghdad by now, no question."

The people I'd worked with in the capital had the very same opinion, which they were careful not to share with any of the reporters who were snooping around. One of the first things I'd been told after arriving in Baghdad was to be real damn careful when it came to the press, and in fact, I'd had a tense encounter with a TV reporter on my first day in country. But I was also told that because we were supporting them, the Iraqi Army and the Peshmerga were regrouping. I said, "They seem to be getting it together now, though."

"Maybe so. But it's going to take them awhile. In the meantime, we have to hold this village. The terrain favors us. We're in this narrow valley and the only road out of here has to wind around that big hill two klicks to our south. We've got a Peshmerga squad on top around the clock. Whoever controls that hill controls the valley. The enemy doesn't have artillery, but they do have mortars, lots of 'em, M252s captured from the Iraqis, who before that had gratefully received them as gifts from Uncle Sugar. This vill is easily in range of an M252 on that hill. We're lucky they didn't grab any real artillery. The IA has the M109 and M198 howitzers, and with those pieces the hajis could flatten this place from Bujal while they sit around picking their noses and drinking their morning tea."

Wilson swallowed the last of his chicken and sat back, using his fork to twiddle around with what was left of his mashed potatoes. "And then there's the militia problem."

This was news to me. "Come again on that, Master Sergeant? We've got militia in the area?"

He looked at me for a second, then his eyes widened in realization. He sat back, wiped his lips with a napkin, and then said, "I guess the captain didn't have time to go over that with you." He sighed, then shook his head. "There's some chatter that an Iraqi militia unit might be wandering around out there. Well, there's almost always militia wandering around, but this outfit is said to be near company strength. We're all supposed to be on the same side against ISIS, but these people are always concerned about turf, and who's gonna be on top when the shooting stops, or at least settles down for a while. The Peshmerga say this particular unit is from Kata'ib Hezbollah."

Now it was my turn to sit back. "You're just full of good news, Sarge." It took me a couple minutes to tell him about my encounter with that bunch while serving with the Wolverines a year and a half before.

"Might not be the same unit," he said. "These characters are coming and going all the time. As for their leadership, from what I hear they generally have Iranian advisers embedded with them, at least at the company level."

"So," I said, "we have to worry about Bujal being overrun by ISIS, or maybe by the militia."

"Or, maybe they'll all just go home," Wilson said with a wry, tired grin. "I wouldn't count on that, though."

"Okay, Sarge. Any advice for your newbie LT about how to handle this mess?"

"My advice, sir, is to not be queasy about calling in all the tac air you can rustle up if it hits the fan here. One group or the other is coming up that road, and when they do, we might not have a lot of time, it comes right down to it. Either way, they'll be coming after us with weapons captured from the Iraqis and maybe the Syrians, probably some U.S.-made, too. I doubt if they'll have any armor, but they'll be loaded for as much bear as they can carry. They sure as hell couldn't match up with us if we put a couple of divisions in the field, but we're not gonna do that, not with who's running things back in D.C. If we came in country with a couple divisions of infantry and an armored brigade, combine that with our air and we could take care of the problem in about two weeks."

"It didn't take us long the last time," I said, "or the time before that."

Wilson nodded. "My uncle was in the Air Force in the First Gulf War, back in '91. He flew an A-10 along the Highway of Death and he said it was ducks on a pond for him and his buddies. Why? Because the enemy had no air cover, no appreciable anti-air capability and so they were running for their goddamn lives, that's why. It'd be the same now. Ground forces in strength to push the enemy back along the roads to Syria and the flyboys do the rest. But instead, it's basically just us SF guys out here in the boonies and some Air Force planes down in Baghdad and Navy birds off the carriers in the Gulf." He finished his water, then said, "The guys down the road are vicious bastards and if they're given the chance they'll come through here like shit through a goose. And they're on their way."

"Understood, Sergeant. Thanks for the heads up."

"No problem."

The ODA was headquartered in what had once been the home of the town's top merchant. Unfortunately for him, he'd been a Baath Party member and vanished shortly after the U.S. invasion in '03. The Kurdistan government had confiscated the place and now it was ours for the duration. Four hours after my little conversation with Wilson, I pushed open the door of my room, flipped the switch and was gratified that the overhead bulb flickered on and stayed lit. It was anybody's guess how long that would last. Reliable electricity was just one of the many challenges faced by Iraq these days, one that was not likely to be resolved any time soon. When you have invaders holding parts of your country, things like electricity tend to take a back seat to more pressing matters. I made a mental note to have my lead 18C, Sergeant Samuels, take a look at the local power grid to see if he might recommend some upgrades. Samuels was the more experienced of my two engineering sergeants and probably knew more about blowing things up than keeping a civilian power grid operational, but it was worth a try.

There was so fricking much to do, that was the problem. Jones had given me some responsibilities right after my arrival, but a large part of my duties involved just learning how things were done in a deployed ODA. Now I had to run the ODA. Fifth Group was supposed to be sending another warrant officer here to help out, but like the enlisted replacements, not for at least two weeks, probably more. Until the new warrant got here, it was my show.

I chucked off my boots and lay down on my rack, not bothering to take off my ACUs. If the electricity here was spotty, laundry service was even worse. Everything was done by hand, and we had a couple local girls for that, but they also had their own families to help out, so we couldn't impose on them too often. They'd warned me about all these things during training, of course, but hearing about them and then experiencing them were two different things.

I picked up the Rough Rider's diary. With everything that had been going on since graduation, I still hadn't had time to read any more of it. Its musty old cover seemed to be calling out to me. Were there any more letters in there from Ernie, or my grandfather? What could possibly be in there from the Rough Rider himself that would help me, now? He hadn't been an officer, just a grunt, sweating through his blue cotton blouse and firing that old Krag at the Spaniards. What could he possibly tell me about being the commanding officer of a combat unit?

Frustrated, I put it aside and picked up Sam's last letter. The only internet service we had here was via satellite and our ability to access it was limited. Something about the terrain again. We could get commo with Baghdad and Fort Campbell, but only twice a day, with barely enough bandwidth to allow official comms. Skyping was out of the question. But resupply birds came in every few days and brought old-fashioned mail, among other things, so the families of the ODA had quickly taken to writing letters the way their grandparents had done. It was kind of cool, really. Sam's handwriting was flowing and delicate; she'd paid attention back in grade school when they taught cursive.

Postmarked ten days ago from Minocqua, she was full of chit-chat about what was going on in town. She'd been under the weather a little, missed a couple days at work, but otherwise her job was going well, although she dreaded having to give her notice. We'd talked a lot about that. I'd be based more or less permanently at Fort Campbell, so after this deployment ended in April, I'd be coming home to Wisconsin and we'd be loading up her car and moving to Kentucky. She was putting up a brave front about that but I knew she was a little scared. She'd grown up in northern Wisconsin, gone through school there, started a career there. Now she would be moving to what would amount to another country to her.

But she was tough, she'd acclimate. Getting a job down there wouldn't be a problem, we'd been assured. Base housing was cheap and there were more than a few other amenities that would come our way. We'd make it. Army families had been making it for a long, long time, and so would we.

And Sam had written something that really had hit home with me: *You've changed, Jake, and for the better. That day of your party, I hadn't seen you since graduation. At church that morning, my mother said how good you looked in your uniform. She said I should say hello to you. I was scared, but she talked me into going to your party. I really didn't know what to expect, but that night, and the next few days, were wonderful. I fell in love with you that day we were in the forest, talking and laughing and swimming and just being together.*

I read it again, then folded the letter and laid back on my rack with the letter on my chest. Staring at the ceiling with its peeling paint, I tried to imagine Sam, at that very moment. It would be early afternoon in Minocqua, and she'd be at work. Since the wedding she'd been living at Mom's place, letting the lease run out on her apartment. They were like peas in a pod, and that pleased me greatly. Later on in the evening she'd be in the bathtub, but I tried not to think of her body glistening in the water. I thought of our honeymoon, not all the way up to Isle Royale but to her uncle's cabin on a lake near Eagle River. Three days of fishing, canoeing, making love on the rug in front of the fireplace. They were the best three days of my life. God, how I loved her. And not with the lusty, fake "love" of a teenager, but it was deeper, more powerful. I couldn't imagine my life now without her in it. All the more reason to come home alive, and whole.

Well, tomorrow would be another day, as they say, and I resolved that it would go better than this one. I would take it step by step, and I'd have to rely on Wilson for a lot, at least at the beginning. Yeah, the old sergeant had been around the block more than a few times. Jones had told me a couple stories from their earlier tours together. They'd seem some shit, that was for sure.

I had a feeling we were going to see more, a lot more, and soon. Unfortunately, I was right on the money about that.

CHAPTER THIRTY-THREE

Qaszir, northern Iraq
November 9, 2015

When I stepped outside after breakfast the next morning, I could already feel something was different. No, not just because Jones was gone, but there was something in the air. People were moving about the village with more tension than even the day before.

Bliese, the commo sergeant, was right behind me. He noticed it, too. "What's going on, sir?"

"I was just about to ask you that question, Sergeant. Anything on the air I need to know about?"

"Last commo package was at 0600, LT, and it was just routine."

My MBITR short-range tactical radio chose that moment to activate. *"Badger Actual, this is Badger Nine, do you copy?"* That would be Sergeant First Class Bentler, the ODA's 18F, the intelligence sergeant, and also the assistant to our 18Z Operations Sergeant, Wilson. Jones had used "Badger" as our unit's call sign, and since we were both from Wisconsin, there was certainly no need to change it.

"Copy, Badger Nine," I replied, "this is Badger Actual. What have you got? Over."

"I'm at Station Teyrelaş, be advised we have two Land Rovers inbound your position, ETA ten mikes. No obvious armament. They have flashed the recognition signal, repeat, signal is friendly. Estimate maximum six souls aboard. Wolfhound is passing them through, requests you meet them in the square. Over."

"Copy, Badger Nine," I said again. "Two Land Rovers inbound, assumed friendly. Wolfhound gives passage, is that confirmed? Over." Wolfhound was the call sign for Colonel Ghali, the commander of the

Peshmerga company that was the garrison force for Bujal and this village. He'd been down in Bujal when I got to the ODA, and we hadn't yet met. Now, according to Bentler, the colonel was on Teyrelaş, the hill that commanded the road leading into the village, which was where Bentler had spent the past two days. He was due to be relieved by noon today, one more thing I had to get done.

"That's affirmative, Badger Actual, over."

"Copy that, Badger Nine. Be advised we'll have your relief up there by 1200. Badger Actual out." One less thing to do.

"Company coming, LT," Bliese said. He had a knack for stating the obvious, but I liked him. He certainly knew his MOS, but that was no surprise. It would've been surprising if he didn't know commo backwards and forwards. Before joining the Army he'd worked at a Radio Shack. I wasn't at all surprised to hear that.

"Well, let's go see who it is."

We got to the village square, at the literal end of the road from Bujal, as the two Land Rovers were coming down the slight grade. About one klick past them I could see the Humvee that must have been Colonel Ghali's command vehicle. The Land Rovers swung into the square and pulled to a stop, small dust clouds overtaking them from behind. It had been dry here lately; they said the last rain had come two weeks before. Water usage in the village was starting to become an issue, but these people dealt with it stoically, like they'd been doing for centuries.

The doors opened on both of the vehicles and I had to force myself to stay impassive as I saw the occupants disembark. The driver of the first rig was obviously a local, but the woman who got out from the passenger side was not. Her blonde hair was covered in a scarf that was standing in for a *hijab,* the head covering worn over here by Muslim women. She could've done a better job with it, but at least she wore a long-sleeved shirt and long pants, both khaki and looking much too fresh for these parts. The last time I'd seen her, she was in designer shorts, making absolutely sure her legs were noticed. In the Green Zone of Baghdad, she'd been pushing the envelope, but that was her rep. Up here, though, it would've been a different story, and at least it appeared she knew that.

Bliese must have noticed my reaction to seeing the woman, hard as I had tried to hide it. "You know her, LT?"

"We met in Baghdad," I said.

Just then one of the men from the back seat opened up the rear gate of the Land Rover and brought out a TV camera. "Oh, shit," Bliese said.

"My feelings exactly, Sergeant. She's Jenny Stratton, she works for NBC, and things just got a lot more complicated around here."

I got a break because Ghali's Humvee rolled in right on the heels of the TV crew and he took charge. Clearly, the Peshmerga colonel wanted to establish his bona fides with Stratton right away. That was fine with me. The less I had to deal with her, the better.

During Phase IV of the Q Course, the cadre had brought in a guest speaker, a CNN correspondent, to talk to us about media relations during a deployment. The reporter had not exactly been greeted with hosannas, but what he had to say was important. And at least he was honest. He admitted that a lot of reporters, in particular the TV people, like to grandstand it, especially overseas. Many had an agenda, and their reporting hewed to their preferred line. When someone brought up the name of Jenny Stratton as an example, he just smiled. She was notorious for building her Instagram following to stratospheric levels by regularly posting photos that Uncle John would've referred to as "not quite pinup material, but close enough." She dated A-list Hollywood actors and baseball stars. Her network tolerated it all because the publicity translated to ratings, and ratings meant dollars.

I had only asked one question of the CNN guy: of all the TV journalists he knew who covered the military, how many had ever been in uniform? He thought about that a moment, then shook his head. "None that I know of." That had told us pretty much all we needed to know.

But up until my arrival in Baghdad, the few encounters I'd had with journalists in the field had gone fairly well. The Fox News guy who'd covered the big firefight down in Wasit Province had been pretty fair with us, and I'd run into a lot of people back home who had seen his story. But Stratton had caught me just hours after my plane touched down, and I wasn't in the best of moods. Neither was she, and I tried not to think of what the on-air result would be. Right now, though, I still had a job to do. Jones hadn't briefed me on any reporters sniffing around, and my instructions from 5th Group were to cooperate with the press but not to let them photograph the men's faces unless I was released to do so in a specific directive. And, I noted, the latest package of orders I'd reviewed with Jones had not included any such release.

"Pass the word," I said to Bliese, "the men are not to consent to any on-camera interviews with this bunch unless they get clearance from me."

"Roger that, LT, and thank you. That'll just make it official. And we can blame you for it?"

"By all means, Sergeant." I figured that meant I'd be hearing from Stratton pretty soon.

I saw Ghali directing one of his officers to show Stratton and her crew to whatever quarters he might've been able to scrounge up for them, and then he saw me. When he came over, I saluted and then offered my hand. "Colonel Ghali," I said in my best Kurmanji, which wasn't too great, "I am Lieutenant Dawson, in…." I couldn't remember the word for *temporary*.

Ghali was about five-eight, swarthy and carried a few extra pounds, but Jones had told me my Peshmerga counterpart was a competent officer and looked after his men well. He gave me a smile, showing a gold tooth. "I speak English, Lieutenant," he said. "Some, eh? We will do okay with it."

"Thank you," I said, gratefully. "I am in temporary command of the ODA. Captain Jones has gone home to tend to a family emergency."

"I heard," he said. "His boy, terrible. I have offered prayers for him. He is a good man. It is a hard thing, a son to lose, yes?"

"It certainly is." I knew the Kurds placed a lot of value on small talk, but I decided to take a chance and get right to the heart of the matter. "Colonel, forgive me for being brief, but what is our situation in Bujal?"

Ghali nodded, concerned. "Serious. We must discuss it." He looked at his watch. "Please meet with me and my officers, in my quarters, thirty minutes?"

"Of course, sir."

Ghali had two of his lieutenants with him; his second-in-command was still down in Bujal, and another lieutenant was on Teyrelaş. I brought my 18Z, Wilson, along with Bliese and Bentler, the intel sergeant. Ghali had been given use of a modest home only a block from our billet. He had a map spread out on the table in what passed for the dining room. The Kurds looked grim when we got there and it didn't take long to find out why. After first requesting that the briefing be done in Arabic, to which I readily agreed, Ghali began.

"Captain Shadid has sent a report," he said. Shadid was his 2IC, commanding the garrison in Bujal, about fifty men. The rest of the Peshmerga force, about twenty or thirty effectives, was here in the village. "It is not good news." He pointed at a town on the map. "The enemy is here."

His finger was on a dot on the map with an Arabic name I could read: Mamuzin. Halfway between Mosul, which was in ISIS hands, and the town of Aqrah, a distance of about thirty miles northeast on a relatively good highway. At Aqrah the highway swung due east and ten miles down the road in that direction was Bujal.

"Are they advancing?" I asked.

"Not yet," the colonel said. I looked at Bentler for confirmation, and he nodded. "But," Ghali added, "they could move at any time. There would be no resistance along this road to Aqrah, unless we can have an air strike."

"We can probably arrange that," I said, making a mental note to have Bliese call in the request as soon as the meeting was over. If the enemy moved out of Mamuzin, we could make it a very poor decision. It would all depend on how fast they could move, and that would depend on what they were moving. They never did a march on foot, no more than a few klicks anyway, so for an advance like this they'd have to rustle up enough vehicles to move at least a company, about two hundred fighters, and they could be in Aqrah in an hour. We'd have to move fast to get our air assets in place. "I will see about drone recon," I said. "Once they move, we can hit them on the road when they're well clear of Mamuzin."

"Yes," Ghali said, "but that is not our only problem." He pointed to Aqrah, then traced the highway eastward. "There are no Peshmerga in Aqrah, they're all here in Bujal and then up here." The fingertip followed the squiggly road northward through the mountains, six and a half miles to where we were right now. With nothing but mountains behind us.

"So, the enemy can take Aqrah," I said. The air strike would be the only chance to stop an advance. There were probably air assets available, but this was a pretty busy theater, with much of the action well to our west. Stopping a company of what amounted to mechanized infantry would take a sizable commitment of assets. There would be political considerations, too. There always were. If the Iraqi government considered other towns more valuable, that's where they'd direct their own ground forces and they'd lean on our people for air cover. There were only so many planes to go around.

"Aqrah will be saved, God willing," Ghali said, "if your Air Force can stop them. But the more serious problem is already in Aqrah itself. The militia is there, in company strength. They will not fight Da'esh. Instead, they will abandon the city and come to Bujal. And then they might very well come here."

Ghali must have seen the grim look on my face. Wilson had warned me about this, just the day before. The Peshmerga commander motioned one of his lieutenants to speak. "Lieutenant Tahan is my intelligence officer. Your report, please."

Tahan was only about twenty-five by the look of him, maybe a few years younger, but he didn't look overwhelmed. In my time with the Wolverines, I'd worked with several Kurdish officers and it was clear they knew their stuff. These people had been fighting for generations. Under Saddam they'd been suppressed but had gone underground, many escaping into eastern Turkey, northern Iran, and even farther north to Armenia and Nakhchivan, the autonomous republic that had been fought over by the Armenians and their next-door neighbors in Azerbaijan. I'd made a point of studying the history this time.

Since Saddam's ouster in '03, though, the Kurds had returned and they'd been asserting themselves here in the north of Iraq, pretty much running their own show, which made the Iranians and Turks nervous. Now their country was under attack yet again by murderous outsiders, ISIS—or Da'esh, as the Arabs called them—coming in from the west, and the anti-Kurdish militias from the south. Tahan cleared his throat, then said, "Our best information says the militia is Kata'ib Hezbollah. Maybe two hundred, two hundred fifty fighters. This group is independent of the Popular Mobilization Forces."

I shook my head in dismay. The PMF was a group of Iraqi militias, largely Shi'a but some Sunni as well, that the Iraqi government had formed about a year ago to help combat the ISIS threat. This outfit that was moving on Bujal evidently had split off from PMF control. Could this get any worse?

"Where did they come from?" I asked, dreading the answer.

Tahan leaned over and pointed at Kirkuk, well south of the Kurdish capital of Erbil. "Originally, we had reports of this group forming around Kirkuk. They came through Erbil, with our government's permission, then west toward Mosul, but somewhere between Erbil and Mosul, they swung north."

"They did not engage the enemy," Ghali said with disgust. "Cowardly sons of whores." That surprised me. Unlike Americans, Arabs and Kurds don't throw insults around casually, especially one like that. Ghali was well and truly pissed at these guys.

Tahan's finger continued to trace a path northward toward Mamuzin, then along the same highway we'd looked at a moment before, to Aqrah. "Now they are here, and we believe they will soon move on Bujal. They are heading east. They fear Da'esh is coming all the way here."

"What's their ultimate destination?" I asked as I looked at the map, already suspecting the answer.

Tahan moved his fingertip another forty miles or so to the east. "Here," he said. "The Iranian border."

"They're running for home," Wilson said, speaking for the first time in the meeting.

"Yes," Ghali said. "I would be glad to see them leave our country. I would wave at them as they drove by. I would prefer to show them the sole of my boot, but it would be better to get rid of them entirely and then I could prepare to confront the real enemy if Da'esh advances on Aqrah. But if they see my men in Bujal, they will try to fight their way through."

"Even if you offer them safe passage?" I asked.

"They would consider it cowardice to accept," Ghali said. "They would be showing their true colors to all of Kurdistan." He paused, then said, "Lieutenant Dawson, I have received new orders from my government in Erbil. I must abandon Bujal and let the militia go through. I will pull the rest of my men back, up here."

Beside me, Wilson straightened, as if I could see his hackles rising. "You would leave the city to the militia, Colonel?" I asked.

"It is to let them pass safely through," Ghali said. "My superiors believe it is the prudent course. The militia is desperate, we think. If we block them in Bujal, they will try to fight their way through. Many in the city would die. We would defeat them, yes, with your help, but if we let them go through, the problem solves itself without bloodshed, hopefully."

Ghali must have seen the concern on our faces. He stood a little straighter. "Make no mistake, my friends. My men and I are ready to fight to the death to defend our country, but the larger threat is from Mosul. What would happen if we fight the militia, and we win, but take high casualties? And then Da'esh moves on Aqrah and your Air Force cannot stop them? There are over twenty thousand of my countrymen in Aqrah. I must do what I can to protect them. If I let the militia through Bujal, I can then move my entire force to Aqrah and await Peshmerga reinforcements. If the real enemy continues to advance northward, they must be stopped there."

"I see your point, Colonel," I said, and I did. Commanders have to make tough choices in the field, and in this case, the choice had been made for him. Of course if it went wrong, if Ghali pulled his men out of Bujal and the militia ransacked the town before moving on, Ghali would get the blame. The politicians would make sure of that. He was in a tough spot, and it was my job, the ODA's job, to support him. "We will stand by you, of course," I said. "But I must ask one question of Lieutenant Tahan." I looked the young Kurd straight in the eye. Hell, he was about my age, and now he looked a little frightened. I hoped I didn't look that way to him. "The militia will know there were Peshmerga in Bujal. They'll be told your men went north, not east. Will they follow you up here, to protect their rear?"

Tahan swallowed. "That…is possible."

"I'd say it's likely, LT," Bentler said. I had to agree with him. A minute ago, I'd wondered if things could get any worse. They just had.

CHAPTER THIRTY-FOUR

Qaszir, northern Iraq
November 9, 2015

When it gets dark in the mountains of Kurdistan, it's really dark. At 2100 hours I decided to check the perimeter. The village was maybe one square kilometer, but roughly rectangular, running north-south along the valley. Teyrelaş rose about a hundred and fifty meters from the valley floor, its eastern base crowding the road, and on the west merging into the larger mountain. I could see the lights of some campfires up there at the crest and just below it on the near side.

Wilson was with me as we checked the perimeter in a Humvee. "What's the deal with the name of that hill, Master Sergeant?" I asked.

"Named after a native scavenger bird, LT," Wilson said. "The Egyptian vulture. Smaller than the ones we have back home, and it has a golden head, not a red one. The legend here is that enemies who threaten the village die up there and become food for the vultures."

"Well, that's a pretty picture to paint for your kids at the dinner table," I said. "As hills go, it's a fairly steep one."

"That it is, sir. Grade of about thirty degrees on this side. It's a hike."

"But not as steep on the south side, right?"

"I'd say it's about twenty degrees max over there. Humvees could make it to the top from that side a little easier. This one, too, although I wouldn't want to do it cither way if the people on the top didn't want me coming up."

I made a mental note to climb that hill the next morning. I wanted to see if there was any cover to be had going up this side. Something was telling me that could be important. Right now it was too dark for a sweep with binoculars. No, I'd have to hoof it myself, in daylight.

"How many men up there right now?"

"Ghali has maybe two dozen, sir, and tonight we've got two of ours, Rivers and Thomas, up there."

"Are you a betting man?"

Wilson was silent for a moment, then said, "I've been known to put a few bucks on the World Series, sir."

"What are the odds that the militia will keep going east through Bujal and ignore us up here?"

"I'd say six will get you ten that they'll be heading up this road in the next forty-eight hours."

"So, if you're the company commander and Higher says it's your discretion whether to evacuate and retreat to the east, or come up here to the north, or make a stand, do you stay and defend Bujal?"

Wilson didn't hesitate on that one. "I stay and make my stand there, sir. Knowing the enemy, and what he'll do to my civilians if I'm not there, I hold. Call for reinforcements, harden my defenses as best I can, call for tac air to hit them before they get to me, and whatever the air can't take care of, I finish off when they get to my perimeter. In fact, I can think of three ambush points where we could deal with them inside the perimeter, if they make it that far. I've spent more than a little time in that town. You give me forty-eight hours and I can harden it and make it very tough for the enemy to come through, even if I don't get air support."

"Do we know anything about their makeup? My briefings down in Baghdad said these units could be anything from irregular infantry up to and including tanks."

It wasn't so dark that I couldn't see Wilson shaking his head. "That militia unit doesn't have any armor, we can be pretty sure of that. They've come too far to maintain the kind of supply line you need for even one or two tanks. So here's another wager for you, LT: seven will get you ten that they're the usual bullshit Arab irregular company with maybe a dozen or so technicals with fifties in the beds, then some clowns passing as infantry who wouldn't last two days at Fort Benning." I heard him spit, probably out of frustration, maybe anger. Then he said,

"But those clowns will be armed and they'll be highly motivated. They won't go down easy, and if they get a free pass through Bujal it'll be like Christmas morning, or whatever passes for that over here."

The sergeant paused, then said, with a voice that was quieter but even more determined, "If I evacuated and the enemy came through and killed and raped my people, I'd never forgive myself. I'd wind up putting a bullet in my head, probably. Sir."

I nodded, feeling an odd combination of relief and pity. Relief, because of the caliber of this man beside me, who I'd be relying on so much in the next few days. Pity, because I felt sorry for Colonel Ghali. He was in a no-win situation. In SF, we didn't like no-win situations. There was always a way to win, somehow. You just had to find it.

Now, *I* had to find it.

I said, "That's exactly how I feel. You know Colonel Ghali a lot better than I do. Is that how he's feeling, too? Would he rather stay down there and make a stand?"

"I would bet that's how he feels, LT, but he has his orders. If it's me down there and I get those orders, I follow them, otherwise I'm relieved and the next guy follows the orders anyway. If I follow my orders, I stay in command and that means I'll get another shot at those bastards."

I sighed again. "Yeah, he's got his orders." I checked my watch. Earlier in the day I'd used one of the communication windows to send a message up to the bird and back down to 5th Group's headquarters in Baghdad. "Let's finish this up and get back to our post. The comms window is closing up in thirty minutes."

I was bone-tired when I got to my room two hours later. The comms package hadn't given me any new orders. I typed up a report of the situation and emailed it up to the bird. Maybe they'd have something for me in the morning, but I rather doubted I'd be ordered to take my team and abandon the village and Ghali. That would go against everything we were trying to achieve in this country, everything Special Forces stood for. I'd never heard of it happening, but there was always a first time.

And I had to admit, there was a part of me, deep down inside, that wanted this to be that first time. I'd been in my share of combat since that very first deployment down in Wasit, and I'd made it through in pretty good shape. Some guys went their entire careers–Wilson came immediately to mind–without anything worse than a few scratches and sprains. But Chet Murphy came to mind, too. He'd only deployed once, and now he was in a steel coffin, buried in some Montana graveyard.

And then there were the guys who came back, but not all of them made it. I'd heard the stories, about guys who lost limbs or were burned or disfigured, and their lives were never the same. Best case, they get strong support from their family, their community, and they get treatment and have a life afterward, even if they can't play catch with their kids or make love to their wives. Worst case? It's a nightmare from the moment they wake up and it never goes away, and then it gets worse. They're lying in a hospital bed at Walter Reed when their wife walks in with divorce papers for him to sign, or their fiancée takes one look and turns right around.

Sam wouldn't do that to me, though. I had to hold onto that. Whatever was going to happen up here at the ass-end of nowhere, she'd wait for me, and she'd stick with me. How many times had she told me she was proud to be marrying a warrior? Not only that, a leader of warriors?

One of the things the Q Course cadre had hammered away at us in Phase III was about leadership. My favorite instructor, a former SF colonel who'd put in four tours in Vietnam, had passed around a quote from a former Secretary of Defense, Robert Gates, talking about the principal attributes of a successful warrior leader, that it's not physical toughness or tactical proficiency or even bravery. "Even more important on the battlefield," Gates wrote, "are self-discipline, character, and the ability to earn the trust and confidence of one's comrades, superiors and subordinates."

I had to turn it off somehow, get some sleep, but I was still wired. I had my Kindle e-reader on the shelf, all charged up, and I made a move to reach up for it, but then I remembered something Uncle John had told me, what seemed like years ago, about where I should be looking for guidance. I left the Kindle alone, pulled over my duffel bag and dug around, rummaging blindly through it until my fingers brushed the familiar old leather. I pulled out the Rough Rider's diary, for the first time since it had come back to me. Sitting up in my rack, my thin pillow giving me what comfort it could against the cold stone wall, I opened it up.

Maybe I'd been hoping that reading about my ancestor's adventures in Cuba would be entertaining, maybe even relaxing, to take my mind off the responsibilities I had here, what I felt pretty sure was coming. Well, it didn't take me too many pages to realize that if I was looking for some relaxing reading, this wasn't it.

CHAPTER THIRTY-FIVE

The journal of Charles J. Dawson, con't.

June the 28th, 1898 – The morning after the fight, we buried our dead. I assisted in the digging of the trench, into which the bodies of 16 of our comrades were laid. The only one not there was Capt. Capron, whose remains had been taken back to the beach to be temporarily interred there. After placing the bodies reverently at the bottom, we put palm leaves over top of them.

The chaplain began the service with most of the Regiment surrounding the grave. Nearby, on the road from Santiago I saw a group of women and children, emaciated and forlorn, trudging away from their city. The chaplain read from Scripture and then we sang, "Nearer My God to Thee." Then we began shoveling dirt onto the men. The bugler played "Taps" and a closing prayer was said. It was a moment of extreme emotion. Many of the men wept. These were some of the toughest men I had ever met, bronco busters and sheriffs, foot-ball players and steely-eyed men of business, and they cried like children. Although I had not gotten to know any of the fallen personally, I had met several of them, and now they were gone. Nevermore would they share a campfire with their comrades. Their families would not welcome them home as heroes. Their loved ones would have only the memories of their fallen to comfort them, and I wondered how much comfort they would get from that.

I myself had come close to death more than once during the fight. It could easily have been my body lying down there. The realization sent a deep shudder through me. What had Father warned me about, that day back in his office, when I begged his help to join the Regiment? "There is no romance on the firing line." How right he had been.

Following the funeral, there was not much to do except to prepare for what we had heard might be an encampment of a few days' duration. We moved two miles closer to Santiago and camped along a river known as the Aguadores, as picturesque a stream as one will find anywhere. As we gathered around our campfires for supper, rumors abounded. One, that I later learned was true, was about a Spanish prisoner brought to Col. Wood after the funeral service. An officer, he is said to have told Wood that the enemy was bewildered by the fact that Americans, unlike Cubans, did not break and run in the face of Spanish fire. After his interrogation, Wood turned the Spaniard over to the Cubans, who promptly executed him in the most horrible fashion, by decapitation with a machete.

The heat and humidity are oppressive. Some troopers from Louisiana said this is far worse than they experience back home. The mosquitoes and flies are almost obscene in their number. Men have been falling sick with fever. Some call it "yellow jack," and rumor has it one can die from it, but nobody is sure of the cause. We have been encouraged to boil the water we get from the stream before using it for drinking or cooking, but few men do. I have to confess I am not one of the few. So far my health has been good.

Food is scarce. We have been living hand to mouth. There are no fish in the stream we camp upon and no game to be had in the jungle. A rumor that there were provisions aplenty sitting on the beach back at Siboney became so strident that Lt. Col. Roosevelt himself set off for the coastal town and found over half a ton of beans. He was told they were for the officers' mess, and Roosevelt declared he would take all of them because his officers have big appetites. Of course the beans were distributed amongst all the men and were much appreciated. Some troopers have been inventive in the preparation of native fruits like mangoes, despite warnings from the surgeons that the mango may be the source of yellow jack. We have also gorged on limes when a tree is found.

There has been no tobacco to be had for days now, since Las

Guasimas. Many of the smokers have suffered from lack of it with headaches and insomnia. One trooper brought back a plug of tobacco from Siboney and sold it for thirty times its worth. Some desperate smokers rolled their own, using a noxious mixture of grass, roots, tea and horse droppings.

Every afternoon it rains around 3 p.m., and a Cuban rain is always a downpour. Trails become rivers of mud. Even inside a tent, we are miserable during the rain. Many of the New Mexico and Arizona troopers have hardly seen this much rain in their entire lives. The novelty of it wore off quickly for them. Our boots do not dry and are beginning to rot. As for our feet, they suffer worse than any other bodily part. Officers remind us to keep our feet clean but it is useless in these horrid conditions.

We use the rain to bathe and wash our clothing as much as can be done. We are forbidden to use the river for washing or bathing, or as a latrine, lest we foul it for those who are downstream. Few of us have shaven since departing the ship. We are a motley crew indeed, but even in the midst of such primitive conditions, spirits remain high, to my amazement. As for me, I long for my soft, dry bed back in Platteville. My only solace is that Father campaigned for much longer, at one point, he told me, going nearly a year between leaves home. We are confident we shall be home soon, but there will be hard fighting ahead, of that there is no doubt. We routed the Spaniards at Las Guasimas, but Santiago awaits us, and its defenders will be ready.

June the 30th, 1898 ~ Whether we will have the leadership necessary to achieve victory remains to be seen. Two days ago, Gen'l Shafter himself rode past our camp. It is a miracle that a mule was actually found that is capable of bearing his bulk. I was with some of my Harvard mates, and Wells noted that it appeared Shafter would be better able to carry the mule than the other way around. There have been rumors aplenty about the dithering of the general and his staff. It is no secret that Lt. Col.

Roosevelt has no fondness for Shafter.

Yesterday, I accompanied a scouting party that reconnoitered the last obstacle between us and Santiago, a series of hills the Cubans have named Los Cerros del Rio San Juan. Richard Harding Davis, the reporter, was with us. He is reporting to a New York newspaper and also to Scribner's Magazine. Davis has earned our respect with his willingness to share our hardships since the landing, and he declared the hills to be known as San Juan Heights. There are buildings atop the hills and the Spaniards are fortifying them. They have also been digging trenches along the length of the hill tops. Even from about a thousand yards off, we could see the distinctive white sombreros of the enemy.

We returned to the camp to make our report. I was present when the scouts, led by Capt. O'Neill, briefed Col. Roosevelt about the reconnaissance. O'Neill was very thorough, going so far as to sketch a rough map of the hills, including the Spanish fortifications. At the end of the briefing, he said, "Colonel, if we could bring artillery to bear on the enemy while they are digging, it would go a long ways toward helping us when we advance."

"I am in thorough agreement," Roosevelt stated, "and in fact have already communicated that to the general's staff. I shall do so again, but so far I have seen no movement."

It was more than I could stand. Father had once told me that fighting entrenched Rebels was bloody work indeed, and only by virtue of sustained artillery bombardment could they be dislodged without high casualties on the attackers' side. On the occasions such a strategy was not used, the loss of Union lives was frightful. With Father's words in mind, I said, "With respect, Colonel, we must bring our cannon to bear on the enemy before the assault. Have the general and his staff learned nothing from the Rebellion?"

O'Neill gave me a hard look, but Roosevelt was more understanding. "Your father was an officer in the Iron Brigade, was he not, Dawson?"

I swallowed, suddenly fearful of a rebuke, and then said, "Yes, sir."

"Well, then, certainly the opinion of a veteran of those campaigns must be respected. What would he have said about our current predicament?"

Without hesitation, I said, "Were he here, Colonel, after seeing what we saw to-day, he would most certainly call for the artillery. Every cannon we could muster should be brought to bear. Why else did we bring them to Cuba?"

Roosevelt nodded, as did O'Neill, I noticed. Then the colonel said, "Gentlemen, I appreciate your efforts to-day. I will consult with Colonel Wood and forward a recommendation to General Shafter. I pray that he heeds our words of caution." He paused, holding up a finger, and through his spectacles I saw a hard glint in his eyes. "But, we must be prepared in the event the artillery is not employed as we might like. Because, gentlemen, Santiago is our goal, and to get there we must go up those heights. And one way or another, we shall."

CHAPTER THIRTY-SIX

Qaszir, northern Iraq
November 10, 2015

The next day dawned with clear skies, but they might as well have been overcast, because the mood in the village was dark. By mid-morning, Peshmerga troops were filing in past Teyrelaş, their faces grim. These were the men who'd been ordered to evacuate Bujal, and they weren't happy about it. Ghali and I met with Captain Shadid for his report on the situation down there. Shadid was not the young newbie I'd expected; he was a veteran, nearly as old as Ghali, and it was clear they were on the same wavelength.

Our morning comms pack had come through. As I expected, my orders were to stick with Ghali's unit and do what I could to assist in the defense of Qaszir. Air support might be available if the militia advanced up the valley, but there were political considerations. Kata'ib Hezbollah had significant support within the Iraqi government, and unleashing U.S. air power on one of its units in the field could cause a problem. My translation: don't expect air support.

Unleashing it on ISIS, though, was no problem at all, which was why a strike package was being prepared right now to handle the enemy force that might soon be marching up toward Aqrah. Intel suggested that could be happening within the next six hours. So, I would have some good news to give to Ghali, along with the bad. As it turned out, that was the only good news that would be found at the briefing.

Before turning the brief over to Shadid, Ghali asked if I had any word of pending air strikes against ISIS staging out of Mamuzin. "Yes, Colonel," I said, "I have just received word that our Air Force is ready to confront the enemy." I turned the next part of the briefing over to

Bentler, who explained that our intel had the ISIS company moving out of Mamuzin that afternoon, and that they would be hit when they were ten kilometers out of town. But what Bentler didn't say was that we were concerned about security. Could Ghali's officers really be trusted, all of them? Now was not the time to take chances, so the strike package of two fighter-bombers was loitering near Mamuzin right now, with a drone orbiting the town to keep an eye on things. If the militia started moving out before noon, we'd know there was an informant in this room.

"Very good," Ghali said when Bentler finished his brief. "Now, to the more immediate problem. Captain Shadid tells me that the militia is closing in on Bujal."

The map on the table became the focus of everyone's attention. Besides Ghali and Shadid, there was Tahan, the young intel officer, and two Peshmerga lieutenants. Shadid put a fingertip on the road, two kilometers west of the town. "I have a scouting team still in Bujal," he said. "Their last report was one hour ago. Lead elements of the militia force were two kilometers out. By now, they are certainly within the outskirts of the town."

"What are your scout team's orders, Captain?" I asked.

"They are to observe the militia, but not engage. If they are spotted and fired upon, they are to retreat up the valley as quickly as possible." To Ghali, Shadid said, "Colonel, quite frankly I am concerned about civilians collaborating with the militia. I have told my team not to take any chances. Not to accept shelter or offers of transportation. They have a truck of their own. Above all, to avoid capture. They are also to be on radio silence once the militia enters the town, as they have our frequencies."

Ghali nodded. "Wise precautions." He stared at the map, then said, "The next few hours will tell us the story. Will the militia spare Bujal and keep moving, to the Iranian border? Or will they stay to attack the civilians?" He looked at Shadid. "What is the morale of the people down there?"

"Not good, Colonel," Shadid said, shaking his head. "Many believe we have abandoned them. My men were pelted with fruit and worse as they left town. They believe we have broken our word to them."

Ghali was silent, his head bowed, leaning on the table. He seemed to be staring at the map, but I sensed his thoughts were elsewhere, like Bujal. What was happening there right now? What would happen in the next few hours? It was something I wouldn't have wanted on my conscience, but the man had his orders, and he'd followed them. Finally, he straightened and looked at me. "Lieutenant, do you have any recommendations?"

He was putting me on the spot, but was it deliberate? It wasn't hard to imagine that if things went south in Bujal, the Peshmerga might possibly want to blame their American advisors. Something told me there wouldn't be much of a paper trail following his order to retreat from the town. But, fortunately, Wilson had warned me about this before we left for the meeting, and we'd come up with something we hoped would keep everybody's vital parts out of the fire as long as possible.

"Colonel," I said, "while it is unfortunate we can't help your loyal citizens in Bujal, at least we can protect those who are here. Let's set up a security gauntlet." I moved to the map, putting a fingertip on the dot that represented Bujal. "It's ten kilometers from Bujal to Qaszir. We should have a recon team here, two kilometers up the valley. If the militia gets that far, they're coming all the way. We can then pull the scouts back to our perimeter, which should be here." I moved my finger to Teyrelaş "We should fortify the hilltop. We have no artillery, but we do have mortars. We must assume the militia does as well. If they take the hill, they can use their mortars against us here in the town. They would have the M252, the mortar we have supplied to the Iraqi Army, and we would be well within the weapon's range from the hilltop."

Ghali nodded. "Very good," he said. He turned to Tahan. "Major, set up the recon team at two kilometers up from Bujal. Also, make sure the hill is fortified. How many men are up there now?"

Tahan didn't hesitate. "Twenty-two, sir, plus two of Lieutenant Dawson's men."

"Increase our complement to forty men," Ghali ordered. "How many mortars do we have?"

"With the six that Captain Shadid brought from Bujal, we now have eight."

"Put four on the hill." Ghali looked at me, then at his officers. "Brothers, we will hold this town, or we will die in its defense. We withdrew from Bujal, but here we will stand and fight." He looked at me. "And we will fight with our American allies at our sides, yes, Lieutenant?"

"You can count on that, Colonel."

CHAPTER THIRTY-SEVEN

The journal of Charles J. Dawson, con't.

July the 1st, 1898 – We have marched perhaps five miles since my last entry, yesterday morning. Shortly after I finished my notes, the Regiment was roused to vigorous but organized activity by our buglers, and we began striking our camp and preparing to move out. Word came through by mid-afternoon that Col. Wood had been elevated to temporary command of the 2d Brigade, as its leader, Gen'l Young, had been felled by fever. So has Gen'l Wheeler. Lt. Col. Roosevelt is now in sole command of the Regiment.

We were issued three days of rations and told to leave behind anything we could not carry. A shortage of mules meant that what beasts were available were tasked with carrying our machine-guns and a weapon that had not been used at Las Guasimas, a pneumatic dynamite gun. Once made ready, we had to wait beside the road for the longest time. It was terribly disorganized, as nobody seemed to know which units were to march at what time. More than once I saw Roosevelt ride by on his horse, Little Texas, his demeanor one of cold fury despite the oppressive heat.

Finally, we began the march, following two regiments of Regulars, the 1st and 10th Cavalries. Before the march began, our own troopers mingled with the men of the 10th, Negro soldiers whose officers are all white men. Nonetheless, the officers seem to treat their men fairly. The one I saw up close was a hard-looking lieutenant with a thin mustache. After passing by our location on foot and ordering his men to muster up ahead of our Regiment, he stopped to take a drink from his canteen, then cursed when he discovered it was already empty.

I offered him a drink from mine. He accepted with a grateful nod, took two brief gulps, and handed it back to me. "Thanks," he said. He offered his hand. "John J. Pershing," he said. I accepted the handshake and told him my name. He nodded and moved forward to join his men.

One of our troopers said to me, "So, you met Black Jack. He likes those nigger troops, I hear. That's why they call him that. I hope to hell he keeps 'em in line to-morrow."

Something in his voice betrayed an attitude that I found disquieting. "They look like first-rate troops to me," I said. "I suspect the Spanish bullets that are fired at us will pierce dark skin as easily as they do white." He grunted and moved away.

The march was tedious and suffused with stoppages, during which times we would generally sit or lie alongside the road, such that it was. The jungle was close upon us on both sides. With no prospect of a breeze, the heat and humidity were worse than ever. I nursed my canteen and hoped no one else's would go dry as Pershing's had.

At one point, close to dusk, we espied the most amazing sight. Past the front of our column, a balloon rose into the air, with two men in a basket suspended underneath. Word quickly came down the line that it was a Signal Corps craft, designed to observe the enemy's position from above. Next to me, Burdwell spat onto the ground when he saw the balloon. "Well, if the Spaniards didn't know where we were before, they do now," he said. My nervousness increased, and for the next half-hour expected to hear the sound of enemy artillery at any moment. But, no reports came, and we marched on.

Finally, about an hour past dusk, we came upon a hill named El Pozo. I had seen this while on the reconnaissance mission. Now I knew we were about a mile and a half to the east of San Juan Heights. The word came down from the officers and sergeants that we were to camp here, but to stay quiet, and fires for cooking were forbidden. Burdwell and I erected our tent and after we gnawed on some hardtack, we prepared to retire. My Texas friend crawled inside first and I was about to join him when Sgt. Lie appeared. He said I was to report to Lt. Kane, and to bring my rifle.

Lie led the way to Kane's tent. In the light of the full moon, we had no problem negotiating our way through the tents of the Troop. In the distance, I could see the vague outlines of the blockhouses atop the Heights, partially illuminated by campfires. Evidently the Spaniards had no fear of being shelled at night.

The Lieutenant was standing outside his tent, a pipe in his mouth, but it was not lit; the Troop's last ounces of tobacco had been smoked and chewed a few days before. As always his uniform was immaculate. In spite of the miserable conditions of the past few days, the lieutenant never failed to turn out in fine order, and unlike most of the Troop he managed to shave daily. The sergeant announced me in a low voice and I came to attention, my Krag in the Order Arms position, and saluted. "Private Dawson, reporting as ordered, sir," I said, remembering at the last moment to keep my voice low.

Kane approached me so we could converse quietly. "At ease, Dawson." When I assumed the Parade Rest position, he smiled underneath his brushy handlebar mustache and removed his pipe. "Relax, son." When I had done so, somewhat loosening my stance, he continued. "I have some good news and bad news, Private."

My heart almost seized in my chest. I thought immediately of Father. Although no mail had gotten through to us since we had landed at Daiquiri, maybe the Lieutenant had somehow gotten word that Father had fallen ill, or worse. Was I to be shipped home?

"The bad news first," he said. "You are on sentry duty for part of the night. Sergeant Lie will show you to your post. You will be relieved at midnight."

My relief was palpable, and must have been obvious to him, because I could swear I saw a moonlit twinkle in his eye. I asked, "And the good news, sir, if I might?"

"Your effectiveness in the battle at Las Guasimas was noted by Sergeant Lie and others, including myself," he said. "I forwarded your name for promotion, and today I was informed by the Colonel that it has been approved." He extended his hand. "Congratulations, Corporal."

An hour later, with some two hours left at my post, my excitement at the promotion was still with me, although dampened by then with fatigue. It had been a long, wearying day. I struggled to remain awake, even though I did not sit down, or even lean against one of the trees that dotted the hill. It was not beyond the realm of possibility that the Spaniards could choose a nighttime assault of El Pozo, thus the sentries. I had just emerged from the shade of a tree when the moonlight revealed a form moving down the hill toward me, from the encampment. I had been given instruction in how to challenge anyone approaching the camp, but this person was heading from within. My orders did not differentiate between direction, so I took a stance with my Krag at Port Arms and whispered, "Halt! Who goes there?"

The figure stopped some ten yards distant. "Colonel Roosevelt," the form said, in the voice that everyone in the Regiment was by now familiar with.

Still, my orders were clear. Anyone approaching the perimeter was to be challenged. "What is the password?"

"The word is 'crimson.'" The school color of Harvard. He was correct.

"Advance and be recognized, sir."

Roosevelt came closer, and I could see moonlight glinting off his spectacles. "Well done, trooper." He peered at me. "Dawson? From Wisconsin?"

"Yes, sir."

He clapped me on the shoulder. "I understand you have been promoted. Congratulations, old man."

"Thank you, sir."

He gently motioned me around to face outward from the perimeter, toward San Juan Hill. The Spaniards' fires were dwindling. "All quiet, Dawson?"

"Indeed it is, sir. Except for the jungle, of course." We were by now familiar with the nighttime sounds of Cuba: various peeps and shrieks, and the occasional snarl of a predator. But there had been none of the sounds humans make in the jungle, such as the slight clatter of a canteen hitting its owner's belt, the snap of a twig under a boot, the inevitable curse resulting from a stumble.

Roosevelt was silent as he contemplated the night along with me. Finally, I said, "The word is we will be assaulting the heights to-morrow, Colonel."

He said, "The word is accurate."

After another moment, I ventured to inquire about something I'd been wondering about since we encountered the enemy at Las Guasimas. "May I ask a personal question, sir?"

Roosevelt hesitated, then said, "You may, Corporal."

"Are you scared, sir?"

I heard him inhale, then let his breath out slowly. For a moment I feared that I had offended him. Certainly he had proven his courage in battle already during this campaign. But then he said, "I have often been afraid, Dawson. Certainly as we approached the enemy the other day, I felt some measure of fear. I have no death wish, despite what some of my critics claim."

"How do you deal with it, sir?"

"Well, I was afraid of many things when I went out to Dakota. Grizzly bears, gun-fighters, and failure, especially. But by acting as if I was not afraid, I gradually ceased to be afraid."

"That's good advice, sir."

"It is natural to feel fear, Dawson. I'm sure your father did, many times. Each time we face our fear, we gain strength and courage, and confidence in the doing." He clapped me gently on the shoulder again. "I have every confidence you will acquit yourself well on the morrow, and that we shall carry the day. Now, I must check one or two other positions and then retire, although I might have some trouble getting to sleep."

"Not from fear of the morrow, though," I said, hoping he could see my grin in the moonlight.

He must have, because he returned it, with that amazing set of teeth under his mustache. "Oh, no. To-morrow will be our day, Dawson." He gestured toward the Spanish positions. "When we have taken those heights, the glory will be ours. Napoleon said that history is written by the winners. We shall be writing ours soon."

The Colonel bade me good night and assured me we would meet again on the heights the next day. As he walked away to the next sentry's post, I could not help thinking of an obscure book I had read just the summer before, a French translation of a treatise by an ancient Chinese general named Sun Tzu. In it, he had written, "Victory is reserved for those who are willing to pay its price." I wondered if Lt. Col. Roosevelt had read the same book. I sincerely hoped so.

CHAPTER THIRTY-EIGHT

Qaszir, northern Iraq
November 10, 2015

The Air Force came through. About noon, an AC-130 Spectre gunship began orbiting the village and Bliese was able to establish commo. The ISIS company that had taken Mamuzin began moving out along Highway 3 toward Aqrah at 1030 hours. Five klicks outside the city limits, they'd been hit by a pair of Air Force F-15E Strike Eagles from 39th Air Base Wing out of Incirlik. The fighter-bombers dropped ordnance on the ISIS column, knocking out a total of fifteen technicals and troop trucks. The gunship finished up by using its Gatling gun to hose the survivors as they tried to reach cover off the road or flee back to the safety of Mamuzin. Some may have made it; the Spectre had stuck around for an hour, just to make sure the enemy didn't regroup with assets they'd left in town to make another run for Aqrah. By noon, they concluded that nobody would be making a second effort to advance. Estimated casualties: around a hundred enemy fighters KIA, a couple dozen more wounded. Ambulances coming to get the wounded had been allowed to retrieve them and head back to Mamuzin.

All told, it was a big win for the good guys. The ISIS unit that was their northeastern spearhead had been devastated, relieving pressure on the Peshmerga to reinforce Aqrah. But it also meant that there was probably someone within Ghali's command feeding intel to the other side. We'd specifically predicted an afternoon movement by ISIS out of Mamuzin, and they'd come out early. But was it due to a warning, or just a desire to get rolling, perhaps taking Aqrah by surprise? There was no way to know for sure. We would just have to keep an eye on things. The next test would be with the militia unit that was occupying Bujal right now.

Could a Peshmerga officer in Ghali's command be in contact with both the ISIS company and the militia? That seemed unlikely. Master Sergeant Wilson, the most experienced man in the ODA, didn't think so. Maybe one or the other, he said, but almost certainly not both. At the moment, we had no way to know for sure, and no definitive proof that the ISIS unit's early movement was the result of getting a heads-up from someone here in Qaszir. The local phone line out of the valley was still working. We didn't use it, but a Peshmerga traitor certainly could. I had a hard time thinking it might be Ghali himself, but I told Wilson that from now on we had to assume that one of the Peshmerga officers had turned. If that was the case, Qaszir could be in serious trouble. I decided to visit Teyrelaş myself and see what was going on. If we couldn't hold that hill, we were all in deep shit.

Wilson would stay behind in the village while I took Bentler and Bliese with me. The 18Z was in charge of helping the Peshmerga fortify the village. They didn't have a lot to work with but it was better than relying on the Teyrelaş platoon to hold the line against a militia advance up the valley. And just in case, I told Wilson to have a couple of the men scout avenues of retreat up into the mountains, but keep it as quiet as possible. That wouldn't be easy; the villagers were nervous and keeping an eye on our movements.

They weren't the only ones. Just before leaving with my two men to head up to the hilltop, I was cornered by Jenny Stratton. She was looking a little more ragged than she had after rolling into town the day before, but she still did her best to project a regal presence. I saw her coming as we were heading toward what passed for our motor pool, where the ODA's two Humvees were parked. I told Bliese to bring the vehicle around and kept Bentler with me. There was no way I was going to talk to this woman without having someone else to verify the conversation.

"Lieutenant Dawson," she said when she got close, "if I didn't know better, I'd say you've been avoiding me." She didn't have her camera or sound guys with her, so that was a good sign. She still had to be dealt with, though, and I had to tell myself to keep it professional.

I forced a smile. "Not at all, Ms. Stratton. Welcome to Kurdistan. It's a little late, I know, but I've been pretty busy."

Today she had another long-sleeved shirt on, but this one was white. Sweat stains were already in evidence around the armpits, and I made a silent prediction that this look would never be featured on her Instagram page. Strands of blond hair trailed from underneath her makeshift hajib. I knew this wasn't her first time in the theater and wondered why she hadn't found a local woman to show her how to wear it properly. "I asked three of your men for interviews last night," she said, her green eyes sharp and accusing. "They all turned me down."

"I hope they were polite about it," I said.

"They were," she said. "They also told me they didn't know where I could find you."

There would be kudos going out to all the men at our next meeting that evening, and I also had to admit I felt good about being able to stay off Stratton's radar as long as I had. But now it couldn't be avoided. "We all have different tasks here," I said. "What can I do for you this morning?"

"I hear that there's a militia unit in Bujal, and they're coming up here. And they're not necessarily friendly," she added.

"That's three things. I can confirm the first part," I said carefully, "but not the second and certainly not the third." My short time in the Green Zone had included a briefing about the Iraqi militia, and we were always to assume they were friendly toward all Coalition and Peshmerga forces in the country, until proven otherwise. In other words, until they started shooting at us.

"Well, if the second and third things turn out to be true, will you let me know?"

My first inclination was to tell her to get in line, at the back; my first obligation, after all, was to our Peshmerga allies, including these villagers. But having the press on your side is not a bad thing. I'd been told during the Q Course that journos in the field could be a pain in the ass and sometimes even interfered with combat operations, to the point where they assumed they knew what had to be done and weren't shy about saying so. Maybe it would be a good idea to cultivate Stratton. Every hour drew us closer to a possible confrontation with a hostile militia unit. The story of that confrontation would eventually be told, and I wanted to make sure the SF part of the story was related as fairly as possible.

I nodded. "Certainly. In fact," I said, "I'm going to inspect our emplacements on Teyrelaş right now, if you'd care to accompany me."

That seemed to catch her by surprise, causing an eyebrow to go up. But then she smiled. "That would be fine. If you could give me five minutes, I'll be back here with my crew and our vehicle."

I pointed down to her designer boots. "How good are those things for climbing?"

She was turning back toward her quarters, but stopped and looked over her shoulder at me. "They should be okay, why?"

"Because when we get to the bottom of the hill, we'll be hoofing it the rest of the way." I couldn't resist adding a smile.

She took it as a challenge, returning my smile with a cocky version of her own. "You're on, Lieutenant."

Hiking a hill with a thirty-degree grade is not easy, but if you're in reasonably good shape it shouldn't be hard, either. I'd done much tougher hills during training and while with the Wolverines. Bliese and Bentler had already been up here a few times, they'd told me. I figured Stratton was in pretty good shape; her Instagram account included a few bikini shots that led me to conclude either she was one of the all-time biggest winners in the gene pool lottery, or she was very familiar with the inside of a gym.

Her camera and sound guys, though, were another story. They were huffing less than a hundred meters from the start of our climb and asked for a break. Stratton covered for them by declaring this was a good place to shoot some footage. "I'm putting together my first report about this village," she told me. "We'll get some pretty nice video from up here."

She was right about that. The mountains soared around us, and Qaszir looked small and vulnerable down in the valley to our north. Overhead, an eagle circled, keeping an eye on the humans below. I'd grown up with eagles all over the place in northern Wisconsin, mostly bald eagles and a few goldens, but this one seemed bigger. The TV people were doing their thing, so I took a moment to glass the bird with my binoculars. It was pretty good-sized, more golden in color than the ones back home. I'd have to ask around about this one. I lowered the binocs as the eagle soared behind a nearby outcropping. From up there, with its keen eyesight the eagle could see everything that moved down here. I sure could've used its help now. What was going on farther south, down the valley? We'd heard no reports from the security team that Ghali had ordered Tahan to send down to the two-klick line.

Stratton quickly got her team organized and they filmed for about three minutes. I was anxious to get moving, but at the same time I had to concede, grudgingly, that she knew what she was doing, and was clearly in charge, without being a hard-ass about it. She got a few words from me, had the cameraman sweep the valley for a panoramic shot, then said, "Okay, guys, that's a wrap. Let's get going, I'm sure the lieutenant and his men have better things to do than wait for us."

Beside me, Bentler muttered, "Got that right, honey." I gave him a look that I hoped was halfway between humorous and stern.

"Thanks," Stratton told me.

"No problem," I said. "Let's keep going to the top, okay? I'm sure you'll be able to get even better footage up there."

It was tough going as we climbed past the hundred-meter mark. There were a few scrubby trees on the hillside but mostly it was gritty soil and rocks. A lot of rocks, some the size of small cars. Many were loose, and in some places outcroppings jutted from the inside of the hill. It would've been extremely difficult to get a Humvee up here, considering the terrain as well as the grade. In my mind's eye, I pictured an infantry assault. There was plenty of cover to be had, but it was a long haul. A couple hundred meters on flat ground was a lot easier, even under fire, given reasonable cover and especially with enough ground to flank the objective. On this hillside, though, it would be tough indeed. That meant we had to keep Teyrelaş at all costs.

We were all winded when we got to the top. Stratton had hung right in there, but she was breathing hard. Her two techs were still thirty meters behind us. I didn't have time to wait for them. With Bliese and Bentler beside me, I got my first look at the peak of Teyrelaş.

The top was studded with rocks and outcroppings, like the side, but it had been worn down by generations of goats' hooves and Kurdish feet. Shaped roughly like an oval, maybe fifty meters across, about forty meters from where I stood to the lip on the far side, leading onto the southern face of the hill. There were three separate structures, stone and wood huts that had been cobbled together by long-gone goat herders who didn't want to sleep out in the open if they were stranded on the top overnight. Each was about six or eight meters square, spaced roughly the same distance apart. As I looked them over, I had more trouble than I thought in catching my breath. The air seemed thinner, even though we were only seven hundred feet above the valley floor. Then I remembered that the floor was already at about five thousand feet of altitude. Right now we were more than a mile above sea level.

The Peshmerga had fortified the huts as best they could, but they sure as hell weren't anything like bunkers. One or two mortar rounds apiece would be all it would take. They were being used as shelters now, and that's all they were really good for. Yet I knew from experience that having some type of structure at your campsite meant something, psychologically. Besides the obvious benefits of shelter and storage, they lent a sense of permanence, and the older they were—and these were old, for sure—the better.

I did a quick head count. There were supposed to be two dozen men up here, two Americans, the rest Peshmerga. I spotted my guys right away. My two weapons sergeants, Koser and Amans, had the duty today. Koser was trotting over; I saw Amans working with four Kurds, positioning a mortar tube. Amans was the youngest member of the ODA, an X-Ray who'd gone for Special Forces from the get-go after enlisting. As for the other Peshmerga, some were manning a pair of machine gun emplacements near either end of the hilltop, some were sitting around near the huts, dozing or eating.

"Good morning, sir," the 18B said. I'd continued Jones's policy of disdaining salutes, which were rarely rendered within ODAs in the field. "Welcome to our little bit of heaven."

"It seems to be underpopulated," I said. "I count twenty Peshmerga. Should be twenty-two, and a little while ago Colonel Ghali ordered an increase in strength up to forty."

Koser shook his head. "News to me, sir. We had two men head back to the vill about an hour ago, both reported having stomach problems."

"And one mortar tube," Bentler said. "Should be a total of four up here, LT."

I saw Koser's eyes widen appreciatively, just as I caught a whiff of Jenny Stratton's perfume, almost but not quite overwhelmed by her sweat. "Hello, ma'am," the weapons sergeant said, nodding.

I made the introduction, then motioned Bliese to join me as I led him away from the group. "Try to raise the colonel," I said. "I want to find out what's going on up here."

CHAPTER THIRTY-NINE

Qaszir, northern Iraq
November 10, 2015

Colonel Ghali told me that he assumed Major Tahan was still organizing the reinforcement of the hilltop. He'd check on it. I ended the transmission, then put out a call for Master Sergeant Wilson. No answer. One of the engineering sergeants, Samuels, responded to my next unit-wide call. Wilson and the other 18C, Thomas, were up in the foothills of the mountains somewhere, scouting one last possible evacuation route. That left only Samuels and the medical sergeant, Rivers, in the village. Of the nine soldiers in the ODA, including myself, five of us were currently on the hilltop. I didn't like that situation at all, especially with Tahan unaccounted for and the Peshmerga reinforcements nowhere to be seen.

I was glad to see Stratton and her crew interviewing two of the Peshmerga soldiers, so I took the opportunity to huddle up with my men near one of the huts. None of the Kurds were in earshot. "All right, gentlemen," I began, "I'm starting to wonder what the hell's going on around here. Anybody with any insights, no matter how crazy they might sound, I'm ready to hear 'em."

"These guys are getting nervous," Amans said. He was only twenty years old, looked maybe sixteen, but if he'd come into Special Forces as an X-Ray, he had to have something on the ball. This was his first deployment. In his rundown of the ODA members, Captain Jones had noted Amans was still raw but eager to learn and a hard worker. Certainly he'd done a good job with that mortar emplacement, from what I could see. From that edge of the hilltop, the M252 commanded a good piece of the valley to the south. Four or five more of those tubes up here would make me feel a lot better, though. Where the hell were they?

Amans had been thinking along the same lines. "We can't hold this hill with just one tube, Lieutenant," he said. "These guys aren't bad, but they need more live-fire training. I wanted to fire some practice rounds but their sergeant said no. Even on these mountainsides there might be goat herders, he said."

"I haven't seen anybody on these mountainsides, no matter when I've been up here," Koser said. "We need to sight in the weapon. Three rounds down near the road would do the trick. It's not exactly full of traffic down there."

"I'll talk to Ghali about it," I said, "but we need to get a full complement up here, both men and mortar tubes." I looked at Koser and Amans. They'd been up here since the previous afternoon. Conditions weren't a hell of a lot better down in the village, but at least they could get a hot meal and a shower down there, and sleep in a halfway decent rack. Unfortunately, I couldn't spare anybody right now to relieve them. "Are you two okay with staying up here till tomorrow morning?"

"We're good to go, LT," Koser said immediately. Amans looked a little hesitant, but said nothing.

"All right. I'll get your relief up here no later than 0800 tomorrow. You two have pulled more time up here than anybody else, from what I understand, and I hate to ask you to do more right now, but if the militia comes up that road in the next twelve hours I want men up here who know the terrain. Do the best you can to zero in the mortar. How many rounds do you have for that tube?"

"Fifteen, sir," Amans said.

"Hell, that's not nearly enough." I knew from experience that a well-trained American mortar team on its worst day would run through fifteen rounds in two minutes or less. "I'll see about getting more up here, along with the additional tubes and crews." I turned to Bentler and Bliese. "I want you two to hustle down there to the village and hook up with Samuels and Rivers. See if you can raise the master sergeant and have him RTB right away. I want to have one more look around up here before I head back down."

Koser nodded towards Stratton and her crew. They were shooting footage from the far side, looking south. "What about the journos, LT?"

"I'll take them down with me," I said. "I don't want them wandering around up here any longer than necessary. As of right now, they don't go anywhere without an escort from the ODA, at least one man."

Amans cracked a smile that pushed his freckles up around his nose. "I'll take the first shift, Lieutenant," he said.

"Joe, you're up here with me till tomorrow morning," Koser said. "You must've forgotten that when you imagined yourself helping that babe with her laundry."

I couldn't help smiling, just as Amans' expression turned to disappointment. "Don't worry, Joe. If she needs a back rub to help her get to sleep, I'll send for you."

Half an hour later, I rounded up Stratton and her crew to begin the trek down the hillside. She seemed pleased with the work they'd done up here, and I consented to a short interview about the strategic importance of Teyleraş. Nothing was said about the militia in Bujal. Just as we were starting down, I got a radio call from Wilson. He and Thomas had returned to the village, and he'd found something interesting that he wanted to talk to me about when I got back to our post. I asked him to check with Ghali to see if there was anything new about Tahan and the hilltop reinforcements.

I couldn't shake the feeling that something was really wrong here. I wanted to hustle down the hillside and get back to the village, but had to take it relatively easy due to the journos. About halfway down, Stratton asked for a water break. Her two crew members, Henderson with his camera and Oakley with the sound gear, were having trouble. They were both Americans and this was their third tour in Iraq. I offered a power bar to the camera operator, a slender, bearded guy with wire-rimmed glasses, and asked, "First time up in these mountains, Henderson?"

"Yeah, for both of us," he said. He peeled the wrapping off the bar and took a healthy bite. He was about to drop the wrapper on the ground when he saw me looking at him. The wrapper went into a pants pocket.

"Your other tours, did you ever get out of the Green Zone?"

"A few times," he said. "It's a little different up here," he added with a self-conscious grin. But grin or not, he and his buddy were hurting, and grateful for the rest break.

I walked away from them a few steps and looked back up at the hilltop. The eagle was back, soaring high above. The best overwatch capability in the animal kingdom, no doubt about it. What I wouldn't give for a drone right now, I thought.

Stratton approached me. "You're looking rather pensive, Lieutenant," she said.

"Just wishing I had a drone up there, ma'am."

"Tell you what, if you agree to stop calling me that, I'll tell you my real age," she said, somewhat playfully.

"Okay, Ms. Stratton," I said. "You have a deal." Hey, I was curious, in spite of everything that was going on at the moment. SF veterans had told me that on deployment, when there was so much to do and the stress level was high, a little relief was necessary, even a couple minutes' worth.

"First, you have to guess," she said. The look in those green eyes was no longer professional. It was flattering, I suppose. The glamorous TV star was flirting with me.

"Thirty-two," I said, purposely coming in lower than what my honest guess would be. And as I suspected, it worked on her, just like it did for every woman over the age of twenty-three or so. They all wanted to be perceived as younger than they were.

"Add three."

I nodded, giving her a smile. "Had me fooled," I said. But not by much.

"And you?"

"Twenty-six next April," I said. There was a pause, as if she was waiting for something, and I decided I didn't have time to mess around.

Just in case she had something more personal in mind for later, I wanted to get it out there and deal with it. I said, "In the movies, this would be the part where she asks the soldier if he's ever been with an older woman."

There was the glint in those eyes again, and now a sly grin to go with it. Was she coming on to me? I hoped not. "But this isn't the movies, is it, Lieutenant?" she asked. "Even if you might like it to be."

"It most certainly is not," I said, "and what I'd like us to be doing right now is getting a move on. I've got a lot of work to do."

She looked almost relieved, but said nothing as we started down. We'd gone only ten meters when Henderson stumbled over a rock. He yelled in pain as he fell and the camera went flying. Stratton made a dive for it, but came up just short. The camera bounced off one rock and smashed into a larger one. Pieces of metal and plastic went flying.

Stratton picked herself off the ground, looked at the debris and said, "Well, fuck."

I went over to help Henderson up. He tried putting weight on his left leg and gasped. "Looks like you sprained the ankle," I said. "Put your arm around my shoulders, I'll help you get down. My medic will take a look at it."

"Th-thanks, Lieutenant."

We took a couple steps and I saw that Stratton hadn't moved. "Get it together, Stratton," I said. "Salvage what you can and let's go." I almost said it as, "Move your pretty little ass," but held that back. Uncle John would've been disappointed.

CHAPTER FORTY

Qaszir, northern Iraq
November 10, 2015

I found Colonel Ghali at his headquarters, and he told me Tahan had everything under control. There had been an "unavoidable delay" in mustering the reinforcements for Teyleraş, but the colonel had been assured that the hilltop would have its full complement of troops and mortar tubes by local dusk. What about the security detachment at the two-kilometer lookout on the road to the village? In place, the colonel said.

I advised Koser and Amans on the hilltop about the situation and then met with the rest of the ODA in our quarters. The main room was used as our makeshift Tactical Operations Center. I'd been in a few TOCs and this one was probably the simplest in existence. We had two laptop computers available, pretty much worthless except for the morning and evening windows when we had satellite access to the internet. For whatever reason, the techies back in Baghdad hadn't been able to come up with anything better. Using the telephone landline was out. Not only was it notoriously slow for internet service, it was unsecure. Bliese's commo gear included the AN/PSC-5 SPITFIRE radio, a very reliable device, but its line-of-sight capabilities were useless this deep in the valley, except for communicating with aircraft orbiting overhead. It did have satellite access capability, though, and that was our lifeline during the daily windows. The ODA just had to make do with what was available, and that was par for the course on deployments. I never thought I'd miss the crude TOC we had with the Wolverines in Turkey, but by comparison, what I had to work with now was like going from the original *Star Wars* of the seventies to a *Flash Gordon* serial from the thirties.

Wilson reported that the last evac route he'd scouted could be used to get the Kurds up into the mountains if the militia was about to overrun the village. The Peshmerga could fight a holding action while the ODA took care of the civilians. The latest head count was two hundred and forty souls, about two-thirds women, the rest either elderly men or kids under thirteen. All military-age males had been conscripted into the Peshmerga months ago, although there was talk some of them had avoided service by joining a militia unit. Another thing for me to worry about; if any of those men from Qaszir were in the Kata'ib Hezbollah company now in Bujal, they would know every nook and cranny of this valley, including everything the enemy would need to know about taking Teyleraş.

After the briefing, we went to the mess hall. The cooks were still working, a good sign. In fact, there'd been no indications that any of the civilians were bugging out. In many ways it looked like business as usual in the village, but the Peshmerga soldiers were definitely not moving out toward the hilltop. At 1800, a check-in with Koser confirmed that no reinforcements had yet shown up. I decided to give Ghali and Tahan another hour to get it together. Later on, I'd have a lot of regrets about that decision.

By then it was getting dark in the valley, with local sunset an hour before. Rivers, the medical sergeant, had been on the "Jenny watch," as the men were already calling it, since we'd returned from the hilltop and he'd treated Henderson's ankle. I decided to go over there and take the duty for a while. Bentler would relieve me in two hours.

The journos had been given quarters in a two-room house, previously used by a Kurd family that had since gone next door to bunk with relatives after the husband and father had gone into the army. Stratton had one room and her two crewmen had the other. For meals and meetings they used Stratton's room, which had the only sink and running water. The latrine, a two-holer, was out back. Indoor plumbing had come to the village just five years before, I'd been told, but a sewage system was still a long way out. I found Rivers waiting outside the front door. "They just finished dinner, LT," he said.

"How's Henderson's ankle?"

"Sprained, but not too bad. A day or so on crutches, if he has to get around, then he should tape it, and he'll be good to go."

"Where he's going to go will be the question," I said. "If we have to bug out up the valley, can he make it?"

"Not on his own. His buddy can help him, if they can both hump some of their gear."

"If it comes to that, carrying their gear will be the least of their worries. Go get some chow, Doc."

I knocked at the door. Stratton opened it, and she looked about as dazzling as one could expect, under the circumstances. Her hijab was off, allowing her light brown hair to flow down to her shoulders. Even without makeup, she looked good. Beyond good, in fact, now in a tee shirt with a UCLA logo and cargo shorts that showed off her legs to great effect. In deference to the bare stone floor, she wore white socks. "Good evening," I said. I nodded at the shirt. "Your alma mater?"

"Yes, class of '02," she said. "Come on in, Lieutenant."

I entered, noticing that her bed was made. A backpack leaned against the far wall, its top pocket partially unzipped. The strap of a bra hung out of it. Her stylish boots, which had indeed done the job for her on the hill, were set next to the backpack, one boot tipped over. There was a wooden chair, an antique chest of drawers, and against the near wall, an ancient sink with a cabinet underneath. A table with two chairs was in the corner past the sink, and another rickety cabinet hung on the wall. A plate with remnants of a meal sat on the table. "All the comforts of home," I said.

"If your home is Appalachia in the Depression, maybe," she said. "Have a seat, Lieutenant. Can I offer you anything?"

"I'll stand, thanks. I hope you didn't bring liquor into the village."

"Don't worry," she said, "this ain't my first rodeo." She padded over to her backpack and took out a bottle of water, unscrewed the cap and saluted me. "Cheers."

I noticed that the connecting door to the room her crewmen shared was closed. "I heard Henderson will live," I said.

"His pride is hurt worse than his ankle," she said, sitting down on the bed. It was chilly, and I assumed the place was heated by a wood or coal stove in the next room; I'd seen a stovepipe coming up out of the roof over that side. Stratton surely valued her privacy, but I would've thought that staying warm would be more valuable to her. For a California girl, she was showing remarkable tolerance for the cold, although it was having an effect, if the increased elevation of the U and A on her shirt was any indication.

I averted my gaze, saying, "Were you able to salvage anything from the camera?"

"As far as any new video, it's toast, but Henderson says the memory card is intact, so when we get back to Baghdad we can pull out the footage we've already shot. And I brought a backup, just in case, a minicam. It's a good one, with plenty of battery life, thank God."

"Good to know," I said. "I assume you're aware of the situation in Bujal?"

"Yes, Colonel Ghali filled me in yesterday, over dinner."

I couldn't help smiling. "Dinner? He moves pretty fast."

She shook her head, smiling. "He was a perfect gentleman. Despite what you might have heard, Lieutenant, American female journalists are not constantly being hit on when we're on assignment. And the men aren't, either, for that matter."

"Well, like we said up on the hill, this isn't the movies."

"You're making me self-conscious, standing there." She pointed at the table. "At the very least, pull up one of those chairs, take a load off. As long as you're my babysitter, I can make use of the time to get some work done." She got up from the bed, retrieved her backpack and pulled out a note pad and pencils. When we were both seated again, she asked, "You don't mind, do you?"

Truthfully, I did, but I was mindful of maintaining good relations with the press. "No, fine, go ahead," I said. "If something is classified, I'll let you know."

She smiled. "I'm sure you will, but my first question probably isn't even getting near that." She flipped back the cover of her notebook, then a couple pages. "Among the Peshmerga, you're known as the *Dargiran Siwar,* the Rough Rider. I assume that's because of your great-grandfather?"

A year ago, that question might have prompted a heated response from me, but times had changed, and maybe I had, too. In fact, I'd heard it from one or two of the Peshmerga since my arrival in the village. "My great-great-grandfather, actually," I said. "Yes, he was one of the original Rough Riders, served in the Spanish-American War. Charles Dawson was his name."

"Did he survive the war?"

"If he hadn't, I wouldn't be here."

She scribbled on the pad. "He served under Teddy Roosevelt, I assume?"

"Roosevelt never liked being called that," I said. "It was always 'Theodore.' His wife got away with calling him 'Thee' now and then."

Stratton raised an eyebrow. "You've done your homework on him," she said.

"Charles thought highly of him, so I thought it would be a good idea to find out more about him myself."

"Interesting." She wrote another line, then said, "Did your ancestor leave any papers, photos, things like that?"

"Yes, in a diary."

"Really? Do you have it with you? Can I see it?"

"He really did, and yes, I have it, and no, not a chance." I softened the blow with a smile. "Sorry. Family tradition, Dawson eyes only."

"Okay, I'm good with that. So, after your research about Roosevelt, what do you think of him?"

I didn't hesitate. "We could sure as hell use him now," I said, and immediately wished I hadn't. I could almost see the headline: *American officer disses Commander in Chief.* "Don't quote me on that," I added. She smiled, a little more broadly this time, and made a show of crossing out a line on her pad. "How about a little quid pro quo?" I ventured.

She gave me a look for a long three seconds, then said, "Okay, sure.

What do you want to know? You already know my age, which I don't normally tell men. Besides, it's no secret, it's on my NBC profile online and Wikipedia and God knows where else. And my measurements are out there, too, which you probably know already."

"No, I don't," I said, "and I don't really care."

She put her pad down on the bed next to her and leaned back slightly, enough to emphasize her chest. I wanted to believe that part was unintentional. She said, "Sorry, but I call bullshit on that, soldier."

"I really don't," I said, honestly. Stratton was good-looking, to be sure, but I had a wife back home, and in a beauty contest, Stratton would come in second to Sam. A close second. "Besides, I've seen your Instagram shots, and I know how tall you are, so it's really just basic math from that point. But I've got better things to do. Since you brought up the subject, though, why the bikini shots? You're a good reporter, from what I'm told. Why do you need to sex it up like you do?"

She sighed, then leaned forward, elbows on knees, and shook her head. "If I had a buck for every time I'm asked that," she said. Then she sat up again, giving me a look that could've been called defiant. "I posted one and it got a lot of hits, so I did a couple more and my Q Score went through the roof. That's a test used to measure the strength of someone's brand."

"I've heard of it," I said.

"So, the higher the Q Score, the higher your ratings when you're on the air, and the better position you're in when contract time comes around. That's the theory, anyway. So far, it's worked for me."

"It's about the money, then."

She shrugged. "A girl's gotta eat," she said. Another sigh, then, "To be honest, if I could, I'd delete them all tomorrow, or whenever the hell we get back to some semblance of civilization and I can get online. They don't have WiFi here, believe it or not."

"I hope you do," I said. "Let your work do the talking."

"I really wish I could, Jake. I hope you don't mind if I call you that. Now that we're talking about my body, we should be on a first-name basis, don't you think?" There was silence between us for a few seconds.

I wondered where this might be going, and then we were saved by a knock at her door. I got up, pulled it open and there was Wilson.

"Lieutenant, you have to come with me, please."

Behind me, I heard Stratton get off the bed and walk over. I asked, "What's up, Master Sergeant?"

"It's Colonel Ghali, sir. He's dead."

"*Dead?*" Stratton gasped.

"Him and Captain Shadid."

Holy…Then something clicked into place. "Where's Major Tahan?"

"He's missing," Wilson said. "Almost certainly heading for Bujal. Twenty minutes ago, Koser reported seeing a Peshmerga vehicle tearing ass down the road, heading south."

CHAPTER FORTY-ONE

Qaszir, northern Iraq
November 10, 2015

Nobody reported hearing any gunfire, but Ghali and Shadid had both been shot twice in the head and once in the torso, at close range, evidently with a silenced weapon. They were in Ghali's headquarters, and there were no signs of a struggle. Tahan must have gotten the drop on them, although Shadid had been able to draw his pistol. He hadn't gotten off a shot, though.

Wilson, Bentler and I looked on as Rivers examined the bodies. The medical sergeant took several photos, then came over to where we were standing. I'd posted two men to keep the Kurds outside. At this point, although Tahan was the prime suspect, I couldn't rule out the possibility that one or more of Ghali's lieutenants were in on it. I doubted any of the enlisted had been involved. Like virtually all Arab armies, the Peshmerga's officers tended to keep their distance from their enlisted soldiers, one of the major challenges SF teams always faced when working with indigenous forces in the Middle East. I'd sent Samuels and Thomas to round up the lieutenants. Right now, they had the four Kurds under guard in the next room. Wilson had been questioning them while I watched Rivers work.

"What's it look like, Doc?" I asked the medic.

"My guess is that he fired on Ghali first, one round to the chest. Shadid was on the other side of the table. He reacted quickly enough to draw his weapon, but not quickly enough to return fire. He took a round to his upper chest, near the left shoulder. That tells me the shooter was bringing his weapon around and snapped off a quick shot as he saw him turn. Then he put one round in the head."

I turned to Wilson. "Master Sergeant, what's up with the other officers?"

"They all deny knowing anything about it," he said. "One of them was on his way to the latrine out back, heard a noise that may have been the silenced weapon being fired, came in and saw the bodies, but not the shooter. Then he hustled over to our TOC to ask for help. The other three were elsewhere in the village. One was rounding up the unit's remaining mortar tubes, the other two were having chow."

I shook my head. "We'll have to question them separately. Do you trust them enough to let them return to duty?"

"Not in the slightest. This will have to be reported up to Peshmerga headquarters in Erbil, and of course to 5th Group in Baghdad. Under normal circumstances, we should secure the crime scene and keep the lieutenants confined and under guard. But these aren't exactly normal circumstances."

"No, they're not," I said. "It looks like it's Tahan, though. And if any of the lieutenants were in on it, why didn't they book it with him?"

Bentler said, "Good question, LT, but we can't discount the possibility that Tahan's accomplice might have been ordered to stay behind, just to keep an eye on things, maybe disrupt our efforts here, while the militia moves up the valley."

"You think they're on their way?" I asked Wilson.

"I think we can damn well count on it," the 18Z said. "Tahan delayed reinforcing the hill long enough to get to nightfall. I'd say it was likely that Ghali was calling him on the carpet for it. So, it might've been impulsive for Tahan, he might've panicked and opened fire."

"A silenced weapon points toward premeditation," I said. "In any event, Tahan's gone, the Peshmerga's two highest-ranking officers are dead, the rest of the officers arc out of the picture, and the enlisted out there don't know what the hell's going on."

"It's a major league goatfuck, all right," Bentler said.

"You have a talent for understatement, Sergeant."

We were quiet for a moment, contemplating the brutal scene in front of us, and the brutal circumstances it had thrust upon us. Then, the master sergeant spoke. "Lieutenant, you're in charge of the village now, including the Peshmerga. What are your orders?"

Back in Phase III of the Q Course, we'd been given all kinds of scenarios to deal with. This was one of them. You're in the field with your ODA, the guerilla or government unit you're working with takes casualties and its officers go down. What do you do? You take charge until the locals' higher authority can provide replacements for the missing officers. It's up to the ODA commander to keep it together until then. Easier said than done, of course.

But everything about being a Special Forces officer was easier said than done.

"Find the top sergeants of the Peshmerga unit and bring them to our TOC," I said. "At some point we're going to have to trust somebody. I can't have our guys guarding their officers all the damn time. Erbil will be sending a team up here to take over the investigation, but not until tomorrow. Pick a couple of the ranking non-coms and put them in charge of the prisoners. And we have to seal the crime scene, somehow."

From outside, we heard a muffled sound that might've been firecrackers going off, but nobody used firecrackers around here. That meant only one thing. "Ah, shit," I said.

We hustled outside and all of us looked to the south. The sounds were louder, and definitely gunfire. A flash of light from the top of Teyleraş was followed seconds later by a boom. "That's a mortar round for sure," Wilson said.

I led the way toward our TOC on the run, and halfway there, in the village square, my MBITR radio squawked. *"Badger Actual and all units, this is Badger Three, Station Teyleraş is under attack, repeat, we are under attack. Estimate enemy force at two-platoon strength."* Koser's voice was as calm as could be expected, but he had to shout over the sounds of gunfire in the background. I also heard the thump of the Peshmerga mortar. Amans wasn't wasting time getting his team in the fight.

Doors were opening in the buildings surrounding the square, and civilians were coming out, looking to the south, some pointing. A woman began to wail. "Badger Three, this is Badger Actual," I said. "Can you hold? I can get reinforcements to you in thirty mikes."

"Negative, Badger Actual, the enemy has achieved tactical surprise. I have at least four friendly KIA and three wounded. Badger Four is manning the mortar tube, but I think it's too late for that, sir."

I didn't hesitate. Hesitation meant lives lost. The reinforcements that should've been there eight hours ago might've made a difference, but it was too late now. "Badger Three, this is Badger Actual. Evacuate the position, immediately. Destroy the mortar if you can't take it with you. Don't waste any time. I repeat, evacuate the position. Do you copy?"

"Affirmative, Badger Actual, I am evacuating the hilltop. Badger Three, out."

CHAPTER FORTY-TWO

Qaszir, northern Iraq
November 10, 2015

It was nearly 2300 hours when I got back to the TOC. One last meeting with the ODA and then we'd all try to get some shuteye, with the exception of Samuels and Rivers, who had the first two-hour security watch. It would be a short night for everybody.

This would be just a wrap-up of the evening, making sure everybody was on the same page. I'd invited Jenny Stratton to attend; after talking it over with Wilson, I'd decided that having the journo recording as much as possible would be the best way to make sure the truth would be told about what had been happening here, and what was going to happen.

"All right, let's go over it one more time," I said. I leaned against one of our wooden tables, solidly built, an anachronism in itself in this village. "Sergeant Koser, tell me about the Peshmerga."

The 18B weapons sergeant knew the Kurds about as well as anybody. He was on his third tour in Iraq and his Kurmanji was very good. He and Amans had successfully evacuated the sixteen Peshmerga survivors from Teyleraş, bringing four wounded men down with them, leaving four dead behind. Koser was pissed, mostly at himself. The enemy had come along the mountainside with half its force, catching the defenders by surprise. The tripwire security element that was supposed to be down the valley? Never happened. As soon as the enemy engaged from the flank, and on higher ground to boot, the rest of the assault force had come in, hauling ass up the road in trucks and charging up the hillside on foot. But I'd told Koser to forget about it. Now, he said, "They're in about as good a shape as we can expect, LT. They were shook up about their commanding officers getting killed, but their sergeants are pretty solid. They'll be ready to go tomorrow, whatever happens."

The enemy had been quiet since taking the hilltop, but we couldn't count on that lasting much past daybreak. They hadn't come all this way just to sit up there and watch the village. Shortly after sunrise, they'd be getting their mortar tubes ready to fire.

As I saw it, we had three options: retake the hill, hold in place and defend the village if they attacked, or evacuate. I was leaning toward Plan A. There were all kinds of tactical reasons to retake Teyleraş, but there was also a psychological one: the Kurds needed a win. They'd voluntarily, if reluctantly, given up Bujal, and now another of their towns was in danger. I'd talked to their ranking sergeants myself, and they were determined to defend this place and retake Bujal. One thing at a time, I'd told them. But they were ready.

Our operational orders said nothing about taking offensive action against an entrenched enemy force, but the tactical realities of the situation had changed. I started thinking that it might be time to issue a FRAGO, a fragmentary order. First, though, I needed more info. "Sergeant Thomas, how about the perimeter defenses?"

The 18C engineering sergeant looked tired, as I'm sure we all did, but it showed more in him. The ten-year SF veteran from Tennessee had been working hard, helping the Qaszir villagers to improve what little infrastructure they had, and now preparing the town to resist a mortar barrage and infantry assault. He had his helmet off and scratched his scalp, which showed at the crown through his close-cropped brown hair. "Not much out there in the way of natural defensive positions, LT," he said. "Just one option as far as entering the village, as we know, coming right up that road. We've cobbled together some IEDs that could slow them down. Close-in to the first buildings, we've situated Claymores on either side of the road. Between us and the Kurds we've got four, and we've staggered them to form a gauntlet." The Claymore mines were lethal weapons indeed, firing hundreds of steel balls at an attacking force, but they could only be used once.

"It'll come down to how many casualties they're willing to take,"

Wilson said. "If they come in at company strength, a hundred fifty, a hundred seventy-five fighters, we can degrade them by about thirty percent before they get to the wire." The master sergeant was speaking figuratively; the southern boundary of the village had no wire, no barriers of any kind.

I nodded. "All right, so we can make them pay a heavy price, but it would still come down to house-to-house. How many Peshmerga can we put in the box?" Our Area of Operations, which was now pretty small, was always referred to as "the box."

"Their sergeants took a head count," Koser said. "They can put seventy-four effectives on the line. Another twenty or so have wounds or injuries that limit their combat capability, but we can use them to evacuate the civilians."

"So, we'll be outnumbered, more than likely," Bentler said.

"If they've moved their entire force up the valley by now," I said. "Sergeant Bentler, do we have any indications about how many they have on the hilltop?"

"From what Tom and Joe reported about their assault, I'd say seventy to eighty men," the 18F intelligence sergeant said. "As to the rest of their force, the Peshmerga have put some scouts up on the mountainsides. No indication so far that their main force has gotten within five klicks of Teyleraş. But they could very well have another platoon coming in to reinforce the hilltop."

I threw the next question to the group. "Any guesses as to what they'll do?"

Wilson said, "My take is they'll soften us up tomorrow morning with a mortar barrage. The rest of their force will be coming up from Bujal and then, when they figure they've done what they can from the hilltop, they'll come in here to finish the job. No later than noon."

I looked at my 18E, Bliese. "Anything new from 5th Group?"

The communications sergeant shook his head. "They acknowledged receipt of our evening intel upload, but no new orders. They're getting in touch with Peshmerga HQ in Erbil about Ghali and Shadid."

"And nothing about getting a bird of some kind, a drone, whatever, upstairs so we can get some real-time commo?" With an orbiting platform overhead, manned or unmanned, we could communicate directly with 5th Group, and anybody else we wanted to. But we couldn't put one up there ourselves.

"They said they'll try, LT. I've been listening on the hour. Nothing as of 2300. I could try transmitting, just in case the bird is up there."

Wilson said, "We should avoid that. If the enemy picks up our transmission, they could determine that we don't have real-time commo and then they'll know we can't get air support. If they think they might get a five-hundred-pound can of whoop-ass dropped on them, that might keep them from advancing. At the very least they'll be thinking about it."

"Sooner or later, they'd figure it out," I said. "Bleez, listen again at midnight, but then get some rack time."

"Roger that, LT."

I looked over their faces, the faces of tired, but determined men. Experienced combat veterans, almost all of them. I checked my watch: 2335 hours. In twenty-five minutes, it would be November eleventh. Veteran's Day back home. I'd usually been able to call Uncle John on that day, just to shoot the breeze. He always attended the community service of appreciation at the National Guard armory. I'd always thought I'd be able to join him there someday and stand up with the other vets. Or would they be reading my name on Memorial Day next May?

In a corner in the back, Jenny Stratton stood quietly. The night had cooled off; it might get down to the mid-forties, and she'd put on pants and a jacket. The hijab had stayed off. What did it matter, at this point? She wasn't recording the meeting, but she was following every word, taking notes on her pad. She looked scared. Certainly not the cocky TV star who had arrived the day before. I wondered if she'd ever been this close to a real combat action. Somehow I doubted it.

I thought of my ancestor. The diary was in my quarters. Old Charles and his buddies had faced an entrenched enemy on a hilltop, too. If they hadn't done anything, the Spaniards would've kept the high ground, unleashed their artillery on the Americans down below, maybe gotten reinforced from Santiago with enough men to drive the invaders away, back to the beaches. It could've gone to hell in a rocket if Wood and Roosevelt had sat around, waiting for something to happen. But they hadn't waited around.

They had attacked.

I made a decision.

"We're going to regain the initiative," I said. "Tomorrow morning, we take Teyleraş back."

The village was blacked out, and with no moon above, the stars were all we had for light as I walked Stratton back to her quarters. It was almost midnight. She pulled her jacket tight around her against the cold. Off to the south, Teyleraş loomed, a hulking shadow a shade darker than the mountains behind it. Earlier, there'd been lights on its crest. Campfires, flashlights, as the militia dug in. I thought the chances of them attacking at night were slim, but had ordered the blackout anyway. Our southern perimeter had a dozen Peshmerga, plus two of my ODA, on guard.

"Do the Kurds know you're attacking in the morning?" she asked.

"Not yet," I said. "Operational security. First light is about 0600. We're going to muster them at 0500. If we can start up the hill at first light, we can use it to our advantage. Maybe catch them half asleep up there."

"And you'll evacuate the village?"

"Just a precaution," I said. "If the assault fails, we'll fall back here and defend the vill, but either way, it'll be better to have the civilians up in the mountains. You and your crew can assist with that."

"Henderson and Oakley will," Stratton said. "I'm coming with you."

We were almost at her door. I stopped and she turned to face me. "Out of the question," I said, my voice low, but firm.

"Jake, it's my job. I have to go. This is the biggest story of my career." Her voice took on a mockingly dramatic tinge. "It's the story of these people, and of a small band of Americans who are fighting against great odds to save them." She paused, and in the dim light, I could see she had a tight smile. "It sounds melodramatic, but it's true. They'll eat it up back at the network. But it's more than just about ratings, in case you were thinking that. Nobody back home knows what's going on here, with the Kurds. Nobody seems to care. Jake, they need to know, and they damn well need to start caring. So, I'm going with you, even though I'm scared as hell."

"It's my job to keep you safe," I said.

"No, it's your job to take back that fucking hill and save these people," she said. I could almost see her eyes flashing. "The militia will kill them all if they trap them here."

"Jenny–"

She reached out and touched my cheek. I almost stepped back, but didn't. She held the touch for a moment, two, then said, "'To free the oppressed.' That's your motto, isn't it? Special Forces?"

"Yes, it is."

"Then you will keep them free tomorrow. You're the Rough Rider. You and your men, you're all Rough Riders. You'll do it. And I'll tell your story." She leaned forward, kissed me on the cheek, and went inside.

CHAPTER FORTY-THREE

The journal of Charles J. Dawson, con't.

July the 1st, 1898 – The most exciting and terrifying day of my life has nearly gone, and I am alive to tell the tale. The Lord above saw fit to protect me through my great trial, although many of my comrades are now with the angels above. It was only some 16 or 17 hours ago that they, like me, were rousted from fitful slumber by the sergeants and officers for 4 a.m. reveille, without a bugle. As a newly-minted Corporal, I had to join in that duty. Without lighting fires for breakfast, we consumed the remainder of our hardtack. None could tell when we would eat again.

The mustering of the men commenced, and for this I was paired with another Corporal, Edwin Coakley, a colorful fellow from Kentucky. I had previously met him at Camp in San Antonio. He is a veteran of campaigns against the Indians in the West, also against the tribes above the border in Canada and even claims to have marched with Republican revolutionaries in Brazil.

The roll had just been called when a battery of artillery was heaved to the top of El Pozo by teams of draft horses. Even in the early-morning gloom, it was an inspiring sight to see the four big guns being brought into position. The pieces were situated, and then we all waited. At 7:30, the sound of artillery came rolling over us from the northwest. This was the beginning of the Regulars' assault on the town of El Caney, which had to be taken to ensure the Spaniards could not reinforce San Juan Heights from Santiago.

Not long afterward, the battery on El Pozo, commanded by Capt. Grimes, fired its first rounds. The roar was enormous, as was the cloud of smoke. The artillerymen reloaded and fired again, and again, a dozen volleys, with no apparent effect on the Spanish positions on the two hills. Then all of a sudden, shells began to explode over our heads. The smoke from our pieces allowed the Spaniards to zero in their location, whereas the enemy was using smokeless powder. One shell burst over one of the buildings on top of El Pozo and eviscerated several Cubans on the roof. Anyone who had not found cover by now raced to hide in whatever manner they could.

Our Troop was in dire straits at this point, exposed as we were to the Spanish guns, and we might all have perished were it not for Lt. Col. Roosevelt, who had mounted Little Texas and rode amongst us, rallying all with a cry to follow him. He had taken a piece of shrapnel on one wrist; I saw blood, but he ignored it as he led us down off El Pozo to the north, into some underbrush. Along the way we passed wounded men, some horribly maimed.

The duel of the big guns ceased, and the officers began sorting out the Troops and re-forming the men into lines of march. We set out upon a muddy road in the direction of the Heights. The heat was already fierce, and we were ordered to drop our packs. Ahead of us was the Aguadores, and men were fording it. Our Regiment had to wait for the Regulars ahead of us to cross, and the Spaniards had divined where we were. Mauser rounds and artillery shells ripped through the trees and brush around us. We had to stand in formation as we waited our turn. It was my responsibility to help keep the men together and as calm as possible. I recalled Roosevelt's words from the night before; if I could project a brave front for the benefit of the men, could I then control my own fear? I found that I could, and that the fellows needed me to do so. I saw several of them vomiting up their breakfasts, others unable to control their bladders, and still others seemingly as content as if on a Sunday outing in the park.

Someone shouted and pointed overhead, and there was the observation balloon we had seen previously, this time being pulled along the road in our direction. It was yellow and quivering, with a single officer suspended in the basket below. It was also telling the Spaniards our exact location. Beside me, Sgt. Lie exclaimed in his native Norwegian, *"Gud forbann de idioter!"* I later learned that meant, "G-d damn those idiots!" He added in English, "They should just paint big words on the side, 'Here we are!'" Indeed, the enemy fire increased. Within the ranks, some men fell, wounded by shrapnel.

Roosevelt had seen the balloon, too, and I heard him cursing it to high heaven as he rode past our column. At the head of our Troop was Lt. Kane. Roosevelt pointed at him, then ahead toward the river. "Lieutenant! Cross the river now, on the double-quick!" We reached the river but had to halt there, as several troopers ahead of us were stopping to fill their canteens. I myself took mine off my belt and was about to unscrew its top when I saw the despised regimental adjutant, Lt. Hall, ordering the men to cease their replenishment and keep moving. Amongst our ranks, thirsty men cursed his name. It was only much later I would learn that Hall had been under orders.

I was across the river when someone behind me yelled, "There she goes!" I turned in time to see the balloon falling as Spanish bullets perforated its skin. The officer in the basket was screaming at the handlers on the ground to pull him down, but he crashed into a tree and was enveloped by the hissing, deflating device.

We marched out of the jungle and into a small valley containing what appeared to be a road. That took us westward for about one-half mile to the base of a hill that was the easternmost of the two that comprised the Heights. By now it was nearly noon. The enemy was still firing upon us from entrenchments on this hill and the taller one about 500 yards to its west. Making things worse were the snipers, who had stayed hidden in the trees through which the entire army had marched.

Roosevelt ordered the Regiment to take cover as best as possible in this draw. There was barbed wire on either side. I found a spot along the creek that was a tributary of the Aguadores. Already soaked with sweat above the waist and drenched below from fording the river, I could not have cared less at this point about getting any more wet.

At the top of this hill was what appeared to be a ranch house and a few other structures, and three large kettles. The Spaniards had dug trenches in front of the buildings and were using them effectively. I could hear the ping of American rounds that struck the kettles. Next to me, my tent-mate Burdwell took a look. "G-d damn, Charlie," he said, "how in hell are we going to get those beaners out of there?"

"I don't know," I said, "but we'll have to take them somehow."

At that moment, a trooper ten yards to our right rose from his crouch to aim at the hilltop. There was a sound like a whipsaw, and his hat flew forward along with the top of his head. "Sniper to the rear!" someone shouted. Men turned to face the new threat, but all we saw were the trees of the dense jungle a few hundred yards behind us. The Spaniards' use of smokeless powder made it nigh impossible to see their hiding places.

Lt. Kane, scuttling like a crab, came down the line to us. Oddly enough, I looked first to see if his uniform was dirty; at long last, it was showing the effects of the march and the mud. "Dawson! Burdwell! I need you to get back there and take out that sniper!"

"Where is he, Lieutenant?" I asked, fear starting to crawl through my gut.

He pointed behind us. "I believe he's in that first group of trees. Can you take him? You men are two of the best shots in the Troop."

"We'll get the bastard, sir," Burdwell said. All I could do was nod.

"Very good," Kane said. "Take him out and get back here. We shall be going up this hill any time now, gentlemen." He grinned at us, his teeth showing below his brushy mustache. "I would hate for you to miss the fun of the assault. Good luck!"

Burdwell and I scrambled up the low bank and looked at the trees Kane had pointed out. I thought I saw a flash from one of them, very briefly. "See that, Charlie? There he is!" my Texas friend yelled.

"There's damn little cover, Lee," I said. The grass was about two feet high. It would have to be enough.

"We'll go after him like we were Apaches. Saw 'em do it a couple times when I was a kid. Follow me!"

I picked out four troopers nearby. "You men!" I shouted over the fusillade of rifle reports, using my new authority as a Corporal. "Give us covering fire!" I turned to follow Burdwell as I heard the selected men slosh through the creek to take positions.

Burdwell crouched, then sprang and ran low, zig-zagging his way forward ten yards. I took an opposite tack, not wishing to give the sniper two easy targets. I watched my friend carefully and mimicked his clever moves as we advanced. He never went more than twenty or thirty feet, never rose above a scrabbling crouch, and dove down at the end of each burst, and almost always in a different direction, although once or twice it was the same, just to keep the Spaniard off-balance. And it worked. Rounds chewed into the earth near us, but never closer than four or five feet. The covering fire of our comrades undoubtedly helped.

We got to within a hundred yards of the trees. I saw a wink of light from one, and then another from a second tree. "There's another one!" I yelled to Lee, who was prone about twenty yards to my left.

"I'll take that one!" he shouted. "Look 'em over close, Charlie! Look for any movement or color that don't look like a tree."

I focused on my targeted tree. It was about twenty feet high, with a relatively thick cover of palms. I would have given my entire inheritance for a pair of field glasses. It seemed fruitless, but then I caught an unnatural movement. There! In a swing, with grass being used as camouflage, but not enough to conceal the Spaniard entirely. I aimed carefully. The swing was still, but there was a cross-breeze that I would need to account for. I forced myself to calm my breathing. I saw his Mauser come up, sighting on a target. The breeze moved a palm frond in front of him, and it must have obscured his view because he held fire. When the frond moved away, I squeezed the trigger. My Krag discharged and I knew the shot was true before I saw the Spaniard's rifle fly from his hands. He tumbled over backwards out of the swing, trailing grass as he fell. I thought I heard him cry out just before he hit the ground.

The shout of a berserker tore through my throat, and then I found my voice. "Got him, Lee!" I looked to my left, just in time to see Burdwell aim and fire. Another cry, another thump, and my comrade loosed a very authentic Texas yell of "Yee-haw!"

"Let's get back!" I said. "Stay low, there might be more snipers out there." We rose and began running back to our mates at the base of the hill, zig-zagging all the way. The four troopers who had covered our action whooped and slapped our backs as we rejoined them.

Roosevelt was there, on Little Texas. He had doffed his khaki jacket and was wearing the same blue shirt as the rest of us, his pants held up by white suspenders. His blue bandanna with white polka-dots was tied to the back of his hat. "Well done, you men!" he yelled to us, his big teeth flashing. "By Godfrey, that was some fine shooting!" He wheeled his horse around. He doffed his hat and waved it to attract the attention of the troopers, but it also drew even more attention from the enemy. Mauser rounds zipped around him, but incredibly, none struck man or horse. "Get ready!" he shouted. "Boys, this is the day we repeat what we have done before! You know we are surrounded by the Regulars. They are around us thick and heavy." He glanced back up the hill, and then spurred his horse forward a dozen yards. Wheeling again, he shouted, "Don't forget where you belong! Don't forget what you are fighting for! Your reward is not here in the present, but our glory will be in the future!"

CHAPTER FORTY-FOUR

Qaszir, northern Iraq
November 11, 2015

Luck was with us at first. We managed to muster some seventy of the Peshmerga to gear up and join the assault team. Their sergeants were right on the ball; I got the distinct impression they'd told their men to be ready. The remaining troops were ordered to start gathering the civilians for evacuation when we commenced the assault. The militia mortars would have to concentrate their fire on us, rather than go for the villagers.

There was one unexpected break that helped us fill in a few critical blanks in our intel. At 0445, I found the Peshmerga master sergeant to tell him to start mustering his men. He reported that one of the lieutenants had broken during the night. The traitor was now being held separately from the other officers, and when the sergeant showed me to the rogue officer's quarters, it became apparent that he'd been helped along his path to confession. His face was bruised, his lips and uniform blouse bloodied. They'd made no attempt to clean him up.

I sent for Koser to help with translation. The man said that Tahan had indeed killed Ghali and Shadid. The turncoat major had been working with Kata'ib Hezbollah for maybe two years, and he'd recruited the young lieutenant just a few months before. Money had been paid to the lieutenant's family in Erbil, and more was promised. The lieutenant's job was to help cover Tahan's escape, and disrupt the Peshmerga's response to the militia as much as possible. What he hadn't anticipated was being taken into custody right away.

What did he know about the militia unit how holding Teyleraş? Only what he'd been told by Tahan, which wasn't much beyond what we already knew or had surmised. As to what kind of force was on the hilltop right now, he had no clue. But he did tell us that the militia was determined to wipe out the Peshmerga here. Tahan had alluded to some sort of overall plan to disrupt and weaken the Kurdish government in Erbil, taking advantage of the ISIS invasion. The militia unit, seemingly gone rogue, was actually following specific orders.

"Ask him who is advising the militia," I told Koser.

Koser hesitated. "With respect, LT, does that matter?"

"It could," I said. "What kind of leadership they have up there might very well tell us how motivated they'll be to hold the hill."

Koser nodded and asked the question in Kurmanji. The lieutenant appeared to think for a moment, then spoke. "He says Tahan told him the militia has Iranian advisers," Koser said.

An old, familiar chill crept up my spine, working its way up, tingling the hairs on the back of my neck. I fought to tamp it back. "Any names?"

"Fermendarê Îranê kî ye?"

The battered young officer was eager to answer. His left eye was nearly closed, but the right one was bright, maybe with hope that the Americans would protect him from his own countrymen. He nodded, saying, *"Erê, erê! Ya sereke got ku navê wî bû Mazdaki."*

"He said, the major told him the Iranian was named Mazdaki." When I didn't say anything, Koser asked, "You know the name, sir?"

"Yeah," I said. "All right, we're done with this guy. Thank him for his cooperation, tell him we'll do what we can for him when the investigators from Erbil get here." Without waiting, I turned and headed for the door. I knew the guy was as good as dead; the Kurds took a dim view of treason. But, I had more immediate concerns right now, and he'd just added some big ones.

It was still forty-five minutes before official dawn when the assembled Peshmerga troops set out for the foot of Teyleraş. In the gloom, it was hard to read the faces of the men, but I didn't have to. Men marching into battle always look the same, no matter their nationality. There's fear and uncertainty, determination and confidence.

Every man processes his emotions differently.

I remembered a movie I'd seen a few years back, about a Roman outpost at Hadrian's Wall in second-century Britain. A platoon was mustered to go outside the fort on a rescue mission, and the filmmaker had done a great job of capturing the tense emotions of the men. Nineteen hundred years later, the weapons and body armor had changed, but not the men.

Like me, the Roman commander in that picture had just arrived to take over the post. Like me, he faced a ruthless enemy, massing for an attack. But unlike me, that Roman had no idea who his opposing commander was. He was a stranger, someone without a face, an unknown entity. But I knew exactly who that man up on the hill was, the man endangering my soldiers, my allies, the villagers I had to protect. Mazdaki, the Iranian Quds Force officer. A Guardian Lieutenant Colonel, last I'd heard. Maybe he'd been promoted since then.

Whatever. He was the man who'd commanded the enemy force in my very first firefight, down in Wasit Governate, southeastern Iraq, four and a half years ago. The man responsible for the deaths of twelve Iraqi soldiers, and one American: my best buddy, Chet Murphy.

This couldn't be about revenge. This couldn't be about killing the man who had evaded us down in Wasit, somehow surviving not one but two Apache runs, the man who had lived to take over a Kurdish village not too far from here three years later, tormenting its citizens and holding an American teenager as a slave. No, this couldn't be about him.

At one time, the Iranian had lurked inside me, always there, constantly whispering, striving to keep me from my goals. My soul had been consumed by thoughts of revenge. But I'd forced myself to beat him back, drive him away. My instructors had helped. They'd taught me how to confront him, acknowledge him, and put him aside. The final blow had come when I'd been reading about my great-great-granddad's commanding officer. Theodore Roosevelt had said, "Unless a man is master of his soul, all other kinds of mastery amount to little."

I looked south, toward the brooding hill, the imposing mountains behind it. No lights up there, not yet. Unbelievably, the enemy was sleeping in. So far, the advantage was ours. We needed to exploit it. I needed to have all my wits about me, to focus on the mission. Always the mission.

And yet…"We're coming, Mazdaki," I said softly, almost unable to hear myself over the sounds of the men's footsteps alongside me, the creaking of their gear, the nervous clearing of a throat. "We're coming, and you're going to die."

CHAPTER FORTY-FIVE

The journal of Charles J. Dawson, con't.

We waited. The heat was bad enough, but making matters worse, far worse, was the constant shelling, and the rifle fire from the Spanish entrenchments. A cacophony unlike anything I had ever heard, and I hope to hear it never again. Troopers were almost helpless to evade shrapnel from enemy artillery, bursting overhead or into the ground nearby. We clung to whatever cover we could, wishing we could burrow into the ground, cover ourselves up and end this madness. Troopers wondered aloud, and profanely, about the reasons why our own artillery could not deliver any decisive blows to their Spanish counterparts. As the hour wore on, the language from the men grew even more foul, such epithets as I had rarely heard, and I must confess I added a few choice verbs and adjectives of my own to the frustrated conversation.

But we knew our only course was forward. We simply had to await the order. More than once I saw Roosevelt riding past the line. On one such trip, Burdwell yelled at him, "Colonel, when are we going to charge?"

"I wish they would let us start!" our commander replied. "Stand fast, men! Our time is coming, very soon!"

There were still snipers out there, although more of our troopers were following the example set by Burdwell and myself, going back through the grass to bring the Spanish sharpshooters to heel. One such mission, tragically, was necessitated by the fatal shooting of Troop A's Capt. O'Neill. The word came down the line that he had taken a sniper round in the mouth, only minutes after declaring to his men that there was not a Spanish bullet in existence that could kill him.

Finally–finally!–the order came down the line to advance. Lt. Kane himself came to each group of men in the Troop to give the word. Men began to rise from their pitiful hiding spots and move ever upward, toward the red-tiled building at the top of what we were now calling Kettle Hill. Slowly but surely we moved, a rush forward for several yards, a crouch or a dive into the ground for a few seconds, then up and forward. We encountered the tall grass again, but also wiry brush and even cactus plants. We had to ford yet another small river, which I later learned was the San Juan, with water up to our waists.

Burdwell stayed on my left. To my right was Arthur Cosby, a New Yorker who was also a Harvard man, one of the group who had befriended me on the train to Texas. The three of us were advancing together, and about a quarter of the way up the hill, Cosby was rising from the ground when his hat started to blow off with a breeze. As he reached up to adjust it, I heard a sound like a wet slap and he went down with a cry. I was only five feet away. I went to him. He had rolled on his back, clutching his bleeding right hand. He also had a hole in his blouse, and I saw blood there, as well. "You're hit, Arthur," I told him. A Mauser bullet had gone through his hand, creased his temple and drilled into his chest, below his right collar-bone. "You need to get back to the rear," I said.

"No," he said, while staring unbelievably at his hand. "I cannot. I must advance."

"For God's sake, Arthur! Go back, man! That's an order!"

He looked at me, somehow managing a tight grin through his pain. "Well, Corporal, I guess I shall." I helped him to his feet and he started back down, trying to stay low.

Across the broad expanse of the hill, I saw troopers to my left and right advancing. The Regulars were on our right, and at first I could not see them joining us. Were the Rough Riders assaulting the Spaniards alone? Roosevelt was everywhere, still mounted on Little Texas, still drawing enemy fire, and miraculously still unharmed, except for his wrist wound.

He was waving his hat with the fluttering bandanna, exhorting the men, encouraging the reluctant, praising the determined. Finally, with a roar, the Regulars began to advance.

Rush forward, drop, sight my Krag and fire, reloading when necessary. The shouts of men, the crackling of rifles, the distant boom of artillery, the odd pinging of rounds striking the kettles, even the neighing of Little Texas, all combined into a whirlwind of sound that I shall never forget. Some men shouted with glee, others with terror. Wounded men cursed or cried out for their mothers. Onward we pressed, even as our comrades around us fell. At any moment, I expected a Spanish bullet to end my life. Still, I advanced. I do not know what drove me. Duty, to the Regiment and my comrades? The deeds of my father? The righteousness of our cause? The deep desire within my soul to prove myself worthy? Perhaps all in one. But I did not feel fear. The moment I began the assault, all fear within me vanished.

There was a wire fence some forty yards from the summit, like one we had surmounted at the base of the hill. The first Spanish trenches were ten yards farther up. Roosevelt was at this point about ten yards to my right. He dismounted his horse and leaped the fence, using one post to support himself. I used a similar tactic to get over, and then I espied a Spaniard rising from the trench. He brought his Mauser to his shoulder, looking at Roosevelt. "Colonel! Get down!" I shouted. He heard me and immediately crouched. The Spaniard fired, his round passing harmlessly over Roosevelt's head.

I brought my Krag up and squeezed the trigger, but the firing pin clicked on an empty chamber. I tossed the rifle toward the Spaniard, who saw it and was startled, enough to keep him from firing again at the Colonel. I charged the trench and leaped onto the Spaniard, bowling him backward, his Mauser flying from his grip. I caught a glimpse of three of his comrades farther along the trench line, all climbing out of the pit and scrambling away, toward the top. The man I had knocked down glared at me with furious brown eyes. He shoved me off and got to his feet. I quickly regained mine, in time to see him reaching for a knife at his belt. Without conscious thought, I evaded his backhanded slash, stepped in and delivered a left-right combination, right on the button, and he went down. Burdwell came to the edge of the trench, aimed his Krag and put a round in the man's chest.

I looked around to see Roosevelt rushing past me, aiming his pistol at two retreating Spaniards. He fired twice, and one of the men fell. I later learned that his pistol had been retrieved from the wreck of the Maine.

We reached the summit. The remaining Spaniards had fled. I saw the guidon of Troop E, and several Regulars, including Negro troops from the 10th Cavalry. Roosevelt quickly began to organize the men, because our fight was far from over. To the west, the highest part of the ridge line loomed. San Juan Hill, about five hundred yards distant, was still in enemy hands, and from its blockhouse and trenches, they were directing rifle and machine-gun fire at us. The Colonel shouted orders, directing our fire toward the blockhouse.

How long were we up there? Only minutes, perhaps. We saw hundreds of blue-clad men, Regulars, advancing slowly up one face of San Juan Hill. Then we heard a deep-throated, rapid drumming sound from the base of the hill, too quick for artillery. Spanish machine-guns, somehow down there? Roosevelt studied them, then leaped to his feet, slapped his thigh and shouted, "It's the Gatlings, men! It's our Gatlings!" And indeed it was, a detachment of Gatling guns, firing up the slope toward the Spaniards, bringing cheers from our throats.

But even with the support of the Gatlings, the Regulars advancing toward the summit were being hard-pressed by the defenders. Next to me, Burdwell sighted his Krag and fired two quick rounds into the distance. "Can't do much from here, Charlie," he said. "Too damn far."

"We're going to have to go over there and root them out," I said.

As if he had heard me, Roosevelt stepped to the front of our men, raised his pistol and shouted, "Now, by God, men! Let's charge 'em, G-d damn 'em!"

CHAPTER FORTY-SIX

Qaszir, northern Iraq
November 11, 2015

Between the ODA and the Kurds, we had about ninety troops for the assault. I thanked God that I'd had the foresight to climb the hill myself. Was it just the day before? Two days? I couldn't remember, a combination of fatigue and excitement crowding against unnecessary thoughts. I'd slept maybe four hours, taking time to read from the Rough Rider's diary before killing the light.

Unlike his assault, ours began in pre-dawn twilight, and there was almost complete silence. But I felt the same emotions he did. And like him, I felt no fear. Old Charles and his mates had to assault two hills against an entrenched enemy, in broad daylight. We had a few advantages that he didn't. We had no Gatling guns, but we did have mortars: four tubes were set up behind covering rocks at the base of the hill, with Sergeant Amans in charge of the battery. He'd sent one of his Peshmerga soldiers up the mountainside opposite Teyleraş to be his spotter. Now, Amans was waiting for my signal to open fire.

I'd spread the assault force out across the face of the hill, taking the middle position. The ODA was interspersed with the Peshmerga, except for the RTO, Bliese, who stayed with me. At 0530 he'd managed to get uplinked to the satellite and sent my latest report to 5th Group, along with my intention to assault the hill. By the time we were ready to move out, he'd yet to receive a response. I told him we couldn't wait. I'd tried direct voice commo over the sat phone, but the frequency was somehow too garbled to be reliable. Even if I'd been able to request air support, by the time Baghdad could vector in a fighter-bomber or a gunship, it would be full daylight and any element of surprise we might've enjoyed would be lost.

A gunship would've been able to chew up the hilltop and make our work easy, but I couldn't discount the possibility that the Iranians had brought along some MANPADs, portable anti-air missiles. From my time with the Wolverines, I knew they had Russian-made Igla and Strela versions, which could cause trouble for a slow-moving target like a Spectre gunship. In any event, it was a moot point. We were going up, and we wouldn't have air support.

But we had the mortars.

Stratton was behind me, geared up with a helmet and body armor. A pistol was holstered at her hip. She'd assured me she knew how to use one, and I ordered her not to draw unless her life was directly threatened. Throughout the march to the hill, I'd heard her whispering as she recorded the scene.

We climbed the hill for fifteen tense minutes, taking our time, but maintaining a steady pace. Slipping on loose rocks might not only injure a man, but start a rockslide that at the very least would alert the enemy. I had to assume Mazdaki had put sentries out. I would've put a couple squads of them around the hillside, about thirty or forty meters from the top. We were about halfway to that point now. So far, there'd been no response. Could it be possible that they'd bugged out? That would've required some sort of lights, though, in the deep dark of the mountain night, and our own sentries would've seen them. No, they were still up there, it was almost as if I could feel them.

I had to maintain radio silence until the last second, so I'd told the men to rely on hand signals, passed down the line. With me in the middle, leading the way, I could signal to my left and right to halt, take cover, or advance. When I judged we were about a hundred meters from the peak, maybe fifty from where the line of sentries might be, I signaled a halt. All down the line, men stopped in place and hunkered down, bringing their weapons up.

I lowered my night vision goggles. The ODA had been issued the new panoramic version, and now I used them to sweep the hillside in front of us. And there they were: two, four...six sentries, spread out on a line for about fifty meters, and about fifty in front of us. Most certainly, they didn't have NVGs themselves, or we would've been spotted already.

I activated the SEND function of my MBITR tac radio and whispered, "Badger Four, do you read, over?"

"Badger Actual, this is Badger Four, read you five-by-five, over."

"Badger Four, prepare to fire. Acknowledge, over."

"Badger Actual, we're ready to go, over."

"On my mark." I looked along my line, first left, then right. The men were spread out, in firing position, behind whatever cover they could find or prone. "Three. Two. One. Execute."

From behind us I heard the telltale thump of a mortar launch, followed closely by three more. Amans had zeroed them on the hilltop as best he could. His spotter on the opposite mountainside would guide him from here.

Ahead of me, the ghostly green images of the militia sentries began to move, and I heard shouts.

I clicked my SEND button again, the signal to the men. All of the ODA were on the circuit, along with the Peshmerga sergeants. "Badger Actual to all units, engage on first round impact." I switched off the goggles and raised them up to the front of my helmet. The view went from black with shades of green to shades of gray.

On the top of the hill, a mortar round exploded, then another. The next two overshot the target, but I didn't wait. I sighted my M4 on where the nearest sentry had been and squeezed the trigger.

CHAPTER FORTY-SEVEN

The journal of Charles J. Dawson, con't.

A valley separated the two hills, covered with grass, with a pond at the bottom. Atop San Juan was a low building fronted by trenches from which the Spaniards were firing at us. I saw Roosevelt run down the hill, leap the fence and continue onward. Burdwell and I rose and ran after him, but few others did. Had they not heard the Colonel? One trooper yelled for everyone to follow, moments before his head was torn asunder by a Mauser round.

Roosevelt had run some hundred yards, with only myself, Burdwell and a few other men behind him. When he turned, he realized the rest of the Regiment had not heard his call to charge. He ordered the three men nearest him to drop and wait, and about fifteen yards behind them, Burdwell and I did as well.

As we waited, firing at the Spanish fortifications, the incoming fire was murderous. I saw each of the three men ahead of us get hit, but none mortally. Burdwell cried out; he'd been winged in the left shoulder. "It's just a crease, Charlie," he said to me. Moments later, I felt a blow to my head, like I'd been hit a by a rock, and my hat flew off. A round had sliced open my scalp, just at the hairline on the right side. I saw stars, but although I realized that I'd been hit, I somehow sensed it was not serious. "You're bleedin', Charlie," Lee said to me. He crawled closer and peered at my wound. "Didn't get the bone, I don't think," he said. "Give me your bandanna, I'll wrap you up." I took off my sweaty bandanna, wiped my eyes and forehead, and then handed it to him. Within moments, he had dressed my wound and stanched the blood.

I knew not how much time had gone by since Roosevelt went back to get the rest of the men, but I soon heard a bugle call, followed by a cheer and the stamping of hundreds of boots on the ground. I glanced behind me, and here they came: Rough Riders, Regulars, white men and black men, all shouting, with Roosevelt leading the way. Lee and I rose, as did the wounded men in front of us, and joined the thundering mass. From several of our Indian fellows came war whoops, thrilling and inspiring.

We came to the pond. Several men were ahead of Roosevelt by now, some going around to the pond's right, others splashing through its knee-deep waters. Lee and I, rushing to catch up, chose the water. The steep mass of San Juan Hill rose before us, more than two hundred yards to the top, with no cover save the knee-high grass. But no matter. To our left, on the southern face of the hill, the Regulars were advancing slowly. The Gatlings had ceased their fire, not wanting to endanger friendly troops as they neared the summit.

The enemy's fire was steady at first, but then began to slacken. When we'd closed to perhaps a hundred yards or so, we saw Spaniards abandoning their trenches. We pursued them with even greater vigor. When Burdwell and I reached the top, men of almost every Troop in the Regiment were already there, including Roosevelt, of course, and officers and men of the 10th. The defenders had fled down the hill, westward toward Santiago.

By now it was mid-afternoon. I was overcome with fatigue and thirst, and I was not alone by any means. While some men searched the trenches and the blockhouse, the rest of us took rest wherever we were. I managed to get into a spot of shade on the east side of the house. I drained the last of the precious water from my canteen and wished mightily for something to eat. Even more hardtack would've been welcomed, but we had left our haversacks along with our packs long before we'd started the assault of Kettle Hill.

The nearest Spanish trench was only fifteen or so feet from the summit, and I had walked partially through it to reach the blockhouse. Bodies were strewn everywhere, nearly all of them felled by shots to the head. A testament, I supposed, to the marksmanship of the Regiment, especially the Westerners, who had clearly shown their superiority to most of the Easterners during training back at Camp. But the results were ghastly. Not just the blood, but the grayish, lumpy matter that had been their brains. That morning, I thought, those men were having their own breakfast, thinking about the battle to come, doubtless wishing, like all of us, for this war to be over so they could go home, in their case across the sea to Spain. Now, they never would. But many of ours would not go home, either.

Our efforts for the day were far from over. Roosevelt mustered the men and we moved off the hilltop to the west, coming to the edge of the ridgeline. Before us, less than a mile away, was Santiago itself, its white buildings looking sleepy and peaceful. A city of some 40-thousand, we'd heard. Beyond the town, I could see warships at anchor in the harbor. The retreating Spaniards had fallen back to their last line of defense, trenches and earthworks protecting the city. Were we going to charge them, too? Now we would be going downhill, into the teeth of the enemy, which had doubtless been reinforced from the city. Nearby, I saw Pershing, the captain from the 10th, gazing upon the enemy lines through binoculars. "They have machine-guns in place down there," he said. "It would be suicidal to attack without artillery support."

We were held back, thankfully. I saw a tall officer lead a couple dozen troopers another hundred yards or more toward the Spanish works, but they were called back. I learned later that the officer, a Lt. Greenway from Troop A, had wanted to assault the works and take the city. He should thank the Lord that he was recalled before the Spaniards opened fire. Greenway was a foot-ball star at Yale, but that line would have been much harder than any line he ran into on the gridiron.

We were still taking fire from the dug-in Spaniards, so the Regiment was ordered to fall back to the summit of the hill, and we occupied the trenches used minutes before by the enemy. Some of us were put to work carrying the bodies of the Spaniards from the trenches and depositing them into the blockhouse. The bodies of fallen Americans were also laid out there, on the opposite side from that facing the enemy. It was like the aftermath of Las Guasimas, only worse. Troopers filed past them, looking for comrades, stopping to say a few words over them, many weeping.

It was at that somber location that I found McGee, my erstwhile boxing opponent, for the first time that day. He was kneeling next to the body of a fellow Coloradan. I commiserated with him for a moment, then said I was off to find a medical officer to treat my wound. I had a frightful headache, but hoped it was more from fatigue and sun than from the wound itself.

"Don't let them take you back to the rear," McGee said. "The medical tents are back there, and you don't want to see what's going on." He said the day before, he'd helped transport a man suffering from a serious leg wound, incurred during the shelling of El Pozo, to a medical tent. "They took one look at the fellow and up on the table he went, and out came the saw. When they were done they tossed his leg onto a pile outside." McGee paused, obviously still shaken by that gruesome sight, and that of his dead friend before him now. Then, he said, "G-d damn, Dawson. No wonder my daddy took to drink. No man should go through this."

I could think of little to say, except, "We're going through it together, my friend. We will survive it together."

CHAPTER FORTY-EIGHT

NBC News Special: "The Charge that Saved Iraq," part I
May 29, 2016

Good evening, I'm Tom Brokaw. On a chilly morning in the mountains of northern Iraq six months ago, a small group of American soldiers faced overwhelming odds against an entrenched enemy. Along with about seventy troops of the Peshmerga, the army of the Kurdistan Regional Government, nine U.S. Army Special Forces soldiers had to protect a remote village populated by some two hundred Kurdish civilians, mostly women, children and elderly men.

The motto of Special Forces is, "Di oppresso liber," "To free the oppressed." On that morning in the region of Iraq known as Kurdistan, those nine Americans were the only hope for freedom held by some seventy-five soldiers of the Peshmerga and the civilians in the village of Qaszir. The Americans had limited communications with their headquarters, and no hope of air support or reinforcement. Facing them on a hilltop overlooking the village were nearly one hundred fighters of the virulently anti-Kurdish Kata'ib Hezbollah militia. NBC News correspondent Jennifer Stratton was the only reporter in the village. This is her story of Operational Detachment-Alpha 5237, Charlie Company, 2nd Battalion, 5th Special Forces Group: nine Green Berets who risked their lives to defend a remote place no Americans had ever heard of.

STRATTON: I had arrived in Qaszir just two days before, coming north from the town of Bujal, which was on the verge of being overrun by the militia. The Peshmerga had abandoned Bujal to the advancing Kata'ib Hezbollah, hoping the militia would simply march through and continue eastward, to the border with Iran and safety from advancing ISIS forces. It was a huge gamble, one the local Peshmerga commander had been forced to take, under orders from his superiors in the provincial capital of Erbil.

Col. Azwer Ghali, the Peshmerga commander of the region encompassing the northern districts of Kurdistan, was Stratton's host when she and her team arrived in Qaszir on November ninth, 2015. He consented to an interview with her that evening.

GHALI: My orders from my government in Erbil were to abandon the cities of Aqrah and Bujal to the militia. The militia's appearance in the area was an unstable addition to an already dangerous situation. An advance force of Da'esh fighters had taken the city of Mamuzin, only some forty kilometers southwest of Aqrah. Our forces in the region were thin. I have to admit that the rapid advance of Da'esh from Syria had been a big surprise for my government and the national government in Baghdad. Our forces were slow to respond. The American withdrawal in 2011 weakened the Iraqi military substantially. We were not ready, but they were pulled out anyway by their government in Washington. Many in Iraq welcomed this, but many did not, especially here in Kurdistan. The Americans had freed us from Saddam, and protected us from the insurgents after that. Now there was a new threat. Our fears were proven to be warranted.

Now, this militia unit is suspicious to us. The organization has not been friendly to Kurds in the past and this unit, like most, is advised by Iranian Quds Force officers. Iran's hatred of the Kurdish people is well known. I wanted to defend Bujal, but was ordered to let the militia through, in hopes they would proceed eastward to Iran. Just in case they turn north, my men and I, along with our American friends, are prepared to meet them here, at Qaszir.

STRATTON: Only hours after granting me that interview, Colonel Ghali was murdered, along with his second-in-command, Captain Shadid. The prime suspect was Major Tahan, the unit's intelligence officer. He was identified as the killer by a Peshmerga lieutenant whom he had recruited as an accomplice. Tahan fled the village in a Peshmerga vehicle on the afternoon of November 10, apparently going to Bujal and joining up with the militia force. It is not known if he participated in the attack on Teyleraş, the hill overlooking the village. As of this date, he is still at large and is presumed to be in Iran, under the protection of the Iranian government.

A small group of U.S. Army Special Forces soldiers, under the temporary command of 1st Lieutenant Jake Dawson, was in Qaszir, having assisted Ghali's command for several months as it prepared to defend the Aqrah region from the advancing ISIS forces. Dawson had arrived in the village only a few days before, when the team's previous commander had been summoned home to the U.S. due to a family emergency.

STRATTON: Lieutenant Dawson was reluctant to speak with us when we arrived in Qaszir. This is not unusual for Special Forces troops, whether they're deployed or in training back in the States, but the day after my arrival, the lieutenant allowed us to accompany him on his personal reconnaissance of Teyleraş. From this video, which we shot that day, you can see the looming mountains that hem the valley in. Teyleraş itself is more of a mountain than a hill. Colonel Ghali had emphasized the importance of the hill in the defense of the village, and had two dozen of his men occupying the hilltop.

DAWSON: You can see that this is pretty rugged country. Only one road leads to the village, northward from Bujal, and this is the end of the road. There are some trails leading north from Qaszir up into the mountains, but it would be tough going, especially for the elderly in the village and small children, and that's about all they have left here, along with the mothers. But we're preparing to evacuate up there anyway, just in case.

STRATTON: Can you hold this hill, Lieutenant?

DAWSON: Our Peshmerga allies are very competent soldiers, ma'am. I have at least one of my men up here around the clock, in direct communication with us down below at our TOC, that's our Tactical Operations Center. With the reinforcements Colonel Ghali has ordered, we should be able to hold the hill and protect the village, if the militia comes up here.

STRATTON: Are they coming?

DAWSON: I hope not. I hope they keep going east, to Iran, and leave these people alone. We can hope for the best, but we have to prepare for the worst.

And "the worst" is what indeed happened. The Peshmerga's top two officers were murdered, the hilltop was not reinforced, and on the night of November tenth, the militia moved up the valley and attacked Teyleraş, taking the hilltop and killing four Peshmerga defenders. The rest, along with their two American advisers, were able to retreat back to the village.

STRATTON: Lieutenant Dawson had ordered the four remaining Peshmerga officers, all lieutenants, to be held under guard after the murders of Ghali and Shadid. One of them confessed to his part in the crime, but the other three could not be entrusted to resume command positions within the ranks of the defenders. That left Dawson, a veteran of two previous combat deployments to Iraq and one to Afghanistan, in overall command of the defenders.

Only twenty-six years old, Dawson's family has a rich U.S. military history. An ancestor received the Congressional Medal of Honor for service with the Union Army in the Civil War. Another fought with Theodore Roosevelt and the Rough Riders at San Juan Heights in Cuba in 1898, another was a decorated Marine Corps fighter pilot in World War II and Korea. Dawson's grandfather was a Special Forces sergeant who was killed in action in Vietnam in 1972. Lieutenant Dawson's legacy was known among the Peshmerga, and they called him *Dargiran Siwar,* roughly translated as "Rough Rider." When I asked him about that, the lieutenant declined to comment, except to say that he was proud of his family's legacy of service, which includes his father, a former member of Congress. But his top sergeant was more than willing to talk about his young commander.

Master Sergeant Robert Wilson retired from the Army in February 2016 after twenty-two years of service. While on deployment in Iraq, Wilson and other members of ODA-5237 worked with local Peshmerga troops, helping to advance their training and plan their missions, while also providing much-needed medical and engineering help to the

Kurdish communities they stayed in.

WILSON: Twenty-two years in the Army, the last fifteen in Special Forces, and I loved every minute of it. Total of thirteen overseas deployments, plus a couple tours Stateside as an instructor. I could've stayed in another two years, maybe three, working as an instructor, but the time just felt right. I had some close calls in Kurdistan, and I didn't want to tempt fate too much longer. There would've been an ODA that needed an 18Z for a deployment, they would've asked me, and I would've said yes, and that might've been the tour I didn't come back from. As it is, now I'm home, and my wife and kids are starting to get to know me again.

When we heard 5th Group was sending us a new officer right out of the Q Course, we wondered what kind of guy we'd be getting. Besides me, there were seven other sergeants in the ODA for that deployment, one of them on his first tour, the rest with multiple deployments. The word was that Lieutenant Dawson knew the ropes, had been over here a couple times and that was a big plus. And he'd been with the 75th Rangers, a top-notch outfit, so we figured he had already learned what a lot of new officers need to learn about where they're operating. He knew the territory, and more importantly, he knew the people we were working with. And most especially, he knew the people who were coming up that valley.

Most officers are captains before they come to SF. Usually the 2IC is a warrant officer, but we'd lost our warrant when he was wounded by an IED. When we heard a lieutenant would be coming in as Captain Jones's new 2IC, we knew he must have a lot on the ball, and it didn't take long before we'd have to find out. When the captain was called home, that put Lieutenant Dawson right into the frying pan. Usually the men wonder how something like that is going to turn out. We didn't have time to wonder about it.

STRATTON: The militia's successful assault of the hill overlooking the village was a serious blow to the American team and the Peshmerga force, which had suddenly lost its two most experienced officers.

WILSON: I'd never run into anything like that before. Lots of the indigenous you work with in SF don't like their officers. Hell, there's some American soldiers who don't like their officers, either, but this was the first time I'd run into a situation where the commander and his 2IC were gunned down in cold blood. Blue-on-blue during a firefight, yeah, I've seen that, but this was bad. Came at the worst possible time. The lieutenant had to step up to the plate. We all had to.

I'll say this now, something I couldn't say when I was in uniform, but somebody sure as hell dropped the ball in Baghdad. First, somebody in the Iraqi government turned those militia clowns loose up in Kurdistan, knowing full well they had Iranian leaders who were not averse to hunting Kurds. The Peshmerga lieutenant who turned said the whole thing was part of a plan to destabilize the Kurdish government, and you know the Iranians were behind that all the way. The Iranians were behind a lot of the (deleted) going on over there, but there were too many influential people in the government in Baghdad who were in Iran's pocket. As to the leadership we have over here, and what they were doing about it? Don't get me started.

And second, there was no way we shouldn't have been able to get some air support up there. Yes, the commo was (deleted) up, those mountains made it tough to get through to 5th Group, but Captain Jones had asked for all kinds of help and we never got it. If we'd been able to call in a couple fast-movers to come up that valley after Teyleraş was taken, they could've solved the problem in about five minutes, and a lot of brave men on our side would be alive today. My experience? When an SF force on the ground asks for air support, it's gonna come down to two things: available assets, which is a given, but right behind that is how sexy the target package is. And in this case, I wouldn't be surprised if there'd been someone in Baghdad telling our people that our air would be better directed elsewhere.

So when the lieutenant told us that night that we'd have to re-take the mountain the next day, nobody complained, nobody questioned it. We all knew it had to be done. It was either that or defend the village when the rest of the militia came up that road, and with them using the mountain for their mortars, we'd have been in deep (deleted). A lot of civilians would've died. There's no way we could've evacuated all of them up into the mountains.

STRATTON: I decided to go along with the assault force. My cameraman was injured and couldn't climb the hillside, so I had him and my sound engineer assist with the evacuation of the village. But I had to go. The lieutenant objected, but then he wound up giving me a helmet and body armor and a sidearm. I knew the risk involved. There was a good chance of being wounded or killed, but I wasn't going to sit back and observe from a safe distance. The way things were in that valley, no place was safe.

It was early on the morning of the eleventh, Veterans Day back home, when we started out from the village. I was able to get a brief interview with Lieutenant Dawson as we started out.

DAWSON: I really don't have time for this, Jen–Ms. Stratton.

STRATTON: Just a few quick words, Lieutenant.

DAWSON: All right, but we need to keep moving.

STRATTON: How confident are you in the ability of your Peshmerga allies?

DAWSON: Is that a serious question?

STRATTON: There's been fratricide within their ranks, and–

DAWSON: I have full confidence that every soldier will perform to the best of his ability, whether he's wearing a U.S. flag patch or a Kurdistan patch. You get one more question, and then we stay quiet until we begin the assault, okay?

STRATTON: If the assault fails, will you be able to retreat and get the civilians out of the village in time?

DAWSON: We're not going to fail.

STRATTON: But, what if–

DAWSON: You have a lot to learn about Special Forces soldiers, Ms. Stratton.

When we return, the charge up the heights of Teyleraş.

CHAPTER FORTY-NINE

The journal of Charles J. Dawson, concluded.

August the 8th, 1898 – I am exhausted beyond all measure, but also delighted. We are going home, at long last. We are aboard the transport ship Miami, bound for Long Island, New York. I am delighted to be sailing northward, to cooler weather and the safety and comfort of America. I am also delighted to be alive to complete this record. So many of my comrades had to stay behind, interred in the loamy ground of Cuba.

The fighting continued, albeit intermittently, for another dozen days after our successful assault of San Juan Heights. The Colonel (who was made officially so by the War Department during the campaign) had the Regiment occupy a campsite on the ridgeline facing Santiago, a site we promptly dubbed Fort Roosevelt. We were the closest U.S. encampment to the enemy, meaning we took the brunt of the Spaniards' fire from their works at the edge of the city. While we repulsed one Spanish charge against us later on the 1st, we were never given the order to move against the city proper. As we bedded down that night in the trenches, covered in what amounted to slime, drenched by rain and still hungry even though we'd had a meal made up of captured victuals from the Spanish officers' quarters on the hilltop, we did not yet know how many casualties we had taken on that long, dreadful day, or that more were to come on the morrow.

The next day, Col. Roosevelt called for volunteers to root out Spanish snipers, who still infested the jungle to our rear and were taking a frightful toll, even of medical personnel, despite their Red Cross brassards. "These brigands are courageous," Roosevelt said when he addressed us, "but also wantonly cruel and barbaric. You are to eliminate them without mercy." I stepped forward, but my tent-mate Burdwell could not; he had been assigned to a wagon detail, sent to the rear to round up equipment left on the march. (He was pleased, declaring that being a mule-skinner meant he would be allowed to use his entire repertoire of profanity, which is impressive, without fear of rebuke.) The sniper hunt was to be conducted by several teams of two, and to my surprise and delight, I was paired with McGee, who had quickly shrugged off his wound from Las Guasimas and established himself as a crack shot in his Troop. As for my own head wound, a surgeon had disdained stitching it up, but had cleaned and dressed it well enough that I could wear my hat over the bandage and return to duty.

McGee and I set off to our assigned sector. It was again hellishly hot and humid, and by now the water we were able to find was far from pure, so we were reluctant to quaff it in any real quantities. After an hour of patrolling our sector, we heard the by-now-familiar report of a Mauser from a tree-line up ahead. We hit the dirt and advanced on the enemy. I had filled McGee in on the successful tactics used by me and Burdwell previously, and they worked again. Inexorably, we closed on the Spaniard's position, which was finally revealed to us when my fellow hunter drew a shot that missed, but which revealed the sniper's location to me exactly. I dropped him from 100 yards.

Wary of other snipers that might be nearby, we advanced cautiously, as our orders were to ensure that no wounded men escaped. We found the Spaniard crumpled at the foot of the palm, a bloody hole in his blouse. His neck was twisted at an unnatural angle, doubtless the result of the twenty-foot fall from his swing. I knelt over him to search his person for any documents or souvenirs; we were to bring back proof of each man brought down.

Suddenly, McGee, who was standing nearby, shouted, "Christ Almighty!" Before I could react, I heard the roar of his Krag, followed almost instantaneously by the bark of a Mauser from above. The trunk of the palm tree seemed to explode, showering me with shards of wood. Fortunately, my battered campaign hat protected my head, the brim covering my face except for the last inch or so of my chin. Something stung me there, and in my chest and forearms. I sat back onto the ground with a grunt.

Above and behind me, I heard a groan, then a plaintive cry: *"Madre de dios! Por favor, no me dispares!"* There was a clatter, and a thump. The Spaniard had dropped his rifle to the ground.

I heard McGee sigh. "Don't shoot him again!" I gasped. I looked up into a tree some thirty yards away and saw the sniper. Blood soaked the front of his blouse near the shoulder.

"The Colonel said to eliminate them," McGee said. "No mercy. You heard him, Dawson." He raised his Krag and aimed, then sighed again. He uttered a mild oath, lowered his rifle and motioned to the Spaniard. "Come on down, Pedro. We'll get you fixed up."

We helped the prisoner to the nearest medical tent. We never saw him again. By the time the detail reported back to the Colonel the next day, eleven Spanish snipers had been killed. I was the only American who had sustained even a slight wound. Some of the men bragged about how they had brought down their targets. One, an Arizonan from Troop B named Goodwin, told of how his partner, a Negro soldier from the 10th, had slit the throat of a wounded Spaniard. McGee and I, by mutual agreement, said nothing about our experience, other than to report our one confirmed kill.

I had more than enough killing, by that point. Although the Spaniards traded rifle fire with our line sporadically throughout that day and the next, their fate was sealed on the morning of the third, when we heard a long series of rolling booms, almost like thunder, coming from the harbor. We learned later that it was naval gunfire. The Spanish admiral, Cervera, had decided to make a run for the open ocean. His fleet was decimated by our naval squadron, waiting for just such an opportunity.

Over 300 Spanish sailors died, versus just one American.

At noon that day, a flag of truce was raised over our lines, as Gen. Shafter sought parley with the Spanish commander, a brigadier named Toral. Shafter, we heard, threatened to shell the city if his terms were rejected. We all laughed at that, but without much humor. The previous day, word had spread through the ranks that Shafter had wanted to pull all troops back from the Heights, closer to the beach, perhaps to resolve the wretched supply situation. Not only were we virtually without food, our ammunition was running dangerously low as well. The withdrawal was vigorously opposed by Roosevelt, of course, but also by Wood and Wheeler, and they carried the day. Now, Shafter was bluffing about bombarding Santiago, as all his siege guns were still in the holds of the transport ships or sitting quietly on the beach at Siboney.

The Spaniards did not know that, though, and so the bluff worked, at least giving us time to rest. First, we cheered the news of the Spanish fleet's defeat. The regimental band played "The Star-Spangled Banner" from the top of San Juan Hill, and we all celebrated. But then we went back to work, fortifying our trenches, positioning our two machine-guns and three of the Gatlings, all the while hoping none of us would have to fire a shot again.

July the 4th, our Independence Day, saw Cuban civilians fleeing Santiago by the thousands, almost all women and children, fearful of the threatened bombardment. They were allowed through our lines and comprised a most pitiful sight. We heard tales of no food in the city for days due to the blockade, of people eating cats and rodents. That day we also heard more grim news: Col. Roosevelt reported to us, and in a dispatch to Shafter, that our Regiment had lost 92 killed, wounded or missing. Sadly, a few of the dead included men who had been pushed beyond their limits and took their own lives.

The truce lasted another six days, and at four o'clock on the afternoon of the tenth, the Spaniards resumed fire. We retaliated, and our artillerists finally produced results, using the pneumatic dynamite gun to silence several enemy batteries and devastate some of his trenches. The truce resumed at noon on the eleventh. Once again the guns fell silent as the generals passed notes back and forth. Our tents finally arrived, just in time to shelter us, in a manner of speaking, from a violent thunderstorm that evening. Burdwell himself had found our respective caches of gear and we slept under cover for the first time in over a week, and even with the pouring rain and roaring thunder, we slumbered as if dead.

Despite our exhaustion and privation and the growing threat of sickness in the ranks, Roosevelt kept us on our toes. We heard stories of some regiments of Regulars taking it easy, but not us. Nobody resented the discipline. Every one of us by then recognized that without the Colonel's leadership, our casualties would have been far worse, and his own personal courage had long since been established. He was among the men almost constantly, day and night. When the man had time to sleep was a mystery.

Burdwell and I were in our trench on the night of the thirteenth when Roosevelt came by, slogging through the mud. "How are you men holding up?" he asked.

We were filthy, exhausted and ravenously hungry, but we knew he had shared all of our trials, and what's more, now carried the responsibility of the entire Regiment on his shoulders. We said, "We're just fine, Colonel."

"Bully!" he cried, flashing those now-famous teeth. His uniform was just as ragged and dirty as ours. Accompanying him on the inspection was Lt. Kane, who was, as always, spotless and clean-shaven. "It should be over soon, gentlemen," Roosevelt said. "Carry on."

And indeed, it was. At noon the next day, a rolling cheer swept the ranks. The Spaniards had surrendered the city. It was, at long last, over.

We should be home in a few days. There is a camp on Long Island, where we shall be under some sort of quarantine. Nobody knows when we'll be mustered out and allowed to return home. It is possible that we could be re-formed as a Regiment and sent to the island of Porto Rico, where the Regulars are now engaged, or back to Cuba, this time for an assault on Havana. The Spaniards have no hope of victory, yet they have not surrendered their colonial capital. There is some talk among the Regiment about returning to the island to finish the job, but it is empty talk indeed. Nobody really wants to go back. I certainly do not. But, of course, if ordered to do so, we shall.

At least we now have new uniforms, issued to us just yesterday. Enormous bonfires were made to burn our original duds, which had been reduced to filthy rags. All of us were able to bathe in Santiago Harbor before embarking on the voyage. Some of us went into the city to purchase supplies or souvenirs, although it being a Sunday, most shops were closed. The city would have had some charm under peacetime circumstances, I could see, but even though it had not been shelled, its people were in a sorry state. Their mood, however, was buoyant. The hated Spaniards were gone. Freedom had finally come. We received many thanks, handshakes and kisses. Then we set sail. Gen. Wood, having been promoted, stayed behind with a regiment of Regulars to garrison the city. Who knows how long American troops will have to remain here, to keep order and help the Cubans learn how to run their own country? Hopefully not long at all, but I fear these people have a long way to go.

This voyage may have the same problems we experienced on the Yucatan, from what seems like years ago. There is hardly room for all of the troops, the food is bad, the water most foul. Yet we don't seem to care that much. "At least nobody is shooting at us," McGee said a little while ago, as we stood at the railing, watching Cuba disappear into the Caribbean haze.

There is talk that Roosevelt will be running for the governorship of New York. Some of our lads from that state say he would be unbeatable in such a race. "Hell, why stop there?" Burdwell said. "He should be the next President. Better than that old coot we've got there now." Ordinarily I would not appreciate criticism of President McKinley, but if the haphazard planning and calamitous logistics of this entire campaign are any indication, the White House and War Department could certainly use some new blood.

If the Colonel does run for the presidency in 1900, he shall certainly have my vote. But that is perhaps the only part of my immediate future that I am sure of. After this experience, can I return to the campus in Madison to resume my studies? Should I? Yes, I should and I will, because I have promised Father. And yet, two more years of schooling, and then Law School, sound dreadfully dull, by comparison with what I have just been through. Joining Father's law firm and living in quiet, charming Platteville has its positive aspects, though. I will be doing important work in my community, and each night I will return to my clean, dry home, with plenty of food on the table and a soft bed awaiting me. And, as McGee said, nobody will be shooting at me.

Will this experience, this trial by fire, make me a better student, a better lawyer? Eventually, a better husband and father? The people of Cuba will soon have their freedom, and I helped them achieve it. I will always be able to point to that with pride. But I also realize the wisdom of what Father told me that day in his study, when I begged his help in applying to the Regiment. War is indeed hell, and no nation should engage in it except as a last resort, to defend itself, and its helpless neighbors. No doubt Father's Civil War experience shaped him as a man, and a wonderful man he is. If my time in uniform can help me achieve only half of his greatness, it will have all been worthwhile.

The foot-ball players will doubtless cheer my return to campus and will anxiously await my tales. What shall I tell them? As fond as I had grown of some of them before I left, they cannot possibly measure up to my comrades from the Regiment. These are the finest men I have ever known. We served under a man who I believe, and dearly hope, will become one of the most inspiring leaders in American history. The friendships I have formed with Burdwell and McGee, Wells and Dean and others will last forever. When the day comes that we finally part our ways, there will be many a tear shed, hugs and handshakes exchanged, and promises made to reunite down the road, when we will raise a glass to comrades lost. We will always have this time, this experience, and these memories.

We will always be Rough Riders.

CHAPTER FIFTY

NBC News Special Report: "The Charge That Saved Iraq," part II

STRATTON: Lieutenant Dawson ordered the mortars to launch their first volley. Two of the four shells impacted on the top of Teyleraş, in the midst of the militia force, and that's when Dawson and the entire assault force opened up. The militia sentries were eliminated in seconds. I shot this footage as the firefight began.

On the tape: That's Lieutenant Dawson leading the assault. It's another hundred meters to the top. Mortar rounds are impacting. The mortar team is zeroing in on the enemy emplacements. Oh God, this is…that explosion! A man just went flying, parts of him! The men, the Peshmerga, they're actually whistling something.

In studio: The Peshmerga soldiers are whistling "*Ey Requîb,*" the anthem of Kurdistan. It means, "O Enemy!" In English, the first verse ends, "Let no one say the Kurds are dead, they are living, they live and never shall we lower our flag."

WILSON: I trained indigenous troops and fought with them all over the world, and the Peshmerga are some of the best anywhere. These guys were ready to march to the gates of hell, and that's exactly what we did. You're going up a hill with very little cover and the enemy has machine guns up there. You know you probably aren't coming back down, but you keep going. It was either that, or die in the village.

STRATTON: The militia were slow to react. Dawson's decision to assault the hill had caught them off guard. Later, prisoners said that their Iranian advisors told them the Peshmerga would not move without the Americans to lead them, and the Americans were too cowardly to act.

WILSON: If they'd been ready, if they'd had night vision, we might not have made it.

DAWSON *(on the tape)*: Come on, men! We're almost there! *Ji bo*

Kurdistanek azad!

STRATTON: The lieutenant shouted in Kurmanji, "For a free Kurdistan!" Many of the Peshmerga took up the call.

WILSON: The lieutenant was the first to reach the top. I was about thirty meters to his left. Two of the Peshmerga in my squad had been cut down. I got hit in my left leg, went down, got back up, kept going. Thank you, adrenalin. The lieutenant went over the little berm they had up there and into the midst of the enemy.

STRATTON: I was right behind Dawson as he charged. I've never been so scared in my life, but these men, if they were scared, they didn't show it. The Peshmerga were fighting for their village, for their country. The Americans were fighting for them, for their brothers.

The scene at the top was chaos. I had my camera in one hand, had drawn my sidearm with the other. I got to the top and a militiaman came at me. He was screaming. He had a rifle with a bayonet. I just reacted, I aimed and fired.

(On the tape.) My God, I just shot a man! I just sh–

WILSON: The lieutenant had spaced us out properly. The mortar barrage had torn them a new (deleted), that's for sure, but there were plenty of them left alive up there to deal with. We'd lost about a quarter of our force on the way up, but when the rest of us got up there, we had the advantage in numbers, and the momentum. Some of the enemy took off down the south slope, back the way they'd come. The rest of them, though, fought damn near to the last man.

STRATTON: You can see the chaos. That's the only way to describe it. I tripped over the man I'd shot, but kept my camera, and used him for cover without even thinking about it, as I recorded the scene. You can see the Peshmerga, fighting hard, and the American Green Berets. They're ruthless, but they're efficient. And there's Lieutenant Dawson. He's fought his way to one of the three shacks on the mountaintop.

WILSON: I took out two of the enemy as soon as I got over the berm. I checked to my left, saw the other squads coming over, the ODA leading the way, keeping them as organized as possible. I saw Sergeant Koser go down, bayoneted....two fighters with bayonets got him.

(Pauses, wipes his eyes.) Sergeant Thomas took care of them.

STRATTON: The lieutenant was fighting, but also directing his men, all around him. He was getting closer to the middle shack.

WILSON: We knew that's where the Iranian officers would have their headquarters. It was the most logical place. The enemy on my flank was falling back, heading for the opposite side, trying to escape over that berm and flee back to Bujal. But the Peshmerga weren't gonna let them.

STRATTON *(on the tape)*: They're running away! The militia, they're—an officer is trying to rally them. There he is! He has a different style of uniform. Has to be the Iranian officer. There's one of the Americans! He's charging the officer!

WILSON: I looked and there was Joe Amans. He was our cherry, the youngest guy in the ODA, first deployment. He was with his mortar team down at the base, then he left the Peshmerga sergeant in charge after the first volley and came up the hill after us. He ran all the way. I saw him leap over the berm, pause a moment, and then he saw the enemy officer and took off after him. Joe was a just kid, an X-Ray, came to SF right out of high school, great kid. He really admired the lieutenant.

SGT. JOSEPH AMANS: I was ordered to stay with the mortar team, but the Peshmerga sergeant was a good guy, he knew his stuff, and I knew the lieutenant would need my help up there. So I ran like hell—I can say that on TV, right? Yeah, okay, I ran like hell and made it up there. My first firefight, I wasn't gonna miss it. I was locked and cocked. I saw the master sergeant on my left, the lieutenant ahead on my right. The TV gal, Stratton, she was down, using a body for cover, but I saw she was okay. Then I saw the officer. He was firing an AK, took down one of the Peshmerga, then the rifle jammed. I saw him draw his sidearm. The lieutenant was ten feet from him, going hand-to-hand with a militia guy. I saw the officer aim at the lieutenant. I aimed and fired at him, but I was too quick, just got him in the shoulder, just winged him, but I kept him from shooting the lieutenant. Then my weapon jammed.

STRATTON: I saw Amans charge the Iranian officer. Tried to take him down, but the officer used some sort of judo throw on Amans, flipped him over his hip. Aimed his sidearm, point-blank, but then Lieutenant Dawson tackled him. They both went down. They struggled.

WILSON: I saw Amans make his damn-fool run at the Iranian, saw him get tossed aside like a doll, he was a dead duck right there, but the lieutenant came flying in and took the guy down. I was running over, but I was still maybe twenty meters away. Saw the lieutenant draw his knife, stab the officer in his side. Got in a couple, then I heard the gunshot.

AMANS: The lieutenant had him down on the ground, had his knife out, stabbed the guy twice, but then there was a pop, the lieutenant grunted. He brought his knife up and got the guy in the throat.

STRATTON: The militia had broken. Most of them were dead or dying. A few had escaped to the south, down the side of the mountain. The Peshmerga were screaming, firing after them. I saw two of them shoot wounded militiamen on the ground. Another militiaman was trying to surrender. He was about to be executed, but one of the Americans stepped in between the two, saving the life of the militiaman.

WILSON: I could see the lieutenant was in bad shape. I yelled for our medic, Sergeant Rivers. The Iranian was dead, and from his uniform I could see he was a lieutenant colonel in their Quds Force. The lieutenant's KA-BAR knife was sticking out of the side of his neck. With the lieutenant down, I was in charge of the assault team. I made sure Rivers was working on him, then I went around to the men. We had to treat the wounded, secure the prisoners, and above all secure that damn hilltop.

AMANS: The lieutenant was conscious. I went over to him. I…*(wipes his eyes)*. I told him I was sorry that I didn't get the officer first. He said…he said, "Don't worry about it, Joe." Then his eyes…closed.

EPILOGUE

The letter of John Dawson, Gunnery Sgt., USMC (ret.)

July 4th, 2026

To my descendants,

To start with, I should tell you that this is the first letter I have written in about forty years, and I'm not even writing it. I am dictating it to my wife, Jackie. We tried having me speak it into the computer, but it turned out all wrong, so she is transcribing it on the keyboard. That's the word she used, "transcribing." I'm told that's hardly ever done anymore, but she did it a lot as a young lady in her career.

On this 250th anniversary of our country's birth, I wanted to tell you one final story. I will be gone soon. Jackie doesn't want to type that part, but I insist, so she does. If I make it to October, I will turn 79 years of age. I hope I do. The old ticker has been giving me more problems in the past couple years. The doc says I could have a transplant, but to hell with that. Give the heart to some young guy or gal who has their whole life in front of them, that's what I told him. I'm just an old gunny whose time is almost up, so I am putting these thoughts down now. I have never added anything to the diary, and I figured it was high time.

I've lived a damn good life and have no regrets, except that I didn't meet Jackie about twenty years earlier. She has been a wonderful wife to me. I'm just sorry we couldn't have kids together.

What could I write about? Whoever's reading this, do you want to know about how it was in Vietnam, when I was in the Corps? I don't think so. I wasn't a hero, like my brother. Yeah, I was at Khe Sanh, but you can read all about it in the history books, or whatever they use for books now. I just did what I could to survive and make sure my Marines survived, and most of them did. The ones who didn't, a day doesn't go by I don't think of them, and it's been, what now, damn near 60 years? So, I'm not going to tell you any of my stories, except this one, which happened way before I went into the Corps.

This is the story of how three generations of Dawson men came together when one of them was a little older than I am now. That would be my grandfather Charles. It was the summer of 1959 and he had just turned 83. He wanted my dad, Ernie, to take him on one last trip, and for me and my older brother, Dennis, to come with us. It was important, Gramp said. So, we came along. My dad was 39, Dennis was 15, I was closing in on 12. I was a young kid, but my memory of that trip is still pretty damn sharp.

Dennis and I knew our grandfather was a special guy, and not just because he was in the war, that would be the Spanish-American War, but because he was our grandfather, and a hell of a grandfather he was. One of the most prominent men in Platteville, Wisconsin, a lawyer who'd helped a lot of people over the years. He'd made enough money to live a pretty comfortable life, but that wasn't what made him special. He was a guy we learned a lot from, me and my brother, about how to be a good man, a good husband and father, a good professional. He led an honorable life and showing us how to do that was his greatest gift to us. He never sat us down and lectured us, but he led by example, which is the best form of leadership. So, when he asked my dad to put this trip together, my dad didn't hesitate.

We flew to New York City, the first airplane flight for me and Dennis. Our dad was a hotshot fighter pilot in two wars, so he knew all about flying, and the first half of the flight he said the pilot should be doing this, he should be doing that, until Gramp told him to put a lid on it. We landed and Dad rented us a car and we went to a hotel and rested up, got a good night's sleep. We'd never been to the Big Apple and Dad promised us we'd see the sights, including a game at Yankee Stadium, but first things first.

So on our first morning, we hopped in the car—a '58 Olds, I remember that, a real boat, and of course a gasoline engine, no satellite radio, no GPS, and someone actually had to drive the car—and we went to the village of Oyster Bay on Long Island. Dad was at the wheel, which was always an adventure because Dad drove a car like he flew a fighter plane, which is to say he took a few chances, but this time he kept it under control. Oyster Bay was a pretty little spot, a lot like the small towns we knew in Wisconsin. We drove to a cemetery. It was a warm day, I remember that. We parked and Gramp led the way. He had to use a cane, but he was getting along pretty good. Dad stayed with him, making sure he didn't stumble and fall.

Gramp said he'd been there before, but that was forty years ago, for a funeral. He remembered the spot, though. Led us up a little hill, and Dad wanted to help him but Gramp said, "No, I climbed a couple hills with the man up there and I didn't need any help then and I don't need help now." Of course I knew that he was talking about something he'd done when he was a young man, not a guy in his 80s, but he went up that hill on his own, Dad right next to him, me and Dennis trailing behind.

There were lots of trees, and it was very pretty. Very solemn. We came to a gravesite, two graves, one headstone, surrounded by a metal fence. There were a lot of flowers on the graves. Gramp went right to the fence and leaned up against it. Dad was on his left, I was on his right, then Dennis. Gramp looked at the headstone, and then he lowered his head and he started to cry. His hand wobbled on his cane, and I put my hand over his, to steady him.

I looked at the gravestone, wondering who it could possibly be who would cause my grandfather, the most disciplined man I've ever known, to break down, and when I saw the names, of course I understood.

THEODORE ROOSEVELT
and his wife
EDITH KERMIT

The dates of their lives were listed under their names. I don't remember them now, but TR was only 60 when he died, that I do remember. Not very old, at least how I think of it now. Back then, my dad was an old guy, and he wasn't even 40 yet.

Gramp pulled himself together. He took out a handkerchief, wiped his eyes, blew his nose. Dad's hand was on his shoulder, steadying him. Dad looked misty-eyed, too, and that was a big shock to us, because our father was the toughest guy on the whole planet, for a whole lot of reasons. Just a week before, we'd been in Platteville on Saturday night, coming out of the Avalon after seeing a movie, and Mom was with us. A couple of college guys were walking by, on their way to the taverns on Second Street, and one of them made some crack about Mom and my dad dropped him like a bad habit, one-two, then he dropped the other guy with just one to the gut, and he led us up the street to our car as if nothing had happened. You didn't mess with my dad.

I'd read about Roosevelt in school, how he was President of the United States way before I was born, how he'd done this and that. I tried paying attention because I knew my grandfather had known him personally, served under him in the Rough Riders, but to be honest, I spent most of my fifth grade year thinking about playing baseball and getting a kiss from Donna Mae Solum, the prettiest girl in the class, and not necessarily in that order.

But Gramp knew all about Roosevelt, had some pictures of him on the wall of his library back home, and a lot of books about him, including a couple Roosevelt had written and signed himself. And now, at the gravesite, he said, "You know, his wife was a wonderful woman. Came to see us in Tampa, I remember it like yesterday. Raised a fine family. Served me a cup of tea and cake on the porch of their house, the last time I visited. That was after their boy Quentin was shot down over France, summer of 1918. I came here to pay my respects."

"You knew Mr. Roosevelt, right, Grampa?" Dennis said.

"Yes," Gramp said. He was quiet a moment, then he said, "Boys, the men he led, our Regiment, was the finest group of men I've ever known, and the Colonel was the finest of them all. If he had asked us to follow him into hell, we all would've gone, no questions asked."

Later we had lunch in Oyster Bay, and Gramp bought us each a couple books about Roosevelt in a little bookstore. Then we went to Roosevelt's house, Sagamore Hill. Gramp always called him "the

Colonel," not "the President," because he said that's what Roosevelt wanted, what he was most proud of, and that's saying something because he was a hell of a president.

Nobody had actually lived at the house for more than ten years, since his wife had died. Today it's one of those National Historic Sites, but that came a few years after our visit. Somehow Gramp had arranged a tour, a personal one just for us, and another big surprise was that it was conducted by Roosevelt's grandson, Kermit Roosevelt Jr., who I found out many years later had been a spy with the CIA. Anyway, I paid attention during the tour and it was just about the most interesting thing I'd ever seen. I wanted to sit in the chair at the Colonel's desk in his library, but Gramp said, "Nobody here is worthy to sit in that chair."

When the tour ended, we sat out on the porch. There were a couple rocking chairs, which Gramp and Dad took, and Dennis and I sat at their feet. We had some lemonade, and Gramp told us stories about his time with the Rough Riders, which we'd never heard before. About the training camp, and the ride on the train, the voyage by sea to Cuba. The landing, the march, the first battle. He told us about the heat and the bugs and the sand crabs. The bullets flying past him. His friends, wounded and killed.

My grandfather was never much of a storyteller, not like my dad, but that day he told those stories so vividly, I could almost see everything, like a movie. I could see the men taking cover from the Spanish artillery. I could hear the sounds of the shells exploding, the screams of the men when they got hit. It was only about eight or nine years later that I was hearing those sounds for real, in Vietnam, and I'll tell you, knowing that my grandfather, and my own dad, had made it through shit like that, it helped me out. I knew they'd made it, and their courage gave me courage. No doubt in my mind, I'm here today because of them.

I made it home alive from Vietnam, but Dennis didn't. He just kept going back. Had to finish the job, he told me before his last tour. In a lot of ways, I wish it had been me instead of him. He was twice the man I was.

But, anyway, Gramp told us about San Juan Heights, and hunting the snipers, and how he saved Roosevelt's life by taking down that Spaniard on Kettle Hill, and how he nearly got killed himself. He pointed to the scar on his temple, where hair never did grow, and finally we knew how he got that scar. He talked about how the men suffered. He talked about his two best buddies, Burdwell from Texas and McGee from Colorado, both of them gone by now, he said.

We went to Montauk, farther toward the eastern end of the island, where Gramp's regiment was quarantined when they got back to the States. There's a marker there. Gramp wanted to walk around. He pointed out where his tent was, where the mess tent was, where Roosevelt's headquarters tent was. Gramp said he was summoned to that tent one day, a week after they arrived, and the Colonel told him personally that he'd been promoted to sergeant. It was the proudest day of his life, he said. He told us about how they were about to be released from quarantine and getting ready to go home, and how all the men chipped in and got the Colonel a statue by Frederick Remington, "The Bronco Buster," and how they presented it to him as a surprise in front of his tent. We had seen that statue in the house.

"The Colonel shed a couple tears when he saw it," Gramp said, "and then he gave us a little speech. When he was done, he went around and shook hands with every one of us, and he remembered every name. It was right here, on this spot," Gramp said, poking down into the ground with his cane, and he started to cry again. Dad steadied him on one side, Dennis on the other.

"Do you remember what he said to you, Gramp?" I asked.

"Yes," Gramp said. "He said, 'Sergeant Dawson, it has been an honor to serve with you. I owe you my life.' And I said, 'Colonel, the honor has been mine, sir.'"

Gramp was quiet after that, and we went back to the car. Dad was driving, Gramp was in the passenger seat, Dennis and I in the back. Dennis asked if he'd visited Roosevelt at the White House when he was president, and Gramp said he had, twice, and also saw him at Rough Rider reunions, starting with the first one, 1899 in New Mexico. And then Dad said, "Your grandfather was there in Milwaukee the day

Roosevelt was shot."

We begged Gramp to tell us that story, but he shook his head. Dad told us later, when we were at Yankee Stadium and Gramp was resting back at the hotel, how Gramp had been in Milwaukee during Roosevelt's campaign in 1912, and how he had helped the Colonel into his car outside the hotel, and a guy came out of the crowd with a pistol and shot Roosevelt in the chest. Gramp said if he'd just been a little faster, he would've been able to take the bullet himself. "Good thing he didn't, boys," Dad said, "because otherwise we wouldn't be here today."

"Did the Colonel die?" I asked, forgetting the date on the tombstone.

"No. He insisted that my father drive him to his speaking engagement, and he spoke for an hour and a half, with a bullet in his chest, and then he went to the hospital. Now you think I'm a tough guy, boys? There was one hell of a tough guy, let me tell you." Well, I remember a little about that game, the Yankees beat Kansas City and I think Mickey Mantle hit a home run, but that story about Gramp, that really stuck with me.

A few days later we all flew back to Wisconsin. We had some stories to tell our friends back home in Platteville, I'll tell you. Nobody believed us. But in sixth grade that fall I gave a report about the book Gramp bought me in Oyster Bay, Roosevelt's own account of his time with the Rough Riders. I even pointed him out in the famous picture of Roosevelt and the Rough Riders atop San Juan Hill. Gramp is the fourth man to Roosevelt's left. You can just see the top of Gramp's hat. His buddy McGee is next to him, and you only see his hat, too. The teacher said it was all true, and said my grandfather was a war hero. That made me a pretty big deal for a while, and I finally got that kiss from Donna Mae.

Gramp died just about a year later. A lot of people came to his funeral, including two old Rough Riders. Gramp got full military honors, a rifle salute, the whole bit. My grandmother had died a few years before, so when they folded the flag, they gave it to my Aunt Edith, Gramp's oldest daughter and my dad's sister. My cousin Ted has it today, on the mantle of his home in Lancaster.

I miss my grandfather. I miss my dad, too. He died in 2004. Doesn't seem that long ago, but it was 22 years. I think about both of them every day. I'll be joining them soon. Then we'll be able to swap stories for eternity.

Fayetteville, N.C.
October 2041

"Sergeant Dawson? May we have a few words, please?"

The tall young woman turned. The reporter, three inches shorter, stared up at the soldier, then said, "Seth Brown, NBC News."

"What can I do for you, Mr. Brown?"

He held up his minicam. "Just a couple minutes? I was sent by Ms. Stratton, personally. Did you get her email?"

The soldier smiled. "Yes. Her invitation to join her on the *Today* show. I'll check with my captain, see if I can get a few extra days' leave. But right now, I don't have much time. My family is here, and I…well, give me a second." She adjusted her green beret, still getting the fit just right. It had only been on a few minutes, after all. She tucked one last strand of blonde hair up underneath it, then nodded.

The reporter smiled. She was such a good-looking woman, and yet the stories he'd heard about her, and her father…He pressed a button on the camera. "We're here in Fayetteville, just outside the arena where the most recent Army Special Forces class has graduated, and the most notable graduate is Sergeant Susan—"

"Excuse me, but it's Sergeant First Class, and I doubt if I'm 'notable.'"

"Yes, pardon me, Sergeant First Class Susan Dawson. Sergeant, congratulations. How does it feel to be the first woman to become a Green Beret?"

"I'm grateful to all the soldiers I went through the Q Course with, and to the training cadre. And of course, to all the men and women I've served with since joining the Army. I never would've made it without them. By the way, I was never given any breaks due to my gender."

"And, Sergeant Dawson, we know your family's legacy of service, going back almost two hundred years, all the way back to the Civil War. You're the first woman in that line of decorated warriors. Do you consider yourself a trail blazer, now that you've broken one of the few remaining glass ceilings in–"

Her eyes narrowed, and the reporter felt their power, so much that he stopped in mid-sentence. He was not the first to be cowed by that stare, and would certainly not be the last. "Mr. Brown, I am a soldier in the United States Army. That's all that matters. Thank you."

She turned away, leaving the reporter holding his camera, still recording as she walked away. She saw her mother and her grandparents. They waved, smiling broadly.

They met her in the midst of the celebrating graduates and families. The autumn sun went behind a cloud, and nearby a band began tuning up. The mother knew she didn't have much time before the music would begin, and she wanted to have a minute with Susan. But first came the hug.

"Oh, honey, I'm so proud of you."

"Mom." It was the only word the soldier got out before the tears started. She'd thought of her mother so many times these past three years. On the long ruck marches, through the brutal combatives training, the maddening navigation evolutions. The long deployments. Through the dark nights and the hot days, the rain and the mud and the snow. Through the firefights, the explosions. The death and destruction. So many times, only the thought of her mother's strong, comforting arms had kept her sane, kept her going. That, and thoughts of her father…

But there were others to hug, too. Reluctantly, she let go of her mother. "Grandpa. Grandma." She hugged them both, together. Grandpa Dawson was seventy-four now, but looked ten years younger, and her grandmother was still the gentle soul she'd always been. Her grandfather had a small package under his arm. "What have you got there?" the soldier asked.

"In a minute, honey," her mother said. She took a tablet out of her purse. "First, this message…" She stopped, composed herself, then continued, "…this is for you." She handed her daughter an ear bud, then pressed a button on the tablet.

A holographic image appeared above it. The soldier gasped, putting a hand to her mouth. The man in the image, whom she resembled so much, smiled at her. "Hello, Suzy," a voice said in her ear. It was his voice, the one that had read stories to her at bedtime, had cheered her on at her track meets. The voice she'd heard over the phone, calling from faraway lands, lands that she herself would be visiting now.

"Daddy…."

"I wish I could be there to see you today, honey," the image said. "I'm looking down on you right now. I know you believe that."

She stifled a sob. She had to be strong. For him. "Yes, Daddy, I do." He was in his uniform, with the silver oak leaves of a lieutenant colonel on the shoulder tabs. She looked at the rows of ribbons, and there was the one for the Distinguished Service Cross, and the one for the Silver Star. She didn't see the light blue one, with the stars, worn by a very select and honored few. Of course it wouldn't have been there, yet…

"I know that this is a special moment for you," he said. "Your mother is there for you today, like she's always been. You have her strength, Suzy. Your mother is a warrior, too."

She smiled at her mother, crying now as she held the tablet. "She sure is, Daddy."

"I'm very proud of you. If you're seeing this, it's because you have achieved something special, wearing the uniform of our country. It's something I didn't quite understand for a while, but once I did, I knew that nothing would please me more than to see my own child serve our country, too. And now, you are serving the same cause I did, that our family has done for nearly two centuries. You are defending our nation, and the cause of liberty. Wear that uniform with pride. There's nothing like it in the world."

She couldn't help it. The tears started again. "I know, Daddy. I know."

"If it's the uniform of an airman, aim high. If it's a sailor's, sail not for self, but for country. If it's a Coast Guardsman's, you're always ready. If it's a Marine's, *semper fi.*" She heard her grandfather sniff. Her father continued, "And if it's Army green you're wearing," he said with a wink, "remember the motto. 'This, we will defend.'" The man in the hologram smiled. Such a sharp image, like he was really there, floating before her. "And now it's time for me to go, honey, because I know you have a mission, and you will always complete the mission with honor, because you are a Dawson. That's what we do. Jeremiah was at Gettysburg, Charles went up San Juan Heights. Ernie was in the skies over the Pacific and Korea. Dennis was in the jungles of Vietnam. Your grandfather had his mission in the halls of Congress. As for me, well, I went to a lot of places. And to help you on your mission, we have something special for you. Cherish it always, as I have. Goodbye, Suzy. Always remember that your father loves you, and trust in God that we'll meet again."

The image faded. She hugged her mother again, hard and long, and the tears were tears of joy.

"This is for you," her grandfather said, handing her the package. She unwrapped it carefully. The breeze carried the smell of the old leather to her. She held it reverently, feeling its timelessness, its strength. The band began to play. Around her, a hundred voices began to sing, and she proudly joined in: *"Fighting soldiers, from the sky..."*

AUTHOR'S NOTES

Northwest Wisconsin
May 2019

The Spanish-American War was fought, and won, entirely within the space of a few months in 1898. The Secretary of State, John Hay, called it "a splendid little war." His boss, President William McKinley, wasn't that thrilled. "War should never be entered upon," he said, "until every agency of peace has failed." McKinley knew a lot about the subject, having served in the Union Army throughout the Civil War, surviving some of that bitter conflict's most harrowing combat.

One of McKinley's sub-cabinet appointments, upon taking office in 1897, was Theodore Roosevelt, the young, hard-charging police commissioner of New York City, as assistant secretary of the Navy. For his part, Roosevelt had no reservations at all about war in general, and war in Cuba in particular. He said, "A really great people, proud and high spirited, would face all the disasters of war rather than purchase that base prosperity which is bought at the price of national honor." Just before taking his new job in Washington, he had written to his sister, Anna, about the potential of war with Spain over Cuba: "I am a quietly rampant 'Cuba Libre' man." He had little faith that the Cuban people would be able to govern themselves, but the goal should be to kick the Spaniards off the island, and things would then work themselves out.

Entire forests have been felled to print books about Theodore Roosevelt, and he wrote quite a few himself. And yet, I didn't really know a lot about him until I was well into my own adulthood. I had seen his bust on Mount Rushmore as a young teenager, and undoubtedly read about him in history books during my school days, but my interest in him wasn't truly piqued until I saw the movie *Rough Riders*, released in

1997 as a two-part event on the TNT television network. Tom Berenger played TR, and play him he did, right down to the pince-nez. It was a stirring tale, and it prompted me to find out more about this man who was so eager to leave his wife and children and go to war at the age of thirty-nine.

Roosevelt would go from Army service to the New York governor's mansion to the vice presidency and then to the White House, all in just three years' time. His rise was meteoric, to say the least. The Republican Party, fearful of TR's tendency to shake up the establishment, put him on McKinley's re-election ticket in 1900 to get him out of the way. (McKinley's original VP, Garret Hobart, had conveniently died late in 1899). The vice presidency in those days was rarely good for anything, and few VPs ascended to the big job. Still, some Republican bigwigs were nervous. Ohio Senator Mark Hanna, who had engineered McKinley's first campaign, said that putting TR on the ticket would mean "there's only one life between that madman and the White House."

It didn't take long for Hanna's fears to be realized. The McKinley/Roosevelt ticket won easily, and on September 6, 1901, barely six months into his new term, the president was shot at close range while shaking hands at the Pan-American Exposition in Buffalo, N.Y. The assailant, an anarchist named Leon Czolgosz, had lost his factory job during the economic turmoil of 1893 and regarded McKinley as his oppressor, even though the financial crisis had come during the administration of Grover Cleveland. McKinley lingered for eight days before succumbing to his wound, and Roosevelt, who had been climbing a mountain in the Adirondacks, was summoned to Buffalo and sworn in as the nation's 26th president. A month away from his forty-third birthday, TR was, and remains, the youngest person ever to hold the highest office in the land.

Roosevelt was elected to a full term in 1904 by a landslide, but declined to run again in 1908, honoring a promise he had made after assuming office. There is little doubt that he would've won again. Instead, he went to Africa on safari. During his absence, he soured on the performance of his hand-picked successor, William Howard Taft, and in 1912 he challenged Taft for the GOP nomination. Despite winning most of the primaries, Roosevelt was denied the nomination by the party's old pols in the proverbial smoke-filled room, so he ran at the head of the new Progressive Party. Taft stayed in the race, and with him and TR splitting the Republican vote, the election went to the Democrat, Woodrow Wilson. Taft finished a dismal third. Even a cursory analysis of the state-by-state returns from that election shows that combining Roosevelt's votes with Taft's would have provided more than enough electoral votes to defeat Wilson. That prompts another question in the historian's favorite parlor game: how might history have changed? But that is a subject best visited at another time.

Roosevelt dealt with defeat by sailing to South America to explore an unknown tributary of the Amazon, an adventure that nearly cost him his life. One can hardly imagine a former president embarking on such an expedition today, but TR was not your ordinary ex-president, just as he was not an ordinary anything. The story of that trip is thrillingly told by Candice Millard in *The River of Doubt: Theodore Roosevelt's Darkest Journey.* TR survived the trip, just barely, and suffered ill health as a result of it, undoubtedly shortening his life. When 1919 arrived, his name was already being bandied about by Republican Party insiders as the favorite for the nomination in 1920, but Roosevelt died in his sleep just six days into the New Year.

I had long toyed with the idea of writing a novel featuring Roosevelt, as other writers have done. He makes a prominent appearance, for example, in Harry Turtledove's 1997 alternate-history novel *How Few Remain,* which includes a memorable confrontation in the 1880s between young rancher Roosevelt and former president turned Marxist Abraham Lincoln. (It's complicated.) In the same genre, Robert Conroy's 2003 novel *1901* shows TR as president, repulsing a German invasion. And just a few years ago, writer Adam Glass and artists Pat Olliffe and Gabe Eltaeb collaborated on a series of graphic novels featuring TR in the "steampunk" genre, where he teams up with other prominent Americans of the Gilded Age, including Thomas Edison,

Harry Houdini and Annie Oakley, for a series of rollicking adventures. (My first thought upon reading the first issue: Why didn't I think of this?)

I wanted to keep my story grounded in reality, though, and finally came up with the concept that led to *The Heights of Valor.* Rather than make it a novel strictly about TR and the Rough Riders, I wanted to connect it somehow to modern times. Roosevelt's policies as president still have a profound influence on us, more than a century after his administration, but I wanted to explore the possibility that an individual Rough Rider might have a long-lasting influence, too, albeit on a smaller scale.

"Legacy" is a concept that doesn't appear to hold much sway in America these days. It seems to have been shoved aside, along with other old-fashioned ideas like "honor" and "integrity." Although it is impossible to measure such things quantitatively, I think it can safely be said that a person's family legacy–that is to say, the impact of his or her family's history on the individual's modern actions–is a lot less evident these days than it used to be. Part of it has to do with distance. It is much more likely now for people to live far away from their grandparents, for example, and thus they cannot easily learn important lessons from them or hear stories about their ancestors. I was very fortunate to grow up within a few miles of both sets of grandparents, and learned much from them, both directly, in the form of stories and lessons, and indirectly, by observing how they led their lives with simple dignity and honor.

The next generation, though, is a different story. Our own children grew up separated from their grandparents by more than a thousand miles. Our first grandchild, who will have celebrated his first birthday shortly before this book's release, will grow up more than a thousand miles away from us, although his paternal grandparents are close by, fortunately. And ironically enough, even with instant communication that allows people to talk to virtually anyone in the world, studies show that young people today are lonelier than previous generations. If they're lonely, they're certainly not learning valuable lessons from their parents or their grandparents.

History has always been my favorite academic subject. I asked myself, "What were those people really like? Were they that much different from us?" No, they weren't. I have found that while times change, people generally lack far behind history's pace. Certainly, today's Americans have far different, and undoubtedly better, ideas about things like race relations and women's rights than did most Americans of the 1890s, but it can also be said that the average Americans of the Gilded Age were concerned about pretty much the same things their descendants would be in the first quarter of the 21st century: making a living, raising their children, building a better future. There were criminals and cutthroat business tycoons and crooked politicians just like today, but there were also honest men and women who worked hard to make the world a better place, also just like today. I think it's important to know how we became the people we are now, to understand how their times shaped our own. And of course there's much truth in what the Spanish-American philosopher George Santayana wrote back in 1905: "Those who cannot remember the past are condemned to repeat it."

My own great-great-grandfather, like Jake Dawson's, was an Army combat veteran, although William Tindell's service with the 43rd Wisconsin in the Civil War didn't put him in harm's way too often, which I suppose is a good thing. He never won any medals, and when the war ended he came home to southwest Wisconsin and started working on the line that eventually produced me some ninety years later. That line now reaches two more generations into the future, with my daughter and grandson. When little Pasquale James Marolda is the same age as my father is now, it will be the year 2102, well into what I sometimes think of as *"Star Trek* time." What legacy will he inherit from his mother, back through me and down the centuries to William, the Civil War vet? Hopefully, it will be the same one that Jake Dawson learned from his family's diary: a legacy of service, sacrifice, and honor. We needed those qualities in the 19th and 20th centuries to meet the challenges that came our way, as individuals, as families, as a nation. We for damn sure need them today, as my grandfather might have said, and I have a feeling we'll need them in the 22nd century, too. They might seem quaint, but they never go out of style.

The author at the Rough Rider memorial, Arlington National Cemetery.

ACKNOWLEDGEMENTS

A novel is always a collaborative effort. The writer may do all the writing, but at the very least he learned his craft from someone, and was helped out along the way toward publication of his or her work. The particular work you're holding in your hand now would not have happened without the support and encouragement of some close friends and fellow authors. Thanks go out to fellow authors Donna White Glaser, Darren Kirby, Marla Madison and Jodie M. Swanson for their honest, unsparing critiques and insights.

More often than not, the research that goes into a novel is almost as much fun as the writing of the book itself. Thanks to having a globe-trotting wife, I frequently get to do research on the road (or water, as the case may be), and this time was no exception. In the fall of 2017, I spent a pleasant few days in New Mexico with my son-in-law, Mike Marolda, researching the Rough Riders in the town of Las Vegas, which not only has one of the country's best archives of Rough Rider papers but was also the location for much of the photography of a favorite TV series, *Longmire*. So in addition to hunting down places where the show was filmed, Mike and I got to ride horses near Santa Fe, explore Fort Union National Monument and haunt some intriguing antique stores as part of my never-ending quest for TR memorabilia. In one, we hit the jackpot, and today a bust of Roosevelt in his Rough Rider uniform sits atop a table in my writing room, presented to me as a birthday gift by Mike and his wife, my daughter Kim. Thanks again to both of you for your companionship and support on this journey.

And speaking of Las Vegas, a heartfelt thanks goes out to the City of Las Vegas Museum, Administrator Cabrini Martinez and her staff, especially museum specialist Michael Rebman, for being very kind and tolerant hosts for my long day of research in their meticulous archives.

To my cousin, CW4 Scott C. Witz, U.S. Army (ret.), thanks for your expertise and your honorable service to our country.

I am especially indebted to the following authors for their often-brilliant work on the U.S. Army's Special Forces, both from the Vietnam era and today, as well as the life and times of Theodore Roosevelt, especially his time in the Rough Riders:

Edmund Morris, *The Rise of Theodore Roosevelt, Theodore Rex,* and *Colonel Roosevelt*

Theodore Roosevelt, *The Rough Riders*

Mark Lee Gardner, *Rough Riders—Theodore Roosevelt, His Cowboy Regiment and the Immortal Charge up San Juan Hill*

Dale L. Walker, *The Boys of '98*

Tim Brady, *His Father's Son—The Life of General Ted Roosevelt Jr.*

Dick Couch, *Chosen Soldier—The Making of a Special Forces Warrior* and *Sua Sponte—The Forging of a Modern American Ranger*

Tom Clancy, *Special Forces*

SFC Frank Antenori, U.S. Army (ret.), *Roughneck Nine-One—The Extraordinary Story of a Special Forces A-Team at War*

And, of course, Robin Moore, *The Green Berets.*

My brothers, Alan Tindell and Brian Tindell, both offered their thoughts early on in the process and helped shape the course of the book. I have been fortunate to travel with them in recent years, and since we're all kind of nuts about history, we spend a lot of time exploring battlefields and museums. In 2011, Brian and I rode through Theodore Roosevelt National Park in North Dakota on horseback and visited the sites of TR's ranch houses, along with the saloon in nearby Wibaux, Mont., where the future president knocked out a menacing cowboy with a one-two combination. Four years later, Alan and I made a pilgrimage to TR's gravesite on Long Island and explored his home, Sagamore Hill, along with the excellent museum that is housed in the nearby home that was once owned by his oldest son, Ted Jr. You can read about these adventures in more detail, along with seeing lots of photos, on my blog at www.djtindellauthor.com. To keep up with what else is going on with me, and to find out about my other books, please visit my website, www.davidtindellauthor.com. I always list upcoming events where I can be found talking about my work, selling books and generally making a nuisance of myself, and you're welcome to stop by and say hello.

And finally, none of this would be possible without the love and support of my wife, Sue. You can read about our travels together, along with her fascinating solo trips, on her travel blog, www.travelleaders yournextjourney.blogspot.com.

COMING SOON

What's coming up? Well, I have the next books in the *White Vixen* and *Quest* series just about plotted out, but I've already begun serious work on a stand-alone project whose genesis came with a family trip to Colorado way back in the summer before my freshman year in high school. We toured the U.S. Air Force Academy, and occasionally I've wondered how my life would have changed if I'd followed my father's advice and matriculated there. The theme, along with the title, drew inspiration from TR's most famous speech. Here's the first chapter of *The Man in the Arena:*

It was a hot day and they were just about ready to head in off the river when Coles had an idea. "We need to catch ourselves a big one," he said, casting his line one more time. The cork plumped near the stump they'd been fishing for the past half-hour. Sitting on the seat back by the motor, Trace tipped the bottle up to his lips and drained the last of his beer.

"Waste of time, bro," he said. "We should rack it up for the day. Cold one and a burger at Freddy's, over on the Iowa side, that's what's waitin' for us."

"Just a little more time. Got me a feeling there's a big cat down there."

Trace just shook his head. Everybody who'd ever fished cat on the Mississippi hereabouts knew you'd never get one this time of day. They liked cooler water, so this time of day they'd be down deep. That's why you put out your set lines in the evening and took them in in the morning, not the other way around. But what the hell. All they'd gotten so far today were a few bluegills, tethered helplessly to their stringer over the side. Trace watched his own cork sitting quietly about ten feet left of the stump. Not a bite for the past half hour. He wanted to get this done, get home and clean up for his date with Emma. It was his twenty-fourth birthday tomorrow and she'd promised him a special present. Her kids were with their grandma so they'd have the place to themselves and Trace was counting on breaking some furniture with her.

There was only one other boat nearby, a nice fifteen-foot flat-bottom, big 30-horse Evinrude motor on the stern, one guy on board. Trace didn't know what he was doing different, but it was working, he was hauling in some nice ones, had to be six or eight just since he'd arrived about twenty minutes ago. The guy didn't look like your typical fisherman. Big fellow, wearing a tee shirt and a ball cap. There were lots of big guys with ball caps and tee shirts on the Mississippi, but not like this one. He was built, and Trace had caught a glimpse of the shirt when the guy had motored by them. What the hell did USAFA stand for?

Coles whipped his pole up with a triumphant yell. "Got one!" And damn if he didn't. Trace sat up as Coles reeled the fish in, his pole bent over nearly double. Big lunker, for sure. "Get the net, bro!" Coles shouted. As Trace set his own pole down, he glanced across the water and saw the big guy watching them.

It took Coles a good two minutes to land the fish, and sure enough it was a catfish, a nice one, maybe ten, twelve pounds. Trace had heard about some real whoppers coming up on set lines or hauled in by guys fishing near the lock and dam a few miles north. This one wasn't like those big ones he'd heard about, but it was big enough. Trace worked his way to the edge of the boat, almost falling in. That last beer, he thought, might've been one too many. But he was still sober enough to stay dry and reach the net down into the water. Coles worked the fish over into the net and Trace lifted it up.

"Damn, a nice one," Coles said. He hooked a finger into the cat's mouth and lifted him out of the net.

"Don't let him bite you," Trace warned, but Coles just laughed. He held the struggling fish up and removed the hook from the cat's lip with his other hand.

"Gonna keep him?" Trace asked. He wasn't much for cleaning fish in the first place and cat were the worst. No scales, you had to skin them and there were those barbs on the mouth that could slice your hand open, Trace had seen it happen to his uncle once. "A bitch to clean," he said. If Coles wanted to keep him, that was okay, but Trace wouldn't clean him, he'd take care of the bluegills they'd caught. They were easy.

The look of victory on Coles's face dwindled. He pushed his Packers ball cap back as he held the fish. "Well, shit," he said. Trace knew that look. Coles was thinking, and he wasn't the easiest thinker in the world, so it took some effort. Still thinking, Coles reached for his beer. Trace could see there was half a bottle left. Coles picked it up, then stopped, and he smiled at Trace.

"Gonna let him go?" Trace asked, hopeful. He really wanted to wrap this up. Emma and her furniture were waiting.

"Yep," Coles said, "but I don't wanna waste this beer." He held the fish over the water. The cat was still alive, Trace could see his gills heaving. The mouth was open. The one eye Trace could see looked blankly out at him. Then the eye seemed to widen a bit more as Coles started pouring the beer into the cat's mouth.

"Jesus, Coles," Trace said, "what the hell?"

Coles laughed. "Hot day, let's give him a cold one!" He wasn't able to get all the beer into the cat, it struggled mightily and then tore itself away from Coles's finger and splashed back into the water.

"That's it, we're done," Trace said. He was up for a good time as much as the next guy, and sure, he'd done some dumbass things in his life, but pouring beer into that fish…He reeled his line in and reached for the anchor rope. As he did, he happened to glance over at the other boat. The big guy was watching them. Something about his face had changed, and the look sent a chill up Trace's back. "Let's get the hell outta here," he said.

"All right, candy-ass," Coles said. "Freddy's?"

"Yeah, okay."

They came out of Freddy's and made their way down to the pier. Big cheeseburgers and a couple more beers apiece had them walking a little slowly. Coles was laughing about some lame joke he'd heard inside but Trace didn't think it was very funny. And when he saw the big guy waiting for them on the pier, he knew this wouldn't be very funny at all.

The guy was sitting on a bench, one leg over the other. His ball cap was pulled low and he was wearing sunglasses. There was a symbol on the ball cap, Trace didn't recognize it. As they got closer, he saw the symbol had some wings and a star with a red dot in the middle of it. Looked like some kind of military shit. By itself, not very unusual, lots of guys wore caps with military patches or ARMY or something, and some of the guys wearing them had actually been in the service, but this guy looked like the real deal, especially when he stood up. He was six-five easy, and his tee shirt, the one with USAFA across the front above another symbol, fit him like a damn glove. The guy had a mustache with some silver in it and he was not smiling.

"Hello, boys," he said, when Trace and Coles got to the pier. The tall guy was standing right in front of them.

Coles was still feeling it from the two beers he'd had inside. "Excuse us, mister," he said, kind of smart-ass like. Trace had the distinct feeling that was a big mistake, to say it that way.

"Saw you out there catching that catfish," the man said. His voice wasn't the deepest Trace had ever heard, but close enough. And there was something about it, like the guy was used to being paid attention to.

"Yeah, it was a big one," Coles said. "Ten pounds, easy."

"Decided to catch and release?" the guy asked.

"Yep. The sporting thing to do," Coles said. He was a good six inches shorter than the tall guy and the last time Coles had seen the inside of a weight room was high school football, and that was coming up on six years ago now. This guy, on the other hand, looked like he might just live in a weight room.

"Wasn't very sporting to poison the fish with that beer," the guy said. Trace couldn't see the guy's eyes behind the sunglasses, but he expected they were staring at Coles pretty hard. The guy reached into his back pocket and pulled out a cell phone. "Amazing devices, these phones," he said. "Pretty good cameras on them. Can zoom in real nicely. Got a nice shot of you with that fish. Another nice one of the license number on your boat."

Oh shit, Trace thought, they were using his dad's boat. His dad was gonna skin Trace alive.

"Yeah, so?" Coles said.

"But my service provider isn't all the best around here," the guy said. "I only had one bar out there, so I had to come ashore here to get enough bars to call the Iowa DNR. They have jurisdiction, since we were on their side of the river, and they were very interested in my report. Should have a game warden here any minute now."

"Uh, we'd best be going," Trace said.

The man looked at him. "You're not going anywhere, son, not quite yet. Maybe the game warden will want you to go with him, though."

"Back off, mister," Coles said. Trace knew the signs and Coles was showing them all, just like the last time he'd been in a bar fight. That hadn't turned out well for the drunk who'd been coming on to Coles's girl that night. Trace had a feeling this little encounter would be different.

He was right. The big guy just smiled and said, "We're just going to wait here for the warden, boys." Coles reached out to push the guy aside, and then in the blink of an eye, he was on the ground, his hand twisted up behind him, and the big guy was holding on with what looked like hardly any grip at all. He put his phone back in his pocket and pointed at Trace. "Sit down over there on that bench."

"Yes, sir." Trace backed up to the bench and sat down, very glad that his dad would be the one doing the skinning, and not this guy. His dad would probably let him live.

***

Publication dates for upcoming books have not yet been finalized, but here's a tentative schedule:

The Bronze Leopard, book 3 in the *White Vixen* series, 2020
The Man in the Arena, 2021

Quest for Redemption, book 3 in the *Quest* series, 2022

Made in the USA
Middletown, DE
17 June 2022

67131252R00239